The Newcomer

Fern Britton is the highly acclaimed author of seven *Sunday Times* bestselling novels. Her books are cherished for their warmth, wit and wisdom, and have won Fern legions of loyal readers. Fern has been a judge for the Costa Book of the Year Award and is a supporter of the Reading Agency, promoting literacy and reading.

A hugely popular household name through iconic shows such as *This Morning* and *Fern Britton Meets…* Fern is a much sought-after presenter and radio host. She has also turned her hand to theatre and toured with Gary Barlow and Tim Firth's *Calendar Girls*.

Fern lives with her husband, Phil Vickery, and her four children in Buckinghamshire and Cornwall.

f /officialfernbritton
y @Fern_Britton
www.fern-britton.com

Fern Britton

The Newcomer

HarperCollins*Publishers*

HarperCollins*Publishers* Ltd
1 London Bridge Street,
London SE1 9GF

www.harpercollins.co.uk

First published by HarperCollins*Publishers* 2019

2

Set in Birka by Palimpsest Book Production Ltd, Falkirk, Stirlingshire

Printed and bound in the UK by CPI Group (UK) Ltd, Croydon CR0 4YY

MIX
Paper from
responsible sources

FSC C007454

This book is produced from independently certified FSC™ paper
to ensure responsible forest management.

For more information visit: www.harpercollins.co.uk/green

In memory of my mum Ruth
1924–2018
Her stories were the best

PROLOGUE

The evening before Mamie Buchanan's corpse was found had been an enjoyable one. Her niece, the Revd Angela Whitehorn, had thrown a gossipy dinner party for her new parish friends, where it was agreed that her aunt was the most entertaining newcomer Pendruggan had ever had.

This may have been due to her rackety stories and her genuine interest in the lives of others, or, more likely, it could have been her inability to pour anything less than very large measures of alcohol.

'Your aunt is an admirable woman,' said a squiffy Geoffrey Tipton, the last guest to say his goodbyes on the chilly, moonlit doorstep of Pendruggan vicarage. 'My God, they don't make women like that any more.'

Angela nodded in agreement. 'They certainly don't.'

'*GEOFFREY!*' The voice of Mrs Tipton came from beyond the gate, making both Angela and Geoffrey jump. He turned giddily. 'Yes, my love. Just coming.' He steadied himself with a gnarled hand on the doorframe. 'Was thanking the vicar for a splendid party.'

'You can do that in a letter. *COME*,' commanded Audrey. She may as well have asked him to heel.

Geoffrey pushed himself from the doorframe and gave Angela a wobbly wave before staggering towards his wife.

Angela gratefully closed the door and walked to the kitchen where Mamie, the belle of the ball, was gaily polishing off a bottle of champagne.

'Good God,' she said theatrically, 'I thought they'd never leave. Last glass before bed?' She pointed the bottle towards Angela.

Angela shook her head and started to load the dishwasher. 'I've already had too much.' Over her shoulder she said, 'You know Mike Bates is in love with you, don't you?'

Mamie sank her glass in one. 'Yes. He told me. And who can blame him, darling!' Her eyes twinkled with laughter. 'I'm very fond of him.'

Robert Whitehorn, Angela's husband, entered with the last of the pudding plates balanced in his hands. 'Mamie, you were outrageous. You mercilessly flirted with the dreadful Tipton man.'

Mamie became her usual heartless self again and leant out of her kitchen chair to drop her empty bottle into the recycling crate by the back door. 'Me?' she laughed. 'Poor dear Geoff. A frightful old bore but such a sweetheart. That gorgon of a wife of his is hard work.' Mamie looked to the ceiling and raised her immaculate eyebrows.

Angela, taking the plates Robert was offering, gave her aunt a fond but exasperated look. 'You are a heartbreaker *and* you got everyone drunk.'

'And there was I thinking I was brightening the dull and unsullied lives of your flock,' Mamie smiled impishly.

Angela's tired grin shifted into a yawn.

'And you are exhausted,' Mamie said kindly. 'You two go up to bed and I'll clear the last bits up.'

'Are you sure?' asked Robert.

Mamie picked up a tea towel and flapped it at the pair of them. 'You've got early church tomorrow. I can lie in.' She kissed her niece and nephew-in-law affectionately. 'Off you go. Bed. Now.'

'Where does she get her energy from?' Robert plumped the pillow under his head, his eyes already closing.

'She's always been the same.' Angela lifted her legs onto her side of the mattress and pulled the duvet up. 'Always.'

It was Angela who found Mamie's body. She had woken at 3.20 with a post-alcohol thirst that needed at least a pint of water. In the dark, she had padded, barefoot and silent, to the top of the stairs and noted a line of light under her aunt's bedroom door. She thought vaguely that Mamie was probably engaged in her usual nightly routine of make-up removal and meditation, so she decided not to disturb her..

Her fingers carefully held the smoothly worn stair rail as she counted the sixteen treads down to the hallway. She and Robert had been in the vicarage only six months but Angela knew by now most of its foibles and peculiarities: the sticky window in her office, the back door that needed an encouraging kick after rain, and the creaking third and fifth treads.

At this hour all was still and silent. The now-familiar warmth of the house wrapped itself around her.

The smell of garlic roast lamb and sherry still hung in the air, and something else. She stopped for a moment and sniffed. Ah, yes. Mamie's perfume. Shalimar. Angela was surprised that it could override even last night's cooking smells, but there it was. The very essence of her aunt.

She reached the bottom step and her naked toes felt the familiar texture of the Indian rug covering the oak floor of the hall.

Confidently, she let go of the wooden sphere on the end of the newel post, and turned left in the darkness, heading towards the kitchen.

It was then that her foot felt something unusual.

Soft.

Fleshy.

Her skin began to prickle.

'Mr Worthington? Is that you, boy?' She knew it wasn't the dog.

She stood stock-still and held her breath. But there was no answering thump of a wagging tail or whiskery nose sniffing her leg.

Fear crawled from her stomach, through her bowels and down her legs. She began to shake.

She was breathing faster and recognised panic. What should she do? Scared to progress further and tread on anything else that might be lying in the dark, but knowing she had to, she reached her foot forwards, feeling for anything else.

What was that?

She drew her foot back quickly.

'Oh dear Lord,' she whispered, and took two quick hops to where she hoped the light switch was.

In the sudden glaring light, she saw her beloved aunt's body.

'*Robert! Robert!*'

*

Robert was dreaming of Venice, sitting in the sun, under the shade of a bougainvillaea and having lunch alone, watching the beautiful women walk by. Where was Angela? He couldn't remember why she wasn't with him, but never mind. He could sit here without guilt. Of course Angela would be very cross if she caught him but it was innocent fun. Then he heard her. Upset. Angry? Her voice was coming in distressing sobs.

'*Robert, oh dear God. Robert! Robert. Robert.*'

The vision faded and he sat up in bed, ready to apologise. It had only been lunch. Nothing more. Angela would understand. But Angela's side of the bed was empty. He ran his hands through his thick, dark hair and heard her shout again, '*Robert, it's Auntie Mamie, she's fallen.*'

A dose of adrenaline hit him and he leapt out of bed. Six foot two, muscular and naked, he sped onto the landing and looked over the banisters. His wife had one hand to her mouth while the other clutched her nightdress to her heart. He saw the body on the rug. Twisted awkwardly. Her eyes half open. A bruise spreading on her temple. He knew she was dead.

He took the stairs two at a time. Stepping round the grim scene, he reached Angela and pulled her to his strong, naked chest.

'Darling. Don't look. Make some tea. I'll call the police.'

'She needs an ambulance.' Angela pushed her way out of Robert's arms. She stepped carefully over Mamie's feet and went to the phone on the hall table. 'Check her breathing, Robert, and fetch a blanket. She'll get cold.'

Robert dashed for the blanket from the back of the sofa, then knelt and checked Mamie's pulse. Nothing. He bent his ear to her nose. She wasn't breathing.

'Ambulance, please.' Angela's voice broke as the emergency operator asked for details.

Robert placed Mamie's lifeless arm gently on her chest and stood up. 'Darling, we need the police as well. I'm so sorry. She's gone.'

Angela took the receiver from her ear and looked at Mamie, lying in her scarlet silk pyjamas, and her legs gave way.

Robert took the phone and gave the emergency operator their address and an assessment of what had happened. He put his hand fondly against Mamie's cool cheek, before pulling the blanket snugly over her as though she was sleeping.

Finally, he collected Angela's small frame in his arms and carried her to the kitchen. Tenderly he lowered her onto her chair by the Aga.

'I'll make tea. The police and ambulance will be here soon.'

'Mamie,' keened Angela, her head in her hands. 'I didn't hear her fall, Robert. I should have heard her. Why didn't I hear her?'

'Darling, it's an accident. Somehow she tripped on the stairs and fell. I don't think she would have known anything about it.' He smiled into Angela's green eyes. 'In a funny sort of way, isn't this so typically her? Exactly the way she would have liked to have gone? After a great party where everyone loved her . . . and full of gin.'

1

Six months earlier

'Penny?' Simon Canter shouted from the bottom of the vicarage stairs, his shirt sleeves rolled to his elbows, a sheen of sweat on his brow.

'Penny.' He shouted a little louder.

He had been emptying and clearing his office for the last three hours and it had not put him in the happiest of moods. 'Penny!'

'What?' Her voice from upstairs was irritated. 'I'm sorting the bloody books in Jenna's room.'

'Where are the bin liners?'

'Under the sink, where they usually are.'

'I've looked and they are not.'

'Oh, for goodness' sake!' she muttered to herself, then shouted, more loudly, 'Have you looked in the box by the back door?'

'No.'

'Well, look!'

Penny was not quite as busy as she was pretending. In truth she had been lying on her daughter's bed for most of the morning, surrounded by packing cases and constantly being distracted by long-forgotten possessions. She had been flicking through her own old copy of Noel Streatfeild's *Ballet Shoes*. She had won it at her boarding school. Her headmistress's inscription still gave her a tiny thrill of pride.

Awarded to Penelope Leighton
For continued improvement in English Literature.
Congratulations
Miss Elsie Bird

Penny had had a difficult childhood. Her father had died when she was young and later she had discovered the woman she had been told was her mother was not. It had destroyed her sense of self-worth and left her with a need for praise and approval wherever she could find it. Even now, reading Miss Bird's dedication to her more than thirty years later, she felt the pleasure of having done well.

It wasn't until she'd met Simon, in her early forties, that she'd found the wonder of loving and being loved in return. And she, a woman who worked in the febrile, emotionally incontinent, ego-driven world of television, had found all that in a vicar! Now Simon shouted again from downstairs, 'They are not there!'

'What aren't where?'

'The bin liners.'

Penny huffily put the book down and went to go downstairs and find the bloody bin bags herself when she spotted them. They were where she had put them, at the top of the stairs.

'Oh, here they are,' she called cheerfully, covering her guilt. Simon was grumping up the stairs.

'Sorry, darling,' she said with a hint of accusation as she met him midway. '*Someone* must have left them upstairs.'

Simon looked tired. His normally clear, tanned face and chocolate eyes were dulled with worry. 'We have less than a week.'

She stroked his balding head and kissed his brow. 'I know. We'll be ready. I promise.'

'I've still got the garage to tackle. What am I going to do with all those tins of old paint?'

Penny placed a hand on his shoulder. 'The new people might want them to touch up any scuffs.' She wiped a string of cobweb from his eyebrow. 'I think you need some elevenses. Everything will look better after a coffee and a digestive or two. Come on.' Taking his hand, she pulled him towards the kitchen.

Outside early spring was dawning on the little patio that Simon had built last summer, with the help of the village gardener, known to all as Simple Tony. The flagstones were warming and a robin was busily building a nest in the early clematis that clambered around the kitchen window.

Penny carried the coffee tray outside and balanced it on top of the lichened birdbath. Pulling up two tatty wicker chairs, she took the edge of her cardigan and swept away the dried winter leaves and crumbly bird poo from the seats.

Setting the chairs side by side, she plonked herself down with a sigh as Simon followed her out with a packet of ginger nuts.

Penny pulled her shoulders back and tipped her face to the sun. 'The sea smells good today.' She inhaled noisily, filling her lungs.

Simon sat down and opened the biscuits. 'Ginger nut?'

She exhaled, shaking her head. 'I'd prefer a digestive.'

'There aren't any.'

She looked at Simon, weighing up whether it was worth the risk of contradicting him by getting up and getting the digestives from the larder where she had put them, or just saying nothing. She chose the latter.

'Not to worry,' she said, and took another lungful of air with closed eyes.

Simon fiddled with the ginger nut wrapper, running his thumb around to find the elusive tape to pull and, while he did so, looked around at his beloved garden, recalling all the hours that he and Penny had poured into it.

The cherry blossom tree marking Jenna's baptism.

The Wendy house under it.

The drift of daffodils, just budding now, planted several autumns before.

Eventually he found the Cellophane string and pulled.

Six ginger nuts sprang out and hit the ground.

Penny opened one eye. 'Bugger,' she said.

He sighed. 'Are we doing the right thing?' He picked up a biscuit and shook the grit off before dipping it in his coffee.

Penny exhaled impatiently. 'Yes!'

'It's Jenna I worry about most,' Simon said, looking at the vegetable patch that he really ought to have dug over by now. 'Taking her away from this. Her home. Her garden. Her friends. The life she has known.'

Penny abandoned her deep breathing and gave him a sharp look. 'How many times are we going to go over this?' She snatched up a ginger nut before the beady-eyed, nest-building robin got it, and bit into it noisily. 'We are *going* to Brazil,' she said. 'It's your dream and we're going to go for it!'

He ran his hand over his head. 'Am I being selfish? What about you and your work?'

Before he could take another bleat, Penny was on him. 'Stop being so sodding negative. I do believe Brazil has running water and electricity and phone lines and the internet! I can run my office from there easily. In fact, it may be better than being here. And Jenna is seven going on twenty-one and bursting for an adventure.'

'She takes after you.' Simon gloomily drank his coffee.

Penny sat up and looked him square in the eye. 'Do you know what she told me last night?'

'No.'

'She told me that her friends at school were collecting things for the children you will be working with.'

'What things?'

'Hairbands, football shirts, pens, notepads, balls, make-up. Stuff that street kids have never had. She's even set up a website with her form teacher, Miss Lumley, so that she can keep them up to date with her blogging and vlogging.'

'Really?' Simon's eyes were shining with emotion.

'Yes, but keep it under your hat and act surprised because I wasn't supposed to tell you.'

He turned his gaze back to the garden and Jenna's cherry tree. 'It is going to be all right, isn't it?'

'It's going to be bloody amazing!' Penny stretched out to take his hand. 'I know I'm not always the greatest vicar's wife in the world, but the important thing is that I am *your* wife and the only one you have. Even the bishop has started to afford me some respect. He managed to look me in the eye rather than my cleavage last time I saw him . . . a huge step for mankind.'

'He doesn't understand strong successful women.'

'Well, he's going to have to. There are a hell of a lot of us about.'

'Supposing the accommodation is even more basic than we've been led to believe? You might hate it.'

'You forget I have spent most of my working life on film locations with a chemical toilet and cold showers. I never get the luxury Winnebago, believe me. Brazil will be sunny, hot, sexy, all the things that you and I could do with.' She smiled at him. 'It's going to be fun.'

He smiled at her wearily. 'Dear God, I hope so.'

Somewhere in the house the phone began to ring. 'Ah, that'll be God now, telling you to buck up,' said Penny. 'I shall say you're out.'

Penny headed for the phone in the hall, dodging round a pile of boots and coats ready for the charity shop, and reached for the receiver.

'Holy Trinity Church, Pendruggan. Good morning.'

'Penny, is that you?' asked the querulous voice of the bishop. 'You were a long time answering.'

'Maybe because we still have the old-fashioned telephone plugged into the wall.'

'You must ask my office to sort you out a modern cordless one.'

Penny gritted her teeth. 'Yes. We were turned down.'

'Have I caught you in the middle of something?'

'Not at all. We are only packing our lives up for Brazil.'

'Of course. Brazil. Simon will be marvellous. He's exactly the sort of man for the job. I must say when I did my ministry in Sudan, many moons ago now . . .'

Penny closed her eyes, preparing to hear another of the pompous old fart's dreary tales of self-aggrandisement.

'The Sudan!' she said. 'How . . . interesting.'

'Oh my word, it certainly was. The people took to me immediately and the more I worked with them in their villages, taking the good news of the gospels with me, the more they truly loved me. I remember a day when a young woman with a small child on her back came to me and asked, in all humility, "Are you Jesus?"'

'Well I never,' said Penny, rolling her eyes at her husband, who was stepping over the coats and coming towards her. 'How charming! You must tell Simon. He's right here.'

'Who is it?' mouthed Simon.

'God,' she mouthed back.

Simon took the receiver from her and shooed her away. 'William. How kind of you to call.'

Penny collected her coffee from the garden, tucking a couple of ginger nuts into her cardigan pocket, and returned to Jenna's room. She was faced again with the scattered detritus of moving her life halfway across the world. There had been tears and fierce negotiations about what could go to Brazil and what would have to stay behind and go into storage.

'But, Mumma, Blue Ted won't be able to breathe in a crate.'

'Oh yes he will. Teddies like to hibernate and it'll be a big adventure for him to be in the big warehouse with lots of other people's teddies.'

'No it won't.'

'Yes it will.'

'But he'll miss me.'

'Well,' Penny had thought on her feet, 'we shall send him postcards.'

'He can't read without me.'

'So you'll have lots of fun reading them to him when we get back.'

At which point Jenna had burst into tears and thrown herself on the bed with Blue Ted beneath her.

It had finally been agreed that Blue Ted and Honey Bear and Tiny Tiger could all go to Brazil in her flight bag, but the Lego, stilts and dolls' house had to go into store.

Standing now in her daughter's denuded room, Penny knew she only had a few hours to make these last books, games and teddies 'disappear' into storage before Jenna returned home from school.

As she worked, her mind picked at the anxiety she felt about leaving Pendruggan. No matter what she had told Simon, the move to Brazil was not going to be easy. She was a woman who liked to be in control of her environment. She needed her work, her hairdresser, the theatre, shops, and her independence. In Brazil she would have none of these safe anchors. She had to admit to herself that she would find it hard.

Simon, by comparison, would be in his element. He had been handpicked to join the missionary team in Bahia, to help the abandoned children who lived on the streets. Some were just babies, cared for by other children. They were exploited in every way imaginable. The Mission gave them shelter, teaching and food. Penny knew that Simon would plunge straight in and immerse himself totally in the work that he was made for, but she privately wondered how she would cope.

When Jenna had first been told about going, she had cried and run to her bedroom. Mortified, Simon and Penny had followed her, expecting a tantrum and refusal to go, but instead they found her gathering her teddies and telling them that they were needed in Brazil. They watched with awe and pride as she lined them up and told them, 'I love you all, you know that, but there are lots of children who don't have a special teddy or a mummy and daddy, so you are coming with me and I shall let you play with the Brazil girls and boys. But not you, Blue Ted. All right? Mummy says Daddy is going to be very important in a Missionary Position.'

Penny smiled at the memory.

And now Brazil was only a week away.

The essentials for their new life were already crated and stowed on the deck of a container ship, crossing the Atlantic.

Penny looked for the big roll of parcel tape and placed the last two of Jenna's belongings – a magic set and a radio-controlled puppy – into the final box, sticking it down securely.

'Right, you lot,' she said, straightening up. 'It's only for a year. Twelve little months and we'll have you out of storage and back here before you know it.' She looked around the familiar room. 'And you four walls, you are going to be home to the new family. Look after them, but don't forget us.'

A woman's voice called up the stairs, 'Hello-o! Anyone fancy a sandwich?'

Penny went to the landing and looked over the banisters to see the auburn hair and freckly face of her best friend, Helen.

'You are an angel. What you got?'

Helen beamed up at her and swung a Marks and Spencer bag. 'Prawn salad, cheese and pickle or cream cheese and cucumber.'

'Crisps?'

'Salt and vinegar.'

Later, the kitchen table strewn with the remains of the ad hoc lunch and glasses of squash, Simon dusted the crumbs from his fleece and stood up.

'Thank you, Helen. Would you think me rude if I whizzed off to the tip? I've got the car loaded and I want to empty it before I pick Jenna up from school.'

'Go for it,' Helen approved.

Penny chipped in, 'There's a pile of bin liners full of rubbish at the bottom of the stairs, if you can fit them in.'

He dropped a kiss onto the top of her head. 'No problem. See you later.'

Penny patted his bum as he went by her. 'Jenna loves it when you pick her up.'

Once Penny and Helen were alone, Helen leant across the table and put her hand over her friend's. 'How are you feeling? Really?'

Penny slumped her head onto the table. 'Exhausted. Anxious. Homesick already.'

'I'd be the same.'

Penny lifted her head. 'Would you? I've tried so hard to keep upbeat for Simon because this is so important to him.'

'Tell me what you're worried about.'

'Jenna getting ill and no decent hospital to look after her. Insects in the house. Snakes. Lizards. Robbers. Earthquakes.'

Helen began to smile. 'So, not much then.'

'And worst of all, I'm going to miss you.' Penny gripped Helen's hand. 'What is a woman without her best friend? The woman who knows all her secrets. Who's going to make me laugh, bring sandwiches, wine and gossip?'

'How do you think I'll feel without you?' countered Helen. 'Who am I going to complain about Piran to?'

Penny sniffed and wiped her eyes. 'You'll just have to strangle him.'

'You're right.' Helen sighed. 'Easier than divorce.'

'You're not married,' said Penny.

'Oh, yeah. Well, I could walk out on him.'

'But you don't even live together,' Penny smiled.

'Thank God!' Helen laughed.

Penny stood and went to the fridge. 'I've got half a bottle of rosé that needs drinking. Fancy a drop?'

'Is my name Helen Merrifield?'

Penny took two glasses from a cupboard and poured equal measures of wine into them.

'To me,' she said, raising her glass.

'To you,' replied Helen. She took a mouthful. 'I wonder if the new vicar drinks?'

'Probably not. She looks a bit mousy. No, that's unfair. Shall we say, natural. No make-up. Very petite. I think she might be one of those women who run for fun.'

'But her husband is a dish.'

'Did I tell you that?'

'Several times.'

'Well, he is. When we met them at Bishop William's, I couldn't believe how handsome he was. Think Cary Grant with a drop of George Clooney.'

'I am.'

'And he's nice. Charming. Very attentive to Angela.'

'What does he do?'

'I think he said he was a political writer. To be honest, I was so busy looking at him that I forgot to listen to what he was saying. I'm expecting you to get all the lowdown and Skype me with every detail.'

'What about the daughter?'

'I didn't meet her. But I think she's around fourteen or fifteen. Something like that. Probably at the fat and spotty stage.'

Helen gave Penny a knowing look. 'You're feeling better. I can always tell. Your inner bitch comes out.'

As they laughed together as only old friends can, a wave of homesickness overwhelmed Penny.

'Oh, I do hope we'll be OK, and that they will be happy here – this house, this village . . . well, I couldn't have been happier here and–'

Helen interrupted her before she could get into a panic. 'You'll be home before you know it. What could possibly go wrong in a vicarage?'

And with knowing smiles, they settled in for a good old gossip.

'Don't use the sitting room,' Penny yelled four days later as Simon put his hand to the door handle.

He blinked. 'I only want to watch the news.'

'You'll have to watch it on the little telly in the kitchen.' She steered him away. 'Also, no using the downstairs loo, or either of the spare bedrooms or your office.'

'But I need my office.'

'Out of bounds, I'm afraid,' said Penny, pushing him towards the kitchen. 'Helen and I scrubbed this house from top to bottom. Forensics would never know we lived here.'

'This is slightly ridiculous. Angela and Robert don't arrive until the day after tomorrow,' Simon said, exasperated.

Penny shrugged. 'Them's the rules, I'm afraid. And tonight's supper is fish and chips from the chip shop because I've cleaned the Aga. And tomorrow night, Helen and Piran are cooking for us. Our last supper.'

Simon took Penny in his arms and squeezed her. 'I haven't said thank you, have I?'

Penny tipped her head up to look at her husband. 'What for?'

'For doing all this for me.' His chocolate eyes behind their glasses took in her deep blue ones. 'For taking on this huge upheaval and not complaining once.'

'Haven't I? I'm sure I have.'

'Shut up. Just, thank you.'

'My pleasure.' She reached up and kissed him. 'Now go and get the fish and chips.'

The following evening, Simon, Penny and Jenna trooped across the village green to Helen's little cottage. Gull's Cry was as welcoming as always, sitting in its beautiful garden, the path lined with lavender from gate to front door. Wisteria was starting to break into flower around the eaves and, as ever, a fat candle sitting in a bell jar shone in each of the two downstairs windows. The thick front door with its heavy metal dolphin knocker opened before they got to it and a small Jack Russell bounded out to greet them.

The silhouette of Piran Ambrose stood framed in the glow spilling from within.

'Come in, come in, me 'andsome.' He shook Simon's hand. They were old and unlikely friends, who had grown up together.

''Ello, maid, come in out of the cold,' he said to Jenna, putting his huge fisherman's hand onto the little girl's shoulder. 'The fire's lit.'

'Hello Uncle Piran.' She smiled shyly at the man she adored and bent down to tickle the little dog. 'Hello, Jack.'

Penny entered last and Piran kissed her cheek. 'All right, Pen? All set for the big day?'

'I think so. Too late if we're not.'

Helen came from the kitchen drying her hands on a tea towel and welcomed them all. 'Piran, open the wine, would you, and there's a bottle of elderflower cordial for Jenna.'

'Something smells good,' sniffed Simon appreciatively.

'Piran has made his famous lobster curry for you,' Helen told them. 'Couldn't let you go without a proper Saturday night supper in you.'

'That was delicious,' Simon said, putting his knife and fork together neatly on his plate.

'You'll be eating some different kind of grub in Brazil, I 'spect,' said Piran, wiping up the last of the curry sauce with a slice of French bread.

'I'm going to miss you, Uncle Piran.' Jenna had eaten every scrap. 'I love your cooking.'

'Now listen, maid, it won't be too long before me and thee are back on Trevay harbour pulling in those mackerel.'

'Can I gut them when I come back? I'll be eight by then.'

'Eight, is it? You'm growing up fast. I tell you what, when you get back I'll have a proper fisherman's knife waiting for you. How about that?'

Penny butted in, 'Is that a good idea?'

Simon stopped her. 'It's a very good idea. Jenna is growing up a Cornish woman and a Cornish woman knows how to use a knife and gut a fish.' He turned to Jenna. 'It's in your blood.'

'Is it?' she asked, looking at her hands and spreading the fingers. 'Cool.'

'Absolutely,' agreed Piran. 'Now, there's a little tube of Smarties in the sitting room waiting for you, as long as Jack hasn't had 'em. You can sit on the sofa and watch some telly together.'

Jenna needed no further encouragement and skipped off, calling Jack to join her.

'It's going to be a big change for her,' said Piran, watching them, 'but it'll do her the world of good. Growing up in a little village ain't always a good thing.'

'It was good enough for us.' Simon reminded him. 'You couldn't wait to come back after you got your Ph.D. Cornish history is in your DNA.'

'True, true. But where would I be if I didn't have you to keep me on the straight and narrow? My best mate a vicar. I'm still in shock.'

Helen placed a cup of coffee in front of him. 'You'd be a bloody rogue without Simon acting as your conscience. He's your Jiminy Cricket.' She handed Penny and Simon their coffees and sat down. 'So how is tomorrow shaping up? Angela and Robert still coming to be introduced to us all?'

'Yes.' Simon spooned some brown sugar into his mug. 'They're staying over in Lostwithiel tonight with an old friend of Robert's. I think they were at school together. Then they'll drive over. Should only take half an hour at that time on a Sunday morning.'

'The handover will be the hardest thing,' said Penny. 'But better to keep it short.'

'You'll have a full church tomorrow, mind,' said Piran, smiling. 'They nosy lot round here will be breaking their necks to check out the new vicar. They'm desperate to see the woman. Audrey Tipton and her wet husband will be front of the queue, you'll see.'

Penny laughed. 'You're so right. And Queenie. I was in the shop the other day and she was desperately mining me for information.'

'Oh God, she'll bring out the ancient mothballed fur coat for the great occasion,' laughed Helen.

'The fur and perhaps the green velvet hat with the feathers and the net veil that she thinks make her look like the Duchess of Cornwall,' chuckled Penny fondly.

'How does she keep going with the post office and all those cigarettes she smokes? I do worry about her. How old do you think she is now?' Helen asked.

'She came here from the East End as an evacuee as a young girl,' said Simon. 'So she must be . . .' he shut his eyes and calculated, '. . . about eighty-five-ish?'

A chill ran through Penny. 'I hope nothing happens to her while we are away.'

Helen tutted. 'Nothing is going to happen to her. She's pickled in nicotine and her mind is as sharp as a razor. She can still add up quicker than a bookie. I promise you, she's not going anywhere.'

'Mumma?' A tired Jenna wandered in, cuddling little Jack like a baby. His paws were limp and his eyes blinking. 'Can we go now?'

Piran lifted Jack from her. 'Bleddy dog. Spoilt, he is.' He ruffled Jack's ears and kissed his nose.

'He loves that dog more than he loves me,' said Helen, shaking her head.

'Well, I've known 'im longer than I've known you. We share history.'

'Bye-bye, Jack,' said Jenna sleepily. 'Bye-bye, Uncle Piran. You won't forget my fisherman's knife, will you?'

'Certainly not. Auntie Helen and I will have it here the minute you get back.'

Saying their goodbyes, Simon scooped Jenna up in his arms, and led his beloved little family back to the vicarage.

Later, snuggled in bed with the lights out, Penny had a sense of foreboding. She fidgeted over to Simon, whose warmth comforted her. He reached an arm around her. 'You OK?' he asked sleepily.

'Yes. Just thinking about how different the village might be when we get back.'

'It'll be the same as always,' Simon told her. 'Nothing changes in Pendruggan. Take it from me.'

That night, Penny had a torrid dream. Their container ship was sunk by a terrible Atlantic storm, taking all their possessions to the seabed. Her father was there and tried desperately to save everything but, after many dives, was finally swallowed into the murky depths. She woke up gasping, but as she lay in her bed next to her sleeping husband, she heard the high-pitched wail of a strong wind coming off the sea and the rattle of heavy rain.

She turned over to be closer to Simon and tried to shake off the bad feeling that still lingered.

'It's just an ordinary Cornish storm,' she told herself. 'And a simple anxiety dream. Everything will be OK.'

Eventually she did sleep, while outside, the storm raged, shaking Jenna's cherry tree and running up the beach on Shellsand Bay to wash away the great walls of the sand dunes.

But when Simon woke, first as he usually did, the sky was the cleanest, washed-out blue, without a cloud. The sun was rising and bringing with it the first promise of summer warmth.

In the kitchen as he waited for the kettle to boil, he opened the back door and saw the wind-strewn leaves of Jenna's cherry tree on the lawn and the slender necks of the daffodils bent to the earth. But today was not a day to grieve over nature. Today he needed all his emotional strength to hand his flock over to their new caretaker, Angela.

2

'Well?' The suspense was killing Robert. 'Are we going to Cornwall?'

Angela's heart was racing, the pulse in her throat throbbing. She lifted her eyes from the letter in her hand and said, in a quivering voice, 'Yes.'

Robert ran to where she stood in the hall. 'Woo hoo.' He lifted her off her feet. 'Congratulations.' He squeezed her hard and without letting her go called up the stairs, 'Faith! Mum got the job! We are going to live by the sea for a whole year!'

'Great,' came the muffled reply.

'Well, come on. Come down and I'll make a celebratory breakfast. Bacon sandwiches all round!'

'Dad, it's Saturday. I want to sleep.'

'Let her be,' said Angela fondly.

'But it's already eleven. She should be down here with us, celebrating.'

'Darling.' She kissed the top of his handsome head. 'Put me down and we'll have breakfast together. Just the two of us.'

'I'm so proud of you.' He gave her another tight hug, then set her back on her feet.

A short while later, Robert placed the bacon sandwich in front of her. 'Tea or coffee?'

'Tea, please.' Angela bit into the soft white bread and butter, and found the bacon crispy and warm. 'The food of the gods,' she said.

Robert put a mug of tea in front of her, then sat down with his own sandwich and coffee. 'The vicarage is going to feel huge after this little house.'

'It will.' Angela looked out of the kitchen window onto their tiny but neat courtyard garden. 'I shall miss this, though.'

'Oh, I won't,' Robert said through a mouthful of bread. 'Farewell west London, hello west coast.'

'You'll miss work.'

'No.'

'Yes, you will. It's your meat and drink.'

He wiped his mouth with a piece of kitchen towel. 'We have talked all this through. Finish your sandwich.'

'When will you let work know?'

'I'll talk to Gordon on Monday. It won't come as a surprise. He told me you'd get the job.'

'He's been so good to you. To us.'

'Yeah. He's a good bloke.'

Angela stirred her tea. 'And you are sure? About having a year off?'

He put the last of his sandwich in his mouth. 'Absolutely. All those dark rainy nights standing on College Green or outside the door of Number Ten, shouting questions that won't or can't be answered to politicians who are as clueless as the rest of us.'

'I'm not sure Cornwall will offer any of the excitement you're used to.'

'But I shall have a new job. Househusband extraordinaire . . .'

'Not quite as exciting.'

He shook his head. 'Look, you have always been there for me, never minding when the office ring at ungodly hours to send me out on a story, never refusing a camera crew a bed for the night, always taking the burden of domestic responsibility. It's my turn to look after you.'

Angela put her hand on his knee and her head on his shoulder. 'I am so lucky.'

'The good people of Penwhatsit are luckier.'

'Pendruggan.'

He raised his coffee mug. 'To my wife. The vicar of Pendruggan.'

She laughed. 'Vicar for a year, anyway. I hope I can do it.'

Robert grew serious. 'Darling, Ange.' He took the hand she had on his knee and lifted it to his lips. 'What you will be doing is a million times more worthwhile than any television news report. You are doing yourself and me and Faith proud.'

'I hope Mum would be proud of me too.'

'She's smiling down on you as we speak.'

3

Penny took a last look around her bedroom as she rummaged for her emergency packet of tights in her flight bag.

'I hope Angela will like this place,' she muttered uneasily.

Simon poked his head round the door. 'Hurry up. I want us to get to church before Angela arrives. Jenna's ready.'

'I had a ladder so I've got to put these new ones on.' She sat on the bed and rolled the expensive flesh-toned, ten-denier tights gently so as not to snag them.

'We've got to go.'

'I can't hurry this. They snag so easi— oh shit, look what you've made me do.' She glanced up to find he'd already gone and glanced back to see the pull in the fine mesh. 'Bugger, bugger.'

Jenna came in wearing her new grey, buttoned coat, white socks and red shiny shoes. 'Come on, Mumma, Daddy says he's going without you.'

Penny pushed her feet into her taupe suede heels and grimaced at the pinch on her little toes.

'OK, OK. I'm ready.' She got to her feet, tottering slightly, then gained her balance. She sucked in her core muscles and made her way down the stairs in Jenna's wake.

Simon was fussing with his dog collar. 'Does it look all right?'

She gave him a once-over from top to bottom. 'Perfect. How about me?'

Simon was already looking for the door keys. 'Hmm?'

'Will I do?'

Without turning his head, he replied, 'Yes, yes. Lovely as always. Right, let's go.'

The birds were singing in the churchyard and tulips and forget-me-nots were pushing their way up among the damp headstones. Simon strode ahead of Penny, deep in thought. Penny saw the tense set of his shoulders and the nervous way he had of reaching up to smooth his bald head. She understood that today was going to be difficult for him, difficult for them all, and her love and empathy flowed to him. The last couple of months had been fraught with things to organise and she had done her best to take the strain of the domestic arrangements from him.

Goodness only knew how the caretaker vicar, Angela, was feeling. Pendruggan was to be her first proper parish. The poor woman hadn't even seen the vicarage yet, not in the flesh. Penny had shown her around on FaceTime but that was it. To make things easier, Angela and Robert had been delighted for Penny to leave her furniture behind so that there was the least upheaval for them all.

And now, the day to hand over the vicarage had arrived.

Penny and Jenna caught up with Simon as he unlocked the side door into the vestry. 'Nice and warm. Good,' he said, hanging his coat on the worn wooden peg above the radiator. He checked his watch. 'Ten minutes before they are due.'

The door connecting the vestry to the main church opened and a well-built woman wearing a tweed suit and a steel head of hair strode in. 'Morning, Vicar.'

'Ah, good morning, Audrey. Thank Geoffrey for turning on the heating, would you. Most grateful.'

Audrey was at her most domineering. She was feared by almost everyone, Piran being the exception. She turned her gimlet eyes to Penny, who immediately felt inadequate. 'Mrs Canter, perhaps you can solve the mystery of my floral decorations?'

Penny swallowed hard but stood her ground. 'Do you mean my clematis?'

Audrey found the most withering of challenging looks in her arsenal of withering looks. 'I do. Please explain.'

Penny stopped herself from buckling. 'My early clematis has just come into bloom and I thought it might, er,' she searched for the word, 'soften the structure of your altar arrangements.'

'Soften?' Audrey boomed.

'Yes, the, erm . . . boldness of your design was, er . . . striking indeed, but maybe a little too harsh for the . . . welcoming theme of the day?' she ended limply.

'Harsh, Mrs Canter?' Audrey Tipton took a step towards Penny but was interrupted by the arrival of her husband, Geoffrey, a man so henpecked and blustering he was known by the villagers as Mr Audrey Tipton.

'Ah, Audrey, there you are,' he panted.

Audrey became alert. 'Are they here?'

Simon swallowed nervously and felt for his dog collar. 'Angela has arrived?'

'Where?' barked Audrey.

'Just parking,' replied Geoffrey.

Audrey moved to get through the vestry door and out to greet them ahead of Simon, but Simon beat her to it. Penny smiled sweetly and pushed past Audrey too, pulling Jenna behind her. 'Welcome to Pendruggan,' beamed Simon as Angela got out of the front passenger seat. 'How was your journey?'

'We were a little early.' Angela smiled at her husband, Robert, who was stretching his legs and closing the driver's door. 'So we went down to Trevay to have a look at it. So pretty.'

Robert walked round the car and shook Simon's hand. 'Hello. Good to see you again.'

Penny stepped forward and kissed Angela. 'Welcome, at last!' She turned to Robert, who was even more handsome than she remembered. She tried not to gush. 'Hi, Robert. Welcome to Pendruggan.'

Out of the back seat unfolded a tall girl wearing a pair of super-tight white jeans, a crop top and a leather biker jacket. Her hair was long and streaked. Her face had all the sullen chubbiness of a teenager but Penny could tell she was a chrysalis ready to emerge as a beautiful woman.

'And this our daughter, Faith,' said Angela proudly.

'Hello,' said Penny. She pointed to Jenna. 'And this is our daughter, Jenna.' The Tiptons were pushing forward now, Audrey ready to assert her status as head of virtually everything in the village.

And then she saw Robert and gulped.

Tall, dark and handsome. His navy-blue eyes took in the sight of the gathering crowd of gaping villagers. A devastatingly attractive smile grew on his lips.

Angela introduced him, 'And this is Robert, my husband.'

Penny swore later that the gathered women, and a couple of the men, fairly swooned.

Simon, totally oblivious to this sudden swirl of sexual tension, took Angela's arm and chatted his way with her into the church. 'I am so looking forward to meeting every-body.'

The church was packed. Penny, in the front pew, had Jenna on her left, Robert on her right and Angela on his right. She couldn't help but notice that not only did Robert look good, he smelt good too.

The congregation stood for the first hymn as Simon, the church warden and the choir processed from the back of the church to the altar.

Penny looked around for Helen and Piran but couldn't see them. Nor could she see Queenie. A spasm of worry unsettled her again. What if something had happened to her? Were Helen and Piran calling an ambulance?

Robert noticed her fidgeting. 'Are you OK?' he whispered. 'Can I do anything to help?'

Biting her lip, she shook her head. 'Just looking for friends who should be here,' she whispered back.

The service continued with Penny's mind dithering between anxiety about Queenie and trying not to flirt with Robert. There was little space on the pews today and she was very aware of his muscular thigh and strong left arm pressed against hers.

It wasn't until the second hymn that the ancient door at the back of the church cracked open and Helen and Piran crept in. Helen gave Penny a little wave and mouthed a sheepish, 'Sorry.'

Penny wondered what had kept them. Maybe they had overslept. And where was Queenie? Another chill snapped at her heart. Was the dear old thing OK? And where was this sudden anxiety coming from? Queenie could never resist a village occasion. Especially a chance to give the new vicar a once-over. It took all of Penny's willpower to stay put and not get up to go to look for her.

Simon climbed to the pulpit.

'How wonderful to see so many of you here today. I suspect it may not be my sermon you have come to hear but, more likely, you have come to get a good look at your new vicar.' He paused for the laughter. 'I shall ask her to stand up and give us a twirl. Ladies and gentlemen, the Reverend Angela Whitehorn.'

Angela clasped her hands to her chest in embarrassment, but stood, blushing and smiling.

The congregation scrutinised her. Medium height. Very slender. A kind face framed by a short, pixie cut. No make-up. Nails sensibly short and unpolished. She was wearing a knee-length black dress with dog collar, black tights and shiny black Mary Jane shoes. The majority conceded that she looked all right for the job. She sat down and Penny noticed that Robert immediately took her hand and held it proudly.

'Let me tell you about Angela,' continued Simon. 'Upon graduating with an English degree from Manchester University, she joined the prestigious *Manchester Evening News* as a cub reporter. It was there, across a crowded newsroom, a handsome young politics writer caught her eye.' Simon looked down to where Robert was sitting. 'And became her husband. You may recognise him from his appearances on the television news. Stand up, Robert.'

Seeming embarrassed, Robert stood, so tall no one needed to crane their neck. He gave everyone a little wave and sat down again, whispering into Angela's ear and making her giggle.

Simon continued, 'A few years after they married, Angela began her path to ordination. This is her first parish as an ordained priest.' He looked down from the pulpit at Angela and smiled. 'It's only on loan, though!' Laughter came from the congregation and Robert put his arm around Angela's shoulder and pulled her to him. Penny shifted uncomfortably, feeling envious. Simon continued, 'Over the next year you will get to know Angela and Robert and their daughter, Faith, very well and they will also get to know you. I have trust and faith in you all to continue to build the fellowship within our community, and when Penny, Jenna and I return you will have many good things to share. Now, let's sing one of my favourite hymns, and suitable for today, I feel, "To Be a Pilgrim".'

After the service, Penny was still scanning the crowd for Queenie.

Simon and Angela were in the middle of the church, swamped by a deluge of curiosity and goodwill. Robert stood next to Penny, watching as his wife and her husband played the crowd like rock stars.

'Your friends got here then,' he said.

'Yes. But actually, I'm still a bit worried about one of our villagers. She runs the village post office and stores. It's not like her to miss something like this. She'd be wanting to know all about you and Angela. She is very nosy and loves all the gossip but is very kind too. We all love her.'

'Maybe she's busy?'

'She'd never be too busy for this.'

'I'm taller than you. I may spot her. What does she look like?'

'She'll be wearing some ghastly hat, probably green with feathers, and she has a distinctive scent of mothballs and tobacco. Oh, and she hasn't lost her cockney accent even though she's been here for ever.'

'She sounds quite marvellous,' he laughed.

'Oh, she is.' Penny spotted Helen and Piran making their way towards them. 'Helen, this is Robert. Robert, this is my best friend, Helen, and her partner, Piran.'

Piran shook Robert's hand with his natural distrust. He was always darkly suspicious of strangers, and this one looked a bit too pleased with himself. Too tall. Too good-looking. Too well-dressed. And Piran didn't like the way Helen was looking at him all dewy-eyed. He'd have to keep a watch on this one. "Ow do?' he growled.

Robert, used to other men's wariness, struck up a conversation about the weather while Penny got Helen's attention. 'I'm worried about Queenie,' she said quietly. 'Where is she?'

Helen shrugged disinterestedly. 'She's fine. I saw her earlier.' Her gaze wandered back to Piran and Robert. 'Piran's jealous.'

Penny ignored this and continued, 'But why isn't she here? Did she say?'

'Who? Queenie? No. I say, Robert is a bit of all right.'

'Where was she? Did she look OK?'

'Yes, yes, fine. Normal Queenie.'

'Will you stop staring at Robert?' Penny hissed. 'It's embarrassing.'

'I'm not staring,' Helen grinned.

'Yes you are. You are starting to drool. Stop it. Anyway, you already have the most handsome man in Cornwall.'

'Yes, but it's fun to see his nose put out of joint,' Helen giggled.

'I pity poor Piran, and Angela,' Penny said virtuously. 'As soon as everyone settles down and sees Robert as the nice, faithful husband he is, the better.'

Helen looked knowingly at her friend. 'You fancy him too! Don't deny it.'

'I may have referenced his appearance once or twice, but it's the inner person I see,' sniffed Penny.

'Yeah, yeah,' Helen laughed. 'Whatever.'

Penny continued. 'And Angela is going to be wonderful for Pendruggan. She's sweet, obviously caring and conscientious. You are lucky to have her.'

'So you won't want me to send long emails to Brazil about them then?' Helen asked cheekily.

Penny pursed her lips, then said frantically, 'I shall definitely need you to send gossip at least hourly. I don't want to be horrible, but you wouldn't automatically put them together, would you?'

Helen laughed. 'You are a bad girl.'

'I know. But you love me.' Penny looked anxious again. 'We only have a couple of hours before the taxi picks us up. We have got to show Angela around the vicarage, settle them in, and Simon has booked a table at the Dolphin for a "welcome" lunch.' Her eyebrows twitched anxiously. 'Would you and Piran join us for lunch? Give me some moral support? Please? And I want to find Queenie to say goodbye.'

Angela and Simon approached them. 'It's such a beautiful church and I promise I will take care of it and the congregation.'

Angela smiled, tucking her arm into Simon's. 'It feels such a happy place.' She looked over to Robert and Piran. 'Don't you think so, Robert?'

'I do indeed,' he agreed.

Simon locked the empty church and solemnly handed the ancient, heavy key to Angela. 'There. That's yours.'

Angela carefully put it in her small handbag. 'I will look after it with my life.'

Walking out of the churchyard, Simon, with Robert and Piran chatting beside him, noticed that there wasn't a soul in sight. Not a single one to wish him *bon voyage*. All had drifted away back to their homes and Sunday lunch. He was surprised and a little hurt, but he supposed the morning in church had been his farewell.

Penny, walking behind him, felt his disappointment. It was unkind. They were obviously yesterday's people now. Even Queenie hadn't bothered to show up.

She watched as Jenna demonstrated her cartwheels to Faith on the village green but Penny's mind began to slip into a future she couldn't yet imagine. What the hell were they doing going to Brazil?

'Wouldn't you say so, Pen?' Helen was talking to her.

'Sorry. What?'

'The Dolphin is female friendly. It's OK, as a woman, to go to the Dolphin for a drink or a sarnie and not raise eyebrows.'

Penny roused herself. 'Oh, yes. Don and Dorrie are wonderful.' She forced herself to sound relaxed. 'It really is lovely.' They approached the gate of the vicarage. 'Well. Here we are. Your new home.'

At the front door, Simon put his key in the lock and pushed the door open.

'SURPRISE!!!!' A great wall of noisy voices and the smiling faces of Pendruggan villagers hit him. People were blowing hooters and throwing streamers so that, in moments, Simon was covered in coloured paper and hugs.

And, halfway up the stairs, like the Cheshire cat, sat a smiling Queenie with a tray full of her famous pasties.

'Sorry I didn't make church, Vicar, but I was busy making these for you.'

Simon was sucked into the crowd as Penny wiped her eyes and waved at Queenie.

'You didn't think she'd honestly miss a send-off like this, did you?' asked Helen.

'Did you know about this, you cow?' said Penny, unable to stop the tears of relief. 'I thought the worst.'

'Oi,' Queenie cackled as she reached Penny. 'What you crying for?'

'I missed you in church,' Penny smiled, 'I was worried for you.'

'You thought I was dead in me bed, didn't ya? Don't lie.'

'Of course not. It's just that I'm going to miss you.' Penny hugged the old lady, feeling her whiskery chin tickle her cheek.

'Come on, you silly girl, there's a huge buffet spread out for you all in the lounge.'

'Not my clean lounge! That's out of bounds!'

'Well it ain't now.'

4

'Well, that was a surprise,' Penny said, taking Simon's hand as they settled in the back of the people carrier taking them to Heathrow. 'I'm quite exhausted.'

He stroked her hand as he took a last look at the village green and gaggle of people waving from the vicarage garden. 'It was quite wonderful.'

'We'll sleep well on the flight.' Penny yawned and turned to Jenna, who was rubbing her nose with Blue Ted. 'You OK, Pidge?' she asked.

'Faith is nice,' said Jenna sleepily. 'She liked my bedroom. I don't mind her using it because she said she would show me how to put make-up on when I come back.'

Simon swivelled his shocked eyes towards Penny, who put her arm across Jenna's shoulders and hugged her. 'What fun. But no nicking my expensive stuff.'

Jenna giggled. 'Your make-up is for ladies with wrinkles. Faith told me that. She's got proper young stuff. She's even got a purple lipstick.'

'Wrinkles? I haven't got wrinkles.'

'Because you hide them with the wrinkle make-up.'

Simon nodded. 'She's got a point.'

Penny elbowed him hard in the ribs, but Jenna hadn't finished. 'And when I showed Faith inside your make-up bag she said that her mummy uses that white cream on her moustache, too.'

'You showed her my make-up bag?'

'Well, she's family now, isn't she? By the way, can I have a mobile phone because Faith says I can ring her any time when I'm in Brazil.'

Simon spluttered, 'I don't think so, young lady.'

'We'll see,' said Penny.

Angela and Robert closed their new front door as the last of the party visitors went home.

'They are nice people,' said Robert, taking Angela in his arms. 'I like Helen.'

Angela tucked her head under Robert's chin. 'She is nice. I like Piran, too.'

'Do you?' he asked. 'My jury is out. He did suggest we go fishing. But much too macho caveman for me.'

'Don't be silly,' said Angela. 'Do you think they'll like us?'

'I think they will love you.' Robert kissed her hair.

Angela laughed. 'And you! Everybody loves you.' She paused. 'Listen.'

Robert listened. 'I can't hear anything.'

'Exactly. Not a sound. No traffic. No aeroplanes. No music. Just the peace of the Cornish countryside.' Angela stretched up to kiss him. 'Glass of wine?'

Faith was at the kitchen table, surrounded by the remains of the party food. She was munching the end of a pasty and flicking through her iPad. 'Wi-Fi here is useless.'

'Good.' Angela tickled her daughter's head as she passed and began opening cupboards, looking for wine glasses. 'Would you like a small glass of wine? Special occasion and all that.'

Faith cheered up. 'Yes, please.'

Robert sat across the table from her. 'What do you think then, Faith? Like your room?'

'It's nice apart from being baby pink.'

'You'll get over it,' laughed Robert.

'To us.' Angela raised her glass.

'To you.' Robert tipped his glass to hers. 'This is your gig and Faith and I are happy to be the back-up team,' He swallowed the pale white wine. 'Nice.'

'Mamie sent it to us. House-warming present.'

'When does she get here?' asked Faith.

'Tomorrow. She's bringing Mr Worthington with her.'

Faith clapped her hands. 'I've missed him. We can explore the village together. Apparently the lane by the side of the church goes down to the sea and a nice beach, Jenna told me.'

'I might make a picnic for us all. If it's not raining.' Angela looked around her. 'Lovely kitchen, isn't it? I'm a bit afraid of the Aga, though. Never used one before. Is anybody hungry?'

'Those pasties filled me up. I had two.' Robert patted his stomach. 'How about you, Faith?'

'I think I'll have a bath now that I've got my own en suite.' She picked up her iPad and strolled to the door.

'Well, don't take all the hot water because Daddy and I will want one too.'

'Gross,' said Faith with a curled lip. 'TMI.'

'Married people do take baths together sometimes, you know,' Robert called after her.

Faith ran up the stairs. 'La-la-la-la, I can't hear you.'

'Well, that's got rid of her,' smiled Robert. 'Come and sit next to me.'

'I've got stuff to do.'

'No you haven't. The removal men are delivering our meagre essentials tomorrow and I know you don't have to make any beds up because, thoughtfully, Penny told me that she had done them already.'

'I know,' Angela sighed gratefully.

'So, sit here and give me a cuddle.'

'Can't we just lie on the sofa, and watch television?'

Robert checked his watch. 'That's a point. Chelsea were playing Tottenham earlier. We might get the highlights.'

Robert woke the next morning in the unfamiliar bed in the unfamiliar room. The mattress was supportive but seemed to mould to his body. The pillows were the perfect mix of comfort and yield. The duvet exactly the right weight.

He stretched his limbs, feeling the blood tingle through his body, then relaxed once more.

The light creeping over the top of the curtains drew long, bright fingers over the Victorian corniced, whitewashed ceiling. The walls were painted in a subtle eau-de-Nil, which high-lighted the old and uneven plaster. He wondered, as men do, about the workmen who had built this vicarage. How long it had taken them. The families they went home to, covered in sawdust and sweat. They had done a good job. The outer walls were built of sturdy granite and slate. The inner walls probably plaster and lathe with horsehair to bond and insulate.

He closed his eyes and pictured the men working in this room. Caps on. Tweed jackets. Aprons over trousers tied at the ankle. Feet shod in sturdy boots.

They might have sat right where he was lying, eating pasties and smoking pipes.

How many of them had gone on to fight in the Great War? How many had returned? How many were remembered?

He somehow felt connected to them, through the house: now was his turn to make these walls his home. Well, Angela's turn really . . .

He reached across for Angela and carefully folded himself around her, feeling the strength in her sinewy back and shoulders and the warmth of her hips on his thighs. His hand reached round and held her taut flat tummy before travelling up to stroke her small breasts. He kissed her neck and she stirred.

'Good morning, my love,' he whispered.

'Hey,' she whispered back with her eyes still closed.

'Do you want anything?'

'What are you offering?'

'Coffee? Tea? Me?'

'Faith will hear us.'

'I'll be quick and quiet.'

'Smooth talker.'

Somewhere in the village an engine at full throttle disturbed the moment. It was getting closer and slowing into a lower throatier gear.

Robert and Angela knew at once, even before the two-tone horn set the churchyard crows chattering. Robert rolled onto his back and looked at the ceiling before saying, 'Bloody Mamie.'

The Jensen Interceptor drew to a halt outside their gate. Robert and Angela listened as the car door opened and slammed shut. A feminine, well-educated, husky voice shouted up, 'Hellooo! Anybody home?'

'Put your pyjamas on, quick,' ordered Angela as she flew out of bed and over to her dressing gown. Fastening it round her, she went to the open bedroom window and looked out. The village green, thick with dew, sparkled fresh and green at her. A murder of crows, roused from their sleep by the noise of the engine, flapped and cawed furiously from the churchyard.

A tall woman dressed in a tight pencil skirt, white blouse, with too many buttons undone, and a wide patent leather belt gripping her waist, looked up at her.

'Darling.' She opened her arms wide. 'Am I too early? I have come straight from the dullest dinner date in town. A banker. Three ex-wives. Last one dead. Died of boredom, I suspect. But anyway, the sunrise was so divine I decided to drive straight down. Missed all the traffic. The old Jensen really opened up. If it wasn't for the traffic cop stopping me I'd have been here even earlier. He was terribly sweet, though. Turned out he was a Jensen fan and wanted to know all about her.'

Angela was still fighting with her dressing gown sleeve. 'Were you speeding? Is that why he stopped you?'

Mamie shook a white chiffon scarf from her coiffed blond curls and looked sheepish. 'Maybe. A little. But he was awfully nice. Just a little ticking-off. Wasn't that sweet? Aren't you going to open the door and let me in? Mr Worthington is dying for a pee.'

'An Aga, darling!' cried Mamie as if she were looking at the crown jewels. 'God, I am so jealous. I've never stayed anywhere long enough to have one of my own, but darling Jeremy's mother – you know, the one who was married to the Home Secretary – cooked divine things on hers.'

'Oh, good,' said Angela, who didn't have a clue who darling

Jeremy was. 'You can show me how to use it then.' She reached for the big old steel kettle. 'I can just about boil this on it.' She lifted the left-hand lid of the Aga and plonked the kettle on it.

'Now, darling, don't be silly. You know I don't cook. By the way, has my early arrival interrupted a little something between you and Robert?'

Angela pulled her dressing gown closer around her. 'No.'

'Ah.' Mamie smiled wickedly. 'It's just that you've got it on inside out.'

Angela blushed and then began to laugh. 'Oh, Mamie, I am so pleased to see you.' She hugged her aunt.

'Me too,' said Faith, arriving with a yawn. 'Group hug, please.'

Mamie held her arms out for the three-way embrace. 'Look at you. So beautiful, and so tall.'

'Children do tend to grow,' said Robert from the doorway. 'Hi, Mamie. Welcome to Cornwall.' The group hug separated and Mamie gave Robert the once-over.

'Robert, you look divine in pyjamas. I had you down for a sleeping-in-the-buff kind of man.' She raised an eyebrow saucily at him as Faith made a retching sound and Angela changed the subject.

'Where's Mr Worthington?'

'In the car. Sleeping. Dreadful company. And he has had the most unpleasant attack of wind all the way down the motorway, so try not to breathe around him.'

Faith was already out in the hall and wrenching open the front door. Within moments a long-legged, shaggy wolfhound with caramel eyes and a dignified face lolloped in. Faith followed behind. 'Your car does smell terrible, but Mr Worthington says he's very sorry.'

Angela sank to her knees and fondled the big wise head

in her lap. 'Hello, boy. Welcome to your new home. You've come to live by the seaside. Shall we go walkies on the beach later? Shall we?'

Mr Worthington thumped his long, feathery tail on the kitchen tiles and held a leg up to have his elbow tickled.

Breakfast was a busy mêlée of boiled eggs and gossip as Mamie demanded to hear all about the new people of the village.

'Queenie sounds like my kind of gal,' she affirmed. 'We'll be great friends. Get her out on the tonk and I'll know everything there is to know in a flash. And what about you, Robert? What will this year in Cornwall bring you?'

'I am here purely as Angela's wingman.'

'Not going to put your journalistic talents to use?' Mamie liked to get straight to the point. 'I am certain that the local news outlets would love to have the famous Robert Whitehorn on their books.'

'Oh, no, no. My first priority is to get Faith settled into her new school.'

Mamie turned her shrewd eyes to Faith. 'When do you do your GCSEs?'

'Mocks are in the summer term,' Faith said, scowling. 'Real ones next year.'

'A bit disruptive for you, then?'

'My old school is keeping an eye on the syllabus down here, before I go back there. It should be fine.'

Mamie nodded slowly. 'Just promise me one thing.'

'What?'

'You work hard and you don't give your parents any trouble. This is a big year for your mother. Her first parish. She needs this to go well and for you to respect that. Got it?'

'Got it.'

'Good.' Mamie stood up decisively. 'I am going to unpack. Have a shower and get out of these townie clothes.'

'Don't you want to have a rest? You haven't been to bed,' said Faith kindly.

'Good God, no. I've never needed much sleep. Time for that when I'm dead. Now, Faith, take that dog for a pee, please. He stinks. Robert, you wash up. Angela, get dressed. I want to see this new church of yours.'

5

The vestry key, heavy and old, had a knack to it that Simon had showed her but Angela now couldn't remember.

'The previous vicar told me the trick but . . .' she turned the key and wiggled the old latch to no avail, '. . . I can't think what it was.'

'Give it to me,' said Mamie. Angela stepped aside as her aunt lifted the latch and pulled the door up and outwards. She turned the key. The door opened smoothly. 'I think it's one of those doors that changes with the weather,' she said to an astonished Angela. 'You'll get used to it.' She stepped into the vestry. 'God, it's cold in here.'

'The heating's on a timer.' Angela was looking for the light switch. 'Just a couple of hours twice a day, to keep the old place ticking over.' She found the old brass light switch and flipped it down with a pleasing clunk. A dim, unshaded single bulb, hanging from the ceiling, began to glow. 'It'll warm up in a minute. Let there be light and all that,' said Angela, hoping that Mamie wouldn't hate everything. 'And I think the bank of lights switches over by the door there turns on the main lights.'

Mamie peered at the plastic panel and pushed each switch down.

Angela opened the inner door to the church and found the nave and choir fully lit. 'Oh, good. They are the right ones.'

Mamie walked in and took in the beauty of the old church with the late morning sun making the jewelled, stained-glass windows glow.

Taking her time, she stepped towards the altar, heels clicking on the cardinal-red floor tiles. She gazed up at the vaulted ceiling, motes of dust drifting through the sunbeams.

'It's beautiful,' she breathed. 'Imagine all the weddings and baptisms and funerals that have taken place here.' She turned to Angela. 'It's perfect and you are perfect for it.'

An anxious Angela asked, 'So you like it?'

Mamie sat on a pew. 'Darling, I am bursting with pride.'

'Would Mum like it?' Angela asked as she sat next to Mamie.

'She'd hug herself with joy.' Mamie put her feet up on the pew in front of her. 'Bloody cold, obviously, but this is exactly where you belong. I can feel it. There is good karma here. I like the smell too. Beeswax. God, if your mother *were* here she'd be polishing every day.'

Angela grinned. She pointed at a needlepoint kneeler lying at her feet and examined the motif of a lamb watching a bright star in a night sky. 'Wouldn't she love making one of these?'

Mamie nodded. 'Oh, yes. She'd have the stitch-and-bitch club up and running. Knitting for beginners, forcing the poor grannies and young mums into creating hideous pram blankets and woolly hats.' She sighed. 'I miss her.'

Angela looked towards the altar and sighed. 'This is one of those times when I want to ring her. Tell her all about it. I find myself actually reaching for the phone at times. Let her know how Faith is doing. How happy I am with Robert . . . Silly, isn't it?'

Mamie took her niece's hand. 'I do the same. Very often. I miss her more than I can say. I have so much to thank her for.' She rummaged the depths of her pockets. 'Three years this October.' She pulled out a packet of cigarettes and a gold lighter. 'Can I smoke in here?'

'Probably not but I won't tell.'

Mamie lit up and blew a plume of smoke into the still air, then turned her concerned eyes towards Angela. 'How are you?'

Angela watched the smoke rise in the still air. 'OK.'

'Only OK?'

'I haven't cried for almost a fortnight.'

'And the tablets?'

Angela looked at her hands. 'Good. Half the dose now. Dr King keeps an eye on me.'

'And who will keep an eye on you while you are here?'

'I can call Dr King any time. But we generally chat once a week. It helps. Sometimes I'm fine, sometimes I am drowning in the grief of missing Mum and other times I am totally numb. Dr King says it's all normal.'

'Do you talk to Robert when things are difficult?'

'I try not to. It worries him and he feels helpless so . . .' Angela rubbed at her forehead, not wanting to break down in front of Mamie.

'When we were little, your mum and I, she was the good

daughter. If there was washing to hang on the line, she'd do it. If Mum needed her feet rubbed, it was her she wanted. It caused more than a little sibling rivalry between us, I can tell you.'

Angela smiled. 'Mum told me you were a bit of a rebel.'

'A bit! The uncomfortable truth is, I was jealous of her. Her beauty, her sweetness, her brains. Her smooth complexion. She had no need to rebel. Everyone loved her.'

'She told me she envied your independence.'

'Oh, I was independent all right. Lipstick, boyfriends, the Rolling Stones, cigarettes and gin. Insisting that everyone called me Mamie rather than Marjorie.'

Angela laughed. 'Is it true that you tried to get Mum to change her name too?'

'Oh, yes! How could I have a sister called Elsie! I went on and on at her. Ellie. You must be called Ellie. Mamie and Ellie sounded infinitely better than Marjorie and Elsie.'

'And yet you were so close as you got older.'

'We were. She was my best friend. I could tell her anything and she'd never judge me.'

Angela nodded. 'She told me that when Dad died, you came straight home to be with her.'

'Where else would I be? Anyway, being a chalet girl in Klosters might have sounded good but it was a terrible job. The men were all randy, but ugly, and the women were all skeletal bitches.'

Angela laughed. 'I can imagine you arriving, all glam in white salopettes and fur boots.'

'I brought her a bottle of Nina Ricci L'Air du Temps from duty-free. To cheer her up.' Mamie inhaled her cigarette deeply then stubbed the butt on the tiled floor. She noted Angela's raised eyebrow. 'Don't worry. I'll pick it up before we go. So

I gave her the perfume and she hugged me for it and, shortly afterwards, we discovered you were on the way.'

Angela bent down and picked up the discarded cigarette butt. 'What would she and I have done without you?'

'Well, you'd have been called Tracey, for a start!'

'What?'

'Yep. It was the name of the midwife who delivered you. Terrible idea. So I gave her some better options. Sadie. Eloise. Tuesday.'

'Tuesday?'

'Well, you were born on a Tuesday. Anyway, she said no to all of them and then I thought of Angelina because you were such an angel, but your Mum preferred Angela so here we are. And, as it happens, the perfect name for a perfect vicar.'

'I will be happy with being a half-decent vicar.'

Mamie put a comforting arm around her niece and kissed her hair. 'Darling, your mum and I couldn't be more proud of you.'

'Thank you.' Angela's eyes pricked with tears. 'I wonder if I have been incredibly selfish. Asking Robert to take a year out. Disrupting Faith's school life . . .'

'Now stop that!' Mamie reached for her bag and drew out her packet of cigarettes. 'That is self-indulgent nonsense and you know it.' She lit another cigarette and with it between her teeth said, 'You, my girl, are a brave and wonderful woman. Robert will survive; in fact, I think he's very grateful to be out of his rut for a bit.'

'It's not a rut! Mamie, the Prime Minister calls him Bob. The BBC are thinking of sending him to Washington to be their correspondent. He is important. I'm just a rookie vicar who has landed in a tiny rural parish and who isn't so certain that it's the best thing I could have done.'

'You might like to have a few joss sticks burning in here,' Mamie said.

'Don't change the subject. I'm trying to tell you how scared I am. This could all turn out to be a huge disaster.' Angela clenched her hands anxiously.

'My darling girl, I may not have faith in your God, but whoever she is, she has faith in you. This is simply a test of that faith.'

Angela angrily brushed away a stray tear. 'It's hard. Believing in something that others think is a fantasy. People judge me. Think I am naïve. Mad.'

'Who thinks that?'

'You. Robert. Faith. Old friends. I've been asked so often, *If there is a God, why does he allow war and violence?* I can only say that we were given the Ten Commandments to live by but God gave us the free will to follow them or not. Not much of an answer, is it?'

Mamie sat silently, mulling this over, then said, 'If I believe in anything it is the innate goodness that lies inside humans. You will lead this parish by example.'

Angela took a deep breath then sighed. 'I will try.'

'You're only human.'

'Yeah.'

'So what about some joss sticks?'

'No.' Angela smiled weakly.

'Why not?' Mamie shrugged.

'Because I am an ordained priest in the Christian Church. Not an old hippy like you.'

'So pompous and pious,' Mamie teased. 'There's nothing wrong with a joss stick. Great for meditation. Why wouldn't they be great for prayer? Tell me where in the Bible God says, *Let there be no joss sticks?*'

'Fire hazard.' Angela sniffed. 'And please don't stub that cigarette out on the floor again.'

'Sorry.' Mamie stood and walked up the aisle. 'Nice vibe in this building. I can see you bringing fun and spirit to this place. It may not be an inner-city area but it will have its own problems. Humans like to make a mess of their lives and all human mess will be here exactly as it is in any other parish.' She walked back to where Angela was still sitting. 'All joking apart, darling, I know you will make a difference. Whatever that difference may be. Too late for me, of course. God gave up on me years ago. But he likes you.'

'He likes all of us, even you,' Angela said fondly.

'Don't try and convert me. It's much too late. Now let's get out of here, I want to see the beach.'

They went back to the vicarage and picked up an excited Mr Worthington and Faith. The latter was in a tiny jumper and hot pants.

'Put some clothes on. You'll catch your death out there,' Mamie ordered.

'I'll be fine,' said Faith, wrapping an extra-long scarf round her neck.

'It's raining,' her mother told her. 'Put your coat on.'

Faith did as she was told, grumbling, 'You're so boring.'

'Speak for yourself,' Mamie said, propelling her to the door.

The weather had turned from the early sunshine and bright blue sky to a grey accumulation of grim-looking clouds. Shellsand Bay was at its bleakest. As the three women, with Mr Worthington bounding ahead of them, neared the beach, the wind pummelled their faces and the roar of the waves filled their ears.

The weak sunshine layered strips of colour across the

wrinkled sea. Steel grey, bright silver, and oily green met and mingled, changing with the dance of the wind.

The white-capped waves hissed as they bumped on the shore, their rhythm soothing and hypnotic. Dozens of smooth pebbles chasing and flipping as the tide sucked the water out again.

Mamie took off her wedge-heeled gold trainers, revealing tanned feet with scarlet-painted toenails. 'Paddling, Faith?' she called above the strong breeze, not blind to the fact that Faith was shaking with the cold, her bare legs, sticking out from under her far from sensible coat, covered in goosebumps and turning blue.

'No.'

'Well, Mr Worthington and I are going in. Come on. What about you Angela?'

'No, thank you.' Angela's chin was down inside her jacket.

'What's wrong with the pair of you? When you've lived with the Inuits your blood thickens. Hold my shoes.' She handed them to Angela. 'Come on, Mr Worthington.'

Excitedly, Mr Worthington dashed ahead, stopping to circle back for her every few seconds. He spotted a piece of driftwood and wrapped his jaws around it, sand and all, plonking it at Mamie's feet.

She obliged and threw it high towards the water line.

Angela and Faith watched her from the drier sand.

'Inuits?' asked Faith. 'What, like, living in an igloo?'

'Hmm.' Angela frowned slightly. 'I can't always tell which of her stories are real, embroidered or simply fiction.'

'Who was supposed to have given her that fur coat again?'

'A man she met in Marrakesh. He told her it had been left behind in a restaurant by Rita Hayworth, who had never returned to claim it.'

'Who's Rita Hayworth?'

'The most alluring film star of her day.'

Faith wrinkled her nose. 'Weird.'

'Nice coat, though.'

'Yeah, like wearing dead animals on your back is like a good thing. As if the poor things were, like,' Faith raised the pitch of her voice to mimic a small mammal, 'oh yeah, please murder me and wear me as a coat. I'd be honoured.'

'Well, let's not get into that right now. That was then and this is now and Aunt Mamie is Aunt Mamie and . . . oh my goodness, she's fallen over.'

Mamie had been bowled over by an overenthusiastic Mr Worthington and was now on her knees clutching at the shifting sand as a huge wave crashed over her, soaking her hair, leaving her gasping for breath, and tugging her further out.

As Faith and Angela ran to her, shouting, 'We're coming. Hold on,' they heard strong footsteps racing behind them. Angela turned and saw Piran.

'My aunt! She's fallen in,' she shouted.

Piran made no answer. He simply ran to the water's edge and strode into the icy waves. Mamie had found her feet and was staggering in the swell but the next wave knocked her over again and pulled her further out. Piran shouted to her but his voice was just a rag on the wind. Now up to his waist, he plunged in, swimming with admirable strength, as Angela and Faith were later to attest, towards a helpless Mamie.

'He's got her,' shrieked Faith to her mother, panting. 'Hang onto him, Auntie Mamie,' she shouted.

At last, Mamie was towed in, arriving breathless and tumbled.

'Oh goodness.' She rested on Piran's shoulder, trembling and trying to pull her hair from her eyes. 'How can I thank you?'

'What the bleddy 'ell do you think you were doing, woman?' Piran said tersely, gripping her shoulders and pushing her off him.

Mamie let go of him and pulled herself up straight. 'Thank you so much for saving my life. Very kind of you. Though you are hardly Prince Charming.'

Piran saw the coal-like glitter in her eyes. He glared back. 'And you're no Cinderella.'

Angela looked from one to the other. 'Please. Stop. It's all been a shock.' She put her hand on Piran's arm. 'Thank you for saving my aunt, Piran. Perhaps you'd like to come back to the vicarage where I can give you some dry clothes and a hot drink?'

'Thank you, no.' He shook out his sodden jumper and looked up the beach to where Mr Worthington and a Jack Russell were chasing each other. 'Jack, heel.'

'Please send my love to Helen.' Angela attempted a smile. 'It was so good of you both to come to the party yesterday.'

'Had to give Simon and Penny a good send-off, didn't we? We'm going to miss them.'

Angela felt squashed. 'Yes. Well. Simon has left big shoes to fill.'

'Too bleddy right he has,' Piran retorted.

Jack sauntered up and sniffed at Mamie's leg. Her arms aching, her teeth chattering, her heart banging, she could only watch as the little dog raised his rear leg and peed on her foot.

Piran wiped a demon's smile from his face with a huge

hand. 'Come on boy,' he said, his eyes still dancing with amusement. 'Home.'

'What a horrible gorilla of a man!' Mamie complained as she squelched through the back door.

'I'm going to run you a bath,' Angela said. 'Give me your clothes and I will launder them.'

'What an absolute oaf,' Mamie said emphatically, peeling off her sodden things.

'Who is?' asked Robert as he ambled into the kitchen and backed out again at the sight of his aunt-in-law in bra and pants.

'Don't be so priggish,' responded Mamie. 'Never seen a woman in her underwear before?'

Angela gave him a warning glance. 'Make yourself useful and put the kettle on. Mamie fell into the sea and Piran saved her.'

'Good old Piran.'

'I saw nothing good in the man.' Mamie's anger grew and filled the kitchen. 'He was unspeakably rude to me and insulted Angela.'

'Really?'

'I don't think he meant to. It was all very heat-of-the-moment stuff,' said Angela, moving to the kettle that Robert had ignored. 'Tea? Anyone?'

'Tea?' Mamie was unimpressed. 'I need some brandy.'

'Robert, please get Auntie Mamie some brandy and fetch her dressing gown and a warm towel from the airing cupboard.'

'The pink silk wrap on the bathroom door, Robert,' Mamie added. 'Toot sweet, if you could. I'm freezing my jacksie off here.'

*

After a hot bath and a change into warm pyjamas, Mamie came downstairs to find the sitting room fire had been lit. A proper afternoon tea was laid out on the piano. Cheese sandwiches, ham sandwiches, scones and cake. Angela was setting down the teapot.

'Angela, what a spread,' Mamie exclaimed. 'The country is doing you good.'

Angela sat heavily on the sofa and sighed. 'The leftovers from yesterday's farewell party for Simon and Helen. I hope the sandwiches are not too curled at the edges.'

Robert entered with an armful of logs. 'Simon has a fine log store round the side of the house.' He crouched in front of the crackling grate and balanced a log onto the blaze. 'Very impressive. Simon knows what he's doing obviously. A good log store takes understanding and time to . . .' he looked up at the unimpressed faces of Angela and Mamie and changed tack, 'Ah. There you are, Mamie. Better after the bath? Another brandy?'

'If you don't mind. Then I shall tell you all about this afternoon's misadventure.'

After he'd heard the story, he was torn between respect for Piran and a desire to go round and punch his lights out. 'I had my doubts about the man when I met him yesterday.'

'Did you really?' Angela contradicted. 'I thought you said you were looking forward to going fishing with him.'

'Going fishing with him and liking him are two entirely different things.'

'He's a swine.' Mamie tipped the brandy into her mouth and held out the glass for Robert to refill.

Angela plonked the remains of a Victoria sponge onto her plate and sat down. 'I think he was in shock. Remember, Robert, when Faith was small and we lost her in that hypermarket in France? When we found her you shouted at her until you were hoarse.'

'That was with relief.'

'Quite. And I believe that Piran was feeling the same. Relief. Shock. The poor man was only out on a walk with his dog and ended up fully submerged in the icy Atlantic, saving the life of a strange, fully clothed woman.'

Mamie growled, 'I was the victim.'

Angela pulled a face of disbelief. 'You have never been a victim. I shall go and see Piran and Helen tomorrow and pour oil on troubled waters. We have only just arrived and I want to be friends with everybody. I want this year to be a success.' She glared at her aunt and husband. 'You two have to buck up and be nice. Understood?'

Mamie pursed her lips and looked over at Robert. 'I suppose I could,' she said reluctantly. 'If Robert will.'

'I will,' answered Robert slowly. 'Just as long as no one else takes a pop at either of you.'

'Good. That's sorted.' Angela smiled at them both and pushed a large chunk of Victoria sponge into her mouth.

Two hundred yards away, across the village green, Helen was having words with Piran in her cottage.

'How could you? You have insulted Angela by suggesting she's not welcome here, and you have been extremely rude to an elderly lady.'

'She ain't no lady. I can tell. Smelling like a tart's boudoir and pouring herself all over me when I put her down. You should have seen her face when Jack cocked his leg on her foot. Priceless.'

Helen picked up Piran's wet jumper from the rail of the Aga and threw it at him. 'Goodbye.'

Piran caught the jumper in astonishment. 'Now what's got into you? I thought you was cooking supper?'

'I am cooking supper. But not for you. I don't like it when you go all Neanderthal. Go to the pub and get something there.'

'But my trousers are still damp.'

'Well, go back to your house, get changed, and then go to the pub.'

Scowling, Piran went to the door, whistling up Jack behind him. 'Come on, Jack. Someone's had a sense of humour failure.'

Helen winced as he slammed the front door. Piran was one of the kindest, gentlest men she had ever met. But, unfortunately, he still had rather a large slice of chauvinism in his blood.

Helen abandoned the idea of making a lasagne, and took a Scotch egg, some salad and a bottle of wine out of the fridge. Putting the small meal together she went to her snug front room and turned on the television. A romantic comedy starring Ryan Gosling was just starting. Helen settled into the sofa and balanced her plate on her lap. She took a sip of wine and put her feet up.

'He'll be back,' she said to herself. 'Idiotic man.'

6

'Good morning, darling.' Mamie put her face around the door of Angela's office where Angela was on her knees stacking books onto Simon's emptied shelves. 'Sleep well?'

'Always.' Angela heaved herself up and kissed her aunt. 'How are you after yesterday? No bruises or chills?'

Mamie laughed her throaty laugh. 'It'd take more than a dunk to kill me off. And in retrospect, my rescuer was rather handsome.'

Angela shook her head. 'He's taken.'

'My dear, I have never stooped to stealing a man.'

'Well, don't start now, please.'

'Even when John was having a "break" – I think that's the modern term – from Yoko, I told him firmly, no.'

'You mean . . .?'

'Yes. And he was sweet. But so was she.'

Again Angela shook her head in amazement. 'Why have I never heard about that before?'

'One forgets all that one has done in one's past,' Mamie

replied airily. 'I am going to explore the village shop. Get some stamps . . . and some local gossip.'

Queenie was sitting in her comfy old armchair in the Pendruggan village store chatting to Tony, the village gardener.

'So I wants some window boxes this year. Make the shop entrance even more enticing.'

Tony scratched his nose. 'Do you want me to write things down?'

'Help yourself to one of them notebooks on the shelf behind you and there's me pen on the counter. I was thinking apricot geraniums.'

Tony sat back down and opened the school exercise book he'd found. 'I'll write that down.'

'And maybe some light blue pansies.'

'Right you are.'

'And African marigolds. My husband loved marigolds. Now he did have green fingers. Just like you.'

'Mrs Merrifield says that too. I don't know what she mean. Mine fingers are brown,' said Tony, looking at his weather-beaten hands.

'Yes, but that's what makes them green.'

The bell above the shop door rang and Mamie entered, distracting Tony from this puzzle.

Queenie was on her feet in a flash. There was nothing she liked more than a stranger.

Mamie towered over Queenie's arthritic frame. 'Good morning.' She flashed her most charming smile.

'Good morning,' replied Queenie, looking the glamorous woman up and down critically, absorbing every detail to recount to her customers. She folded her arms and hitched up her bosoms. 'Can I help you?'

Tony was sitting with his mouth open, entranced. 'Is that your Jensen Interceptor sports car outside the vicarage?'

Mamie smiled. 'Yes. Do you like cars?'

'No. But I like yours.'

'Thank you.'

'A 1976 seven-point-two litre,' he recited.

'Yes. My goodness,' smiled Mamie. 'You sound very knowledgeable. Would you like a ride in it?'

Tony bobbed his head down quickly, blushing furiously. 'No. I don't like going in cars. They make me all bobbled up.'

Mamie put her head to one side and assessed this man-child in front of her. 'I see. But perhaps you'd like to look at it one day?'

Tony, keeping his head down, nodded. 'Yes.'

'Any time you like.' She stuck her hand out. 'Hello. I'm Mamie. I am the new vicar's aunt.'

Tony kept his hands by his sides and, without looking at her, said, 'I'm Simple Tony. I do gardening. But I like washing cars.'

'What a marvellous thing.' Mamie took her hand back. 'She needs a good wash and polish. When are you free?'

'I'll go home and get a bucket and a sponge now.' He looked at Queenie. 'Am I allowed to?'

'Of course you are.' Queenie was pleased to get Mamie all to herself. 'Off you go.'

The two women watched him leave, his dark shiny hair as sleek as a mole's.

'He'll do a good job. Don't worry,' Queenie reassured Mamie.

'I'm sure he will.' Mamie looked around at the shelves in the shop and took in the time warp of goods on offer. Blakey's heel studs. Bra strap extenders. An impressive news stand laden with gossip magazines. Faded stationery items. Tinned mandarins, frankfurters and processed peas. A vast display of cigarettes, vapes and pipe tobacco. Cheap plastic dolls and boxes, small and large, of jigsaw puzzles. Mamie twirled on the spot to take it all in. 'This isn't a village store,' she breathed in admiration. 'This is an *emporium*.'

'Oh, yes, me duck, it is that. I can send a parcel to Peru from me post office counter and feed you a homemade pasty, all in the same five minutes.' Queenie moved a tatty lamp with a pink-fringed shade out of the way and took herself behind her ancient wooden counter. 'So, how can I help you?'

Mamie pointed a fiery red fingernail at a jar of red sweets. 'May I have a quarter of the aniseed twists, please?'

Silently Queenie weighed her up. She recognised something in the woman in front of her, one gossip to another. 'What have you really come for?'

Mamie held her hands up in surrender. 'I'm new and want to know the ins and outs of the village.'

'Take a seat.' Queenie pointed at Simple Tony's empty chair. 'I'll put a pot of tea on.'

'Coffee, love?' Robert nudged the office door open with his elbow. Angela had filled all the bookshelves but the very top one, and was now balanced on a chair with several hardbacks in her hands. 'Let me do that,' he said.

She reached up on tiptoes but still couldn't quite reach. 'Couldn't find the stepladders.'

Robert put the mugs down on the desk. 'Come down. I'll do it.' He put his hands on her waist and effortlessly lifted her to the floor. 'Drink your coffee.'

'Thank you.'

She sat and watched as he pushed the books into their new home. 'Any more?'

She shook her head. 'Done.' She sipped her coffee and put a foot on his lap as he pulled the chair he'd been standing on closer and sat down.

He rubbed it gently. 'Where's Faith?'

'In her room grumbling about the Wi-Fi. Has the Sky TV man fixed the telly?'

'Oh, yes. My fifty-four-inch pride and joy is now receiving all the favourites and *Love Island.*'

'Couldn't we lose that one?'

'And lose Faith too?'

'Life would be quieter . . .'

He nodded. 'And cheaper.'

They quietly acknowledged this truth.

Robert broke the silence. 'Nice view of the village green from here.'

'Mr Worthington likes it.'

'Where is he?'

'On Faith's bed.'

'I thought we said no . . .'

'We did but he persuaded me she needed him.'

'You're too soft.' He stopped rubbing her foot. 'Other one.' She swapped. 'That's why I love you,' he said. 'I love all of you. Even your cheesy feet.'

She smiled. 'I can't thank you enough for coming all this way. Uprooting yourself, and Faith, to support me.'

'I am a saint.'

'You are!'

'Is there a Saint Robert?'

'Yes. I'm looking at him.' She drained her coffee and took

her foot back. 'How many more boxes have we got left to empty?'

'The last few are in the sitting room. Only my books. I thought I'd put them on the shelves by the fireplace?'

'I'll help you and then we could take Mr W for a walk?'

There was a sharp knock on the front door. 'And so it begins.' Robert stretched his arms above his head. 'A parishioner. I'll bet a fiver.' There was a second impatient knock. 'Definitely a parishioner. I'm off to hide in the sitting room.'

On her own, Angela opened the front door.

Audrey Tipton pushed her way over the threshold. 'Ah, Angela. I must talk to you.'

Angela was zipping through her mental Rolodex, trying desperately to remember the woman's name. She finally got to it. 'It's Audrey, isn't it? Do come into my study.'

Back in the village store, Queenie was rolling a cigarette. 'And that's his story.'

'So he doesn't mind being called Simple Tony? Only it's very un-PC.'

'It's what his mum and dad called him and he's happy. But don't think he's stupid. Far from it. Innocent. Trusting. Kind. But *not* stupid. He has his odd little ways but, by God, half the gardens in this village, let alone the churchyard, would be in a terrible state if it weren't for him.'

'And he looks after himself?'

'Oh, yes. He has a little shepherd's hut in Polly's garden. She's at Candle Cottage. Ambulance paramedic and white witch. Lovely woman. She keeps an eye on him. And next door to her is Helen. Londoner, like me. Came down a few years ago after her husband had done one too many naughties.' She cocked an eye at Mamie. 'You get my drift?'

'I do.'

'Well, she's going out with Piran. Lovely bloke. Kind as they come.'

'I've met them.' Mamie pulled a face. 'He pulled me out of the sea yesterday. I fell in.'

'Did you?' Queenie was all ears. 'How'd you manage that?'

'A dog. A stick. A big wave.'

'Oh my Gawd. I bet Piran weren't too happy about that.'

'No, he wasn't. He was rather rude and told me off.'

Queenie began to laugh. A warm wheezy chuckle that ended in a coughing fit. She wiped her eyes and the corners of her mouth with a small handkerchief, then tucked it back under the cuff of her cardigan.

'He don't like strangers.'

'Clearly. Handsome bugger, though.'

'Keep your hands off.' Queenie frowned. 'He's Helen's.'

Mamie laughed. 'Darling, that's not my thing. I made a promise to myself when I was young. So many men with "attachments" are only too keen to cheat, but it's the women they pursue who get the blame.'

'Ain't that the truth.' Queenie crossed her arms and gave Mamie a hard stare. 'So, tell me your story.'

'So you see, there is an awful lot of work left to me,' Audrey boomed, 'because the village rely on my organisational skills and artistic flair, constantly.'

Angela was trying hard not to quail. 'From this list,' she held the five A4 pages in their clear document case that Audrey had thrust upon her, 'I see there are many things.'

'Indeed.' Audrey buttoned up her tweed jacket and brushed the pleats of the matching skirt. 'Now, if I may just take a look around . . .'

'Around?'

'Yes,' Audrey said in astonishment that this mousy woman should challenge her. 'I am keeping an eye on things while Rev Canter is away.'

'There is no need,' Angela said firmly, moving to open the study door and get this woman out of her home.

Audrey was not used to being disobeyed. 'Mrs Whitehorn, this is not a slight on your abilities . . .'

'Please call me Angela or *Reverend* Whitehorn.'

Audrey's lips tightened. So did Angela's.

Robert's voice called from the sitting room, 'Ange. Come and have a look. Is this OK?'

Audrey took her chance and pushed past Angela, heading for the sitting room.

'Mr Whitehorn. Good morning,' she announced triumphantly. 'I just dropped in to talk one or two things through with your wife.' She advanced towards the tall, dark and handsome Robert. 'I'm Audrey. We met at the vicar's leaving party.'

Robert responded firmly, 'Or, as I like to call it, the new vicar's welcome party.'

Audrey surveyed the room. Much as she hated to admit it, Penny Canter had good taste and had left the room perfectly furnished while removing only the more personal possessions. She walked to the bookshelves and inspected the titles.

'I have a penchant for crime stories,' Robert felt obliged to explain. 'Love a good murder mystery.'

Audrey scanned the spines of the books, then spun on her heel to face him. 'I've had the most marvellous idea. You shall give the WI a talk on crime writers and great detectives of literature. I'll check the diary and find a suitable date.'

'But I have never given a talk to the WI, or anybody else for that matter. Let alone on crime. I could perhaps talk about my work as a political writer?'

'Well, that's two talks you will give. What a productive morning. Now I must get on, good day to you both.'

Queenie was engrossed in Mamie's life story. 'You never did.'

'I certainly did.' Mamie leant closer. 'He was absolutely charming, but a rogue.'

'I loved his voice. I had lots of his records. Gave them to a boot sale.'

'He sang "Fly Me to the Moon" once, over dinner. He was on the tonk, of course. Never truly sober.'

Queenie gave a whoop of joy. 'You've lived, entcha! Did you ever meet Elvis?'

'We locked eyes over a crowded room once. He was a man with grace and animal magnetism.' Mamie halted at the memory, then sighed. 'But he was with Priscilla so . . .'

'Cor, I'd've been at him like a rat up a pipe.'

'Queenie! You shock me.'

'I haven't had such a good chat for ages.' Queenie settled into her chair, groaning slightly as she stretched her old legs in front of her. 'Getting old is no bleeding fun, is it?'

'Speak for yourself,' Mamie laughed. 'By the way,' she pointed at Queenie's tobacco pouch and Rizla papers, 'have you ever smoked a little pot?'

'You what?' Queenie was bemused.

'Had a little toke? A swifty? A bifta?'

'Are you talking about – marryjuana?' Queenie frowned.

'Well, yes,' smiled Mamie.

'No,' Queenie said slowly, 'but I've wanted to have a go.'

'Then,' Mamie looked around her for prying ears and whispered, 'shall we? Just a little? Excellent for arthritis.'

'Is it? When?'

'I'll let you know when I have some.' Mamie smiled naughtily. 'I haven't done it for years but seeing how good you are at rolling your cigarettes, what would be the harm?'

The two women, both so different outwardly, but inwardly so similar, locked eyes as sisters.

'Grab life by the horns, my mum always said,' Queenie said. 'That's what she told me when I was evacuated from the East End. Gawd, I missed her, but one of bloody Hitler's bombs didn't. That's why I stayed here after the war. Nothing to go back to. Met my husband here and I grabbed life by the horns, like she told me.'

Mamie nodded. 'I think you and I are going to be friends.'

'We already are, girl. We already are.'

7

It was the morning of Angela's first Sunday as vicar of Pendruggan.

Now, she was standing in the vestry, staring into the old speckled mirror at her reflection. 'Do I look all right?'

Robert looked at her with a nod. 'Perfect.'

'My heart is hammering.'

'I should hope so!' he laughed.

'You know what I mean. I'm so nervous.'

'The bloody bells are enough to make anyone nervous. Do they have to be so loud?'

'The ringers are doing a special "welcome" peal. Isn't that nice of them?'

'Lovely.' Robert looked at his watch. 'Right. I'd better find my seat. Faith and Mamie are keeping it warm for me.' He kissed her lips tenderly. 'Love you. Good luck.'

Not long after, standing at the back of the church, she took a deep breath and closed her eyes. The ringing bells in the tower behind her finished on three deep gongs. The vibration shook the ancient stones under her feet and she took a moment to offer a silent prayer of thanks and support.

The organist started the opening notes of 'Lord of all hopefulness' and Angela began her walk down the aisle. Heads turned as the parishioners stood to catch sight of her and offer friendly smiles.

She got through the welcome, grateful that she had decided not to make any major changes to Simon's traditional service. Two more hymns and readings, and now the time had come for her to climb into the pulpit and deliver her first sermon.

In the front pew, Mamie's shaking fingers found Robert's hand. She squeezed it with a nervous smile.

Robert looked up at Angela and winked.

Angela swallowed hard and began.

'Good morning, everyone.'

A few voices returned her greeting. 'Morning.'

'I must say I am a bit nervous to be standing in front of you this morning.'

The congregation smiled back, giving her some confidence.

'I am very new to this as I was ordained only at the end of last year, but I feel so lucky to have landed here in Pendruggan. My first proper job as a vicar. And the first woman to preach here. You may have had some misgivings about me coming here and want to know something about me. So here goes. Robert, my husband, and I have been married for almost twenty years. We met when we were both working for a paper called the *Manchester Evening News*. Fresh out of university, I thought I'd found my career. The cut and thrust of the newsroom excited me. There wasn't a cat up a tree or a lost dog that didn't get my full attention. My sympathetic interviews with devastated pet owners and my incisive writing skills led me to have none of my stories ever printed. All spiked by the editor, a seasoned hack with a bottle of Scotch in his desk drawer and a tongue as sharp as vinegar.

'One afternoon, following my regular daily routine of chasing a story, typing it up, having it rejected and spending half an hour in the ladies weeping, I bumped into an impossibly handsome man, who was heading to the Gents' as I came out of the Ladies'. By the time I got back to my desk, the office gossip machine was red hot. All the women were discreetly powdering their noses and applying lipstick, but I had no such tricks to employ. There was nothing in my bag that would camouflage my swollen red eyelids. My friend Tess, sitting opposite me, whispered a name. Robert Whitehorn. The new political correspondent.

'From that day on he became the office pin-up. Funny. Talented. Handsome, and mysterious. He politely declined all offers from the office vamps of a drink after work and skirted any questions about his private life. This made him one hundred per cent more attractive. I kept out of the way. Why would he be interested in me? The only contact I had with him was the occasional shared ride in the lift or in the canteen coffee queue. He didn't look at me once. But one day, I was rewriting a late story for the editor, who had loudly berated me across a packed newsroom for being a useless idiot, when a cup of coffee was placed on my desk. I looked up to thank whoever it was and nearly choked. Robert was standing there. "I thought you might like one of these," he said. I was so surprised, I jumped up and knocked the desk, which tipped the piping hot coffee all down his trousers. And that is how our romance blossomed.'

'Aahh,' said all the women in the congregation, and a couple of men too.

'We got married six months later and, almost immediately,

Robert landed a job on the *London Evening Standard* so we moved south. I managed to wangle a job in the BBC newsroom as a copy taster, reading through the stories as they came in and passing the more interesting ones on to the news editor. At the newsroom Christmas party I introduced Robert to the head of news and the rest is history. If I hadn't been called to this job, I would have made a great showbiz agent.'

The congregation laughed loudly.

'I dearly wanted to start a family but Faith, our daughter, didn't come easily. After a couple of years we were referred to an IVF, test-tube baby, specialist and on the third attempt, and after many prayers, Faith was born to us.'

Angela glanced down at Faith who was blushing furiously, pursing her lips and frowning. She smiled down at her. 'And now I have embarrassed her.'

Robert reached for Faith's hand but she shook it off, muttering, 'Get off.'

'It was around then that my calling to the Church began to take root. My father died before I was born and my mother had very little time to take me to church, but my faith grew with me hardly noticing. It was just there. Inside me. Seven years ago I told my husband that my life lay in the Church. He reacted by pouring two large gin and tonics. But he never tried to dissuade me. So while he was standing outside Number Ten or Chequers, reporting on the state of the nation, I was at the kitchen table studying until the small hours. He has been my support and mainstay all this time.

'My mother became ill during that time. I suspect many of you have been in a similar position. The balance of keeping a day-to-day life going while bearing the pain and responsibility of watching a loved one suffering and fading. I would be lying if I told you that my faith hadn't been shaken at that time. What use were prayers? Where were the answers? I took six months off from my studies to nurse her. Where was God when she cried out in pain? When she died, my strength deserted me. I became depressed. From being the carer, I became the cared for. Robert and Faith were my carers. A horrible, frightening time for them. I was lost.'

She looked around at the rapt faces of her congregation. 'I can't tell you that I am the perfect woman, wife, mother or vicar, but my relationship with God grew again once I stopped raging at him and slowly began to see the good in our world. Walking over from the vicarage this morning, seeing the primroses in the churchyard, the birds beginning to build their nests, the number of you who have bothered to come here this morning – all these things fill me with renewed energy and a determination to give all I have to you. I stand here and make my promise to you. Whatever happens over the next twelve months, I will do my best to help you. Build an even stronger community for Simon to return to. I'm particularly interested in empowering women. Show them the opportunities within their reach. A chance to fulfil their latent potential.'

A few of the older generation looked around at friends and partners with raised eyebrows and pursed lips, sending the silent message to each other. *Didn't we tell the bishop that a female vicar, with ridiculous modern ideas about equality, would bring trouble?*

Angela saw the exchanges but ignored them. 'Do come and talk to me. I want to get to know you well. Share problems, joys, ideas, anything. I maybe the newcomer but my vicarage is open to all comers.'

A young woman sitting in the body of the church began to clap. Next to her, Helen joined in, starting a wave of applause through the majority of the congregation.

The organist wiped a dew drop from the end of his nose and struck up the opening notes of 'Love Divine, all loves excelling'.

'Darling, you deserve a sherry.' Mamie shooed Angela into the big vicarage sitting room. 'Robert, get her a sherry please, and a G and T for me.'

Robert, on the point of entering the room, made a U-turn, and went to the kitchen.

Mamie relaxed into the sofa and kicked her shoes off. She patted the cushion next to her. 'How did you feel that went?'

Angela sat down. 'I think it went OK. What did you think?'

'Darling, you were wonderful! They adored you. You gave them everything.'

Robert returned with a drinks tray and Faith. Mr Worthington followed and hoisted himself next to Angela, before yawning squeakily and burying his whiskery face in her lap.

'I was just telling Angela how wonderful she was,' Mamie told Robert as she took the G and T from his proffered tray. 'Thank you, darling.'

Robert passed a glass of coke to Faith, who had opened a bag of crisps and was tickling Mr Worthington's tummy, and sat down in an armchair, opening his tin of beer.

'She really was.' He lifted his tin. 'To Angela, the new vicar of Pendruggan.'

'To Angela,' said Mamie.

'Mum,' said Faith.

'My wonderful wife,' smiled Robert.

'I couldn't have done any of this without you, my family,' Angela said, her voice soft.

'Now now, none of that,' Robert chided gently. 'This is your time to shine.'

'And I wouldn't be able to do it if you hadn't taken this year off, away from the job you love,' she said.

He waved a hand airily. 'Piffle. You have stood in my shadow too long. It's time I stood aside.'

'Oh, Dad.' Faith rolled her eyes. 'Women can make their own way now, you know. Like, they don't need a man to "stand aside" to help them achieve things in life. We are liberated from that sort of patriarchal nonsense, you know.'

Robert was hurt. 'That's not what I'm saying at all. Your mother is an independent, free-thinking adult woman, but in the past she has been the partner who has supported me while neglecting, maybe, some of things she wanted to do.'

'Huh. *Maybe?* Listen to yourself, Dad. She *definitely* missed out while you were out building your career. How many times were you home in time to read me a bedtime story? How many times were you already at work by the time I woke up? How many times did you take me to school or pick me up or watch sports day?'

Robert was wounded. 'And who do you think paid for your holidays and looked after you and Mum?'

Angela interrupted them. 'Hey. Stop it. You make me sound like some sort of downtrodden drudge. Let me make this clear. Making a home and caring for you both was and still is, *A Job*. One that I love. I would change nothing . . . other than to still have Granny with us today.'

Faith and Robert were chastened. 'Sorry.'

Angela took a sip of her sherry and leant back into the softness of the sofa. 'Now then, this independent, brilliant, superwoman would like her lunch on a tray, right here, watching a movie. And while you lot make that happen, Mr Worthington and I are going to have forty winks. Scoot.'

*

Later that evening, the phone rang in the hall. The women were watching *Poldark*, leaving Robert to get up and answer it.

'Hello?' he asked tentatively, not certain he would know who was calling.

'Hi, Robert? It's Helen here. Helen Merrifield?'

Robert remembered the attractive woman from Simon and Penny's party. 'Hello, Helen. How can I help you?'

'I was wondering if you and Angela would like to come round for supper this week. Would Tuesday be good? Listening to Angela in church this morning, I was thinking how brave she was.'

'She's a tough cookie,' Robert laughed.

'Yes. And I thought, we tough cookies need to stick together.'

'That's very kind, Helen. Hang on, I'll ask her.' He put the old-fashioned receiver down on the hall table and popped his head around the door of the sitting room.

'Who was it?' asked Angela, not taking her eyes from the television.

'Shh,' snapped Mamie and Faith, who were watching a strapping young man gallop a horse across Cornish cliffs, his ruffled white shirt open to the navel and billowing in the breeze.

'Helen,' whispered Robert. 'Wants to know if we can have supper with her on Tuesday night.'

Angela looked at him with bright surprise. 'Love to,' she mouthed. 'Does she want us to bring anything and what time?'

'What do you want me to put the linen napkins out for? You've only got to bleddy wash an' iron after. Don't make sense.'

Helen, chopping fruit for a salad pudding, said firmly, 'Just do it, Piran.'

'She's the vicar not the bleddy Queen of Sheba, is she?'

'Oh, Piran, please, I simply want to make tonight nice.'

'It's nice without having to put out the bleddy linen napkins.'

Helen pushed a handful of chopped grapes into a bowl and put her knife down. 'What's wrong with you? You normally like a kitchen supper with friends.'

'I don't trust him.'

'Robert?'

'Too smarmy by half.'

'He's charming. And devoted to Angela. Two things you could learn from him, actually.'

Piran chuckled at that. He hadn't seen Helen for a few days and had missed her. He walked towards her and put his arms around her. 'You 'ad smooth and devoted from that womanising idiot you was married to, remember?' He nuzzled into her neck, his beard tickling her. 'But I reckon I suit you better.'

Helen felt her shoulders relax. She had missed him too. 'I need to turn the roast potatoes.'

'They'll be fine for a couple more minutes.'

She ducked out of his arms with a kiss. 'The reason you and I work is because you give me the space to be me and I give you the space to be you.'

Piran's eyes, as dark as the night ocean and as deep, softened. 'I don't say this often, but thank you for putting up with me. I know I'm a pain in the arse at times.'

'Most of the time, actually.'

'But we belong together. I don't know what I would do without you.'

Helen frowned comically. 'Who are you? What have you done with Piran Ambrose? The grumpy, selfish, commitment-phobe I call my boyfriend?'

'If you're gonna be like that, I'm off to the pub then.'

There was a knock at the door.

'That's them.' Helen looked around at the untidied kitchen. 'Shit.'

'All right. All right. I'll let them in.' Piran moved to the door. 'You get a bottle out of the fridge.'

'I do love you,' she said.

Piran growled a bit before saying, 'Likewise.'

'This is so kind of you.' Angela handed her coat to Piran. 'Our first night out for a long time, isn't it, Robert?'

'I can't remember the last time.' He looked around at the inside of Gull's Cry, Helen's cottage. 'This is lovely.'

'Very small,' said Helen, passing her guests a glass of cold wine each. 'But I love it.'

'Typical cottage for this area,' said Piran. 'Villagers round here didn't have money to build mansions like up in London.'

'I love the way the front door opens straight into the lounge, it's so welcoming. And the fireplace is wonderful.' Angela smiled. 'Can I see the kitchen?'

'Sure. It's almost the same size as the sitting room. Come and see.'

'Another Aga! I'm not sure how to use the one in the vicarage. I'm learning as I go but maybe you could give me some tips?'

'Of course.' Helen was liking Angela more and more. 'It's basically like a camp fire. Use common sense. When you have time I'll come over and show you. Penny couldn't get her head round it at the start either but now she really is a good cook.'

Over dinner, Angela had to get something off her chest. 'Piran, I must apologise for our first meeting on the beach, and also thank you for saving my aunt's life. She was very rude to you.'

Helen answered, 'I suspect Piran may have been less than charming to your aunt. He doesn't always remember to take his charm pills.'

'The water was bleddy cold, woman!' Piran said. 'It didn't improve my mood. But I am sorry if I caused offence to an old lady. I may have been a bit gruff.'

Robert stepped in. 'You'd better not let her hear you calling her an old lady. She believes she's still in her prime.'

'She is!' said Angela. 'More stamina than any of us. But she does tend to be free with her opinions and that day she was less than gracious to you.'

'Was she OK? Afterwards?' Piran asked.

'Right as rain,' smiled Angela. 'But thank you again for rescuing her.'

Helen stood up and collected the empty plates from her guests. As she put them in the dishwasher she asked Piran, 'Would you get the fruit salad and ice cream out the fridge, darling?'

'Ice cream? No clotted?' he asked.

'I didn't get any. Did you?' Helen asked pointedly.

'Why would I get clotted cream?' he said, pulling the bowl of chopped fruit out of the fridge.

'Well, if you like it, you can get it,' smiled Helen. 'That's the way things work around here.'

She took the bowl from him and placed it into the centre of the table while he pulled a tub of Cornish vanilla ice cream from the freezer.

Piran sat down and said to Robert, 'Women 'spect us to be bleddy mind readers. Sometimes, I come in here to see Helen, and from the look on her face I can tell I have failed a test I didn't even know I was taking.'

Robert looked at Angela and thought better of agreeing with Piran. 'Well, you know, sometimes perhaps we are just preoccupied with our own things and forget that. I mean, Angela and I have decided to reverse our roles for this coming year. She has always been the one at home, keeping the home fires burning, shouldering the child care. I never had to think about anything domestic. She did it all while I worked in the world I love. Now, I shall do the same for her while she's here.'

'Oh, aye? Gonna be one of them househusbands, are you?' growled Piran.

'Yes,' smiled Robert. 'And happily.'

Helen passed a bowl of fruit to Robert. 'Well, I think that's wonderful. It's high time some of the men in this village had a bit of a shake-up and began to value what the women do around here.'

'Was that aimed at me?' Piran said gruffly. ''Cos you know perfectly well, Helen Merrifield, that I treat all people as equals.'

'I do know,' Helen answered, 'you treat all people equally badly.' She handed a bowl to Angela, laughing. 'And yet, beneath that beard and hard exterior, this man here is the kindest man I have ever known.'

Piran tucked into his pudding with a dark look.

'You are, Piran. And you know it.' Helen took his free hand and addressed Robert and Angela. 'He and the Reverend Simon have known each other since they were boys. They swam, fished and surfed together. When Simon was deciding to go into the Church, it was Piran he turned to. And when the opportunity to help in Brazil came, Piran was the one who encouraged him. And when Piran had a difficult time some years back, Simon was there for him.'

Angela was sympathetic. 'May I ask what happened?'

Piran put his spoon down and rubbed his chin. 'My fiancée was killed by a hit-and-run driver.'

'Shit,' said Robert.

''Twas,' Piran said bluntly.

'It's why Simon and Penny's daughter is called Jenna. In honour of the memory of Piran's girlfriend,' Helen finished.

'That's lovely,' said Angela. 'You must be missing Simon, Piran.'

'Yeah.'

The four of them sat quietly in the low light of the kitchen.

After a couple of minutes Piran got up. 'Fancy a beer, Robert?'

'Erm . . .' Robert checked his watch. 'What do you think, Angela?'

Helen was suspicious. 'Are you going to the pub, or having it here?'

'Oh, here, here,' said Piran, pretending the thought of the pub had never entered his head.

'Go on,' Angela said to Robert. 'I'll help Helen clear up.'

Piran took two bottles of Doom Bar from the fridge and, followed by Robert, carried them into the lounge and began stoking up the dwindling fire.

'You don't need to help me,' said Helen to Angela.

'Oh, come on. We'll have done in five minutes,' smiled Angela, picking up a tea towel. 'You wash and I'll dry. And actually, I'd like to pick your brains.'

'Go ahead.'

'What clubs are available to the women in the village?'

'Clubs? You mean like the WI?'

'Do you have one?'

'Yes, but it's run by Audrey Tipton, who bullies all her members into submission. If you're thinking of infiltrating them, don't bother. It's her way or the highway.'

'I'm thinking more along the lines of somewhere where women can find empowerment. Be heard. Be supported. Get advice. Real women being real women. Discussing everything in a safe space. Parenting, sex, cooking, retraining, keeping fit, a book club, politics, campaigns . . .'

Helen laughed. 'Nothing like that round here.'

'Do you think there would be an appetite for it? If I started a weekly women's meeting?'

Helen put the last plate into the dishwasher and handed Angela a pan to dry. 'Could be. It would be something you'd have to sound out. I'm warning you, Audrey will be furious and she will campaign hard against it.'

Angela put the dried pan on top of the Aga. 'Well, I'm always up for a challenge.' She shook out her damp tea towel and hung it over the rail of the range. 'I've got my first parish council meeting.'

'Oh, yes. Mike Bates, the chairman, told me. He's very excited to meet you properly.'

'He emailed me telling me he was looking forward to hearing "my exciting new plans for the parish".'

'And?' asked Helen, fetching two glasses and a bottle of whisky. 'You'll have one for the road while the boys finish their beer, won't you?'

'Um, OK. Thanks.'

Helen sat opposite Angela and poured the Scotch. 'Sorry I interrupted you. So, the parish meeting?'

'Ah, yes, well, do you think it would be the right place to suggest the women's group?'

'Definitely. I think it could be just the thing the women of Pendruggan need.'

Angela flushed with pride – or with the whisky – raised her glass triumphantly. 'To the women of Pendruggan.'

8

'It's not exactly PMQs, is it?' Robert teased as he cleaned his teeth before bed. 'No tricky negotiation with Europe or the Middle East. It's just a meet-and-greet. All the non-churchgoers want to examine you. That's all.'

Angela stepped out of the shower and took the towel Robert proffered her, toothbrush wedged in his mouth.

'I know but . . .' She wrapped the bath sheet round her. 'It's terrifying. I don't know what they expect of me. Should I sit quietly and just listen at first? Should I go in with all guns blazing and a manifesto for the next year? I don't want to put any noses out of joint.'

Robert had rinsed his mouth and was patting his face dry as he listened. 'You're not scared of Audrey, are you?'

'Yes.'

Angela stood in front of him, her tiny frame wrapped in the towel, her short hair curling over her ears, looking lost and vulnerable. He placed his hands on her wet shoulders.

'You are so adorable, how could they do anything but agree with everything you tell them?'

'But I don't know what to tell them.'

'Shall we workshop some ideas?'

'Don't laugh at me. Actually, I have jotted some stuff down on my iPad. I'll review them in the morning.'

He walked back into the bedroom and pulled the duvet back. 'Come on. Into bed, please. You need your sleep.'

She wandered in to join him. 'I like Piran and Helen, don't you?'

'She's all right but he's a bit too blokey for me.'

'You mean you feel your position as alpha male is at risk?' Angela joked.

'God, no. No. Not at all!'

Angela got into bed beside him and snuggled against his shoulder.

'Sure?'

'Well . . . maybe a bit.'

The following morning, over breakfast, Angela ran her women's group idea past Faith and Mamie.

'Nothing ventured, nothing gained,' said Mamie, digging into her pot of Duerr's thick-cut marmalade. 'You should write it all down.'

'I have.'

'Go for it, Mum,' said Faith, kissing her mother goodbye and bundling up her incredibly heavy school rucksack.

'Thank you, darling.' Angela helped her daughter with the webbing straps. 'Are you sure you need to take all this with you every day?'

'Told you, Mum. No desks to keep things in like in your day.'

'Some things just aren't right. Anyway, what would you like for dinner this evening?'

Faith was rushing to the front door. 'Oh, I meant to tell you, I might be a bit late. There's another newbie just joined school, and I might go have a snack before I get back.'

'Yes, OK. What's her name?' But Faith had already banged the front door and gone.

'She'll be fine,' said Mamie, knowing Angela's maternal anxiety meter had leapt up several notches. 'Now, give me the shopping list and any other jobs you want done today. I don't want you worrying about a thing while at the meeting.'

Angela smiled gratefully.

Robert came in to join them. 'Want me to come with you?' he asked.

'No, no. I'll be fine.' She set her shoulders back. 'I can do this.'

The village hall was on the opposite side of the green to the vicarage. Built between the wars, it had a long history of village meetings, the Home Guard, Boy Scouts, amateur dramatics and more jumble sales than anyone could remember. It sat behind a hedge of elderflower, with wild fuchsia and dog rose laced through its blossoms. Beyond the hedge was a pleasant stretch of well-kept grass where Cubs and Brownies would picnic or toddlers play safely. The hall itself was long and low, made of dark wood, with a raised veranda where men could read the cricket results in the shade and discuss England's sporting chances in football or rugby.

As Angela mounted the steps, she could see, through a window to the left of her, a kitchen with a tea urn already steaming and a group of women chatting as they laid out green china cups and saucers.

She girded her loins and opened one of the double doors.

The smell of small children's feet and creosote took her straight back to her primary school days.

In the hall ahead of her were chairs laid out in ordered lines, facing the raised stage at the other end.

'Hello,' said a man with thinning sandy hair and a red jumper. 'You must be Angela. I'm Mike Bates. Chairman of the parish council. Nice to meet you.' He shook her hand. 'Very good service on Sunday, by the way.'

'Thank you.'

Mike had a slight army bearing, oozing old-fashioned courtesy.

He took her arm. 'Let me introduce you to everyone.'

So many new faces and names to remember. Angela smiled and nodded as she was exhibited to each one.

Eventually she came across Helen, who was holding a cup of tea and talking to a youngish man; his age was hard to tell. He was wearing a boiler suit and holding a glass of Ribena.

'Helen, thank goodness for a familiar face,' Angela said in relief. 'And thank you for a marvellous supper last night.'

'My pleasure.' Helen bent and kissed Angela's cheek. 'Let me introduce you to Tony Brown, the most talented gardener in Cornwall.'

'Hello,' said Angela, holding her hand out to him. 'Are you the same Tony who helps out in the vicarage garden?'

'I'm Simple Tony. That's what my mum and dad called me and that's who I am.'

'Simply Tony? Well, I'm simply Angela.'

Helen intervened. 'No, this wonderful man is known as Simple Tony. That's what he likes to be called. It's what we all call him, although sometimes I call him Mr Brown too. After the great gardener, Capability Brown.'

'How lovely. I am very pleased to meet you, and I hope we see you at the vicarage when you are ready.'

'Right.'

'You met my aunt Mamie in the shop the other day, didn't you?'

'I did.' He drank some of his Ribena. 'I washed her car.'

'Yes. She was very pleased. I'm glad I have met you. I think you looked after the vicarage garden for Simon and Penny. I would like you to keep doing that if you can?'

'I can.' Simple Tony hung onto his glass of Ribena with both hands, and looked at his feet.

'Thank you.' Angela smiled.

'You got a dog?'

'Yes. You may have seen him? A big Irish wolfhound. Very gentle. He's called Mr Worthington.'

'Why?'

'It seemed to suit him.'

Mike bowled up. 'Ah. So you have met this marvellous young man, have you? He has single-handedly transformed my lawn from scrub to bowling green, haven't you, my boy?'

Tony nodded.

'May I borrow you for a moment, Tony?' Mike took him by the arm and began to lead him away. 'I noticed that the churchyard needs a bit of work . . .' Slowly they melted into the gathering crowd.

'You've brought out all the gawpers today,' smiled Helen to Angela.

'Oh dear.' Angela felt her top lip begin to perspire.

'Don't worry. You can't blame them. You are the most exciting thing to happen to us.'

'It makes me nervous,' Angela said. 'I get the feeling they will judge me by Simon's high standards. He is so loved here.'

'Yes, he is. That reminds me,' said Helen. 'I had an email yesterday. From him and Penny. They send their love to you.'

'Are they settling?'

'I think so but Penny said it was all a bit of a culture shock. They will write a longer email soon for the whole parish.'

Someone began tinkling a teacup with a spoon and calling for silence.

'We'll talk later,' whispered Helen. 'Let's find some seats.'

Audrey was on the stage, standing beside Mike Bates at a sturdy table, which was covered with a well-ironed, white tablecloth, a pretty bowl of tulips in front of them.

'Thank you. Ladies and gentlemen,' Audrey boomed, 'would you please take your seats?'

Angela sat with Helen on the end of a row, three from the back.

It took a few moments for everyone to settle. Coats were folded on laps, tissues taken from handbags, coughs quelled with barley twists and at last the room fell into an expectant silence.

Angela stuffed her big bag under her chair.

'Mrs Whitehorn?' Audrey's voice came at Angela like a missile. 'What are you doing there? Your place is here. At the top table. Next to me.'

'Oh God!' Helen's hand flew to her mouth. 'I'm so sorry. I should have thought.'

Angela got to her feet. 'It's fine. No problem.' She walked towards Audrey.

'What were you doing sitting back there?' Audrey said loudly.

Angela smiled at the loathsome woman. 'I was looking

forward to watching you, Audrey. An old hand like you, I could learn so much.'

Audrey screwed her lips up. 'Well, yes, undoubtedly that's true, but we have a place for you here.'

Mike Bates rose from his seat and guided Angela to her correct chair. 'You are next to me, my dear.'

'Thank you. I didn't, I wasn't expecting . . .'

He waved her words away. 'I should have told you before. My fault entirely.'

Audrey began to clear her throat and addressed her audience.

'To those of you who are not regular churchgoers, may I introduce you to dear Simon's stand-in, Mrs Angela Whitehorn. Mrs Whitehorn has joined us today to learn more about how Pendruggan works.'

She turned to Angela. 'We run a tight ship here, but you are welcome you to join in with any of our variety of clubs and activities during your stay here. Any questions you may wish to ask or information on anything going on in the village, I shall be happy to guide you. Not only am I parish secretary, but I also run the Women's Institute, the Pendruggan Players am dram group, and I have been the long-time organiser of the Pendruggan Summer Fayre, our greatest fundraiser of the year. There is nothing you need do other than run the church. Oh, and you needn't concern yourself with the cleaning or flowers either. I, and my merry band of helpers, do all of that too.'

Angela knew a problem when she saw one. And Audrey was going to be a problem.

Audrey continued, 'And now, Mr Chairman, ladies and gentlemen, please give a warm Pendruggan welcome to Mrs Whitehorn.'

Audrey, very pleased with herself, sat down.

Angela reached to the floor for her handbag and iPad. Her bag wasn't there. She stood up to light applause. 'Hello, everyone. In my haste to get to the stage, I have left my bag by Helen.'

Helen immediately looked and found the bag where Angela had pushed it under her chair. 'Here it is.' She held it up.

Angela was relieved. 'Would you fish my iPad out and bring it up here?'

Everyone turned to watch Helen digging in the vicar's bag. 'It's not here,' she said. 'Phone, purse, sunglasses and a book, but no iPad. Sorry.'

Angela felt her heart drop. 'Oh dear. Never mind.'

Audrey smirked beside her. 'A bit of a scatterbrain, Mrs Whitehorn?'

Angela took a deep breath and smiled at her audience. 'Well. Off the cuff is always better, so here we go.'

With malicious pleasure, Audrey asked, 'Are you sure? Public speaking can be daunting . . . for those not used to it.'

This was the grit that Angela had needed to form her pearl. 'Thank you, Audrey, for that warm welcome. And by the way, as I have mentioned before, do call me Angela or *Reverend Whitehorn*, or just plain Vicar. I prefer those to *Mrs* Whitehorn.'

Mike gave Angela a reassuring glance, and she continued: 'Ladies and gentlemen, what a wonderful parish this is. I am very lucky to have this chance to spend a year with you. I want to get to know you all and help the community as much as I can. I am passionate about community and family. Goals and challenges. I know you have a very active WI here,' she glanced down at Audrey who immediately preened at the mention, 'but I wonder if a women's group would be a welcome addition? A chance to sit and share our thoughts and concerns?'

She looked at the faces in front of her and several were looking interested.

Audrey interrupted, 'I believe we have all that covered at the WI.'

'I'm sure you do,' Angela went on. 'But I am thinking of a group where anyone can set the agenda. Relationships, health, concerns over our young adults. Drugs, unemployment. Things that impact our everyday lives.'

Audrey twisted one side of her mouth in sly disagreement. 'I doubt anyone will find that useful.'

'Well, let's see, shall we?' Angela said. 'I am a keen runner. I wasn't always fit, though. Actually, when my mum died I put a lot of weight on. Grief created a huge hole inside me and I filled it with food. I also became depressed and it was my doctor who suggested that regular exercise would help me both emotionally and physically. She set me up with an app that would get me running five K, or three miles, in nine weeks. It actually took me ten weeks and I lost a few pounds and began to feel a lot better. During runs I would talk to my mum in my mind and run through happy memories of my time with her. Gradually my depression lifted. I now run for around forty-five minutes three times a week, and I can't tell you how much it has helped me. I would be so happy to start a beginners' running club if anyone is interested?'

Several hands went up.

'Oh, that's good.' Angela was relaxing and her confidence was building. 'Also, and this may sound a bit *Vicar of Dibley*, but how about an outdoor service of blessing for our pets? My dog, an Irish wolfhound called Mr Worthington, you may have seen him?' One or two people nodded. 'He loves to make new friends, and while the animals make friends we can too.'

Mike Bates grinned. 'Terrific idea. My two cockers would love it.'

Audrey's scalp shot backwards. She was simmering with rage. Who was this appalling woman to come in here and attempt to undermine her grip on village society? And over her dead body would *her* dogs be attending a silly play date.

A woman's hand went up at the back. 'We desperately need a dog poo bin on the village green first.'

'Hear hear,' a man called out.

Almost everybody murmured their agreement.

'Good point. Mike?' She turned to him. 'Is that your domain or can I put my oar in?'

'I'd be delighted,' said Mike. 'The vicar's name will certainly help give the council the nudge it needs.'

Angela was encouraged. 'This is all so positive. Now, there is one last thing I'd like to suggest.'

Audrey clucked her tongue and huffed. Why was Mike Bates just sitting there? As chairman of the parish council, a position she had only missed by a few votes, he should be opposing every single thing this ridiculous woman was saying. Instead he was sitting there like an overgrown schoolboy with his tongue hanging out. She'd be having words with him later.

Angela took a deep breath. 'I notice that the village has no presence on social media.'

'With good reason,' Audrey blurted.

Angela ignored her. 'Would anyone be interested in a Twitter page for Pendruggan? And also a community website?'

Several more hands went up.

'That's so encouraging,' beamed Angela. 'By some miracle,

does anyone here have a good enough knowledge of computers and tech in general to help create both those things?'

At the back, Helen put her hand up. 'I can do a bit,' she said.

'Bless you, Helen. That's marvellous.' Angela put a hand to her thumping chest and sent a silent prayer of thanks. 'Right, I have said enough. Over to you. Any ideas?'

'I could run a cycle club,' said a young man at the back. 'For the children. Teach them road safety and go off-roading for fun.'

'Yes, that's an excellent idea. Come and see me after, would you?' She scanned the room. 'Anyone else?'

Simple Tony put his hand up.

'Yes?'

'I would like to dig out the village pond.'

'Have we got a village pond?' Angela was interested. 'Where is it?'

'On the lane down towards the Shellsand Beach,' said a man sitting in the front row. 'Not much left of it now.'

'Why's that?' asked Angela.

Tony shot his hand up again. 'The water got bad. Them say it was cursed.'

'Who said it was cursed?' asked Angela.

'I don't know who said it.' Tony scratched his head. 'But my mum said that one summer the farmer took his cattle there to drink and they'm all died afterwards.'

'I'm not a believer in curses,' Angela said reassuringly. 'But it sounds an intriguing idea.' She looked at Mike Bates. 'Mike, do you know about the pond?'

Mike shook his head. 'The first I've heard of it. But I am a relative newcomer. I've only been here twenty-six years.'

There was laughter.

Angela turned to Audrey. 'Audrey, how about you?'

Audrey's thin lips had vanished, replaced by a thin slit from which she spat, 'No.'

Angela looked back at the sea of faces. 'Well, if we can find out a bit more about the pond, and as long as there are no reasons as to why we can't dig it out, that might just become a terrific village project. Thank you, Tony.'

Simple Tony ducked his sleek black head in embarrassment and pleasure.

Angela once again scanned the room. 'Anyone else? No? Well, that was an excellent start. If you suddenly get inspired, no matter what that inspiration is, let me know. Ladies and gentlemen, thank you for your time.' She sat down feeling both relieved and excited.

9

'How did it go?' Robert welcomed Angela with floury hands and a brief kiss. 'I've been thinking about you. Any takers for the running club?' He went back to his dough-kneading.

'They were interested, certainly. And they loved the pet service, and Helen has put herself up to create some social media activity.'

'Well done, darling.'

'By the way, have you seen the iPad? I forgot to take it. Had to think on my feet.'

'Nope. Must be here somewhere.' He shaped the dough into a loaf and covered it with a tea towel. 'Thought we'd have fresh bread for tonight.'

Angela was preoccupied. 'Is Mamie here? I wonder if she picked the iPad up.'

'She's out.' Robert rinsed his hands under the tap. 'Does she know how to use an iPad?'

'Rude. In fact, she was asking me the other day about updating her phone.'

'Whatever for?'

'She wants to take photos.'

'At her age?'

Angela gave him a hard stare. 'Stop it. She's only in her seventies. I think. She's always been a bit mysterious about her age.'

'I'm just winding you up.'

'Mission accomplished.' Angela shifted a pile of newspapers on the table. 'I must find the iPad.'

'Fancy a cuppa while you search?'

'Yes, please. Is Faith home yet?'

'No, she's having tea at a school friend's. She told you this morning?' He put his head to one side and gave her a questioning look. 'You *are* getting forgetful, aren't you?'

'No.' Angela was irritated. 'I have a lot on my mind, that's all.'

He held his hands up in defence. 'OK. Understood. Premenstrual?'

She continued walking and said without turning, 'You're on very thin ice.'

Sitting at Simon's desk Angela opened each drawer in turn before looking behind it and under it. Next, she checked all the bookshelves, tipped out her handbag and went through the filing cabinet. No iPad.

Upstairs she went through her bedroom, bathroom and wardrobe. Nothing.

The same with Mamie and Faith's bedrooms.

Back downstairs, she checked the cloakroom, the sitting room and returned to the kitchen.

'Tea's getting cold,' said Robert, who was now scanning the local paper. 'Any luck with the iPad?'

'No.' Angela sat down next to him and pulled her mug towards her, feeling defeated and anxious.

'It'll turn up.' Robert turned to the back pages. 'Things always do. Remember your car keys?'

'That was the removal men's fault. I know I put them on the old hall table.'

'And yet they were in your handbag.'

She rubbed her eyes with one hand. 'I think the move and the pressures of coming here must have muddled me, although the keys were definitely moved. I'm so sure I put them on the hall table.'

He put the paper down and nudged her with his elbow. 'Early onset dementia?'

'Oh, just shut up.'

'Joke, joke. Just a joke,' he laughed.

'Well, it's not funny.' She racked her brains and couldn't think where else to look. 'What time does Faith want picking up?'

'She's going to text me.'

Angela picked up her tepid tea and took a sip. 'Eugh.'

Robert got up. 'I'll make you a fresh one.'

'Thank you, darling.' She leant back in her chair. 'By the way, you know that odd chap who washed Mamie's car the other day?'

Robert chucked a tea bag in a mug. 'Yes.'

'He says there's an old pond in the village that needs digging out.'

'Let me guess, he wants a Big Village Pond Dig?' laughed Robert.

Angela's eyes gleamed. 'That's it! That's what we shall call it! It's exactly the sort of thing to get the community united.'

'Aren't there committees and votes and whatnot to get through?'

'The chairman, a nice guy, Mike Bates, seems on side even though he has never heard about it before.'

Robert passed her a fresh cup of tea.

'Thank you.' She took a sip. 'Lovely. The thing is, we don't know exactly where it is.'

'There must be some old parish records and maps?' Robert lifted the tea towel covering his dough to check on its development. 'Nearly ready. Get your Mike fella to check.'

'Yes, he said he'd do that. Quite fun. Tony says there's a curse on it. A lot of cattle died drinking from it.'

'When?'

'Don't know. It'll be in the records if it's true.'

'Can't you exorcise it? Say a few prayers to chase the curse off?'

'I can certainly bless it. That and the new dog poo bin for the village green.'

'The romance of being a village vicar, eh?'

'Oh, and would you help Helen with setting up the website? She's pretty good but so are you. Between you, you'd do a good job.'

'No problem.' His phone buzzed. 'It's Faith. I'll go and get her now.'

'You do that and I'll give Helen a call. Strike while the iron's hot.'

Piran put the two heavy shopping bags down and knocked on the front door of Gull's Cry. He hadn't seen Helen since the dinner last night and, as much as he'd never admit it, he missed staying over. He knocked again.

'It's open,' she called.

He turned the heavy old handle and bent his head to clear the door lintel. Helen was on the phone. She blew a kiss and continued with the phone call.

'Yes, that would be lovely, Angela. We'll give it a try. God knows if it'll take off or not but thank you for supporting the idea.' She stopped and listened then replied, 'I had no idea we had a pond either but then I've only been here six years. It would be fun to dig it out. I might be able to get some info on the history from Piran . . . Yes, he's good at all that stuff.' She turned and looked at him, smiling at his scowling face. 'He'd be delighted to help. OK, Angela. Thank you. Bye.'

She put the phone down and looked at Piran. 'Have you missed me or are you just hungry?'

'Both, actually.' He held up the bags. 'I'm cooking. Lamb chops, new potatoes, and a couple of beers.'

She went to him and kissed him properly. 'You're like an old alley cat with buttered paws.'

'What's that supposed to mean?'

'It means, you don't ever want to be owned, but you know where the best dinners are.'

He grunted and turned to the kitchen. 'I'll take that as a compliment.'

Helen followed him into the kitchen and began helping him to unpack the bags. 'Did you know there was a village pond here?'

'Of course I did.' He pulled at his dark beard. 'Down between the fields and the footpath to Shellsand. Open that beer, maid.'

She reached for the bottle opener and a glass.

'How come nobody else knows about it?' she asked.

Piran unwrapped the chops and began rubbing oil and seasoning into them. 'There's some old folk tale of a child been drowned in it.'

Helen shivered. 'That's horrible. How long ago?'

'Mebbe a hundred years? When I was a lad, the old farmer told us kids that it was cursed.'

'Is it?'

He looked at her as if she was stupid. 'Of course it ain't. It was a story to make sure none of us were daft enough to get ourselves drowned.'

She took a sip of her beer. 'Simple Tony said it was cursed because all the cattle died after drinking from it.'

Piran shook his head and growled, his gold earring glinting among his dark curls. 'That lad is full of stories. Anyway, why do you want to know about it? Pass me a pan for these potatoes.'

She pulled a saucepan out of the cupboard. 'We had a parish meeting today to welcome Angela and she asked us all to suggest things that the village might like to do.'

'As if we ain't got enough to do. I bet the dog shit bin was mentioned.'

'Of course. And I think that might just happen with Angela in charge. Drink?'

'Beer, please.'

She poured two glasses of beer and continued. 'Anyway, Tony suggested digging the pond out and Angela wants to find out about the history and the stories.'

'Huh.' Piran closed the oven door on the lamb chops. 'And you volunteered me as local historian.'

'Well, you are.'

'I am an archaeologist and, by default, local historian.'

'Exactly. And your office is the local museum where all the county history is kept.'

'Not all.' He drank his beer. 'And don't wheedle me. I can't stand a wheedling woman.'

'I'm not wheedling. I just thought you might like to

help, but if it's all beneath your level of academia then sod you.'

He laughed, his white teeth gleaming from his tanned face. 'Helen Merrifield, you be a funny woman. I'll think about it. OK?'

'Thank you.'

'Hey, Mum,' Faith called as she came home, 'guess what Dad and I found?'

Angela was laying the kitchen table. 'What?'

Faith entered the kitchen waggling Angela's iPad in her hand. 'This,' she crowed triumphantly.

Angela dropped her collection of cutlery. 'Oh, thank goodness. Where was it?'

'On the front seat of the car.'

Robert came in, smiling. 'Under your running fleece.'

'Really? How did it get there? I don't remember taking it out to the car.'

Robert put a loving arm around her shoulder and kissed the top of her head. 'I might have picked it up without thinking. Anyway, it's found.'

Mamie came in from the garden with a bunch of bluebells. 'Aren't these lovely? Smell them.' She saw the iPad in Faith's hand. 'You found it!'

'It was in the car. Robert found it,' said Angela, taking the bluebells and sniffing them. 'These are lovely. I'll get a vase.'

'So,' said Mamie to Robert, 'she's not an elderly amnesiac after all.'

'I did not say that exactly,' Robert said defensively. 'And if it sounded that way, I apologise.'

Angela put the vase of bluebells on the table. 'You are forgiven.'

'What's for supper?' asked Faith.

'I thought you were having tea with your new friend?' said Angela.

'He forgot tell his dad and so we had some crisps, that's all.'

'Another poor stay-at-home husband caring for his family,' Robert said tragically while Angela poked him in the ribs.

'His mum and dad are divorced,' said Faith. 'He stays with his dad three days a week in Trevay, just down the road from the school. The rest with his mum. She's just moved into Pendruggan with his baby sister.'

'Hang on.' Angela halted Faith's flowing chatter. 'This new friend is a boy?'

'Yeah.' Faith stuck her chin out. 'What of it? Can't I have friends who are boys?'

Mamie, who had been calmly preparing a green salad, stepped in before any more could be said. 'I'm sure he's charming. Now go and wash your hands, I have a fish pie in the oven. And before you ask, I haven't made it. I wouldn't know how. I bought it frozen.'

In their bedroom that night, Angela, doing her hamstring stretches, was worrying about Faith. 'It'll be nice for Faith to have a friend in the village,' she said, trying *not* to sound worried. 'Did you meet him?'

Robert came out of the bathroom, turning the light out behind him. 'I caught a brief glance.'

'And?'

Robert got into bed and pulled the duvet round him. 'Oh, you know. Spotty. Thin. Weird haircut. Trousers hanging too low. Pretty standard.'

'Oh.' She started on her triceps. 'What about the father?'

'Didn't see him.'

'Well.' She finished and got into bed. 'I'm happy for her.'

'No you're not.' He reached out and patted her hand. 'You're worried sick. Faith is an attractive young woman.'

'Yes, of course I am. She's only just fifteen.'

'And she is growing up. We have to acknowledge that. Remember what we were like at that age?'

'Speak for yourself,' Angela said. 'It was just Mum and me, and I was never a rebel. Auntie Mamie was the naughty one. She and my mum were like chalk and cheese.'

'It's inevitable that Faith will have a few of Mamie's genes.' Robert turned for his book. 'And look how kind Mamie has been to you since we lost your mum. Hmm? Faith will be fine.'

Angela watched Robert as he opened his book and began to read, instantly engrossed. How lucky men are, she thought. They can so easily put stuff out of their minds. Faith was everything to her. Her very reason for living. After trying for three years, and having two miscarriages and two failed IVF attempts, Faith had arrived safe and sound. Angela thanked God that her mum had got to see her grow before she died. She closed her eyes, not expecting to sleep, but she did.

10

The power of the Jensen's engine pushed Queenie into the back of her seat.

'A little bit of G-force,' Mamie explained. 'Wait till I really open her up.'

'Oh my good Gawd, you're like flaming Stirling Moss.'

'Graham Hill was rather more my type. So charming. He told me I reminded him of Honor Blackman. Would you rather I slowed down?'

'Would I 'eck. Get yer foot down, gel.'

The two women were on their way to a secret rendezvous. Mamie had phoned an old friend who had arranged for a friend of a friend to supply her with a little present.

'I was thinking we might stop for a pub lunch after we've made the pick-up.'

'I don't want no gastric pub. I want proper stuff. Scampi in a basket and a shandy. Not goat's cheese and flaming avocado.'

Mamie smiled. 'Your wish is my command.'

Queenie read out the directions. Mamie had taken them down

in her loopy handwriting, and they were now on tiny lanes crossing Bodmin Moor. 'It says take a right at the old garage and it should be four houses along by the telegraph pole.'

'There's the old garage.' Mamie indicated right and drove another hundred yards before the first of the four houses came into view. 'One, two, three and there's the telegraph pole.' She stopped the car and pulled on the handbrake. 'You sit tight. I won't be a minute.'

'I'll keep a look out for the rozzers,' Queenie said with all seriousness.

Mamie roared with laughter. 'Queenie, you are an absolute hoot!'

'I'm serious. If anyone comes along in one of them panda cars I'll blow the horn.'

Mamie got out of the car and disappeared through a respectable-looking wrought-iron gate and up to the door of the respectable house. It opened without her knocking. A middle-aged man in glasses smiled and handed over a small package. Queenie watched as Mamie took an envelope from her handbag and passed it over to him. Queenie took a good look at him from her vantage point. An ordinary man. In his fifties. Good head of hair and glasses. You never can tell, Queenie thought to herself.

Mamie made her way back to the car and got in. 'I can't believe how naughty we are,' she said, settling into the driving seat. 'Any rozzers? Drug squad hiding in the bushes?'

'No. Can I see the stuff?'

'When we get home. But first, it's our scampi lunch.'

The Jensen grumbled into life and Mamie pointed its nose in a direction she hoped would take them to a pub.

'Who was that bloke?' Queenie asked.

'I was told he's a very good doctor.'

'It'll be good stuff then.'

'Queenie,' Mamie was serious, 'we must never breathe a word of this to my family.' She smiled conspiratorially.

Queenie tapped her nose. 'No names, no pack-drill.'

While Angela had the vicarage to herself she had invited Helen over to talk through how the social media sites might be set up.

She prepared some cheese and pickle sandwiches for their elevenses and left them in the fridge, then ran the vacuum round before finally sitting down in her office to catch up on some work. Just after eleven, she heard the front gate open. Looking up, she saw the postman approaching with Helen just a few feet behind.

'Hello. Welcome,' Angela said as she opened the door, expecting to see both postman and Helen. But the postman was already walking back to his van. Helen, however, had a bundle of letters in her hand.

'I told him I'd take them for you,' she said, handing them over.

'Thank you. Come in, come in. I'll just put these on my desk then we can have a coffee?'

Sitting at the kitchen table with the bright morning sun coming in through the open back door, the women sat and chatted.

'It is so kind of Piran to give up his time to look out the pond's history,' Angela said, offering Helen a sandwich.

'He loves all that stuff. He'd like to search the parish records that are kept in the church.'

'He's very welcome.'

'Thanks. He'll be pleased, because he hasn't found much yet, but secretly I think he's enjoying the search.'

'Did a child drown there?'

'He hasn't found any record of that. He reckons that might have been a story put about, an old wives' tale, to keep children away from the pond.'

'I hope so.'

'Me too. However, he wonders whether the pond might have been used as the ducking pond for the village. Sometime in the sixteenth century.'

'Oh gosh.' Angela was very interested. 'The village children would love to hear about that. Witches and witchcraft in the village. What a terrific lesson in history that would be.'

'Oh, yes. Social history brought right up to date. The persecution of women through the ages.'

'Faith would sign up to that. Even her knickers have "FEMINIST" printed on them,' Angela said.

'I approve. Good for her,' Helen smiled.

Angela laughed, then said, 'So, what about the poisoned cattle? Any record of that?'

'Piran found a possible account for that. There was a serious drought around the 1900s and it's probable that the pond not only began to dry out but that any stagnant water would have developed an algae that proved fatal when the animals drank it.'

'Makes sense.'

'Probably didn't do the locals any good either. I shouldn't think there was much fresh water available for humans around that time.'

'Does Piran have any feelings either way as to whether the pond is worth digging out?' Angela finished her sandwich and picked up the teapot. 'Fancy a top-up?'

'Please.' Helen pushed her cup forwards. 'I think he's very intrigued.'

'So it's worth a dig?'

Helen laughed. 'Piran's an archaeologist. He thinks anything is worth a dig.'

Angela began to feel more certain. 'In that case, I shall ask Mike Bates if we can get the ball rolling.'

'By the way, Robert and I have made a start on the village website. I've got a template and the password up and running, and also paired our computers so that we can work on things together while he is here and I'm at home. I have high hopes! Let me know when you have a clear idea of how you want to announce the new women's club.'

'I will, and thank you. It's so kind of you. To be honest, I am rather surprised at how into it Robert is.'

When Helen had left and Angela had the vicarage to herself, Angela went to the peace of her new office and dialled Mike Bates' number. He answered on the second ring.

'Mike Bates,' he said with authority.

'Hi, Mike. It's Angela Whitehorn. I'd like to request permission to excavate the old Pendruggan pond. Can I come over to you now?'

The pub lunch had lived up to all Queenie's expectations (Mamie's too, but in an opposite way) and she was now sitting in the Jensen snoozing as Mamie drove home along the pretty coast road. It was one of those late spring/early summer days when the acid-yellow gorse flowers stood bright against the deep blue Cornish sky. The sea beyond heaved and wrinkled gently, the odd wave cresting far out, and seagulls playing on the wind.

Enjoying herself, she drove past the turning for Pendruggan and continued on the road that would lead to Newquay. She wound down her window to take in the soft breeze. The coconut scent of the gorse and the excitement of that morning's secret assignment filled her with a lightness of being and joy. (And a hefty slice of the guilt of forbidden pleasure.) She'd always been unconventional. Was proud of it. Occasionally it had got her into trouble, but she had always had her sister, and later Angela, as her anchors. Her sister, Elsie, had never judged her. Had always listened to her latest heartbreak or escapade with compassion and love. When Elsie was in her last illness, Mamie stepped up to the mark and swore that she would care for Angela as well as, or better than, Elsie had.

'It's your turn now,' Elsie had whispered to her through the tubes and monitors. 'You and Faith.'

'I promise,' Mamie had said through her tears.

'She is all yours now.' It was getting harder for Elsie to speak.

'I swear on my own life.' And Mamie had kept that vow.

Now she tore her thoughts back to the present and remembered the little bag of cannabis in her bag. Not enough for more than two joints. One each. For old times' sake. Just enough to ease Queenie's arthritis. No one would ever know.

Queenie stirred and sat up. 'I could do with a cup of tea. Where are we?'

'I'm not sure. We're on a mystery tour.'

'No we ain't. Bedruthan Steps is just up here. Lovely National Trust teashop. Fancy a cream tea?'

Angela got back from Mike Bates' just as Mamie pulled in, having dropped Queenie off at the village store.

'Good day out?' she called from her office where she was taking off her coat.

'Wonderful. Finished off with a cream tea,' Mamie said,

shutting the front door behind her. 'Queenie is enormous fun. Totally unafraid of life. She's an icon to modern woman-hood.'

Angela was unsure. 'Really? Queenie?'

'Ah!' Mamie wagged her finger in Angela's face. 'You have fallen into the trap of seeing her as an old lady with bad hips. But what I see is a woman with an enormous experience of life. A woman who takes on challenges as if they were just a basketful of ironing. Open-minded. Courageous. Funny.' Mamie dropped her coat on the hall chair. 'I'm making tea. Want some?'

'Yes. Thank you. Golly.' Angela wrinkled her forehead. 'I may have underestimated Queenie.'

'You won't be the only one.' Mamie swept into the kitchen. 'How's your day been?' she asked over her shoulder.

Angela, following, held up two crossed fingers. 'It looks like I have the sign-off for the biggest community event Pendruggan has held for a long time. A big village event that will get everyone together.'

Mamie filled the kettle. 'Oh yes?'

'Yes! The Big Pendruggan Village Pond Dig has the go-ahead! Well, subject to council approval, but Mike Bates doesn't think that will be a problem.'

'Wow!' said Mamie, hiding her lack of enthusiasm. 'That's wonderful, darling. Thrilling. Now, here's your tea. Take it to your office and tidy up for the day, while I get supper on the go. Robert has left me instructions to defrost a chicken casserole to have with his bread.'

Angela did as she was told and sat at her desk to answer the remaining emails of the day. Pulling her laptop towards her she saw the bundle of letters that Helen had handed to her earlier in the day. She picked them up and flicked through them. There were seven. Three junk mail. Two charity requests. An electricity bill and one, in a blue Basildon Bond envelope, marked personal and addressed to her. She opened it and unfolded the typed message inside.

She read the message with little understanding and read it again. On the page were the words:

YOU ARE NOT WELCOME HERE. GO HOME.

11

Angela folded the note and put it in the pocket of her fleece. Then, opening one of the drawers of her desk, she took the note out of her pocket and pushed it under the collection of greeting cards that she kept for emergency birthdays, etc.

She closed the drawer and sat down. Cold with shock.

Who had the letter come from?

What had she done so wrong that someone, or maybe many people, couldn't come and speak to her? Face to face?

In her mind she went through as many conversations and meetings she could remember. Queenie? No. Mike Bates? Surely not. Helen? Absolutely not. Piran? No, not the sort of man who'd resort to playground tactics. Audrey?

Angela stopped. Audrey was certainly a difficult person. She'd displayed her opposition to any of Angela's ideas at the parish meeting. So would a person so obviously disapproving be snide enough to send an anonymous letter? Angela shook her head. No. Audrey liked an audience. She wouldn't be so cowardly.

Then, who?

Some poor individual who needed help, clearly.

Angela thought back to her time at school and the fashion for chain letters. Hideous, anonymous missives that would insist you would die if you didn't send the letter on to ten other friends, and worry them sick too.

She remembered coming home with one. Her mother took it from her hands and put it on the fire. 'Utter rubbish sent from wicked people who enjoy bringing fear and unhappiness.'

Angela had lived the next few weeks waiting for disaster to come, but it didn't.

How she wished she had her mum with her now.

She picked up her dog-eared Bible from the desk, held it to her chest and prayed for the soul of poor person who had written it.

When she had finished she went in search of Robert. She needed to touch reality.

He was in the old dining room sitting at Penny's desk. She had cleared her things before she had gone to Brazil, and told Robert to make himself at home.

Now, he was working at his laptop, trying to get into the fledgeling village website.

'Hi,' Angela said, sticking her head round the door.

'Arrgh.' His hands flew to his scalp and literally pulled his hair. 'This bloody thing.' He was shouting at the screen. 'I told you what the bloody password is.' He began tapping furiously at the keyboard saying, loudly, 'Bugger bugger bugger.'

'Not a great password,' Angela replied quietly. 'Is this the website for the village?'

'Yes. If I can remember what the bloody password is.'

'Can I help?'

'No,' he said through gritted teeth.

'Helen will know it. Drop her an email.'

His shoulders slumped in defeat. 'What time is it?'

'Late enough to stop working for the day. I was thinking we could take Mr Worthington down to the beach? Blow a few cobwebs away before supper.'

'Yeah. I need some fresh air. Let me just email Helen. She'll think I'm absolute fool.' He typed a short message then closed the laptop lid.

'How cold is it outside? I might take my jumper,' he said.

'I'll get it,' smiled Angela.

'No, no, I'll go.'

'I'm going upstairs anyway to get my fleece. You get Mr Worthington's lead.'

'Thanks, love.' He smiled at her retreating back then bent down to Mr Worthington, who was snoozing at his feet, and whispered into his cocked ear, 'We might get Mum to come with us to the pub for a pint. What do you say?'

Mr Worthington turned his wise old eyes to Robert and licked his lips.

'Good lad. Sometimes we men have to stick together.'

Angela returned with the jumper. 'Ready?'

'Absolutely. Yes. All ready.'

'Got the lead?'

'It's just in the hall. But I can't find his dog whistle – think you had it last?'

'Oh, it'll be there somewhere, probably in one of your coat pockets. Come on then.'

Robert followed her then said, as if the thought had only just occurred to him, 'Fancy a drink in the pub before dinner?'

She cocked an eyebrow at him. 'Maybe. Let's have the walk first.'

The fine April afternoon, walking the lane to Shellsand Bay, held fresh scents of primroses and wild garlic. The campion, its tall spires of pink blooms, waved gently on the soft breeze. Bright clumps of cow parsley shone as white as snow.

'This must have been a peaceful place for villagers to bring their cattle when the pond was here,' said Angela, leaning into Robert's shoulder.

'If there was a pond here,' he answered. 'Stop for a moment.'

She stopped. 'What?'

'Just imagine this two hundred years ago. Hardly changed. The young men and maids . . .'

'Maids?' Angela smiled.

'Stick with me . . .' he nudged her ribs gently. 'Young men and yes, maids, walking through that cornfield.' He pointed up to his right where the fields gently sloped towards the sea. 'Cows and sheep following them . . .'

'Cows *and* sheep?' Angela giggled.

He sighed. 'Look, I'm trying to paint a picture here but if you are going to spoil it then I'll shut up.'

'No. No. Go on. I love it.'

'Right. So. One of the boys, let's call him Robert, is walking down, his heart thumping under his loose shirt, hoping that the maid he has his eye on, let's call her Angela . . .'

'Oh yes, let's.'

'. . . will be there.'

'What's he going to say to her?'

'He's going to tell her that . . .'

'Yes?' Angela lifted her twinkling eyes to Robert.

'He's going to tell her that he loves her.'

'Ah.'

'And then he's going to take her in his arms, carry her to the nearest haystack, lift her skirts and ravish her. With tender passion.'

'Ooh. I like the sound of that.'

Robert bent his head and kissed his wife. 'How about it?'

'It's a bit chilly and I am the vicar.'

'True, true. If we were discovered, me with goosepimpled buttocks, you with . . . well, shall we say your immodesty on display, we'd be drummed out of the village.'

'I might be anyway.' Angela's throat tightened as the thought of the poison-pen letter, which she'd tried to bury in the back of her mind, suddenly sprang forward.

Robert pulled her to face him. 'Why do you say that?'

She told him.

'Why didn't you tell me straight away?'

'I wasn't sure whether to tell you or not. It's too horrible. And I think it must be a hoax or the sender must be very ill. I can't take it seriously. I shouldn't take it seriously.'

'You should. You must go to the police.'

'Oh, no!' Angela was clear. 'No. I don't want to get anyone into trouble.'

'What happens if you get another?'

'I won't get another. Will I?'

'Maybe this nutter is sending them to lots of people but they are all keeping quiet, not wanting to cause embarrassment.'

'Oh, please don't say that. It would be awful.'

'Listen, if someone is picking on you they are bound to be picking on others. Mark my words, you won't be the only one.'

The sun was dropping slowly towards the horizon and the breeze became chillier.

Angela shivered.

'You've got to show me the letter,' said Robert.

She nodded, looking at her shoes. 'OK. But let's just give Mr Worthington a run on the sand first. I don't want to go back home yet. Let it just be us for a few minutes more.'

The beach was empty save for a group of wading seagulls, scavenging in rock pools. They cocked their heads and eyed Mr Worthington with glinting arrogance, daring him to approach them. He didn't. Instead he veered after the tennis ball Robert had pulled from his pocket, running after it as it landed and rolled over the wet sand, sending up a plume of seawater droplets.

Angela had her chin buried in the zipped neck of her fleece.

'Hey,' said Robert, thinking to distract her from thoughts of the anonymous letter. 'Helen had an idea for the name of your women's group.'

Angela gave him a ghost of a smile. 'Oh, yes?'

'The Friends Forum.'

Angela shrugged.

'Do you like it?' Robert asked.

'Forum sounds a bit formal.'

'Hmm. I know what you mean.' Robert racked his brains. 'The Girls Friends?'

'Absolutely not.'

'The Sisterhood?'

'We are not the mafia.'

'Angela's Sisters?'

'Or group of nuns.'

'OK . . .' Robert would not be beaten. 'Angela's Angels?'

'And we could all ride around on Harley-Davidsons? Please!' She laughed.

'OK, how about Angel Friends?'

Robert told him.

'How horrible.' Mike was clearly upset. 'As far as I can see, Angela has been a breath of fresh air to Pendruggan. I have heard nothing but good reports.'

Robert toyed with his empty pint glass, twisting it in circles on the table. 'Maybe we should never have come here. To Cornwall. She misses her friends.'

'Too twee.'

'Well, I rather like it.' Robert put his arm around her. 'Friends are angels in disguise, aren't they?'

'And enemies are devils who hide behind anonymous letters.'

Robert pulled her to him. 'OK, well let's look at it another way. What do you hope the group will achieve?'

'I imagine it as a place of trust. A safe place to discuss everything without being judged. A group of diverse women with a point of view and a desire to help the community near and far.'

'This is sounding like a manifesto!'

'I don't want it to be pious. It's important to stay politically centrist with the focus on helping those who need help.'

'Like Pals?'

'Pals?'

Robert stopped abruptly and clicked his thumb and fingers. 'The Pals! The Pendruggan Association of Ladies.'

Angela thought for a moment. 'I rather like that.' She said the words aloud, letting them roll around her lips. 'The Pals. Let's try it out on a few people and get their reaction.'

'Good. Feeling a bit better now?'

She poked her arm through his, and hugged it to her. 'Thank you. As soon as you have the website up and running, I shall advertise for members. And we need to announce that the Big Village Pond Dig is happening. When do you think it'll be ready?'

'What?'

'The website.'

Robert extricated himself from Angela's arm and picked up the sandy tennis ball Mr Worthington had dropped at his feet. 'Good boy. Shall I throw it again?'

With his head to one side, Mr Worthington raised one eyebrow and then the other.

'I'll take that as a yes, shall I?' Robert threw the ball and Mr Worthington cantered off after it.

'So?' Angela asked, taking his arm again.

'Helen and I need to do a bit more work but it should be soon. Now, how about that pint?'

In the end, Angela didn't go to the pub but sent Robert off with the instruction to have just 'the one' and *not* to discuss the letter with anyone.

'I won't be long, I promise,' he said as he kissed her goodbye and whistled up the dog, who was happy to go out for another sniff about.

Angela watched them go, grateful to have a husband who was not only a lover but also her best friend. As they disappeared into the twilight she went to the kitchen to rustle up some supper.

Robert, certain he was now out of sight of the vicarage, diverted across the green and headed for Mike Bates' cottage. As he walked up the flagged path he could see Mike settling down into a well-worn armchair with what looked like a Scotch in one hand and the TV remote control in the other. Robert caught his eye by waving outside the window.

'Hello, hello,' Mike beamed. 'Come on in. I was just settling down to watch the early news. Want a drink?'

'I've got the dog. I was going to the pub. Wondered if you'd like to join me?'

'Well, that's awfully kind of you. I'd love to. Could do with the walk. I've got a fish pie in the oven. It'll keep for half an

hour or so. Let me get my coat. Mind if along too?'

Mike's boys were a pair of red cocker sp squirmed round the kitchen door as Mike opened to Robert and Mr Worthington for a good sniff.

'Danvers! Davey! Stop that.'

'They're fine. Honestly,' Robert said, protecting his net

The lights from the bar of the Dolphin pub shone invitingly to the two men as they approached the heavy oak door. Landlord Don and his wife, Dorrie, were behind the bar chatting to a customer. Dorrie looked up.

'Hello, Mike. And you must be the vicar's husband?' she said, holding her hand out across the counter. 'Welcome.'

Robert shook her proffered hand and then Don's too.

'What'll you have?' Don asked.

They ordered two pints of Tribute and took them to a table in a cosy corner where Robert hoped no one would overhear him.

The dogs settled themselves on the rug by the fire.

'So,' said Mike, brushing beer froth from his lips, 'you didn't just call on me for a drink in the pub. How can I help you?'

'Ah.' Robert was embarrassed at being found out so quickly but his confidence in Mike's astute and trustworthy nature grew. 'My wife has had an unpleasant letter. Anonymous.'

Mike frowned, shaking his head. 'Oh dear me, no.'

'And I wanted to ask you if this sort of thing had ever happened before?'

Mike looked thoughtful. 'This village is full of some difficult characters but I would be very surprised if one of them would be capable of anything so underhand and unpleasant. May I ask what it said?'

Mike gave him an old-fashioned look. 'And what about you? Do you miss *your* friends? Your work?'

Robert gave a short laugh. 'Gosh, no. I mean this was all about Angela and her vocation. For too many years she has stood in the shadows, allowing me to build my career.'

'You must miss the excitement that your work brings? The recognition? The well-known face of television politics.'

Robert stopped twiddling with his glass and looked at Mike squarely. 'Angela and I made a joint decision. This is the year she can prove to herself and others that she is a good vicar. This is the year that I support her in that.'

Mike nodded sagely. 'I see. That's good and very noble. So, how are we going to make sure that Angela has the best time here?'

Before Robert could answer, Dorrie, the landlady, came by. 'I was meaning to ask, when will the vicar's women's group start? Only, a few of us would like to try it out.'

Robert and Mike shared a quick smile across the table before Robert asked her, 'How many are interested?'

'Gasping Bob's wife and me, deffo.'

'How does Thursday night sound to you?' Robert was excited. 'Seven until nine? At the vicarage?'

'Sounds fine.' Dorrie replied. 'Shall I spread the word?'

'By all means. Angela will be so pleased.'

12

'You're doing a grand job there, young man,' said Mamie the following morning as she walked to the village store.

Simple Tony was filling an array of Queenie's wooden tubs with compost and colourful bedding plants. His sleek head bobbed up. 'Thank 'ee, missus.'

'It's a beautiful day for it.' She smiled at him. 'You look as if you could do with a cold drink. What can I get you?'

'I like Ribena,' he said shyly.

'Then I shall get you one from Queenie's drinks fridge.'

'Thank you, missus.'

'My pleasure.'

Inside the shop, Queenie was balanced on a set of small steps, removing several yellow and curled notices from her window.

'Queenie, be careful up there. What are you doing on those steps anyway?'

'What does it look like?' Queenie said crossly. 'I'm painting my blooming arse pink, ain't I!'

'Oh, now don't be like that.' Mamie put her large shopping bag down. 'Let me help you.'

'If you want to do something useful, put the bleedin' kettle on.'

'Someone hasn't taken her charm pills today, have they?' Mamie retorted. 'And don't put the steps away, I have one or two notices from the vicarage to put in your window.'

'Fifty pence a week per notice and no discounts,' Queenie responded. 'And fetch some of me custard creams.'

'Your blooming niece must be costing the world a few more rainforests with all this paper she's using.' Queenie, now in her shop armchair, was shuffling Angela's notices. 'Running club. Cycle club. Paint the dog poo bins party. Don't she ever stop?'

'No she doesn't,' Mamie asserted. 'We are a very energetic family.'

'You don't say.'

'Sarcasm is the lowest form of wit, darling.' Mamie bit into her custard cream.

'With all these in me window, how'll I display me half-price Easter eggs?'

'Put them away for next year and advertise them as "vintage".'

Queenie laughed her crackly smoker's laugh. 'You're a tonic, you are. Have another biscuit.'

'No, thanks, I'm thinking of my figure.'

'Oh, right. Good job too. No one else is thinking of it. That ship's sailed, love.' Queenie laughed again until it gave way to one of her rasping coughing fits.

'Serves you right,' laughed Mamie, but nonetheless she got up and rubbed her friend's back. 'You ought to see the doctor.'

'He'll only tell me to pack up me smokes. What does he know?' She wiped her mouth with one of the many cotton hankies she always had up her sleeve. 'How many cards does your Angela want to put in me window?'

Mamie counted them. 'Running. Cycling. Poo bins. The Pals. And . . .'

'The what?' Queenie stopped her. 'The Pals. What's them when they are at 'ome?'

'The Pendruggan Association of Ladies.'

'Oh.' Queenie was disappointed. 'Women's Institute by any other name, eh?'

Mamie defended her niece. 'Good God, no. This will be a place where, as women, we can talk about the day-to-day things relevant to all our lives.'

'That's what she told you, is it?'

'Well, she may have said something similar.'

'Boring.'

'All right then. What would entice you to a meeting?'

'Chat. Good chat.'

'You mean gossip.'

Queenie had the grace to agree. 'I want interesting stuff.'

'I shall pass that golden nugget of information on,' Mamie said huffily. 'And you *will* be coming to the inaugural meeting on Thursday. I shall pick you up before seven. No argument.'

She picked up the final card she'd been given to put in Queenie's window. 'This last one is my favourite. The Big Village Pond Dig. Scheduled for the first weekend of the children's summer holidays. Rather exciting, don't you think?'

Queenie looked at her as if she was mad. 'No. In my opinion, if something's buried there's a reason for it.'

'Do you honestly think there may be the drowned bodies

of medieval witches lying in the mud? Mind you,' Mamie added, 'you would have been a prime candidate back then.'

'Oi,' Queenie grumped, 'it's just, like I say, I don't want no trouble brought to this village.'

'What's the worst thing that could happen? It's just a dried-up old pond. Nothing more. Now, let's get these notices up. Got any Blu Tack?'

Once the notices were displayed to their satisfaction, Mamie helped Queenie down from the steps.

'There. Now shall I pop the kettle on again?'

'Yes, please, me duck.'

'And may I buy a Ribena for Tony?'

'I'll take that to him. Check on his planting out there. You get the tea ready.'

Ensconced once more in her armchair, a cup of tea to hand, Queenie rummaged in her pocket for her tobacco pouch. ''Ere, when are we going to have our naughty smoke? Only me knees and hips could do with easing up.'

'I have news on that front.'

'Well, come on. Spill.'

Mamie lowered her voice. 'Where will you be on the day of the Big Pond Dig?'

'Nowhere near that bloody pond, that's for certain.'

'Exactly. And where will everyone else be?'

'Out digging the bleeding pond. What you asking me for?'

'Well, if everyone in the village is taken up with the pond, you and I shall be left by ourselves. Get it?'

Queenie gave Mamie a sly look. 'Oh. Gotcha. Good thinking.'

13

By Thursday afternoon, Angela had worked herself into a state of anxiety over the inaugural Pals meeting.

'I've no idea how many will come,' she said anxiously to Mamie as they shifted the lounge sofa against the corner by the fireplace. 'I suppose we could bring extra chairs from the kitchen.'

'Who have you invited?' asked Mamie.

Angela pushed the sofa the final inch against the wall with her knee.

'Well, Helen put it out on the village website and says she's had two replies. Audrey and Mrs Whatsit from the farm.'

'Evelyn?' Mamie's ears pricked.

'That rings a bell. She's not a churchgoer but I have seen her about. I must get around to visiting her. It's no good preaching only to the converted, is it?'

'No, it isn't.' Mamie pushed her hand through her silver-blond curls. 'I think Evelyn could do with a kind shoulder to lean on.'

Angela looked at her aunt. 'If this is idle gossip I don't want to hear.'

'OK then. My lips are sealed,' Mamie replied. 'Shall I get some kitchen chairs in or not?'

'Let's wait.' Angela's lips twitched. 'So, what have you heard about Evelyn? It may not be true and some strange people enjoy spreading lies behind people's backs, you know.' She had not told Mamie about the anonymous letter and wasn't about to, but suppose this other poor woman was also suffering?

Mamie spilled. 'Evelyn is having man trouble. Her husband has a roving eye.'

'And do you believe that?'

'Yes.'

'From a reliable source?'

'Queenie has excellent sources. Rarely wrong.'

'I might have known it was her.' Angela picked up a cushion and began vigorously bashing it into shape, spreading Mr Worthington's fur around the room. 'I'm shocked at Queenie. She needs to keep her own counsel.' She gave her aunt a sharp glance. 'I hope you haven't been discussing with her what goes on here in the vicarage?'

'Darling. Of course not. Queenie and I are very discreet. No names, no pack-drill. Your grandfather taught me that very early on. Careless talk costs lives and all that.'

Angela didn't believe this for a moment. 'So what have you told her?'

'Nothing.' Mamie was the picture of innocence.

'If I find out that you have been telling Queenie anything about me or Robert or Faith,' Angela was at her most fierce, 'I shall be most disappointed!'

'Understood,' said Mamie meekly as she swiftly changed

the subject. 'Shall I put the kettle on? I think you could do with a cup of tea after all this work.'

Angela's mind immediately returned to the evening's meeting. 'Do you think I should make sandwiches?'

'Certainly not,' Mamie said firmly. 'Guests are best left unfed. It'll stop them hanging around.'

'So just tea and coffee?'

'Much too much work. A family bag of ready-salted from Queenie's and a box of her cheap pinot will be a feast.'

'I'm not sure I can run to a case of wine,' Angela fretted.

'I said *box*, not case. It comes with a little plastic tap on the front and holds about a gallon for threepence. All the rage in the seventies. Filthy to drink but it hits the spot. You and I can have a glass of the good stuff from the fridge. They'll never know.'

'I'm better sticking to water.' Angela went to the piano and fussed with the jug of tulips there, picking up a dropped petal. 'I must keep a clear head.'

In the kitchen Mamie put a cup of tea in front of her niece and opened a packet of Jaffa Cakes. 'Now, tell me, what is the order of play tonight?'

Angela cupped her hands around her mug. 'Six forty-five arrivals. Seven o'clock kick-off.'

'And what are we going to discuss?'

This was the part that Angela was most nervous about. She smiled brightly to cover her anxiety. 'I think we should start with a "getting to know each other" thing.'

'They already know each other.' Mamie was dismissive. 'But if you like, I could get the ball rolling by telling them a little of my life . . .'

Angela's anxiety multiplied. 'That may be a little too racy for them.'

Mamie cocked an eyebrow. 'Have I ever let you down?'

'I'm not saying that you have ever let me down, it's just that your life has been, well, rather less conservative than theirs.'

Mamie reached across the table and put her hand on Angela's. 'Now don't go all po-faced on me. When your mother first told me that you wanted to be a vicar, she made me promise to never allow you to become all holier than thou. And that is a promise I intend to keep. You come from a long family line of liberal, non-judgemental, kind and free-thinking folk and I will not allow the Church to squeeze that out of you. God gave us the ability to laugh at our mistakes and accept people for what they are, and don't you forget it. Now shut up and have a Jaffa Cake.'

Robert stuck his head round the door. 'Is it safe to come in?'

'Of course.' Angela was pleased to see him.

'When does the coven start brewing up?' he asked, rubbing his hands together briskly.

'First arrivals six forty-five,' said Mamie.

He checked his watch. 'That gives me time to avoid them by getting ready to go to the pub.'

Angela gave him a pleading look. 'Can you not stay just long enough to welcome them with me and then go to the pub?'

'I would but I have to meet someone.'

'Who?'

Robert reached for a Jaffa Cake. 'The editor of the *Trevay Times*. He's interested in me becoming the regular food critic.'

Angela rocked back in her chair. 'Really? That's wonderful. Do you want to do it?'

'I do. It means I can whizz you out to dinner once a week. No bill to pay and the extra benefit of a date night!'

'And when you can't take your wife,' Mamie said, 'can you take a glamorous slightly older guest?'

'Certainly. A plus-one every time.' He looked at his watch. 'But I'll have to skip the pleasures of your meeting tonight.'

Angela was disappointed but said, 'You are forgiven.' Robert bent to kiss her as she added, 'Could you take anyone to these dinners?'

'I can't see why not. Why?'

'Well, Helen is doing an awful lot on the social media stuff for the village, so maybe you could take her as a thank you?'

Robert straightened up. 'Providing Piran doesn't lamp me, yes.'

Mamie laughed. 'You'd better get going or you're going to bump into the female hordes wanting to flirt with you. And I have to collect Queenie.'

'And pick up the crisps and wine at the same time?' Angela reminded her.

Robert bent and kissed his wife again. 'Good luck.'

Audrey Tipton was the earliest arrival, ringing the bell with insistence.

Angela was upstairs putting a brush through her hair and adding a little mascara.

'Faith, can you answer that, please?'

Faith, who was coming from the kitchen with a glass of milk and a packet of chocolate Hobnobs, ready to take to her room and do a bit of homework, drooped.

'Do I have to?' she yelled up the stairs.

'Yes, please. I'll be two minutes.'

Faith opened the door and said politely, 'Hello. Please come in. Mum's just coming.'

Audrey took in Faith's long slender legs, tiny shorts and hair screwed up in a bird's nest, and found her wanting. 'You're Mrs Whitehorn's daughter?'

'The *Reverend* Whitehorn's daughter, yes. I'm Faith. Welcome. Would you like to come through to the lounge?'

Audrey shouldered her way in. 'I know my way.'

Faith was no pushover and stepped in front of the gargoyle. 'Wait one moment while I call Mum.' She turned to the stairs and shouted up, 'Muuuum.'

'Who is it, darling?' Angela was hurriedly changing her blouse.

'A woman for the meeting.'

Audrey glowered at Faith's impudence and said loudly so that Angela could hear upstairs, 'This is Audrey Tipton, Vicar.'

Angela appeared at the top of the stairs. 'Audrey. How good of you to come.'

Faith moved to the stairs and rolled her eyes as she passed her mother. 'Good luck, Mum,' she said, then reached her room and closed the door rather too loudly behind her.

Angela stepped down into the hall and noticed that Audrey looked different. Her thin lips were sporting a line of coral lipstick and her eyelids a hint of shiny green eye shadow.

'You look very glamorous, Audrey,' she said warmly.

'I like to keep a standard.' Audrey headed to the sitting room. 'Is your husband with us tonight?'

Angela followed behind. 'No, unfortunately he had another appointment.' Was she imagining a slight droop of disappointment in the Tipton bearing? 'Did you need to speak to him?'

Audrey was surveying the layout of the lounge. 'He hasn't

responded to my emails *re* the WI talk. Get him to contact me. Why is the sofa pushed up against that wall?'

'To make more room. I'm not sure how many people will attend.'

'You should bring the kitchen chairs in. That's what Simon always does when he holds meetings in here.' Audrey walked to the fireplace and ran the index finger of her right hand over the mantelpiece, checking for dust.

Angela felt a stab of irritation. 'I understand that this house is on loan to me but, while I am here, I shall run it the way I feel best.'

Audrey rubbed her thumb and forefinger together. 'If you need me at any time just call. I have a spare key to the vicarage and Geoffrey or I can drop in at a moment's notice. Social engagements permitting.' She walked to the most comfortable of the armchairs and sat down. 'So, what is on your agenda for tonight?'

At that moment Mamie arrived with Queenie, staggering under the weight of two large wine boxes and a bumper bag of crisps. Mamie had overheard the last bit of the conversation.

'Good evening, Aud. Angela has a carefully worked out programme for tonight's events. She has even booked a guest speaker. Me.' She ignored Audrey's horrified expression and carried on. 'Thought I'd get the ball rolling for Angela. I am giving a little talk about my personal experiences of travelling the world. I have met some fascinating people.'

'Really? You?' Audrey spluttered.

'Yes, me.' Mamie smiled combatively as she plonked the wine onto the piano. 'Do you have a problem with that?'

Queenie coughed down a snigger and cut Audrey off at the pass. 'Mamie has got Rita Hayworth's fur coat upstairs.'

Audrey's face twisted thunderously, her hackles up. She had disliked Mamie from the first moment she had set eyes on her. She had told Geoffrey more than once, *That woman and her ridiculously over-painted face. No better than she should be. A woman of her age.* Geoffrey had kept his silence. He rather fancied Mamie.

Audrey sniffed, turning her lips down. 'I despise tawdry revelations.'

'Oh,' said Queenie innocently. 'Shall I cancel your weekly order of *Hello!* then?'

Beneath her face powder, Audrey blenched. She checked her watch, internally struggling with the delicious idea of walking out of this farce, or hanging on to see exactly what was going to happen. She decided on the latter.

'Well, Mrs Whitehorn, I am looking forward to what you have in store for tonight.' She turned to Mamie. 'And my name is Audrey. Never Aud.'

'And my niece's name is *Reverend* Whitehorn, never Mrs,' Mamie replied clearly.

Queenie almost choked.

Angela said politely, 'May I get you a glass of wine, Audrey?' The doorbell rang. 'Mamie, would you get Audrey a drink while I answer that?'

Helen was on the doorstep with two women. 'Angela, may I introduce you to Evelyn? She and her husband own the village farm.'

Angela greeted her warmly. Evelyn was in her forties, she guessed. A pretty, plump woman with the healthy complexion of someone who spent a lot of time outdoors. Her hair was naturally dark with attractive grey streaks, her smile diffident. Angela could imagine that she wasn't happy.

'Mamie, would you also find a drink for Evelyn, please?'

Angela asked before turning her attention to the second person Helen had brought in with her.

'This is Robbie,' Helen introduced her. 'She and Evelyn are sisters-in-law.'

Angela shook Robbie's hand. 'Welcome. You have an unusual name.'

'Short for Roberta,' said Robbie. 'Mad really. I'm married to a man called Robert but everyone calls him Bob, or Gasping Bob on account of his smoking.'

'Oh, yes.' Angela remembered the name. 'I've heard of him. I'm told he has done wonders fixing the church roof at times.'

'He has.'

'Well, let me take your coats and come on through.'

Back in the lounge, Queenie was tipping crisps into small bowls and Mamie was filling wine glasses from the wine box.

She flashed a glowing smile. 'Just in time, ladies. Wine for everyone and then we'll get started.'

Queenie shuffled along the sofa to make space for Evelyn and Robbie. She put her gnarled hand onto Evelyn's arm, and whispered, 'How are you doing, duck?'

Evelyn shrugged and whispered back, 'He's gone out tonight. Probably to you-know-who's.' Her eyes filled with tears and she quickly put her head down to wipe them away.

Queenie passed her her handkerchief. 'You're with friends tonight, duck. Should have you smiling soon. Now drink your wine.'

The final arrival was Dorrie from the Dolphin. ''Ello, all right?' She smiled at Evelyn and Robbie on the sofa. 'Have I missed anything?'

'Nothing at all.' Angela looked at her watch. 'I think we'll make a start, shall we. If anyone else arrives they can easily join in.' She looked at the seven faces in front of her. Not the crowd she had been hoping for but perhaps this number was better. More intimate. She began.

'Welcome to the Pals.'

Everyone looked at each other and smiled.

Angela continued, 'A place where we can get to know each other. Have some fun. Do some good for ourselves and others. Discuss topics of the day, relevant both politically and personally to us as women.'

There was a wary silence.

Angela forged on. 'And what about a book club? We'd pick a book every month then read and discuss it. Reading is such a wonderful way to get a good conversation going.'

Helen smiled warmly but the other women said nothing. Evelyn's face dropped. She looked over at Robbie in desperation. Robbie caught the wild-eyed glance and coughed uncomfortably.

Mamie butted in. 'Well, yes, books and politics can be very interesting, but I propose we first talk to each other about ourselves. Let off steam. Get things off our chests. The one rule being that what is said in this room stays in this room. Understood?'

Helen broke the silence. 'Great idea. There are times when I have plenty to get off my chest, particularly when Piran is driving me mad.'

Queenie laughed. 'I wouldn't kick him out of bed.'

Robbie and Dorrie joined in the laughter.

Audrey, listening to all this with curled lips, said, 'I'm sorry to be the voice of reason here but someone has to be. It sounds very much as if this *women's group* will be nothing more than gossiping over a glass of cheap wine. As for the book club, I've been thinking of setting one up at the WI for a while. What titles will you be offering, Reverend Whitehorn?'

Angela, cowed by Audrey's superior tone, said, 'I wondered if we might start with *Eleanor Oliphant is Completely Fine*.'

'Never heard of it.'

'That's a great book,' said Dorrie. 'Brilliant story.'

Angela was relieved. 'So I hear.'

'I would prefer a Dickens or an Austen,' sniffed Audrey. 'I do not intend to read cheap "chick lit", as I believe it's called.'

'It has sold millions of copies and readers love it,' Dorrie insisted.

Audrey gave her version of a tinkling laugh. 'So did *Fifty Shades of Grey*.'

'Oh my good Gawd,' said Queenie. 'Now them books were something else. Read them twice now.'

'Why doesn't that surprise me?' Audrey sneered.

Queenie ignored her. ''Ere, anyone want to hear Mamie's life story? It'll cheer you up and make your hair stand on end as well.'

Helen said, 'I hear you own Rita Hayworth's fur coat, Mamie. Is that true?'

Mamie smiled. 'Actually, yes. It's upstairs. Shall I bring it down?'

Evelyn and Robbie brightened up.

'Yes, please.'

Mamie stood and went to the door. 'In that case, ladies, I shall go and get it.'

As she left the room, Mr Worthington, unseen despite his size, slunk in and hid under the piano. He loved checking out handbags and here were a few that he hadn't explored. Faith wandered in behind him with a cup of hot chocolate and her phone. 'Can I join you?'

Audrey tutted but all the other women welcomed her. She

plonked herself on the rug by the fireplace. 'Where's Auntie Mamie? She hasn't gone to get her horrible old coat, has she?'

'Yes she has,' said Angela. 'Want a crisp?'

'No. And why does she want to show us all a pile of dead animals anyway? It's disgraceful. No human should wear animal skin.'

'If I had the money, I'd have one,' said Robbie.

Mamie appeared wearing the shimmering full-length coat. Right or wrong, it was magnificent. All eyes were on her.

'Rita Hayworth was given this by one of her many lovers. It's sable. I was given it by the maître d' of a restaurant in LA where she had left it behind. She never came back to collect it. A few months later I happened to be there with dear Marlon,' she paused for dramatic effect, 'Brando . . . and by the end of the evening I was wearing it.' She held the tall funnel collar to her nose and sniffed. 'I always imagine I can smell her perfume.'

''Ere, let me 'ave a whiff,' said Queenie.

Mamie took the coat off and passed it to her.

'I think that's Chanel,' Queenie announced. 'You have a sniff, Evelyn.'

'Maybe,' said Evelyn after some deliberation, before passing it to Helen.

Helen stroked the sable pelt. 'It's beautiful . . . but I agree with Faith. I think it looks better on the true owner.' She held it out to Faith. 'Do you want to touch it?'

'I'd rather stick pins in my eyes.' Faith, busily texting, shuddered. 'And who the hell is Marlon Brando?'

Before long, Mamie had her audience in the palm of her hand. Her stories, whether true or not, were spellbinding.

Creeping out unnoticed from under the piano, Mr

Worthington nudged his whiskery chin into Queenie's handbag, gently pulled out a bag of soft mints, and tiptoed back to his lair.

Mamie was just describing her first visit to the Royal Pink Palace in Monaco, for the wedding of Grace Kelly and Prince Rainier, when the doorbell rang.

Faith jumped up. 'I'll get it.' Moments later she was back. 'Mum, everyone. This is Sarah. She wants to join you.'

A pretty woman in her early thirties appeared, carrying a baby over her shoulder. 'Hello, everyone. Sorry I'm late. The littl'un needed a feed and then her nappy changed. You know what it's like.'

Queenie was agog and patted the seat next to her. 'Come and sit 'ere with me, duck.'

'Thank you.' Sarah gratefully sat down. 'Faith's taken Ben upstairs to watch telly.' She smiled at Angela. 'She's a lovely girl, isn't she? You must be proud of her.'

'I am, yes.' Angela was confused. 'And Ben is?'

'Oh, sorry, yeah, he's my son. Him and Faith have really hit it off at school.'

'Oh, Ben, yes,' said Angela. 'And he's gone upstairs with Faith?'

'Nothing to worry about with him.' Sarah chuckled. 'He's known for a long time that girls aren't his thing. I'd been waiting for him to tell me. It's a tricky conversation to have and I wanted him to be comfortable and able to tell me when he was ready.'

Audrey's eyes widened. 'Your son is queer?'

'Gay, yes,' Sarah said smartly. 'I would thank you for not using any other word.'

'Hear hear,' said Dorrie.

'Faith was so good to Ben when he arrived at the new

school,' Sarah explained. 'Two newbies together. They've really taken to each other.'

'Oh, yes,' said Angela, her anxiety draining away. 'Thank you for having her over after school the other day.'

'Oh, bless. That was at Ben's dad's house. Johnny, my ex. Lousy partner. Good dad.'

Queenie's inquisitive eyes were on the baby. 'So who's this one, then?'

'This is Santi. She's four months old. Her daddy hasn't seen her yet. Well, he has on FaceTime, but we can't always get a signal to the ship.'

Mamie needed more. 'Ship?'

'Yeah. Royal Navy. HMS *Sirens*.'

'My dad was in the navy during the war,' Queenie chipped in. 'He was in the kitchens. Terrible hot down there. Mind you, my mum said he could cook anything.'

'Oh, yeah,' Sarah agreed. 'My Joe says the food is really good.'

'What job does he do?' Angela asked.

'Weapons engineer. *Sirens* is a battleship. I'm not supposed to know where he is at the moment. So I'm guessing the Gulf.'

'When will he be home?' asked Evelyn.

Sarah shrugged. 'A few months yet. Depends on what the powers that be think.'

'It must be difficult for you with the baby, on your own,' Mamie said.

'Yeah. Can be. It's why I came to this village. Thought I'd make some friends. I saw the notice on the village green about this group and thought, "On you go, Sarah, be brave." And here I am. Whose is that beautiful coat?'

'Oh, it's mine,' said Mamie.

Angela stood up. 'What can I get you to drink? Cup of tea? Glass of wine?'

'I could kill for a glass of wine but I'm still breastfeeding the littl'un so a cuppa would be great.'

The conversation in the room bloomed as all the women, other than Audrey, took it in turns to coo over Santi.

In the kitchen, Angela filled the kettle and left it to boil while she went upstairs to check on what exactly Faith and Ben were up to.

They were in Angela's bedroom, lying cuddled together on her bed, watching something on Netflix.

'Oh, hi, Mum.' Faith briefly glanced at her. 'This is Ben.'

'Hi, Mrs Whitehorn.' He lifted the hand that was attached to the arm wrapped around her daughter.

'Hello, Ben.' Angela was out of her comfort zone. 'Faith, can I have a word, please?'

Faith remained glued to the television. 'What about?'

'I just want a word. In private.'

Tutting, and with loud sigh, Faith got off the bed and followed her mother onto the landing. 'We're not doing anything, if that's what you think,' she sulked.

'Yes, I, erm, I know he's gay, which is completely fine but . . .'

'But?' Faith said.

'But I, er, would like to have met him when he arrived, before you brought him up to the bedroom.'

'God forbid we forget our manners.'

'Oh, don't be silly, Faith. You know what I mean.'

'Yes, you mean you don't want me to have friends because you think I might have sex with them.'

'That's not what I mean.' That was exactly what she meant.

'It is exactly what you mean,' Faith flared. 'Just because

your generation was all sex and drugs and Madonna warbling away with her stupid bra on. Nowadays we can have friends of any sex and simply be friends. It's nothing to lose your mind over. Relax yourself. Ben and I are cool. He's great. All girls need a gay best mate.'

Angela wasn't sure if this was a positive or not. 'Is he sure? It might be a phase.'

Faith threw her hands above her head and hissed, 'Homophobic!'

'Of course I'm not, but when you're young you don't know who you really are.'

'Mum. Shut up.' Faith put her hands on her hips. 'People are people. My generation don't define people by their sexuality, ethnicity, religion or gender.'

'Sure. Sure. OK. I totally agree and, erm . . . would Ben like a hot chocolate? Or anything?'

'I'll ask him.' She raised her voice. 'Ben . . .'

'Yeah.'

'Mum wants to know if you'd like a hot chocolate?'

'Yes, please.'

The front door opened and slammed shut below them.

'Hellooo. Is it safe to come home?' Robert's voice.

Mother and daughter froze.

'Don't say anything to Dad,' Faith pleaded. 'He'll only make one of his stupid jokes.'

They listened as Robert walked away down the hall and opened the sitting room door to a chorus of greetings from the Pals, who were thrilled to see the most handsome man in the village, up close.

When Angela returned to the sitting room, Robert was holding Santi and charming the lot of them.

He spotted Angela by the door and winked. 'Takes me back, this.'

Angela stepped into the room. 'I'm not sure either of us could do the sleepless nights again.' She went to Robert's side and looked into Santi's sleeping face. 'But she is beautiful.'

Sarah checked her phone. 'Look at the time! I must get Santi and Ben home. School tomorrow. Where is Ben?'

'I'll find him,' smiled Angela.

As everyone gathered at the front door ready to leave, Angela said, 'One more thing I had forgotten to say. On Saturday morning I'm starting the Couch to Five K running club. Very simple. Lots of walking interspersed with short bursts of jogging.'

Dorrie put her hand up. 'I'd love to.' She looked at Robbie and Evelyn. 'You'll come, won't you, girls?'

'Oh, I don't know . . .' said Evelyn.

Helen said, 'I'll give it a go.'

'Think about it,' Angela said. 'Meet on the village green at nine o'clock. Then back for a coffee here by nine thirty.'

'Sounds interesting,' said Robbie.

Audrey pulled her tweed jacket a little closer to her chest and said, 'Geoffrey and I are very keen on Canadian Air Force exercises. Been doing them for years. So we won't be joining you.'

Finally Angela shut the front door on her new group of Pals and walked, tired but relieved it had all gone well, to the kitchen where Robert was making himself a cheese sandwich.

'You'll get heartburn,' Angela said.

'I like to live dangerously.' He wrapped the block of cheese in cling film and put it back in the fridge as Faith wandered in. 'Ben seems a nice boy,' Robert told her.

'Yes,' Faith said, directing her words at her mother. 'He *is* nice.'

'All boys are nice until they touch my little girl, then they are dead,' he laughed.

'Daaaad.' Faith rolled her eyes. 'Ben's gay.'

'Ha! Oldest trick in the book.'

'Oh God, you're as bad as Mum.'

Mamie came in from the garden where she'd taken Mr Worthington for his final pee. She did not look happy and neither did Mr Worthington, who went to his bed and lay down with his back to everyone.

'Your dog has the squits. Minty ones.'

14

Saturday morning's sun held the promise of a warm day. Having been up at the crack of dawn sorting out paperwork, rotas and spending a frustrating half an hour on a fruitless search for the parish cheque book Angela was out on the green doing some calf stretches and warming up her shoulders. When she'd done those she checked her running watch to record the results and set the stopwatch to zero.

She looked around the empty green and then at the church tower where the clock stood at two minutes to nine. Would any of the Pals join her? She gave her neck a stretch and began to jog on the spot, closing her eyes and tipping her head to the sun, enjoying the warmth on her face.

'Hiya.' Helen's voice was close and made Angela jump. She clutched her chest.

'Sorry. I thought you had heard me coming,' Helen said.

Angela kissed her. 'I'm so glad to see you. I thought for a minute no one was joining me.'

'Dorrie's on her way,' Helen said. 'As is Robbie. She said she was hoping to coax Evelyn but . . . I'm not sure.' Helen said nothing about Evelyn's unhappiness so either she didn't know or she was being discreet.

Behind her Angela heard another voice calling, 'Morning!' It was Dorrie, looking very sporty in smart running tights, vest, baseball cap and good training shoes.

Helen laughed. 'I must warn you, Angela, Dorrie is a veteran of several marathons. Practically professional.'

'Get away with you,' smiled Dorrie as she got close to them. 'I haven't done much through the winter so I'll be useless. Hey!' She pointed and waved at Robbie and a reluctant Evelyn. 'Come on, girls,' she yelled.

Robbie broke into a power walk while Evelyn puffed (and huffed) behind.

'Welcome to the brand-new Pendruggan Running Club, ladies,' Angela said.

'I hope you don't expect me to run fast,' said Evelyn with dread. 'I never could do cross-country at school.'

'Evelyn, I promise you that within the next three months, I will have you running non-stop for thirty minutes, at least. But the secret is to start very gently. Literally baby steps.'

'I don't know.' Evelyn looked as if she might cry.

Angela put an arm around her. 'Here's the deal. Try this just once and then see. OK?'

'OK.'

'Good.' Angela looked at the others. 'Dorrie, you can be my front woman.'

'OK.' Dorrie nodded. 'Which route?'

'If we go down to Shellsand, along the beach for a couple of hundred yards to the footpath, up the footpath, back into the village and a lap of the green, we should do two miles.'

'Perfect.'

'Keep the pace slow. Helen and Robbie, stay in the middle

of the pack and Evelyn and I will bring up the rear. The plan is to have a warm-up walk for five minutes, then we jog for sixty seconds, walk for ninety, and repeat that seven times. Don't worry, I will be counting. We cool down with a five-minute walk. How does that sound?'

'Not too bad,' said Evelyn uncertainly.

'You'll be fine.' Angela set her watch. 'OK, let's go. A five-minute brisk walk to start.'

The gaggle of women set off. Angela hung back with Evelyn and began chatting to distract her. 'Beautiful day. Spring here is so lovely.'

'Yes.'

'And Pendruggan Farm has cows?'

'Yes.'

'How big is the herd?'

'We got seventy-two.'

'Goodness. And you know every one of them?'

'Most. My husband and my two boys do most of the milking.'

'Twice a day?'

'Yes.'

'How early?'

'I was up this morning at four thirty. My husband ain't home at the moment. The boys and I did the milking.'

'Ah.' Angela was undecided how to proceed. Should she dig deeper and ask where he was – presumably with another woman – or keep schtum?

She checked her watch and shouted to the women ahead, 'Fifteen seconds to the one-minute run.'

'OK,' they called back, giving her thumbs-up signals.

Angela checked her watch again. 'Sixty seconds starts . . . now!'

Evelyn beside her broke into an amble.

Angela was encouraging. 'Good. Feeling OK? No pains?'

'No,' Evelyn gasped. 'How much longer?'

'Twenty seconds.'

Evelyn kept going.

'And now, walk.' Angela instructed the group before turning to Evelyn. 'Well done. How was that?'

'All right,' said Evelyn.

'Ninety-second walk to catch your breath,' Angela smiled, 'and then we'll do it again.'

'Oh shit,' said Evelyn.

Half an hour later, the women clattered through the back door of the vicarage laughing, red-faced and breathless.

'Well done!' gasped Angela. 'We deserve tea and cake after that.'

'That was fun,' said Robbie, bent over, hands on knees, steam rising from her sports top.

Helen was exhilarated. 'I thought that might be ghastly but . . . when do we do it again?'

'Three times a week for the next nine or ten weeks. By then we will have built up to running three miles non-stop.'

'Really?' Evelyn was wiping her scarlet forehead with some kitchen towel.

'Yes, really.'

Robbie put her arms around Evelyn and hugged her. 'We'll get fit together and hopefully drop a couple of dress sizes.'

Dorrie was stretching her hamstrings. 'That'd be good with the summer coming. I've got a new bikini.'

After getting changed, Angela went into the kitchen and laid out two trays, one with tea and coffee, the other with a large fruit cake.

'I bought it at the Trevay bakers yesterday,' she said. 'Let's take this into the garden, shall we? It's a shame to waste such a glorious day.'

'I'll bring the other tray,' said Helen.

Once they were settled outside in the garden, Robbie started talking to Angela about Evelyn. 'We've known each other all our lives. She's my best friend. I was her bridesmaid when she married my brother, and she was mine when I married Bob.'

Evelyn managed a smile as she munched her slice of cake. 'You're the sister I never 'ad. I don't know what I'd do without you.'

Robbie gave Evelyn a quick and – Angela noticed – over-bright smile. 'Well, you'll never have to do without me, will you, Evie?'

Angela watched as Evelyn reached out for Robbie's hand and squeezed it. 'I hope not.'

Angela instinctively knew that they shared a secret.

Helen was talking. 'So, Angela, shall we arrange our running days now? Get them in the diary?'

Angela dragged her mind back from Robbie and Evelyn. 'Yes. Erm, with the lighter nights, evenings would be good. Say seven o'clock on Monday and Wednesdays, plus our Saturday mornings?'

It was agreed by all.

Mamie came out into the garden with a basket of school uniform to hang on the line. 'Good morning, runners. How was it?'

She chatted pleasantly as she pegged out the laundry and shared a second cup of tea with them before reminding Angela that she needed to take Mr Worthington to the vet's for his check-up.

Quickly, the group broke up, saying their goodbyes.

When they'd gone, Angela asked her aunt, 'Good job you reminded me about the vet's. I thought it was Monday.'

'It is, darling. I just thought you could do with a bit of peace from your new friends. I don't want you giving out too much emotional energy. People can be very tiring. Now, why don't you get out of all that wretched Lycra and have a shower. Faith wants me drop her into Trevay this afternoon with Ben. I rather think he wants a ride in the old Jensen. You and Robert can spend the afternoon together,' she winked, 'without interruption.'

15

The warm Cornish spring brought light winds and blue skies. The hedgerows gradually changed from primroses and bluebells to verdant grasses studded with foxgloves, ferns and buttercups. Children were playing out on the village green until bedtime and early holiday-makers arrived to enjoy the beaches and coffee shops.

Preparations for the Big Pond Dig had begun, with Piran and local builder, Gasping Bob, taking their divining rods down the lane to the beach where they hoped to find proof of a natural spring.

Gasping Bob took a cigarette from behind his ear and lit it. 'If you ask me, this be a wild-goose chase.' He inhaled his tobacco smoke and coughed loudly.

Scanning the surroundings, Piran said, 'I thought you'm stopped those things.'

'I have,' said Bob, scratching his stubbled chin. 'I feel a lot better for it too.'

Piran hid his smile and pointed to the right where the steep fields rose to the north. 'If the water's anywhere it'll be coming out of that slope and running south to the sea.' He pointed to the beach roughly two hundred metres away on their left. 'The verge here gets wider and, looking at that clump of gunnera growing over there, it must be pretty damp.'

Gasping Bob squinted his eyes against the sun and his smoke. 'Aye, gunnera likes to have wet feet.' He pulled two metal rods from his pocket. They were bent at right angles about a third of the way along. He took the short end in each fist and began walking slowly. Almost immediately the rods, swinging free in front of him, crossed themselves. 'There's water 'ere all right.'

Piran nodded. 'Excellent. I'll go further down and walk towards you. See if we can't pinpoint the exact spot and maybe even the size of it.'

He walked fifty metres away and began. He too got an immediate result. Within an hour they reckoned they'd found the perimeter of the lost pond and the possible source of the spring.

Piran shifted a large mass of vegetation and found some boggy ground with water seeping through. 'This could be it. Shall we mark it?'

'Best not,' said Bob, lighting his third cigarette. 'Don't want busybodies tramping through and making a mess.'

'Good point. I'll tell the vicar and Mike Bates, and remind them to keep their mouths shut until the actual dig.' Piran put his rods inside the deep front pocket of his salt-stained fishing smock. 'Right, I think we deserve a pint.'

Angela was out with the running group when Robert collared Mamie as she languished on a garden bench. 'Can I have a word?'

'Of course, darling.' Mamie made room, intrigued. 'What about?'

Robert sat next to her. 'Angela. I think she's doing too much.'

'Really?' Mamie was surprised. 'I thought she was doing very well and taking everything in her usual capable stride.'

'Have you noticed how forgetful she's become?'

'No. Quite the reverse. Her memory amazes me. Why? What has happened?'

'She lost her iPad the other week and it was in the car all along. She couldn't find her watch yesterday but it was where she always puts it, in the dish by her bed, and she forgot she'd put a macaroni cheese in the microwave.'

'Was that the smell?'

Robert nodded. 'It's so unlike her.'

Mamie thought about what Robert had told her and, after a bit, said, 'She's fine. Quite normal. Her mind is spinning with the excitement of her first posting and she has always taken her responsibilities very seriously. She's absolutely fine.'

'Do you honestly think so?'

Mamie patted his hand. 'Yes. I am certain. And I think it's sweet that you are so concerned for her. I'll keep an eye out too, just to make sure. And, if there's anything we can do to take some of the pressure off her, we will. Agreed?'

'Agreed.' Robert looked a little less worried.

'What are her plans for today?' Mamie asked.

'The Big Pond Dig. The gardener boy who came up with the idea . . .'

'Tony, yes?'

'He's been speaking to some woman in the village who says she's a white witch.' He raised his eyebrows and shook his head.

Mamie chipped in, 'Ah, yes. That'll be Polly. She's a para-medic on the ambulance.'

Robert sat back. 'Really? How do you know?'

'My friend Queenie. Apparently Polly is a very good psychic too.'

'Oh, for goodness' sake.' Robert was dumbstruck. 'What the hell is going on this village? I mean, I know I'm not the best Christian on the planet . . .'

'Me neither,' said Mamie. 'But we try hard, to please Angela.'

'Well, quite!' Robert rubbed his eyes with both hands and exhaled through puffed cheeks. 'Which is why all this bloody witchy spell business is bollocks and should be nipped in the bud.'

'Does it? Where's the harm?'

'The harm is that Garden Boy has told Angela that Polly has told him that the pond will need to have its goddess blessed or something, in order for any negative whatnots to be released and . . .'

'We are in Celtic country now,' Mamie said, trying to calm him. 'This is what happens and has happened for thousands of years.'

'That may be so, but if Angela allows it to happen she'll be a laughing stock.'

'Why?'

'*Because*,' Robert finally exploded.

'And you want to protect Angela from ridicule and memory loss and doing too much and making the wrong decisions?'

Robert sagged, his shoulders sloping to his knees. 'Yes. I suppose so.' He sighed, 'I just want her to think carefully about the way she's doing her job. For God's sake, yesterday she was thinking of setting up a champing holiday camp.'

'A what?'

'Exactly what I said. Instead of staying in a youth hostel or B and B, walkers and campers can sleep in a church. Church camping, hence champing.'

Mamie began to laugh. 'Whoever would want to do that?'

'Apparently people do.'

Ever the pragmatist, Mamie shrugged. 'It'll bring in some good revenue for the Church.'

'They'll nick the silver and piss in the font, more like.'

Mamie's laughter was now unstoppable. 'Robert, dear, you are too funny.'

'Why can't she be conventional? A nice garden party at the vicarage with a cream tea and a tombola. How hard can that be?'

Mamie wiped her eyes. 'Brilliant! That's it! We'll have a garden party. You and I will organise it.'

'Will we?' His furrowed, pleading eyes melted Mamie's heart.

'Darling. We can do anything we like.'

'It had better be before the Pond Dig in July, but after the May Day celebrations. Sounds rather fun. Apparently everyone goes down to Trevay and gets pissed. One big boozy pub crawl,' Robert said.

'And you wouldn't want to miss that, now, would you?' Mamie was nobody's fool.

'Well, it's the sort of thing that you have to see once. Isn't it? A nod to my appreciation of local traditions. And I could write a piece about it for the *Trevay Times*.'

'Yes, well, when you tell Angela about how you intend to spend May Day, I would make work the main reason, not the bit about a pub crawl.'

Robert laughed. 'Yes, oh wise woman.'

'So the vicarage garden party has to be after the first of May but before the Pond Dig?'

'Yep.'

'How about her birthday weekend? Middle of June,' said Mamie. 'We could use her birthday as an excuse, so she can't stop us. A perfectly conventional vicar's garden party.'

Robert was relieved. 'Mamie, you are a godsend.'

'A garden party!' Angela threw her arms around her husband.

'It was Mamie's idea too. By the way, you're strangling me. And you're all sweaty from your run.'

'Sorry.' She released him with a kiss. 'What made you think of a garden party?'

Robert's eyes slid towards Mamie, begging for help.

'Well, it sort of came to us,' Mamie said easily. 'We were sitting in the garden, chatting, and it came to us.'

'And,' said Robert improvising, 'so much nicer than going out for dinner or to the cinema. We can do that any time now that I'm the food writer for the *Trevay Times*.'

'Such happy times!' Angela grinned, then frowned. 'The garden needs tidying. I must ask Tony if he would jolly it up a bit. Maybe put some extra colour in with bedding plants? Is that what you put in? And hanging baskets.'

'Leave it all to us,' Robert said smoothly. 'There's plenty of time to plan.'

'And if it rains, we'll need shelters of some sort. Actually shelters anyway, if it's too hot.'

Mamie put a hand up to stop her niece. 'Darling, I have organised more parties than I'll ever remember. Leave it all to me and Robert.'

Angela relaxed. 'It's the nicest thing to happen to me. Thank you both.' She picked up her the trainers she'd kicked off. 'I'm going to have a shower.'

'Do you want anything from Truro?' Mamie asked. 'Only I promised Queenie I'd take her to M&S. She wants to complain about the quality of their knickers or something.'

'No, thanks, Mamie. I've got a lot of planning to do. I've got to do the order of service for the pet blessing, find someone to lead us in the dancing round the maypole . . . That reminds me, we've got to get the old maypole painted and re-ribboned. The mice got to it in the village hall over the winter. And I must see if there are any prayers for cyclists. The Sunday school young bikers have their first lesson this Saturday afternoon.'

Robert looked at Angela then at Mamie. 'See. She's doing too much.'

Angela gave them both a stare. 'No, I'm not, I'm loving it.'

Mamie held her hands up in peace. 'Go and have your shower.'

Robert got up. 'See you both later then. I have an important village meeting on the other side of the green. Helen and I are working on the website all afternoon.'

16

Angela was out of the shower and heating up a can of tomato soup before getting to work in the office, when there was a tentative knocking at the front door.

'Robbie!'

'Am I disturbing you?'

'Not at all. How are you after this morning's run?'

'Fine.'

'I'm sorry that Evelyn didn't make it.'

'She was sorry but she had a lot to do on the farm. My brother, her husband . . .'

'Yes?'

'He's been away for a few days.'

'She must find that hard?' asked Angela, thinking that Robbie might be about to confide in her.

'Yeah. I worry about her. And she worries about me.'

Angela remembered the pan of soup on the Aga. 'Come through to the kitchen. Would you like to share some soup with me?'

'Oh, I'm sorry. I have come at the wrong time.' Robbie

moved as if to go but Angela pointed her towards the kitchen.

'Sit down. The soup can wait. How about a coffee?'

When they were seated opposite each other at the kitchen table, Angela coaxed the obviously anxious Robbie into conversation.

'How can I help you?'

Robbie twisted her fingers around her coffee mug. 'Now I'm here, I feel you might think me a bit silly.'

'I'm sure I won't.' Angela smiled gently. 'Give me a try.'

'Well.' Robbie took a deep breath and spilled her secret. 'I think I might have a lump in my breast.'

Angela's heart missed a beat as memories of her own mum telling her the same thing in the same words, flooded her brain. She swallowed hard. 'Have you seen the doctor?'

'No.' Robbie shook her head. 'I don't want to bother him if it's nothing.'

'But that is what he's there for,' Angela said gently. 'His job is to be bothered. And seeing him will put your mind at rest one way or the other. What has your husband said?'

'I haven't told him. He doesn't like hearing about things like that.'

'I'm sure he'd want to know.'

Robbie fiddled with her coffee spoon. 'I told Evelyn but she got so upset that I lied and told her I was fine. Told her the doc gave me the all-clear. But I didn't see him. She has so much to deal with at the moment. Her husband, my brother, doesn't treat her right.'

Angela understood now the look that Evelyn and Robbie had exchanged the other day.

Robbie began to cry. 'She relies on me, you see. I'm the only person what knows how hard her life is.'

Angela went to her and put her arms around her. 'The best thing you can do for Evelyn then is to see the doctor. I'll come with you if you'd like me to?'

Robbie crumpled. 'Would you?'

'Of course. You can phone the doctor right now. Here. With me. Tell the receptionist you need an emergency appointment.'

'It's not an emergency.' Robbie wiped her nose. 'I can see him next week.'

Angela reached for the kitchen towel and tore a piece off to dry Robbie's face. 'No. Not next week. Today. Monday at the latest. Just to get checked out. We could go this afternoon.'

Across the green at Helen's cottage, Gull's Cry, Robert and Helen were working together on the village website when Robert's mobile pinged a text from Angela.

'Gone to Trevay. Taking Robbie. Back later,' he read aloud. 'Good God, the woman never stops. She told Mamie and me that she had a ton of work to do in her office. Why is she going to Trevay?'

Helen looked up from her computer screen. 'A trip to Tesco or something. Robbie doesn't drive.'

'Which one is Robbie?'

'She's in the running club. Tall? Slender? Gasping Bob's wife. Very quiet. Bob never talks about her. I was surprised when she came to the women's group. Probably glad to have people to talk to.' She returned to her screen. 'Message here from Mike Bates. He's got Digger Pete to lend a hand for no charge.'

Robert was amused. 'Digger Pete?'

'I know. Can you guess what he does for a living? I love it. All the locals have nicknames. Flappy the Fisherman. Skippy Keith. Fred the Fence.'

'So does Digger Pete dig by hand or does he have a digger?'

'He has both. He's the grave-digger.'

Robert leant back in his chair. 'God, I hope it's worth all this fuss.'

Helen laughed. 'Cynic.'

'Well, all this crap with the village witch wanting a ritual midnight cleanse or whatever. And we don't even know if the bloody pond is there.'

'Polly? She's a brilliant paramedic, actually.'

'Polly Wolly Doodle Noodle, in my opinion.'

'Oh, come on, it's all a bit of harmless fun.'

'I don't want my wife, a respected clergywoman, involved with it all. Believe me, being a vicar's husband is hard enough, particularly if you don't entirely buy into the mysteries of Church belief yourself.'

'Don't you?' Helen was surprised.

Robert gave Helen a guilty look. 'Well, not all of it. No. But . . . I do believe in what she's doing. I see the goodness she has and uses in wonderful ways. I'm in awe of her, to tell the truth. She's a much nicer person than me.'

'And me.' Helen smiled. 'How about I make some lunch? Beans on toast?'

'How about I take you *out* to lunch?' asked Robert. 'We've worked hard this morning.'

Helen hesitated, looking at her watch, then made her decision. 'That would be nice. It's such a glorious day.'

'I know just the place.'

Fifteen minutes later, they pulled up to a small wooden building nestling into the lee of the headland overlooking the Atlantic.

There was a large sign with the words 'SeaBay Café' spelt out in light bulbs.

'What a great place,' said Helen, locking her sporty Mini.

'It's only been open a couple of weeks. I've been asked to review it. This is on the *Trevay Times* expense account. I value your opinion.'

'Fabulous!'

Today the sea was emerald green with patches of deepest blue. Small waves curled and thumped onto the rocky beach below and seagulls displayed their consummate flying skills, gliding and hovering on the unseen breeze.

Inside, the shack was pleasingly gloomy, low-lit and peaceful, while outside the sea-facing terrace beckoned them.

They chose a sheltered outdoor table, and settled down with interesting-looking menus.

In the Trevay Health Centre, Robbie and Angela were waiting to be called.

Angela could feel Robbie's tension and tried to distract her with small talk. Eventually a door opened and a good-looking man peered round.

'Roberta Gower?'

Robbie stood up and clutched for Angela's hand.

'Do come in.' The doctor disappeared back into his consulting room, Robbie and Angela following.

'Take a seat. My name is Adam.' He gestured to the two chairs in front of him and folded his hands. 'How can I help?'

Robbie's hand, still holding Angela's, was shaking as she began to explain about finding her lump.

'Well, I think I should take a look. Just pop behind the curtain and take your top off. Lie on the bed and tell me when you're ready.'

As he examined her, apologising for his cold hands, he chatted about living in Pendruggan. 'I know it well. My cousin and his wife live at Marguerite Cottage. Do you know them? Kit and Ella?'

'Yes,' said Robbie, trying not to feel as vulnerable as she was, lying topless under the hands of this handsome doctor.

'I have my alternative health clinic in the garden there. I do a bit of acupuncture, hypnotherapy and stuff . . .' His moving fingers stopped. 'Ah. Is that it?'

Robbie nodded.

He continued to feel the lump then progressed to the centre of her breast and nipple. 'OK. Now can you sit up? Hands above your head.' He looked from one breast to the other. 'OK. Pop your clothes back on and come out when you're ready.'

He returned to his desk. A worried Angela gave him a quick encouraging smile. He unwound the lid of his fountain pen and made a note on Robbie's file.

Robbie returned, tucking her T-shirt back into her trousers. She sat down and fixed her eyes on Dr Adam.

Finally he stopped writing and put the lid of his pen back on, screwing it tightly. 'Well, Mrs Gower, I think we need to get that lump looked at.'

Helen lifted her cider shandy. 'Thank you, Robert, for the nicest lunch I've had in a long time. Cheers.' She chinked her glass against Robert's.

'My pleasure,' he replied. 'Where do you and Piran like to go?'

'Out for dinner?' Helen reached for a strand of her auburn hair, blown by the light breeze, and tucked it behind one ear. 'We never go out for dinner. Piran likes to cook and so mostly we eat at my house or his.'

'Really?' Robert said, surprised. 'I love to spoil Angela when I can. Well, I used to, but she's always on the go with some parish activity or another, and the only time I get her to myself is to take her out. Mind you, I haven't had a chance yet. She's always got something on.'

Helen turned to look at the sea sparkling under a bright sun, whiskers of spray blown from the wave tops, and thought about her relationship with Piran.

'That's nice of you. Angela is very lucky. That's not Piran's thing at all.'

'And are you happy with that?'

'Yes,' she said slowly. 'I am. I was married for a long time to a gorgeous man, Gray, utterly charming and utterly unable to keep himself faithful to me. Piran is loyal and that's worth a lot.'

'Well, your first husband sounds like a fool.'

Helen laughed ruefully. 'Yes, but a charming one. We are still in touch. We share a son and a daughter and we are grandparents to a sweet little girl too.'

'What does Piran make of it all?'

'Oh, he loves our granddaughter, but he can't stand Gray.'

'And neither can I!' Robert smiled into Helen's eyes and she noticed again how handsome he was. She switched her gaze to the sea and its horizon, pulling her sunglasses down to shield her eyes. 'And I remember from Angela's sermon, you met at work?'

'*Manchester Evening News*, in the newsroom. She was a cub reporter and I was on the politics desk. I can see her now. Bundled up in her duffel coat carrying a huge bag. Elfin haircut, luminous skin and the sexiest innocent smile I had ever seen. Believe me, the newsroom was a tough place to be. Heavy on testosterone with the added frisson of three chain-smoking alpha female hacks, all talons and high heels, who were ready to eat her alive. Honestly, I feared for her. This tiny sparrow being circled by vultures. She had nothing to defend her, apart from the duffel coat. No lipstick. No breasts. An innocent in dangerous territory. She was a hard worker, though. Constantly chasing stories that never made the front page. Or the back page. Or the middle page, come to that.

'The editor, an unreconstructed medieval, sexist bully, allotted her a desk in the dingiest corner and delighted in humiliating her when and as he fancied. But, as in all good fairy tales, the heroine finally got her chance to prove herself. She was given a story that everyone else had rejected. An old tramp had been fished from the canal half dead. She sat by his hospital bed for over a week. Nursing him and coaxing his story out of him. Turned out he was a war hero. Had won a VC in Egypt. She came back with the front page, reunited him with old comrades and got him a place in one of the British Legion's care homes.'

'Wow.'

'Yes. She's a hell of a woman.' Robert waved at their waitress and Helen reached for her purse. 'Put that away,' he said easily. 'I told you, this is on the *Trevay Times* expense account. You can dictate your review to me on the way back.'

Angela glanced at Robbie's pale face as they drove from the surgery back to Pendruggan.

'I think it best to let your husband know.'

'Yes. But I might wait until after the tests.' Robbie's hands were clenched tightly in her lap, her knuckles bloodless.

'It's none of my business, I know, but I think he should know before that.'

Robbie swallowed hard but said nothing.

Angela tried again. 'Is there no one else you can confide in? You are sure you don't want to tell Evelyn?'

Robbie shook her head. Angela kept her eyes on the road before gently asking, 'I'm a good listener and I promise anything you want to tell me would go no further.'

Robbie's eyes filled with tears. 'My brother is messing her about and I can't bear to see her so unhappy. We grew up together and now, because of his carrying on with some woman on the side, Evie and I can't talk like we did. He's come between us. He's such an arse. It's not the first time either. She's stood by him twice before, but I told her she should leave him now. But she's scared. The farm couldn't be sold. She wouldn't want to take that away from her boys. So where would she go? What would she live on? I've told her she can come and stop with me and Bob, but Bob is one of my brother's best mates and Evie says she wouldn't want to make things awkward and now . . . I don't know what'll happen if I'm ill.' Her tears flooded down her face.

Angela stopped the car in a grassed-over gateway halfway down the lane. The sea on the horizon was frothing and fierce but beautiful nonetheless. Angela sat silently next to Robbie, instinctively knowing she just needed to cry it all out; sometimes words weren't needed, it was enough to be there. Slowly Robbie's tears stopped and the two women simply sat in the quiet, watching the gulls swirl on the wind and listening to the distant waves crashing into the cliffs, both losing themselves in a moment of true peace.

'The air is so mild today, shall we take the top down?' asked Helen as she approached her flashy little Mini hunkered in the car park.

'I'd love that,' Robert said with genuine joy. So unlike Piran, thought Helen, he hated her car; it was 'too small'. He never wanted the top down – 'If I'd wanted fresh air I'd go out on my boat,' he would say, not knowing how much that hurt her.

She turned the key in the ignition and pressed the roof button.

'So cool!' Robert laughed next to her. He bent over and aimed to kiss her cheek, but as he did so, she moved slightly and his kiss landed on her lips.

'Oh!' She pulled away, hand on her mouth.

He held his hands up. 'I'm so sorry. How embarrassing. That was meant to be a peck on the cheek to thank you for being such great company today. I am really so sorry.'

'It's fine, really.' Helen smiled broadly, refusing to look flustered. 'It was a lovely lunch and thank you again.'

He reached into his inside pocket and pulled out a small leather notebook and pencil. 'Can we take the slow road home? Only I need to write down your thoughts on today's food.'

'OK. We'll take the coast road. I hope you don't suffer from car sickness. There are many bends!'

The high hedges gave way to tantalising glimpses of the sea beyond – the flashes of blues and greens were breathtaking, occasionally distracting Robert from questioning Helen on her opinions on the quality of the lunch and location.

'Out of ten?' asked Robert finally.

'Nine and a half.'

'Aha. And how did they lose that half a point?'

'The Ladies' loo had run out of loo paper.'

'A game-changer?'

'Definitely.'

'And would you go back there again?'

'Yes.'

He closed his notebook and put it with his pencil into his jacket pocket. 'Excellent.' He relaxed back into his seat. 'God, what a great day.'

'Would you like some music?'

'The sound of the wind is enough for me.'

He closed his eyes and as Helen took the turning left into Pendruggan, she glanced at him. Straight nose. Good lips. Dark eyelashes. She felt a flush in her chest.

Oh, no, she realised to herself. *I have a crush on him.*

She pulled up in front of the vicarage to drop Robert off. He protested, 'But we have work to do on the website and the flipping Pond Dig.'

'I can do that later. You need to write your restaurant review.'

'Are you sure?'

'Yes, yes.' Helen tried to sound blithe and carefree. 'Thanks again for a super lunch, and my love to Angela.'

Robert looked at the house, frowning. 'If she's home yet.' He turned back to Helen and leant into the car. 'Can we do this again sometime?'

She thought quickly. 'When we've got the dig and summer and stuff out of the way.'

'Great. See you soon then.' He bent to kiss her once again. 'Bye, Helen.'

Helen put the car in gear and drove around the village green to her cottage with as much speed as was seemly.

She closed the front door and leant back on it, relieved. 'Helen Merrifield,' she said aloud to herself. 'Pull yourself together and stop behaving like a twelve-year-old girl with a crush on your history teacher.' She dropped her bag on the sofa and went to make a stiff coffee. As the kettle boiled she checked her emails. There was one from Penny.

Helen made her coffee, then settled on the sofa to read the news from the friend she realised she missed so much.

Angela took Robbie home to her neat house on the village's small estate.

'Thank you,' Robbie said. She cast her eyes towards the kitchen. 'Would you like tea?'

'I'll make you one. You take your coat off and sit down. It's been a tough day for you.'

Tea made, Angela joined Robbie in her sitting room. Robbie was sitting on her two-seater sofa, staring into space.

'When will your husband be home?'

Robbie looked at the clock on the mantel. 'About six.'

'So you've got a little while. How about a nice bath to relax you?'

'Could do.'

'I do strongly advise you talk to your husband. I'm sure he'll want to know.'

Robbie nodded. 'Mebbe.'

Angela finished her tea. 'All right then. You know where I am if you need me. And I say again, nothing that you have told me will go anywhere. I promise.'

17

The bell on the shop door rang, jolting Queenie from her warm snooze in the armchair by the counter.

'Darling, it's only me.' Mamie shut the door and stood over Queenie in a breeze of Shalimar. 'Sorry. Did I wake you?'

'No,' Queenie snapped. 'I was thinking.'

Mamie pulled up the chair opposite. 'What about?'

Queenie dug her hands into her cardigan pockets and brought out her tobacco roll and cigarette papers. 'I don't know; you've chased them out of me head now.'

Mamie made herself comfortable. 'So, what news from the Rialto?'

'What you talking about? The Rialto? If you want to go to the pictures you have to go to that posh place up on the road to Plymouth. Hundreds of screens they've got up there. You could spend all day going from one film to another, apparently.'

'I'm not talking about a cinema. It's Shakespeare, darling. *The Merchant of Venice*. Dear Larry and Ralph would constantly quote whole chunks of it to me when we'd supper at the Café de Paris.'

'Oh, shut yer cake 'ole.' Queenie licked her cigarette paper. 'My knees are bad. When are we going to have that naughty cigarette?'

'When it's safe to do so. Now tell me, what's the gossip in town?'

Queenie finished rolling her cigarette, popped it into her pocket and, with a glint in her eye, signalled for Mamie to lean forward. 'Gasping Bob's wife, Robbie.'

'Yes, I know,' said Mamie, all ears.

'She's being tested for breast cancer.'

'How do you know?'

'I'm surprised you *don't* know! It was your niece what took her to the doc's.'

'Why did Angela tell you and not me?' said Mamie, affronted.

'It weren't the vicar that told me. One of my friends has a daughter-in-law called Tracey, what cleans at the health centre. She saw them, and happened to overhear an appointment being made for the specialist down Treliske. And now the poor cow is waiting for results of the autopsy.'

'I think you mean biopsy. And which poor cow? Tracey or Robbie?'

'Robbie, of course. Although if Tracey hears anything sooner she'll let me know. Apparently Robbie's that worried she hasn't even told Evelyn, her best friend, because she didn't want to worry her.'

'That's a big secret to keep from your best friend.'

'Yes, but now Evelyn has found out and is all upset that she wasn't told.'

'How did she find out?'

'Robbie told her husband, Gasping Bob, and his best mate is Evelyn's husband, what's having the affair, and Robbie is Evelyn's sister-in-law so, anyway, it was Bob what told Evelyn and now Evelyn is all upset about her best mate Robbie not telling her about the breast cancer.'

'How very complicated. And upsetting.'

'Oh, yes.' Queenie gave a serious nod. 'Very.'

'And when are the results of the tests expected?'

'That's the sixty-four-million-dollar question, ain't it?'

'So we don't know?'

'Nobody knows.'

'I see.'

Queenie gave Mamie a deep and silent stare.

'What?' asked Mamie, feeling discomforted.

'The vicar will know and she's the only way we're going to get to the truth of the matter.'

Mamie found Angela in Faith's bedroom changing the sheets. 'Darling, let me help you with that.'

'I'm nearly done,' said Angela.

'No problem. I like to help. You look tired, darling. How are you? Anything on your mind?'

'No.'

'It's just that I've been thinking. I haven't always appreciated how many things you have to keep to yourself. Confidential matters. Personal matters. It must be so difficult.'

'Not at all.' Angela passed a pillowcase over to her aunt. 'It's part of the job.'

'So you do have secrets? That you've kept.'

'I don't see them as secrets. I feel more that I am a secure bank where people can put their worries and know they are safe with me.'

'That must be very stressful?'

'Not really. No more than I would worry for anybody.'

Mamie smoothed her pillow in its fresh case and placed it neatly at the head of Faith's bed. 'If you ever feel you need to offload any concerns, I am always here,' she said.

'I know and I'm grateful. But some things are not for sharing.'

'Quite understood.' Mamie walked to Faith's window and looked out over the back garden and the fields beyond to the misty horizon. 'I have heard some very distressing news, actually.'

Angela picked up an empty tea mug from Faith's bedside table and a handful of used make-up wipes. 'Do you want to tell me?'

Mamie turned and, taking a gamble and a long, shaky breath, said, 'It's about Robbie, I'm afraid.'

Angela had been incensed that Mamie and Queenie had been gossiping.

Mamie was defensive. 'It's inevitable in a village like this. And it's important that people know so that they can be kind. Anyway, it was Gasping Bob, her own husband, who started it.'

'That is no excuse for passing it round. Gossip spreads like manure and stinks as much as well.'

'Mountains out of molehills,' Mamie said sniffily to Angela's retreating back. Mr Worthington, who had been sleeping in a pool of sunshine on the landing, stretched, sneezed and ambled towards her. 'Your human mother can be so far up her own bum that I can only see the soles of her feet,' Mamie told him.

*

The next women's group meeting happened to be that night, and Angela was anxious that Robbie wouldn't be faced with unwelcome questions.

In fact, the evening turned out to be the best one yet and a turning point in the relationship of Pendruggan's women.

The first to arrive was Sarah with baby Santi and Ben. Faith ran down the stairs and flung herself around Ben before they both went to the kitchen in search of snacks.

Audrey strode in behind them with a copy of *Wuthering Heights* under her arm. 'I strongly suggest that we start the book club off with Brontë,' she told Angela in no uncertain terms.

'We shall put it to the vote with a couple of others that have also been suggested. Thank you, Audrey.'

'I can tell you now, I shall not be reading anything contemporary, even if it has been shortlisted for the Booker Prize and especially not if it has won *any* award.'

'I shall bear that in mind, Audrey. Do please go in. Sarah and Santi are in the living room.'

Audrey stomped off muttering about not wanting to be near any breastfeeding.

Dorrie from the Dolphin pub arrived next with Ella, a beautiful young woman with brilliant red titian curls. 'Angela, I don't think you've met Ella? She lives the other side of the church in Marguerite Cottage. She and her gorgeous new husband are artists!' Dorrie added proudly.

'Come in, come in. How wonderful. Lovely to have you with us.' Angela pointed them to the lounge.

Queenie arrived, looking sheepish. 'I promise to keep my big mouth shut in future, only I didn't know poor Robbie wanted to keep it all secret.'

Angela gently rebuked her. 'It's not a matter of secrecy. It's privacy, Queenie. No one wants their lives discussed by people who don't know the full story, do they? I've said the same to my aunt.'

'It won't happen again.'

'It's not me you need to apologise to, is it?'

'I'll talk to Robbie later.'

'Pick the right moment.'

'I was a Brownie in the war. I got top marks in my kindness badge.'

'Well, go into the sitting room and warn everyone not to say a word, not a word, to Robbie about any of it. Do you understand? I don't want Robbie – or Evelyn, come to that – upset.'

'Got it. Sorry.' Queenie tottered off and Angela could hear her telling the group to 'Keep yer traps shut.'

Finally, Robbie and Evelyn arrived.

'Hi.' Angela ushered them in. 'So glad you came.'

'She didn't want to but I made her,' Evelyn said.

Robbie nodded. 'I know people have been gossiping.'

'I'm so sorry,' Angela said sincerely. 'My aunt and Queenie were part of it. Believe me, I have had words with them.'

'Oh, it's all right.' Robbie looked tired.

Evelyn took over. 'We are here to explain what Robbie's going through. She's got nothing to be ashamed of.'

'No she hasn't,' agreed Angela. 'Come on in.'

As they entered the sitting room, the chatter fell away.

Mamie got to her feet and broke the ice. 'Darlings, you are just in time for a glass of Queenie's finest wine in a box. Now find yourselves a seat and let's have a jolly good time.'

As everyone settled, Angela opened the proceedings. 'Welcome, everyone. Tonight I shall be revealing plans for the Big Pond Dig and also—'

Evelyn interrupted. 'I'm sorry to stop you, Vicar, but Robbie has asked me to tell you how she is and what's going on with her. Is that OK?'

'Of course,' said Angela.

'Right. Well. There's been some gossip about Robbie and sadly it's true. Robbie,' she looked round at her pale friend seated behind her and continued, 'is having tests on a lump in her breast. We go to the hospital tomorrow, with Bob, and will not have any results for another couple of weeks. Robbie is the bravest woman I know and the kindest too. She didn't want to tell anyone, not even me. But she's glad now that you all know. When she knows what the results are, she'll tell you. So, please, don't go asking questions of her before she's ready. Thank you.' Evelyn sat down next to Robbie and took her hand.

'Thank you,' whispered Robbie.

Angela glanced over at Queenie and Mamie and gave them a look that said, *See? And no more gossip, thank you*. Then she put her glass down and began to stand up to begin the meeting proper.

But she was halted again. This time by Dorrie.

Running a hand through her short, spiky blond hair, Dorrie pushed herself out of a chair and rubbed her hands nervously down her sawn-off denim shorts.

'I'd like to apologise to you, Robbie, and also to say how all of us are behind you, supporting you all the way. My Don had a cancer scare last year. Lump in his bollock. Terrified him. He kept it all to himself. Never told us for weeks after he'd found it. Carried on behind the bar, lifting barrels of ale and whatnot. Anyway, I was working in the bar by myself one lunchtime. Full on, it was. Heaving. So I went to look for him for some help. And I found him upstairs, crying. My

Don! Bloody ex-boxer! Anyway, I asked him what the matter was and he told me. He'd been looking at one of my magazines. Reading about a woman whose husband had been in the same situation but didn't tell anyone until it was too late. Scared the bloody life out of him. I marched him down to the doc's and in a couple of weeks the lump was taken out. It was just a cyst. I was so angry with him. How could he not tell me? His bloody wife! Anyhow, I'm sorry that you were not given the privacy you wanted but by God how I wish you had been allowed to.'

Everyone was looking at her in shock. 'Blimey,' said Sarah. 'You poor girl. What a fright.'

'Yeah, well. Don't know why that suddenly all come out, but, Robbie?' Robbie looked up. 'Just to say,' Dorrie continued, 'we're all with you whatever happens and praying that everything'll be all right.' She sat down, pushing her nervous hands furiously through her hair again.

'Well,' Angela looked around, 'if there is a theme for tonight's meeting maybe it is to know that we have friends who will support us in times of need.'

Mamie tipped the remains of her wine down her throat and asked, 'I think we could all do with another one of these, don't you?'

As she filled glasses, hands reached for the small bowls of mixed nuts and crisps.

Angela stood again. 'Right. The Big Pond Dig is—'

But Evelyn interrupted her. 'I've just got to get this off my chest and this feels like the only place I really can.' She closed her eyes for a moment and then said loudly, 'My husband has been a bastard all our married life.'

All eyes turned to her. 'Right now he's with his latest lady friend and I don't know what to do.'

The room was still.

'Do you want to talk about it now? With all of us?' Angela asked gently. 'Or would you prefer to talk to one of us privately, at another time?'

'At our first meeting, you said that anything that happened here would be confidential. Just between us,' said Evelyn, looking with trusting eyes at Angela. 'I'd like to talk now.'

'OK.' Angela spoke to everyone. 'Can we all reassure Evelyn that nothing spoken about in here will be shared with any other person?'

There were nods and murmured agreements all round.

Angela turned back to Evelyn. 'Take your time.'

'I know who the woman is. I hate her. She knows what she's doing. But then so does he. She's not the first. Won't be the last.'

Everyone in the room was looking at each other, not quite knowing what to do. Then, quietly but kindly, a voice piped, 'Is she local?' It was Ella.

'Not in the village. No. Thank goodness. She runs the post office up the top of Trevay.'

'By the school?' chipped in Queenie, who, as a postmistress herself, knew all the post offices in a twenty-mile radius. 'That woman with the big thighs and short skirts?'

Evelyn nodded. 'Yes, her.'

'Oh my good Gawd. What does any man see in her?'

Angela stepped in. 'Queenie, we don't know her circum-stances.'

'Yes we bleeding do.' Queenie was emphatic. 'Bloody woman has had more husbands than hot dinners. Three of her own and plenty of other women's.'

Mamie shushed Queenie and asked, 'How did you find out?'

'He said he was joining the gym. He said evening membership was cheap. He'd been there three weeks when I found his gym clothes and they still had the labels on them. Never worn.'

'But how can you be sure it is this woman?' Helen asked.

'Well, I knew it must be *a* woman because he was shaving every day and began using deodorant. I mean, he's a farmer. A quick shower was the most he'd do normally. But it's what he does when he's seeing someone else.' She dropped her hands into her lap and said without bitterness, 'He hasn't done that for me for years.'

She paused then continued. 'Then there are the secret phone calls in the garden. The total disinterest in me.' Her shoulders sagged. 'I followed him. One night. I followed his Land Rover all the way to her place. She lives above the shop.'

Queenie huffed, 'Knocking shop, more like.'

Angela shushed her.

'It was like in the films,' Evelyn went on. 'Saw her at her kitchen window. Opening the fridge and taking out a beer.' She allowed a stray tear to spill, seemingly without noticing. 'I waited up for him. He came back after midnight. I told him the gym closes at ten thirty. He said he'd had a puncture and had to get a mate out to help. I told him I knew he was lying. He said I was mad. Needed help. I was paranoid. Psychotic. All the usual stuff. He's not a good liar. I've looked up how to spot a liar. It's all there. Covering his mouth with his hand. Denying everything and blaming me.' She stopped for a moment as anger built up in her, and then she let it fly. 'BUT I AM NOT A BLOODY IDIOT!'

'When was all this?' asked Angela.

Evelyn's hands were shaking as she wiped her tears away. 'Three or four months ago.'

'And how are things at the moment?'

'Bad. He still expects his food on the table, his socks washed, he still gets into bed next to me but he doesn't speak. Doesn't acknowledge that I exist. And I can't go on like this.' She buried her face in her hands and began to sob. Mamie got up to tear off a square of kitchen towel, passing it to Evelyn.

'No, you can't.' Angela went and knelt beside the distraught Evelyn. 'You are in a very painful situation.'

'And your boys, do they suspect . . .?' asked Sarah.

'Suspect? They know. His behaviour rubs off on them. My eldest speaks to me the same way he does.'

Angela was shocked. 'What? That must be intolerable, and, not only that, wrong.'

Evelyn shrugged again. 'Made my bed, haven't I?'

Angela didn't know how to answer that.

Evelyn wiped her eyes with the already sodden kitchen towel. 'Well, it's out now, although I suppose you all knew anyway, and maybe I'm glad. It's life, innit?'

'It doesn't have to be,' Angela said firmly.

Evelyn smiled weakly. 'I feel better for telling you all.'

'Well, now that's all cleared up,' said Audrey, who'd been sitting in icy silence for the past half an hour (what a lot she had to tell Geoff when she got home), 'I'd like to put forward my choice for the book club. *Wuthering Heights* is a special favourite of mine and does indeed mirror some of the topics I have heard tonight.'

'Audrey,' said Angela, 'I don't think this is the right time—'

'I have listened, now I wish to speak!' Audrey's piggy eyes swept the faces around her, daring any one of them to contradict her. 'Emily Brontë knew full well the effects of living in a household of secrets and madness. Her themes very much echo village life as we know it today.'

'I really don't think this is appropriate tonight, Audrey,' said Angela quietly.

'Well then, when will it be?' Audrey demanded.

'Next week. I promise.'

'I shall not be available next week,' Audrey snorted.

'Then we shall wait for your return.' Angela looked at her watch. 'We have thirty minutes of our time left tonight. Any suggestions as to how we should spend them?'

Ella put her hand up. 'I'd like to have a cuddle with the baby, please.'

'So would I,' said Dorrie.

'And me,' Helen added.

'You are welcome,' smiled Sarah.

Just before nine o'clock Robert joined them, which cheered them all up. He was looking particularly attractive with a slight stubble, his hair ruffled and bringing the smell of evening air with him.

'Lovely night out there. Mr W and I have been for a walk. Have I missed anything juicy?'

'Nothing at all,' smiled Angela. 'Now would you mind collecting the ladies' coats from the stairs?'

As the women stood and gathered their bags and belongings, they each went to Evelyn with a kind word of support.

'You will get through this,' Dorrie told her. 'And you won't be alone.'

Robbie put her arm around her best friend's waist and walked her to the front door. 'You're going to think us a right pair,' she said to Angela. 'Both of us crocked in different ways. Pair of right ones.'

Angela kissed them both goodbye. 'My door is always open to you.'

A squiffy Queenie followed them. 'Shall I escort you home?' asked Robert kindly.

'I thought you'd never ask!' said Queenie, taking his arm then turning to Angela and saying, 'Well done tonight, Angela. We'll all pull together and get them girls right.'

Angela smiled. 'We will, Queenie. We will.'

Mamie was in the kitchen putting the wine glasses into the dishwasher and giving Mr Worthington the last lick of a crisp bowl.

'Don't let Robert see you doing that,' said Angela, dropping onto a kitchen chair. 'That was rather intense, wasn't it?'

Mamie filled the soap tray and slammed the machine shut. 'It was. But you handled it well.'

'Did I?'

Mamie sat opposite Angela. 'Yes. Very well and I'll tell you why.'

'Go on then.'

'Whatever you have done over the past few weeks in this village, and however you have done it, you have gained the trust of these women. I believe they will keep all that to themselves.'

'Do you think so?'

'Absolutely. But I think you may have to stop them marching on the large-thighed strumpet at the post office and lynching her.'

Angela smiled. 'They wouldn't do that . . . would they?'

18

The next week brought a taste of full spring with warmer days and lighter nights.

Angela found herself alone more often than not, working quietly in her office or doing her rounds of the parishioners.

Mamie was out and about with her 'mood board' planning the garden party. Faith had taken to long walks on the beach, after school, with Mr Worthington and Ben, chatting about whatever it was teenagers found to chat about.

And Robert was spending his time over at Gull's Cry, with Helen, working on the social media pages for the village or at the kitchen table writing up his food column.

The evening before the next women's group meeting, with supper eaten and washed up, Mamie in her room and Faith in the kitchen watching YouTube videos with Ben, Angela wandered into the lounge in search of Robert.

He was lying on the sofa in front of a Rick Stein programme.

'Hey.' Angela ran her fingers gently over his hair.

'Oh. Hi.' He yawned.

'Is there room for a little one?' She lay down beside him

and nuzzled into his chest. 'I've hardly seen you this week.'

Instead of putting his arms around as she hoped, he stretched them out behind his head. 'No. The website is very time-consuming. It should be ready to go fully live soon. Helen is great at the tech side. She's managed to upload pictures of Pendruggan over the years. We're going to go out tomorrow and get some shots taken from the same place as some of the old photos to see the change. We're waiting for Piran to add some historical notes and the research he's got on the old pond for the dig.'

Angela wrapped her arms around him to stop herself from sliding off the sofa, and placed her head in the centre of his chest.

'Oh, has he found anything new?' she asked, interested.

'No.'

'Oh.' She wriggled herself up to look at his face. 'Hello.'

'Hello.' He yawned again. 'What time is it?'

'About half nine?'

'I'd better let Mr Worthington out.' He moved, dislodging her. She let him go and swivelled her body round to sit up.

'Shoo Ben out too, would you?' she asked.

'Is he still here? Why is he always here?' Robert was on his feet and heading to the door.

'He is Faith's best friend.'

Robert, grunting, went off.

Angela turned off the TV and tidied the cushions. Turning out the lamps, she stood by the glass doors leading to the garden and looked out. The trees were clearly outlined by the bright moon, their leaves moving gently to the wind coming up from the beach.

A triangle of light shone on the grass as Robert opened the back door to let the dog out. From behind the glass

Angela watched as Mr Worthington sniffed the scented night and found a shrub interesting enough to pee against. She looked for Robert and saw him in silhouette, one hand in his pocket, the other pressing his phone to his ear. By the phone's light she could just make out a smile crossing his face as he spoke, then listened, then spoke again. Whoever he was talking to made him laugh lightly before hanging up.

She moved quickly from the window, not wanting him to think she was spying on him. She stayed in the dark lounge listening for Ben's departure and the sound of Faith treading the stairs to her bedroom. Finally she heard Robert closing the kitchen door on Mr Worthington before following Faith up the stairs.

She shook herself. What was this? Jealousy? Why was she hiding, here, in the dark? Robert and she were a couple. A loving couple. Rock solid. Forever.

Robert woke her the next morning with a kiss and a cup of hot coffee. 'Morning, darling.'

She opened her sleepless eyes and looked at her handsome husband. 'Hello.' She pulled herself up onto her pillow. 'Did you sleep well?'

'I slept so well I don't remember you coming to bed.'

'By the time I got here, you were out for the count.'

He sat on the edge of the bed and sipped his coffee, looking out of the window, across the village green and – the thought flew across Angela's mind like a burning meteor – towards Helen's cottage.

'Working with Helen today?' she asked, mumbling the words into her mug.

'Yep. We're going to start taking the present-day photos of the village this morning. Lovely day for it.'

'I was wondering,' Angela began, 'maybe we could go out one night this week. Supper? Cinema? There's a film on in Truro that I think you'd like.'

Robert scratched his unshaven chin. 'I don't know. Maybe.'

'It's just that we haven't seen much of each other lately.' She reached a hand out to his thigh. 'I miss you.'

He patted her hand absentmindedly. 'Well, you're so busy always. You're never in, or alone. People coming and going, all wanting something from you.'

'Well . . . yes, but you seem to be out a lot too.'

'Angie, I go out to give you space.'

'I don't like not spending time together.'

He turned to look at her. 'Since when have you been so needy?'

'I'm not being needy,' she said crossly. 'I just want to go out for supper or the cinema with my husband.'

Robert stood up, irritated. 'I'm trying to find a role for myself outside the *vicar's husband* one. I thought getting on with the website would help you.'

'It does,' she said. 'And you have been wonderfully supportive.'

He looked at the bedside clock. 'It's late. I need to shower and get Faith to school.'

Robert didn't come home after the school run.

From her study window, Angela watched as he returned to Pendruggan but parked outside Gull's Cry. He was greeted by Helen, who was tying up some stray rose branches around her beautiful front door.

Biting her lip, Angela was distracted by the ping of an incoming email.

Simon@Bahia.TC

Dear Angela,

How are you finding your parishioners?

I have had some very positive messages of support for you from Mike Bates and Helen Merrifield. Good people.

I'm writing because I have had a difficult mail from Audrey Tipton. First of all I want to reassure you that she is a woman who has presented me with many challenges.

Anyway, she tells me that you have set up a women's group in the village. She believes it is in direct competition with her WI group. To be honest, the WI lot live in fear of her, so if you are offering a more congenial meeting then good on you.

But she has asked me to 'express her concerns' to you. Perhaps you could find a job for her? I know she is desperate to run a book club and she has told me how thrilled she is to have secured Robert as a guest speaker for the WI.

I am quite certain you are more than able to keep her feathers smoothed.

She can be a harridan but beneath that terrifying exterior lies a warm heart – I think!

In other news, life here is a world away from Pendruggan, but we have the exact, albeit Brazilian, equivalents of Audrey Tipton *et al*, running the place. Penny is being very stoic – even when the electricity and water fail, which is often.

You are in our prayers.

Simon xx

Angela read the email through twice. The first time with her anger rising. How dare Audrey Tipton go behind her back? She could fully imagine the tone of her email to Simon. Hectoring. Judgemental. Bullying.

The second time she read it she understood Simon's subtext. Simon was not judging her. Merely guiding her.

When she read it a third time she took her stance. If Simon was asking her not to make a lasting impression on village life, to toe the line, he could ask again. And if Audrey thought she could snitch and undermine, then she would also have to think again. Angela was her own woman and Pendruggan parish was *her* parish and she would bloody well run it the best way she knew and that was to take the lead and not be squashed by petty people who didn't like it.

'Angela,' Mamie called from the hall. 'Where are you?'

'In my office.'

'Ah.' Mamie found her. 'So you are. Darling, Robert is not being very helpful with the garden party preparations. With the danger of dobbing him in, as Faith would say, he has actually done bugger all and so I should like to rope Mike Bates in. Would that be OK?'

'I'm sure he'd love to have you rope him into anything!' laughed Angela. 'He has told me more than once what an attractive woman he thinks you are.'

'Darling, he barely knows me,' Mamie said dismissively.

'But he looks at you. And he likes what he sees.' Angela sighed. 'I will never know what Robert saw in me.'

Mamie wagged her finger. 'Uh-uh-ah. I will have no self-flagellation from you. Masochistic nonsense. Robert adores you. Where is he, by the way?'

'Where do you think? Helen's, of course.'

Mamie pulled up the comfy 'visitor's chair' that Simon had put in the office. 'Oh, do I detect the green-eyed monster? You think your husband is spending too much time in Helen's company?'

'No.'

'Be truthful.'

'He seems to enjoy her company more than mine at the moment.'

'He is working with her on the website,' Mamie said, defending Robert. 'While you are spending all your time here in your office, or out running, or working with the Pals or a million other things, rather than making time for him.'

'I asked him out for a date this week. And he said no.'

'Playing you at your own game.'

'I'm not playing a game.'

'He wants you to miss him so he's playing a little hard to get. That's all.'

'Is it?'

'Of course. I did exactly the same thing with Jack Nicholson.'

Angela had heard this story a million times. 'I know, he kept phoning you for weeks on end for a date, you kept making up excuses not to go and then finally . . .?'

'He stopped phoning.' Mamie touched the pearls around her neck. 'But that was exactly what I wanted him to do in the first place.'

Angela made a noise of disbelief. 'Why did you give him your phone number then?'

'Because I am well-mannered and I didn't want to hurt his feelings.'

Angela sighed deeply then groaned.

'It's a well-known fact men can't handle rejection. Poor little chaps.'

Angela stretched her arms over her head and towards the ceiling. 'Oh, I wish just for a moment I could have had your looks and your fun. But Mum and I missed out on those genes. You got them all.'

Mamie studied Angela carefully, her head to one side. 'OK,

what has brought all this on? Not just Helen and Robert, is it?'

'Oh, I don't know. It's going to sound silly, but I'm feeling a bit . . . lost. Here I am, doing the job I have been wanting for years, in a beautiful parish, with lovely villagers, and yet . . .'

Mamie coaxed her: 'And yet it is not all you expected?'

'Something like that. I can't explain it. I feel rather out there, on my own. I'm giving all I have to the job while losing my family. I barely see Robert, Faith is always out with Ben or in her room with Ben or at Ben's house. I miss her. I miss the chats we used to have before bedtime.'

'She's growing up. It happens.'

'But it has happened too soon. I miss my child. I miss being the centre of her world. When did it happen? When we got here everything changed.'

'Yes,' said Mamie. 'How do you think your mum felt when it happened with you?'

'But Mum and I were always close. I rang her as often as I could afford when I went to uni. Always came home when I could.'

'When you could. Yes. But that's never enough for a parent. You want Faith to be an independent woman, capable of managing her own life, don't you?'

'Well, of course I do.'

'But not right now?'

Angela blew her cheeks out. 'But it is happening right now, isn't it?'

'Yes. It is.'

'So, what do I do? Cut my working hours down and spend more time with the family?'

'And throw away this wonderful opportunity? No! Not

only would you regret it but Faith would be furious. She's having a ball. The beach. New friends. Look at the freedom she has here. You wouldn't let her go walking at dusk on a lonely beach at home, would you? She's safe here, and definitely safe with lovely Ben.'

'And Robert? Is he safe?'

Mamie leant forward and squeezed Angela's knees. 'Safe from Helen, you mean? You are silly. He loves *you*.'

'But he's so handsome and all women fall at his feet. I see it all the time.'

'And has he ever, ever looked at one of them?'

'No.'

'Listen to me. Robert is the kind of man who makes life look easy. He breezes through the Houses of Parliament with his easy charm and clever brain. Some of the greatest minds in the world agree to be interviewed by him because he's intelligent and straightforward. Nothing is a bother to him. *The Times* crossword? He can do it. Build flat-pack furniture? No problem. Have Audrey Tipton fall in love with him? Simple pimple. I don't know what his secret is, but we all fall for it. You and I, my darling, have to work a little harder at life. That is the only thing you should ever feel envious of. He is here for you. Has stepped out of the limelight for you. Is building the bloody website, with Helen, for you. So, as Queenie would so elegantly put it, "Shut yer cake 'ole."'

'Thank you, Mamie. That's what I needed to hear.' She leant towards her aunt and put her arms around her. 'I love you, Mamie. I miss Mum every day, terribly. But at least I have you.'

19

'Ladies, would you please give a warm welcome to tonight's special guest. The chairman of the parish council, Mr Mike Bates.' Angela ushered Mike into the vicarage lounge.

'Good evening, ladies.' Mike beamed at the familiar faces. 'I am delighted to be here.'

Angela ushered him to the comfiest armchair.

Mamie, looking extra glamorous this evening, brandished a bottle of very good whisky towards him. 'You look like a whisky-and-soda man to me.'

Audrey rolled her eyes from the second-most comfy armchair and tutted loudly.

Mike either didn't hear or pretended not to. 'You guess right, Mamie. Just a small one, thank you.'

'Ice?' Mamie asked seductively.

'Rather. Thanks awfully.' Mike pulled at his tie nervously.

'So why are you here, Michael?' Queenie would always voice the question everyone else wanted to ask.

Angela explained. 'Mike has kindly agreed to explain a

little about what will happen during the Big Pond Dig and what he and Piran think we may find. But also, and some of you may know this, Mike fought in the Falklands War. He happened to mention the fact to me the other day and I thought it would be a fascinating story for us to hear from a real-life hero in our midst.'

Mike was embarrassed. 'Well, I don't know about that. I'm rather afraid that you'll think me an old war bore.'

'Not at all,' said Sarah. 'My Joe, Santi's dad, he joined the navy after meeting Simon Weston.'

'Oh, yes,' said Mamie, handing Mike his whisky, ice cubes clinking. 'He was that marvellous boy who got so badly burnt when his ship – *Sir Galahad*, wasn't it? – was bombed. Such an inspiration.'

'I remember it like it was yesterday,' said Queenie. 'We hadn't a clue where the Falklands was. Thought they were up near the Orkneys or something, couldn't believe it when we found out they was down near the South Pole. Penguins and everything.'

'Let's get on with it, shall we,' grumbled Audrey. 'We don't have all night and I have cancelled an engagement to come here and discuss my choice for the first book club.'

'Oh, I had no idea your agenda was so busy,' said Mike. 'Are we all ready?'

Angela made sure everyone had their glasses topped up and Sarah asked Mike if he minded her breastfeeding Santi in front of him. Loosening the grip of his collar from his throat, he said it would be 'absolutely fine'. But he made sure he kept his gaze firmly away from where it was all happening on the sofa.

'You are quite right, Queenie. No one knew where the hell the Falklands were, but very quickly we knew that our training on Dartmoor would not go to waste. The Falklands terrain is very similar. Rocky, craggy, windy, cold.'

'Yomping,' Queenie said knowingly. 'That's what you did, weren't it?'

'Oh, by jingo we yomped. No other way of getting around. Marching day and night with very heavy kit bags. About six or seven stone each.'

Sitting nearest to the door, Angela slipped out of the room, remembering she'd left her choices of book club books by her bed. Mike had told her his war story earlier in the week and she knew he wouldn't mind.

Her bedroom was quiet. The bed inviting. She lay down for a moment and stared at the ceiling. Helen was downstairs and Robert was at the pub. Faith and Ben were in the kitchen cooking pizza. All was well in the world. She closed her eyes.

'Mum? Mum? Wake up. Audrey wants you downstairs.' Faith was gently shaking her awake.

'Oh bugger. How long have I been asleep?'

'Don't worry. Only about half an hour.'

'Oh, thank goodness.'

Faith giggled. 'I don't blame you. No offence but your meetings are boring, aren't they?'

Angela laughed in spite of herself. Then said, 'No. I was just a bit tired, that's all. Be a darling, would you, and top up their drinks. I'll be down in a second. And don't tell them I was asleep.'

Back in the sitting room Angela found everyone in lively discussion. Mamie spotted her. 'Darling, Mike has given us such a thrilling account of war. Truly gripping.'

All the other women agreed: 'Oh, yes, really exciting,'; 'Like one of them films,'; 'But real-life sad,'; 'Very sad, yes.'

Mike was happy it had all gone so well.

'Let me get you another whisky,' Mamie said, whipping his glass away before he could stop her.

Audrey, whose nose was clearly out of joint, said loudly, 'What happened to your wife?'

The chatter ceased and uneasy eyes moved from Audrey to Mike Bates and back again.

'I, er . . .' he began. 'She left me. A couple of years after I left the army.'

'I'm so sorry to hear that,' said Helen, filling the silence with sincerity.

'Water under the bridge, my dear. Probably for the best. Being an army wife is not the easiest job.'

'Not always, no,' said Sarah, passing Santi to Angela as she hooked up her nursing bra. 'But I'd never leave my Joe. I couldn't do that to Santi.'

Mike smiled awkwardly. 'Your Joe is a jolly lucky fellow to have you both. Unfortunately Phyllis and I weren't blessed with children.'

Queenie shook her head sorrowfully. 'It's a shame for you. A crying shame.'

Mike reached for the jacket he'd taken off while describing how he spent two days crouched in a fox hole. 'I'd best be off.' He turned to Angela. 'Thank you so much for inviting me. It's been really super. See you all soon.' He lifted a hand of farewell to the women.

'Let me see you out,' Angela said, and they left the room.

Queenie looked at Audrey and tutted. 'You happy with yerself?'

'I don't know what you mean.'

'You know very well what I mean. You put that poor man in a terrible spot. It was obvious he didn't want to talk about his wife. Shame on you.'

Audrey's cheeks bloomed puce. 'Don't you speak to me like that.'

'I'll speak to you how I bleeding like.'

Mamie stepped in. 'Now, ladies. It was an ill-chosen moment. That's all. I think we can all agree with that.' She turned to Audrey. 'I'm sure with hindsight you would like to admit your mistake, Audrey?'

Audrey looked at the mutinous faces around her and swallowed hard. 'Maybe I chose the wrong place and time.'

'Apologise,' said Queenie fiercely.

Audrey would rather have taken Queenie's shoulders in her hands and rattled her until her eyes popped out but she had the wit to realise she was cornered. 'I apologise.'

Angela came back in and immediately felt the tension in the room. 'Everything OK?' she asked, looking at Mamie.

'All fine. That was very interesting. Sweet man. But now we must choose our book club book, mustn't we?'

Angela took her aunt's words as a coded instruction and did as she was told. 'Ah, yes. As you know, Audrey and I have been discussing the idea of a monthly book club for the last couple of weeks. Are you all still interested?'

Mamie put her hand up. 'It depends on what kind of books. At my age I don't want to tackle *War and Peace*.'

There were murmurs of agreement.

Angela turned to Audrey. 'I know you were keen on *Wuthering Heights*. Is that still on your list?'

'Absolutely.' Audrey folded her large arms over her enormous bosom. 'That or *The Old Curiosity Shop* by Dickens.'

'Two excellent classics,' Angela said.

'What are your choices, Angela?' asked Helen.

'While I love the classics, I thought we might try something a little more modern. Kate Atkinson's marvellous *Life After Life* or *Eleanor Oliphant is Completely Fine* by Gail Honeyman. I have a copy of each here for you to pass round and look at.' She handed them out. 'Audrey, do you have copies of your choices?'

Audrey was wrong-footed. 'Er, no . . . I have forgotten them. Geoffrey didn't remind me.'

'Never mind. Right, ladies, when you're ready we'll have a show of hands for each as I call them out.'

Eleanor Oliphant was in by a mile.

'And what are we supposed to talk about when we've read it?' asked Queenie.

Audrey, desperate to salvage some superiority in defeat, said, 'I shall be looking for your thoughts on the characters, the plotting of the author, and the story's arc. We will share discourse on the relevance of the story to our own lives. I consider myself something of a scholar of the classics and so it will be very interesting to discover if the book you have chosen does indeed have any merit at all. Reading this book will be as challenging for me as it is to you, yet for very different reasons.'

'I will get copies to you all over the next few days,' Angela smiled. 'But for now, I would like to thank Audrey for using her precious time to be here tonight. Now I am sure you want to get home to your husband.'

Audrey found herself being bustled out of the front door. 'I am so grateful, Audrey,' said Angela at the front door. 'Goodbye.'

Angela leant on the back of the closed front door and breathed a sigh of relief. 'What the hell was that all about?' Mamie asked when Angela returned.

Queenie chuckled. 'I know what she's done, girls. She's called Audrey's bluff. That woman will have less time to interfere if she's got books to read. Well done, girl.' She smiled at an innocent-looking Angela. 'That's what you've gone and done, innit?'

'I cannot possibly comment,' Angela said. 'Now, who would like their glasses topped up?'

Once they were all resettled, Angela reached for her iPad. 'Can I just go through some of our summer events? Any feedback or help would be gladly accepted.'

Mamie piped up, 'I have the garden party under control, thank you.'

'I know, and thank you. I'm thinking more about May Day. I know Trevay celebrates it with the procession along the quay and music and dancing . . .'

'One enormous pub crawl, actually. I lose Piran for at least forty-eight hours each year,' said Helen with raised eyebrows.

Angela nodded. 'I wouldn't want to stand in the way of tradition, but I wondered if the children would like to do a bit of dancing on our village green in the morning. Before the Trevay parade kicks off.'

'We used to have a maypole,' said Evelyn. 'Do you remember, Robbie? We used to dance round it when we was at school.'

'Oh, yes. Every year Miss Hunter would shout at us for tangling up all the ribbons.'

'And the boys had to wear ribbons round their arms.' Evelyn began giggling. 'You had a crush on Martin Newton, remember?'

Robbie began to laugh too. 'Oh, yes. He had lovely teeth. My Bob was so jealous he let the tyres down on Martin's Chopper bike.'

Queenie joined in. 'Martin Newton was a tyke. A good-looking boy but a little tyke.'

'Well,' Angela jumped in, 'before you all go off down memory lane, I have found your maypole. Well, Mike Bates found it in the old store room at the back of the village hall. It needs a lick of paint and we need new ribbons because the mice have been at them, but Mike has agreed to let us put it up on the green and hold a small celebration.'

'Does anyone know how to dance round the maypole nowadays?' asked Mamie.

'Hang on.' Helen reached for her phone. 'Let me ask Mr Google.' She typed into the search bar and waited. 'Here we are. Oh, no!' She started to laugh. 'It's sent me to pole dancing.'

Queenie's face lit up. 'That's very clever. I watched a dock-ermentary on that. These girls are ever so strong and they do it with no clothes on.'

'I used to do that,' Sarah said casually, a sleeping Santi on her shoulder. 'And you don't have to do it nude,' she added.

'How did you do it then?' asked Queenie.

'Topless.'

The women looked at Sarah with a mix of admiration and disbelief.

'Before I had the kids, obviously. I'm thinking of training up again just to tighten up my bingo wings and mum tum. Not as a job, as a fitness thing.'

''Ow much could you earn a night?' asked Queenie, the business woman in her surfacing.

'Quite a lot, actually.'

'But you never 'ad those men's hands over you? No "extras"?'

'NO.' Sarah was firm. 'Absolutely not. That is not why I did the job. I needed cash, I was very strong and fit, and I liked dancing. At the time it seemed like a no-brainer. I worked in a nice club where you'd get fired if you did anything like that.'

'And you was topless?' Queenie was fascinated. 'So you got the money tucked into your knickers?'

'G-string.'

'Gordon Bennett, you kept that under yer hat.'

'Except I didn't wear a hat!' Sarah giggled, then looked serious. 'Ben doesn't know and nor does Santi's dad. I'd rather keep it quiet.'

Helen was still looking through country dancing videos on YouTube. 'Ah. Here we are. The twist, the plait, the spider's web . . .'

'On a pole?' Queenie asked mischievously.

'A maypole, yes. Look.'

An hour later they had divvied up the jobs. Queenie and Mamie would source the ribbons and get them nailed to the maypole. Sarah, Evelyn and Robbie would learn the dances and get Gasping Bob to dust off his piano accordion, and Angela asked Helen to help her paint the maypole in traditional barbershop red and white stripes.

'We can get Piran and Robert to help,' suggested Helen, but Angela was firm.

'No, I'd rather just you and me.'

'OK. I'll get the paint and brushes if you like,' Helen said easily.

The meeting broke up soon after, with Robbie quietly telling everyone that the results of her biopsy were due soon.

On Helen's way home over the village green she thought about Angela's negative reaction to her suggestion that Piran and Robert help them with the painting of the maypole. Her intuition was telling her something, but what exactly was it?

20

Life at the vicarage never seemed to slow down. The weather was warming up and the sun seemed to bring out many parishioners from their hibernation.

Mamie's preparation for the garden party was gathering apace and the unused dining room was filling with tombola gifts, raffle prizes, boxes of bunting and all manner of lists and clipboards.

Angela kept out of the way. Three of her own projects were coming together nicely.

The May Day celebration was coming on.

The running club had added Faith, Ben, Sarah and Ella, and the results in terms of the women's fitness were looking good.

And the pet-blessing service was greenlit, having been published on the village website and in the local papers, giving it some good publicity.

'I hope all those who have promised to come actually do come, or it'll be just us and Mr Worthington,' Angela said anxiously.

Faith put her arm around her mother. 'Mum, there will be tons of people, generous people. Perhaps we should, at the end, have a whip-round for the dog-poo bin on the green?'

Angela clamped her hands on her cheeks. 'Oh my! That is genius! But what if nobody comes?'

'Then we don't get a dog poo bin?' Faith laughed at her mother. 'Mum, stop worrying. It will be fine, and if it isn't, no harm done.'

On the morning of the pet-blessing service, the warm early sun rose and cast its golden rays lightly on the fresh green cornfields surrounding the village.

Angela was in the kitchen, back door open, filling small bags with dog treats, cat treats and chopped carrots for any herbivore.

'What about fish and parrots?' asked Faith, finishing a carton of orange juice from the fridge.

Angela frowned. 'Fish? Really?'

'Probably not, but parrots are possible. Shall I put some toast in for you?' Faith mooched to the bread bin and held up a brown loaf and bag of crumpets.

'No, thanks. Do parrots eat raisins?'

'Mum, they either will or they won't, so take some in case.' Faith pressed a crumpet into the toaster and went to tickle Mr Worthington, who rolled over onto his back and offered his tummy. 'No weeing in the church, please. Or sticking your nose where it's not welcome. Understood?'

Mr Worthington answered with a snuffle and a sniff. 'Good.' The toaster popped and Faith went to fetch Marmite and butter.

Angela looked up from counting small bone-shaped

biscuits. 'It's not happening in the church. Dear Simple Tony has mowed the back lawn of the churchyard where there is lots of room.'

'Good thinking. Giving everyone a poo bag too? Just in case?'

'For the dogs, yes.'

'I was thinking more of Queenie,' Faith sniggered.

'Faith! That's very unkind.'

'Lighten up, Mum. Just a joke.'

Angela sniffed and pointed to a pile of small bags. 'You can hand those out to everyone, and collect them up afterwards.'

'Oh Muuum.'

Robert came in from the garden with a bunch of mint and a little posy of roses. 'Mint for the lamb today and roses,' he dropped a kiss on Angela's head, 'for my wife.'

She smiled up at him and inhaled the fresh sweet scent of the mint. 'I've put the lamb in the bottom of the Aga. It should be perfectly ready for lunch.'

'Great. By the way, Piran is away for a couple of days. Helen's on her own so I have invited her for lunch.'

Angela bit her lip. 'Good idea.'

In the churchyard, gathered around a makeshift altar, Angela was amazed at the sight of so many animals arriving. At least twenty dogs. Three cats in baskets. A litter of black kittens with blue eyes. One cockatiel on the shoulder of its owner. Two rabbits on leads. A pony. A donkey. A baby lamb – Angela couldn't help but feel guilty over the lunch in the bottom of her Aga – and a chameleon.

The service was simple. It opened with 'All things bright and beautiful', followed by a retelling of the story of Noah's

Ark, and then Angela quietly blessed each animal and gave it an appropriate snack from her bag of goodies.

The donations to the dog poo bin fund were generous and the amount of dog mess was surprisingly minimal, to Faith's relief, although getting the pony poo into a single bag was rather difficult.

'That'll go on my roses,' Simple Tony said, taking the bags from her.

'Well, that was a great success.' Helen was waiting in a patch of sunshine as Angela said goodbye to all the animals and owners. 'And thank you so much for asking me to lunch.'

'My pleasure,' Angela said guiltily. She tried to remind herself that Helen was a lovely woman. One she had no need to be wary of. After all, she was Penny's best friend. She tucked her arm into Helen's. 'Come on. Let's see how Robert's doing in the kitchen.'

Robert was at full tilt. The table was laid. The new potatoes draining. Early cabbage and spring greens buttered and fresh mint sauce sitting in two small jugs either end of the table.

'Perfect timing.' He kissed Helen first then turned back to stirring his gravy. 'How did the service go, love?' he asked Angela over his shoulder.

'It was wonderful,' Helen replied.

'Excuse me. I just need to wash my hands. All those animals, you know.' Angela went upstairs to her room and shut the bathroom door behind her. Closing the lid of the loo, she sat down and allowed the incipient tears to flow freely.

Mamie clattered in.

'Darling, do you have any hand cream? I can't find any and my hands are in a dreadful state from all the gardening for your party . . . oh my goodness. What's happened?'

Angela turned her face away from her aunt and grabbed a handful of loo paper. 'Nothing. I'm fine.' She blew her nose. 'I think I have a bit of a cold starting.'

Mamie stood with her hands on her hips. 'You can't kid a kidder, Angie. What has happened?'

Angela wiped away a fresh stream of tears. 'It's nothing. It's me being stupid.'

Mamie sat on the edge of the bath. 'Tell me.'

'It's Helen.'

'What has she done?'

'Nothing.'

'So?'

'Oh, it's silly . . .'

'Not still worried about her and Robert?'

Angela looked up with pleading eyes. 'Do you know something?'

Mamie shook her head. 'I only know that Robert adores you.'

'But Helen is so pretty.' Angela began to cry again. 'And I am not as pretty as her and Robert is so attractive and they have been spending so much time together . . .'

'Darling, you've got to stop this. Robert loves you and Helen loves Piran. Robert is not the bonking kind and Helen is too classy. I wouldn't blame her if she had a bit of a crush on him – I think the whole village does. Audrey Tipton certainly does. But for him to cheat on you? Never in a million years. I'd stake my life on it.'

'Honestly? You really think so?'

'I really think so.'

'Are you all right, Mum?' Faith came in. 'Dad says lunch is ready. Have you been crying?'

'Your mother has a headache,' Mamie said. 'And I'm not

215

surprised. She doesn't get a minute's peace to herself. Even this bathroom is like Piccadilly Circus. Tell your father we'll be down in a minute.'

'Poor you, Mum. I'll tell Dad. Can I get you anything?'

Angela sat up straight and gave Faith a reassuring smile. 'No. I'll be fine.'

Mamie shooed Faith out, then said to Angela, 'Come on. You always have me in your corner, no matter what.'

21

The days ticked by and Angela settled down again to concentrate on her work and her family.

Robert and Helen were spending less time together now that the website was up and running, and his job at the *Trevay Times* had expanded into cinema reviews and writing colour pieces on local places of interest. He and Angela even managed to see a film together after a day out in St Ives. But there was a feeling she couldn't quite shake away . . .

May Day arrived and the maypole was carried ceremoniously to the green, where it was placed snugly into its newly dug hole. With a final push, Robert, Don and Piran let it go, whereupon the ribbons fluttered, criss-crossed, wrapped and knotted themselves with glee.

'Oh, for Pete's sake!' Mike Bates was beginning to lose his cool. 'Somebody get hold of those ribbons and secure the damn things.'

Audrey, who adored witnessing others' discomfort, glowed with self-righteous delight.

'I did tell you that ribbons as long as those need to be held in sections and tied securely to the pole before you even attempt to move it,' she crowed.

'Thank you, Audrey,' Mike said with enormous self-control. 'I shall know better in future.'

'I hope so,' she sniffed.

An excitable crew of village children were advancing from the other end of the green, dressed in colourful shirts and shorts, led by Angela and Helen.

'Here we are, children.' Angela grinned. 'The real maypole!'

The children, who had been practising their dancing around a small broom in the village hall, gazed in awe.

'That's bleddy enormous,' gaped a young boy in a cut-down Hawaiian shirt that his mum thought would do.

'Language, Craig,' admonished Angela.

'Sorry, Vicar.'

'Where are their pretty frocks?' Audrey criticised. 'And why aren't the boys in waistcoats?' She shook her head dismissively. 'No, no, this won't do. If you are going to revive an old Pendruggan custom, you must do it properly.'

Two angry spots of colour appeared on Angela's cheeks, but before she said something she would regret, Piran stepped in.

'Right, kids, before your mums and dads arrive, who wants to help unravel the Ribbon Puzzle? 'Tis the tradition of all maypole dancers to get the ribbons sorted out first. And when you've done it, we'll take a big photo of you all, before you do the dancing and get the ribbons all muddled up again. What do you say?'

'Yeeeees!' the children shouted.

'Right, let's get started.'

Mike Bates rocked on the heels of his well-polished brogues

and relished the look of pure fury on Audrey's face. 'Now that's what I call leadership. Marvellous man, Piran, don't you think, Audrey?'

Audrey couldn't speak.

Angela, riven with Christian guilt that she was so happy to see Audrey squashed, said, 'Maybe next year you could help in the design of the costumes, Audrey? But for now, I think they all look lovely.'

'Me too,' Helen added. A sudden flurry of activity outside Pendruggan farmhouse caught her eye. 'What's going on over there?'

Angela turned to see Evelyn hurling a cumbersome suitcase at a man who had his arms up, presumably protecting his face. He was shouting, 'Evie. Stop it. I've come home. To you. I made a mistake.' Evelyn picked up a shoe and threw it at his head. 'Ouch!' he yelled as it landed four-square on his skull.

'Get away. Get out. Get out,' she screamed. 'Just because that tart of yours has thrown you out, don't mean you can come back here.' She picked up the other shoe and threw it but he ducked.

'This is my house, you daft cow.' He began to advance towards her. 'You can't throw me out. It's been in my family for generations. You have no right to be here. In fact, I can throw you out.'

'Don't you threaten me,' Evelyn said.

He kept walking towards her, his face twisted with anger, his voice low and dangerous. 'I can do what I bleddy like to my own wife. Without me what would you be? Another drain on society? I took you in. Fed you. Clothed you. You're nothing.'

Evelyn's bravado began to slip. 'You wouldn't dare. Not with all these people watching.'

He turned round and saw Piran, Mike, Robert and Gasping Bob walking towards him.

'All right, Malcolm?' asked Bob.

Malcolm turned to face the men, arms hanging out at his sides as if he were a cowboy. 'Just a little woman trouble. The silly bitch don't know what's good fer 'er.'

'And what would be good for her?' Piran growled.

'None of your business.'

Mike took a step in front of them. 'Evelyn? Are you OK?'

'Yes,' she said quietly.

'Would you like to come over here and stand with me?' he asked.

'You stay where you bleddy are, woman,' said Malcolm.

'Evelyn? Come over here and we can get you a cup of tea or something. Looks like you could do with one.'

Malcolm turned to stop Evelyn but she held her head up. 'I'd like that. Thank you, Mr Bates.' She walked slowly towards him, leaving plenty of distance between her and her husband.

Malcolm was shimmering with rage. 'If you go with him, don't think you'll be able to come back. I'll get the locks changed tonight. Burn everything that's yours. I'll wipe you out . . . for good.'

'That's enough, Malcolm,' said Robert, who had taken his phone out of his pocket. 'There are witnesses to all you have just said. I am calling the police now.'

'Oh, sod off, you whiny little househusband,' Malcolm taunted him. 'Real men have women to look after them. Not the other way around. You think I'm scared of you? You don't have the balls to call the police.'

'By all means try me, but I suggest you pick up your bag and shoes and leave the village right now.' Robert's finger pressed twice on the nine button of his phone. 'One more and they'll be here.'

Malcolm tipped his head back and laughed. 'Don't you worry. I've got better places to be.' He turned and, collecting his case and his shoes, jumped into his farm truck and sped off out of the village.

Angela and Helen went to Evelyn, who was shaking. 'Thank you, Mr Bates, Piran. Robert, you were wonderful.'

Gasping Bob came to her and took her in his arms. 'I'm so sorry. So sorry. He's been my mate for years but I had no idea how bad things were between you. Robbie said one or two things but I couldn't believe her. That's the first time I've seen him talk like that. Stay with Robbie and me tonight. For as long as you want.'

Evelyn was crying into his shoulder. Her entire body shuddering in shock. 'Robbie don't need me around. Not while she's waiting to hear about . . . you know.'

Bob began to smile and pushed Evelyn away a little so that he could see her face. 'She ain't managed to get hold of you, has she? We heard today. Biopsy all clear. She hasn't got cancer. It's just an ordinary harmless little lump.'

Evelyn's hand flew to her mouth in joy. 'She's OK? Where is she?'

'At home. Go on. She'll give you a cuppa.'

Evelyn needed no more encouragement.

Everyone watched her go while congratulating Bob on Robbie's news.

Even Audrey managed a gracious, 'Please send her my best.'

The church clock struck midday, signalling the start of the May Day festivities. Looking around, Angela could see a group of eager parents and grandparents ready with their phones to capture the highlight of the day.

'Come on, Bob,' she said, taking his arm. 'I'm expecting you to play with even more happiness today of all days.'

'Righto.' Bob lit a roll-up that he'd had waiting behind his ear and picked up his piano accordion. 'Ready when you are, Vicar.'

Twenty children under the age of eleven, in charge of weaving multi-coloured ribbons in complicated patterns to tunes including 'Trelawny', 'D'ye Ken John Peel' and 'The Sweet Nightingale', played by a chain-smoking Cornishman on his ancient accordion, was an experience not to be missed, Angela thought. Proud families laughed and clapped along, taking endless photos and videos.

As Bob played his final rousing chord the children, hot and thirsty and smelling of fresh air, bowed and curtsied and ran to their mums and dads for hugs and the promise of ice lollies.

Mamie, who had missed all the earlier excitement, just caught the last dance. 'Well, that was marvellous and Queenie will be thrilled with the custom you are sending her way.' She slipped her arm through Angela's. 'Now tell me all about what I have missed.'

By the evening, there was not a soul in Pendruggan who hadn't heard about Evelyn and Malcolm.

It would be a while before anyone heard from him again.

But Evelyn had never felt better. Thirty years of bullying had finally been laid to rest and her new chapter was just beginning.

22

The second anonymous letter was among the bundle of birthday cards that Faith brought up to Angela on her birthday breakfast tray.

'Happy birthday, Mum. The postman has been.'

Angela grinned. 'You spoil me.'

'Well, sit up and let me put this on your lap. It's heavy.'

She did as she was told, inwardly smiling at her daughter's definition of heavy – a cup of tea and plate of toast – but she said, 'Thank you, darling.'

Faith, her duty done, already had other things on her mind. 'Right, I'm off. Dad's giving me and Ben a lift to school. Have a nice day doing whatever it is old people do.'

'Charming. And you, darling. Give us a kiss.'

A car horn sounded outside.

'Dad's waiting. I'm going to be late.'

'Kiss me.'

Faith, tutting, kissed her mother, checked herself in the long mirror and left, calling, 'Laters.'

'Love you,' Angela replied.

Tea and toast in bed, with strict instructions to have a lie-in, was heavenly. She picked up her tea and sipped at it, flicking through the birthday envelopes.

The unstamped ones were obviously from Robert, Mamie and Faith.

The majority of the stamped ones had handwriting she recognised.

Unconsciously she sifted through them to find the one from her mother before catching her breath as the pain of knowing there wouldn't be one hit her once again like an express train.

Her mind went to a birthday, many years ago, when her mother and Auntie Mamie, her only family, had taken her out for a trip into London. She'd been about thirteen and deemed mature enough to have lunch at the Ritz followed by a matinée of Gershwin's *Crazy for You*.

Angela lay back against her pillows and closed her eyes. She allowed the happy memory to fill her. She remembered the touch of her mother's loving arm around her as they left the theatre humming the glorious tunes.

She could hear her mother's voice, happy and excited. 'What a birthday treat. One we shall never forget, shall we, Angela?'

Angela would never forget.

Finishing her tea, she put the cup down and went through the cards again, thinking about which to open first.

It was then she saw the letter.

The address had been typed on a white label and stuck to the white envelope. The postmark was blurred.

Curious, she put the birthday envelopes to one side and opened it.

One blue sheet.

Folded in two.

She unfolded it.

Sixteen typed words:

> YOUR HUSBAND IS NOT THE MAN
> YOU THINK HE IS.
> HE KEEPS A SECRET.
> HAPPY BIRTHDAY.

She read it again.

And again.

She turned the paper over.

Nothing more.

She felt a familiar queasiness in her stomach.

The letter was shaking in her hands.

Who was sending these horrible things?

What secret was Robert keeping?

It must be a mistake.

She checked the envelope.

No mistake. It was addressed to her.

Maybe it was Faith and Ben. A terrible coincidence. They had no idea that she'd received one of these before. Having a joke. Yes. The secret must be something to do with her birthday. A present? Or an outing? That had to be it. It was nothing malicious. Just poorly executed.

She put it back in its envelope, and slid it into her bedside drawer.

She'd keep it to herself.

She wouldn't let on.

She didn't want to spoil her birthday.

Or admit that it had upset her.

Given her a shock.

No.

She'd keep it to herself until the secret, her birthday secret surely, was revealed and then they'd all laugh, and that would be that.

She put her breakfast tray, the toast now cold, to one side and got out of bed.

In the bathroom she turned the radio on.

John Humphrys was giving some cabinet minister hell.

Normality.

Reality.

She stepped into the shower and turned her thoughts to the garden party. Only one more day to go. Perhaps they had a surprise planned for that? A hot air balloon ride or a coachload of old school friends, or . . .

Of course she knew who her husband was. They had no secrets from one another. Not a single one. No. Never. She told him everything and he told her everything. Except she wasn't going to tell him about this one. Not yet.

That was the basis of their relationship. They never had time apart. Ever.

So silly.

And yet, if it wasn't Faith playing a game, it was someone very sick.

Someone who needed help.

Someone who knew it was her birthday today.

As far as the village was concerned, her birthday was tomorrow.

The day of the garden party. It had seemed easier to let people think that than have the kerfuffle of two birthdays.

So it must be someone she knew.

She frowned, trying to think of anyone in the village who had exhibited odd behaviour.

Anyone she had upset unknowingly.

She hated herself immediately. How could she even begin to suspect her lovely new friends and villagers?

She snapped the shower from pleasantly warm to icy cold and told herself to forget it. A one-off. She'd got the wrong end of the stick. Or someone else had.

She spent the early part of the morning in her office, distracting herself from the irrational and unwanted thoughts worming their way into her brain.

When Robert had returned from the school run, it had taken every ounce of her self-control not to run upstairs, retrieve the letter and confront him with it.

Instead, she had watched as his car pulled up on the vicarage drive, and met him at the front door.

He had come in, all smiles, with bulging shopping bags and a huge bunch of scented lilies.

'These are for you, my darling.' He placed them in her arms and kissed her briefly. 'I thought they might look nice with some of that mollis from the garden. The lime green against the pink?'

'Yes.' She batted away an unbidden desire to burst into tears.

'Now then,' he said, clanking the shopping bags towards the kitchen. 'I am going to cook you a feast of delights tonight.' He hefted the bags onto the kitchen table and pulled the fridge door open. 'I don't want you coming in and ruining the surprise.'

She had followed him down the darkened hall and was leaning on the kitchen doorframe. 'Surprise?' Her gut twisted.

Satisfied with his survey of the fridge's interior, he took out a bottle of milk, closed the door and went to the kettle. 'Yep.'

Facing her, he flapped his hands and shooed her out. 'Now, you go back to whatever it is you're doing and I'll bring you a coffee.'

Back in her office, Angela tried to put her mind to the church admin that needed putting in order. But the stocktake of communion wafers and rotas for the volunteer cleaners and flower arrangers were not what her brain needed.

Her running shoes were calling to her.

'I told you not to come in!' Robert feigned irritation with her, hands on hips, tea towel thrown over his shoulder.

'Can I fill my water bottle up, please? I fancy a run,' she said, passing her bottle to him.

'Running on your own today?'

'Yes. Running club is tomorrow.'

She took in the explosion of half-prepped ingredients on the huge chopping board (a wedding present from her mum and Mamie to them both seventeen years ago), and a large sauté pan spattering the top of the Aga. 'It smells good in here,' she smiled.

He tapped her nose as he passed her the water. 'Keep your beak out, Mrs Nosy. Have a good run.'

Coming out of the vicarage, she began to run immediately. She usually did a lap of the village green and then either ran to the beach and along the length of its shore, or up the hill, past the Dolphin and through a loop of lanes that brought her back to Pendruggan.

As she was deciding, she heard her name called. Helen was outside Gull's Cry and waving at her. 'Happy birthday, Angela!' she shouted.

'Thank you.' Angela kept her running pace steady.

'Have a lovely day!' Helen shouted back in return.

'Will do!' Angela kept smiling but her brain was asking

her, *How does Helen know it's my birthday? Could she have sent the note? Have she and Robert been meeting up in secret? No. Why would they? Unless . . . STOP, Angela. Don't think about them being together. OK. Is Helen missing Penny? After all, I'm the cuckoo in the nest, taking the place of Helen's best friend. Does she resent me for that? Or does the crush she might have on Robert make her want to stir up trouble? Or, or . . . or maybe I'm just paranoid and whoever sent the note did it for some warped pleasure, never to be heard from again.*

Aloud she said, 'Shut up, Angela, and just run.'

She decided to do her inland run and turned up the steep and pretty lane towards the Dolphin. The landlord, Don, was outside watering his hanging baskets.

'Morning,' she panted as she went past.

'Morning!' he called back.

No birthday wishes from him. So, the letter isn't from him. Unless it is and he's playing it carefully. But why would he send it? Jealousy? Robert is a very handsome man and only the other day he mentioned how lucky Don is to have such an attractive wife as Dorrie. But Dorrie comes to the women's group and I haven't noticed her being overly smitten by Robert. But is she boxing clever too?

Around the bend and out of Don's sight she stopped, bent over, her hands on her knees, tears beginning to form. She dashed them away angrily. 'Stop it. STOP IT,' she shouted in the quiet of the warm and deserted lane.

She steadied herself, took three deep breaths and a mouthful of water.

You are tormenting yourself. Robert has no secrets. You would know if he did. So would Faith and certainly Mamie. Mamie would tell me. She wouldn't let Robert hurt me.

Like the terrorist who wins with threats of destruction, so

this pathetic, anonymous letter-writer was winning by undermining all she knew to be true in her life.

She stood up straight. Rolled her shoulders. Shook her legs and started to run again.

Forty minutes later and only half a mile from home, she passed the closed gates of a house set in a severely manicured garden. From nowhere, two large and drooling Labradors rushed at the gates and barked ferociously, their hackles raised.

Angela stopped in shock and terror.

A familiar voice spoke to them. 'Come along, William, Henry. Quiet.'

The dogs took no notice, continuing to jump at the gates and pin Angela with their evil stares.

Audrey Tipton strode into view. 'Ah, Mrs Whitehorn. The boys are very protective. It's why I didn't bring them to your pet blessing service. Pedigree dogs like these mustn't mix with mongrels. And anyway, I didn't agree with the premise.' She called the quietening beasts to her side. 'Such lovely dogs. Why would anyone have children when they can have doggies as lovable as these?' She bent down to fondle their ears.

'They scared me a bit,' admitted Angela. 'I've often run down here but hadn't seen them before now.'

Audrey curled a lip. 'Running is a dreadful hobby, don't you think?'

'It's not for everybody but I find it very therapeutic.'

'Tennis is so much better. I was a very good player in my youth. But it's golf now. Geoffrey and I are very active members of the golf club. Such a nice class of person plays golf.'

'I imagine so,' replied Angela, thinking how ghastly it must be if they were all Tipton clones.

'But I mustn't stop you, Mrs Whitehorn. Enjoy your run, oh and happy birthday.'

'Thank you. How did you know?'

Audrey was smug. 'There's not much in this village that goes by without me knowing.' She called the dogs to heel and triumphantly walked back towards the house.

Angela picked up her pace once more.

Of course! It could be Audrey. Sharp-tongued and unkind. It would be just like her to write a nasty little note like that. She is exactly the sort of person who wouldn't want a woman vicar in her parish. And she's made it clear she fancies Robert. Who wouldn't? Being married to Geoffrey? Hardly an Adonis. Yes. It must be Audrey or someone in her group of friends. Judging. Criticising. Superior to all others.

Angela slowed to a trot.

What was she thinking?

All these unkind thoughts about innocent people?

This was not why she had been ordained. She had joined the Church because of her faith in Christ's message of love. She wanted to spread that message and make the world and its people kinder, more understanding, loving. And here she was thinking twisted, unkind and hateful thoughts.

She began to walk, taking a good drink of her water. A few yards on was a lichened five-bar gate overlooking the fields that ran down to the sea. She rested her elbows on it and took in the view. Peaceful. The young crops bright green against the cornflower sky. The sea sparkling in the distance. This was her home for now. And her home was filled with three people she loved the most and who loved her. She was blessed. No idiot was going to spoil this day. Or her marriage.

23

At seven o'clock that evening, Robert called Angela downstairs and put his hands over her eyes as he guided her towards the kitchen.

'No peeking, birthday girl.'

The touch of his warm, gentle hands and the timbre of his voice, both so familiar, brought another wave of near tears, just one of several that day. When she had returned from her run he had filled a steaming bath for her, surrounding it with scented candles. She had lain in it and cried with happiness. He insisted that she relaxed until he was ready to call her down.

Faith had wandered in and done her nails for her then shaped her eyebrows. 'Mum, you really need to keep these under control.'

What would she do without her family? Robert was her best friend and champion. The love of her life. Kind. Dependable. And, she admitted, paternal in a way that her own father had not had the chance to be.

He was simply everything to her.

Now, approaching the kitchen blindly, she felt his warm breath on her right ear. 'Just two more steps and then you can open the door. Keep your eyes shut.'

'I will.'

'Promise.'

'I promise.'

He took his hands from her closed eyes, and guided her hand to the door handle.

'Ready?'

'Uh-huh.'

'In you go.'

She pressed the door handle down and opened her eyes.

Waiting for her were Mamie and Faith, and Piran and Helen. They began singing, 'Happy birthday to you, happy birthday to you, happy birthday dear Angela, happy birthday to you.'

Her hands flew to either side of her mouth with joy.

Robert stood behind her and slid his arms around her slender waist. She allowed her eyes to weep their unemptied tears. 'But I'm having my party tomorrow!' she managed.

Helen came to her side. 'Well, that's the party, this is the birthday supper. Two completely different things.' From behind her back she produced a small package. 'I hope you like it.'

Remorse swept through Angela. How could she ever have imagined that Helen could be the malicious letter-writer? She kissed her. 'You never said a word this morning! Thank you. Can I open it now?'

'Please do.'

Inside the carefully wrapped package was a silver bangle with a charm hanging from it.

'It's an Irish wolfhound,' Helen said, then added anxiously, 'Mr Worthington is one of those, isn't he?'

'He is. Oh, it's lovely!' Angela slid it onto her wrist and showed it off. 'Thank you.'

Mamie stepped forward and passed her a glass of champagne. 'Darling, many happy returns and many more of them. I have got you six bottles of this, so I hope you like it.'

Angela took a sip. 'Delicious. Thank you, Mamie.'

Faith was busy picking at a bowl of cashew nuts and told the room, 'I gave Mum breakfast in bed.'

'You did.' Angela remembered the birthday cards and the hideous letter among them and swallowed the flush of anxiety that swept through her body. 'It was a lovely surprise.'

Robert rubbed his hands together. 'Right, everyone. Sit down. Piran, next to Angela. Helen next to me and Mamie and Faith opposite each other.'

Angela was immediately on edge. Why would Robert put Helen next to him? She watched as he pulled the chair out for Helen and said something that made her laugh.

Piran, next to Angela, touched her arm, making her jump. 'Had a good day then?'

She smiled her automatic smile. The one she used for the line of parishioners who waited to shake her hand at the end of each Sunday service.

'Yes. Wonderful.'

Robert was bending over Helen, pouring her another glass of champagne. He looked up and caught Angela's eye. 'Don't worry. I'm coming to your end now. Piran, pass me Ange's glass.' As he poured he kept talking to Helen and spilt the pale bubbles onto the tablecloth. 'Oops. Not paying attention. Sorry.'

Angela took her wet and overfilled glass and drank it swiftly. Piran raised his eyebrows. 'You look as if you needed that, maid.'

'Well, it's my birthday, isn't it?'

Piran sensed choppy waters and held his tongue.

'Helen, I need you.' Robert, his cheeks flushed, was playing the fool. 'You don't mind, do you, Piran?'

'Depends,' he said gruffly.

'I need Helen to be my sous chef and plate up the starters.'

Helen, Angela thought, looked thrilled. 'I would adore to,' she giggled.

Together they fussed about, going in the fridge, sharing a joke about homemade mayonnaise and all the time feeding nothing but a voracious jealousy that Angela had never felt before.

The first course consisted of individual and perfectly sized crudities with a garlicky anchovy dipping sauce.

Helen was in raptures. 'I must have this recipe, Robert. It's incredible.'

'I found it online,' he said. Angela watched him as he watched Helen lick her fingers. 'Bagna Càuda. Literal translation is Hot Sauce.'

Faith wiped her lips. 'Dad, this is the best thing you've ever made!'

Robert looked towards the end of the table. 'What do you think, Ange? I made it for you.'

She couldn't look him in the eye. 'Yum,' she managed, fiddling with the napkin on her lap.

The main course was a huge joint of beef, perfectly pink and seasoned. Robert had made Yorkshire puddings, roast potatoes, fresh peas, sautéed leeks and buttered carrots to accompany it.

'My wife's favourite supper of all time. Isn't that right, my darling?' He looked at her with a faint question mark.

'Thank you, Robert.' She wanted to say, 'No, it's not my favourite. It's *yours*.' She took a mouthful and tried hard to swallow the food and the slight.

When the main course had been cleared, Robert stood up. 'At this point you would expect the birthday pudding, but before I serve it, I want to toast my wonderful wife. Please be upstanding for Angela.'

There was a scrape of chairs as everyone but Angela stood and raised their glasses. 'To Angela,' Robert said.

'To Angela,' they intoned.

'Speech!' cried a slightly tipsy Mamie.

'No, no.' Angela shook her head.

'Come on, Mum!' cajoled Faith.

Angela knew she had to say something or endure this embarrassment a lot longer. Pushing back her chair, she got to her feet. 'Thank you for this wonderful dinner, Robert. And thank you all for giving me an evening I may never forget.' She raised her glass and drained it. She said, 'More wine please, Robert.' And sat down.

Robert pulled a face that said, *Uh-oh, someone's going to have a headache tomorrow*, but he went to the fridge and opened a bottle of pale, Provence rosé. He walked to her and poured it, saying, 'I have a present for you. Would you like it now?'

There was a hush and five faces turned to her expectantly. More than tipsy, Angela leant back in her chair as if challenging him. 'Go on then. Surprise me.'

Robert didn't take his eyes from Angela's face. 'Mamie. Would you make some coffee, please? I've got to go and fetch something.'

He returned with a large, paper-wrapped parcel, which rustled under his touch. He knelt by her side. 'Happy birthday, my love. I hope you like it.'

'Well, come on. Open it,' urged Mamie, filling the cafetiere.

The parcel sat on Angela's lap. Her hands traced the gold embossment. Her fingers found the taped edges and began to pull at the wrapping until a summer dress in gossamer blue-grey chiffon slid out.

Mamie and Faith gasped.

Helen smiled.

'Stand up, Ange,' Robert asked her. 'Hold it up against you.'

It was full length and backless. A high-necked halter giving a demure impression until the wearer turned round.

'Do you like?' Robert whispered anxiously.

Angela had no words. 'Robert. It's beautiful. I love it. And I love you. Thank you.'

He smiled, relieved. 'Thank Helen. She picked it out.'

24

'There you are! What are you doing out here? It's six o'clock in the morning.' Mamie, first coffee of the day in hand, sat next to Angela. 'And why this old bench? It's all damp and rotten.'

'You can't see it from the house,' Angela replied quietly.

'Ah. So you didn't want to be found.' Mamie crossed her Moroccan-slippered feet, pulled her dressing gown closer and took a mouthful of her strong espresso.

'It's not that,' Angela said testily. 'It's just that sometimes I need a bit of bloody peace in my own head. OK?'

Mamie inclined her head. 'Of course. But . . .' she took another sip of coffee, 'Helen and Robert are not having an affair.'

'Oh, for heaven's sake, they most certainly are not. What on earth made you say that?'

'Because I know you and that is why you are out here.'

Angela ran her hands through her short hair. 'Oh, Mamie. Last night was lovely. Robert's present was lovely but . . .'

'Helen chose it.'

Angela gave a wretched nod.

'She has good taste.'

'Yes.'

'But you wanted to think he had chosen it for you, without anyone's help.'

Angela's eyes brimmed. 'Yes.'

'And you want to take the bloody thing back to the shop.'

Angela nodded sadly. 'It's so mean and ungrateful of me. Helen is a friend. Our friend. Our family friend. And she has a loving relationship with Piran. But . . .'

Mamie threw her coffee dregs into the birdbath. 'But nothing.' She put her cold hands around Angela's cheeks. 'Listen to me. Robert. Loves. *You*.'

Angela's expression was far from convinced. 'I love him so much.'

Mamie kissed Angela's forehead before taking her hands from her cheeks.

'Good. Now no more silly talk, please. What's the time?'

Angela checked her small wristwatch. 'Six thirty.'

Mamie pressed her palms on her knees and stood up. 'I am going to brew a large pot of good coffee and you are going to get back into bed and wait for me to bring it to you *both*. OK?'

'OK.'

In the half-light of their bedroom, Angela watched as Robert's chest rose and fell in the innocence of sleep. She crept around to her side of the bed and gently got in, pulling the duvet high around her neck. She longed to reach out for her husband and pull herself closer to him but she was still cold from the garden and didn't want to disturb him. She closed her eyelids and, without expecting to, fell into a dreamless sleep.

*

When Mamie came upstairs with the coffee and found Angela and Robert both sleeping, she left them to it, and took the tray to Faith instead.

'Morning, Faith,' she trilled, putting the tray down on the blanket box at the end of the bed and pulling the curtains open. 'We have a garden party to prepare for.'

Faith, eyes squeezed shut, pulled her head under her covers. 'Close the curtains.'

'It's a beautiful day outside. Come on. I've made coffee. The team of volunteers will be here at eight.'

Faith's hand came from under the covers and, patting around her bedside table, found her phone and dragged it back inside the bed. 'Auntie Mamie, it's not even seven o'clock.'

'Early birds catch the worm. Would you like sugar?'

Faith's head, tousled hair and grumpy expression appeared. 'Sugar is a poison.'

'I know. But it's fun.' Mamie stirred a heaped teaspoonful into a mug and passed it to Faith. 'Drink. It'll chirp you up.'

'Urrggh.' Faith took the mug and drank. 'I'm so tired.'

'Well, you shouldn't be watching Netflix until all hours.'

'Like you don't.'

'That's entirely different. My brain no longer needs to work as it did. I have learnt about as much as I can get in it, and what I can't learn now I don't need or want to know.'

Faith wriggled up the bed. 'OK. What do you want me to do?'

'That's better. I have made lists for different working groups. You and Ben are in charge of putting up bunting, making arrow signs to direct visitors to the downstairs loo and a sign for the loo door. Also, you need to take Mr Worthington on a good walk so that he doesn't do anything embarrassing on the lawn. If there is time after that, you can both help me in the kitchen with making sandwiches. All clear?'

'Yes, Auntie Mamie.'

Mamie patted the long slender legs muffled by duvet. 'Good girl. Sarah is getting Ben over here by eight thirty and I shall have bacon rolls ready for whoever wants them. So, you'd best shake a leg. I don't want your mother to have to do anything today. Understood?'

Angela woke up to Robert's hand running over her tummy and hips. 'Morning,' he mumbled, nuzzling her neck the way he knew she liked.

'Morning,' she replied softly.

Later, as she lay in his arms, she thought about the idea of Robert and Helen together. She saw it now as preposterous and with some apology she said, 'Thank you for last night. It was wonderful. I'm sorry if I got a bit grumpy. I think I had too much wine.'

He hugged her closer. 'You have a lot on your plate. Do you honestly like your new dress?'

'It's amazing.'

'I was nervous that you might not like it. To be honest, there was a lovely little yellow dress with a flowery pattern and buttons down the front. It was the type of material that sort of moved nicely. I pulled it off the rail but by then Helen had found the other one. The shop assistant and Helen were very persuasive. Did I get it right?'

Angela hesitated for a moment. 'I would have liked anything you chose for me. The yellow one sounds lovely.'

'Yes, but the one you have is much more special, don't you think?'

'Maybe it's more Helen than me?'

'I think that's why I liked it. I like to see you looking glamorous. It's not often I get to see you all dressed up.'

Doubts crept back into Angela's mind. 'I'm sorry. I have let go of that sort of thing. Sorry.'

'Well, I've emailed the others and excused you from running club. So you've got all morning to get yourself dolled up.' Robert pulled his arm from under her and swung his legs out of bed. 'I'd better go and lend a hand. I promised Tony I'd help with the pop-up tea shelter. Bless him, he's worked so hard on the garden.'

He went to the bathroom, still talking about Tony's hanging baskets and patio pots while Angela lay in bed and turned the phrases 'I like to see you looking glamorous' and 'You've got all morning to get yourself dolled up' over and over in her mind.

It's true she had let her beauty regime, scant though it had been, go over the years. When was the last time she'd had a pedicure? Manicure? Or shaved her legs?

She curled herself into the foetal position, feeling vulnerable and undesirable. Helen was a million times prettier and more glamorous than she was. Robert was a lot more handsome than Piran was; although, she thought with a small amount of guilt, Piran was a very attractive man in a strong and manly way.

Oh God. Please, don't let Robert leave me for Helen. And please don't let me have these jealous thoughts about Helen either. Thank you.

When Robert had finished getting ready and gone off to find jobs to do, Angela began her personal spring clean in earnest.

25

The garden was filling with guests of all ages. Children were skipping between the legs of adults. Women in summery dresses were chatting and men in shorts were baring white and hairy knees. Angela stood at the landing window looking down at them. The garden really was looking pretty. Pale roses were mingling with deep blue delphiniums and the sweet peas, their canes among a carnival of pansies, were climbing with vigour.

Angela watched as Queenie opened her fold-up chair in the shade and settled herself beside Simple Tony, who was sitting cross-legged on the grass. She fumbled inside her enormous handbag and produced a carton of his favourite drink: Ribena.

And there was Mamie under the pop-up tent, ladling out punch from behind an old trestle table. She had claimed the previous night that it was a secret recipe she had been given by one of the royal Balmoral chefs. Angela could only imagine what was in it.

Faith strolled out from the kitchen into the sunlight

wearing sunglasses on top of her shiny hair, with a strapless boob tube and the tiniest pair of ripped denim shorts, which barely covered her bottom. Angela sighed. Where had her baby girl gone and how had she, mousy vicar, managed to produce such a gorgeous example of womanhood?

Smoothing her dress over her slender hips, Angela began to descend the stairs. Robert and Helen were in the kitchen when she appeared. Robert was leaning on the sink, Helen against a worktop, and they were sharing an easy conversation.

'Hi,' Angela said.

Robert looked up and a slight frown wrinkled his tanned forehead. 'Wow. Don't you look wonderful.'

'Thank you,' Angela said.

'Your dress looks lovely,' said Helen.

'What happened to the one I bought you?' Robert asked.

Angela touched her throat nervously. 'It's just too nice for a garden party. I want to keep it for a special occasion.'

Helen came towards her with open arms. 'You look fabulous anyway.' She kissed Angela and took her hand. 'Come on. Everyone's waiting for you.'

As Angela appeared on the sunny kitchen step, Mamie spotted her and immediately began a round of applause and a chorus of 'Happy Birthday'.

Mike Bates came forward. 'My dear, you look radiant.'

'It's just a bit of lipstick really.'

He turned to face the party. 'Ladies and gentlemen, may I have some quiet, please?'

A gradual hush fell over the guests.

'Our vicar, Angela, hasn't been with us long but I think we can all congratulate her on bringing a new freshness to our village. I am hoping that dear Simon will consider the pet

blessing as an annual event when he returns from Brazil.'
He turned to Angela and said, 'Angela, I thank you on behalf
of all Pendruggan residents, for giving us this year of your
life. And happy birthday.' He signalled to a small girl holding
a delicate posy, who came forward shyly and handed it to
Angela.

'Thank you. How kind of you.'

Happy applause followed before Mamie came to her with
a large cup of punch.

'What's in it?' Angela whispered suspiciously, looking at
the floating strawberries and bits of orange.

'Three of your five-a-day, darling. It will help you mingle.'

Angela took a sip and coughed. 'So this is where the
Christmas Cointreau went?'

Mamie did not reply but took her by the elbow. 'Come
along, we have some fun little contests for you to judge.'

Angela's face creased with anxiety. 'Really?'

Mamie stopped at a table decked prettily with a white lace
tablecloth and four crocheted dolls wearing enormous skirts.
She pressed a red winner's rosette into Angela's hand. 'First
up, a display of crochet work. Darling, which of these
delightful examples deserves first prize?'

Audrey, licking her lips and breathing heavily, hovered next
to a particularly ugly example: a dark-haired dolly in a purple
frock.

'Offerings from my crochet crafters circle,' Audrey told her.
'Such a marvellous hobby.'

Angela took a deep breath. 'Well, how charming. Any little
girl, or boy, would be delighted to have one.'

'These are not toys, Mrs Whitehorn. These are Decorative
Toilette Accessories.'

'Ah.' Angela was confused.

'Yes. These are placed over unsightly spare toilet tissue rolls. Certainly not toys.'

Angela bit her lip to stop laughing. 'Of course, what I meant was, any child would appreciate the fun of them.'

Audrey glared at her before fingering the purple monster next to her. 'So which one wins?' she asked with a malevolent glint in her eye.

'Well, let me have a good look at them.' Angela bent close to the figures and tried her best to find the one that was the least unattractive.

'Mum.' Faith pushed in between her and Audrey. 'Can Ben and I take Mr Worthington to the beach?' She glanced down at the loo paper dolls. 'Gruesome or what!'

'I am judging them, Faith.'

'Oh, well, the pale pink one is the least offensive, I suppose. So, can we go to the beach?'

'Yes. Don't be too long.' Faith skipped off and Angela caught Audrey's piggy eyes. 'And do you teach the crochet, Audrey?'

'Of course.'

'I thought as much.' Audrey's face was a picture of triumph. Angela continued, 'Because the purple one has the look of a professional's work.'

Audrey's lips twitched into a half-smile. 'Well yes, that one is mine. I was inspired by a portrait of Marie Antoinette.'

'How interesting.' Angela nodded. 'So you will understand that my decision must exclude yours because it is in a class of its own, and I would like to award the prize to the Pale Pink Lady.'

Mamie gave Angela a sideways glance and muttered, 'God, I am so proud of you.'

Audrey was puce, stuck between the conflicting emotions

of triumph and defeat. Mamie swore later that Audrey had actually growled before Mamie had swept Angela off to judge Best Buttonhole.

The afternoon wore on in a pleasant haze of sunshine, the Mums n' Dads hula-hoop contest and mountains of cucumber sandwiches and scones.

Feeling light-headed, Angela found Sarah sitting on a blanket in the shade with baby Santi sleeping peacefully in her large pram.

'Oh, how I'd like to be in her position,' Angela said, sitting next to her. 'Fresh air, covers off and legs akimbo.'

'How much punch have you had?' smiled Sarah.

'A bit too much, I think.'

'I've been keeping my eye on the new arrivals.' Sarah shifted her gaze in the direction of a burly man in his late forties with a can of strong beer in one hand and a peroxide blonde with plump thighs in the other.

Angela squinted at them. 'Oh, no. That's Malcolm. Evelyn's husband.'

'I wondered.'

'With the postmistress from Trevay?'

'Looks like it.'

'Where's Evelyn?'

'I'm not sure.' Sarah scanned the garden. 'Oh dear. She's just come out of the kitchen. See?'

Angela scrabbled to her feet. 'I'll cut her off. Warn her.'

Sarah put out a hand. 'Too late.'

The two of them watched helplessly as Evelyn stood immobile, stricken by the sight of her bullying husband and the public evidence of his mistress.

Afterwards it was agreed that Evelyn had shown tremendous turn of speed. Like quick-fire, she rushed at the shameful pair and began battering them with her 'good' handbag.

Angela ran to them. 'Evelyn. Evelyn. Come away. Stop.'

Evelyn, momentarily distracted from her attack, turned to see who was calling her. As she did so, her brutish husband pulled his right arm back and with clenched fist began to swing a punch at her. He didn't complete the move. Piran was already behind him and held back the muscled arm.

'Don't you touch her,' Piran threatened as he pulled the man back in an armlock. 'You were a bleddy bully at school and I should've knocked seven bells out of you on May Day when I had the chance.'

'Malcolm!' screamed the girlfriend as Evelyn squared up to her again. 'Stop her. She's mad.'

Robert arrived and put himself between the two women. 'What the hell is going on? Angela, call the police.'

Evelyn wasn't finished. The worm had well and truly turned.

'You're welcome to that pig. You're not the first and you won't be the last. He's not only a cheat, he's a bloody liar. I've had enough of being lied to, knocked about, made to feel worthless. He's all yours.'

The shackled Malcolm struggled fruitlessly to escape Piran's iron grip. 'Lou, don't listen to her. She's mad. She needs help. I've told you that already. You have to believe me.'

Lou stood confused and in turmoil. She asked Evelyn, 'He hit you?'

'Many times.'

She turned back to Malcolm. 'You said you'd never done it before. You said it was a mistake.'

'She's telling lies. I never hit her.' Malcolm was beginning to bleat.

Evelyn asked with a quiet triumph, 'He has hit you too, hasn't he?'

'Yes,' Lou said to the collective intake of breath of the bystanders. 'So that's why he came back to me on May Day. You had thrown him out?' She was slowly piecing it together. 'What else has he told you?'

'He's told me you're leaving the village to go and live in Brighton.'

'Brighton?' Evelyn began to laugh. 'This is ludicrous. Why'd I go to Brighton?'

'To look after your sister.'

'I don't have no sister, love. He's spinning you a yarn.'

'What?' Lou's face paled as she turned to look at Malcolm. 'Is there anything you've told me that's not a lie?'

'Lou, I told you. She needs help. She's mental,' smarmed Malcolm as Piran held him tighter. 'Ow. You'm hurting me,' Malcolm yelped.

Lou lifted one foot back and swung it forward, kicking Malcolm painfully on the shin.

'You cow,' he spat at her, hopping on his good leg. 'That's GBH, that is.'

Evelyn held out a hand of friendship to Lou. 'Get rid of him. I didn't have the strength for a long time.'

'You're pathetic, that's why,' Malcolm stumbled. 'I should have finished you off years ago.'

Robert spotted two policemen rounding the corner of the house and entering the back garden. 'Good afternoon, Officers. This is the gentleman you may like to speak to.'

Later, Mamie stretched out on the sofa, her sore feet on a cushion. 'Well, that was a garden party to remember. And weren't those policemen gorgeous? I rather enjoyed giving my witness statement, particularly when they asked me for my phone contact.' She sipped her gin and tonic. 'Thank God Evelyn won't be seeing that bully for a long time. Did you see how tight those handcuffs were? Not what I had expected at all. Reminds me of summers in Mykonos back in the seventies. I remember, during one party, Peter Sellers rocked up and of course took an instant shine to me. My boyfriend at the time had no idea who this guy was so – Angela, are you OK, darling?'

Angela was looking very pale. 'No, I don't feel good. Too much sun, I think.'

'Too much of Mamie's punch, more like,' laughed Robert from his armchair, where he was trying to find the football scores. 'You're dehydrated.'

Angela gritted her teeth. Irritated. 'Well, if you had not spent the afternoon hanging around Helen you might have hung around me and made sure I was all right.'

Robert turned to look at her. 'I beg your pardon?'

'You heard.'

Mamie held up a warning hand. 'Now now, you two.'

But Angela was finding her groove. 'I saw you. Laughing. Sharing your little jokes. It was embarrassing.'

Robert turned back to the screen. 'As I recall, you were too busy playing Mother Teresa to your Pals girls. You so enjoy doling out love and prayers, don't you?'

'I beg your pardon?'

'I'm not talking about this now. We'll talk tomorrow after you've had a good night's sleep.'

'I will not be dismissed like that. I think this is an excellent time.' Angela's head was swimming. 'Bloody fabulous Helen. With her excellent taste and freckles, choosing my birthday present that you should have chosen.'

Robert put the television on live pause and folded his arms. 'Is that why you didn't wear the dress?'

'What do you think?'

'I think you will regret this in the morning.'

Angela, truly riled, shouted, 'Are you having an affair with Helen?'

Mamie sighed. 'Darling, we've discussed this. You know Robert loves you.' She turned to Robert. 'Don't you? Tell her.'

Robert was shocked. 'Hang on. You have discussed this? You have discussed that I may be having an affair with Helen?'

'Well, you did spend a lot of time with her when you were getting the website up and running,' Mamie said.

Robert was aghast. 'I cannot be trusted with any woman I spend more than five minutes with? For God's sake! What the hell is going on here?'

Angela was feeling sick. 'What is the secret you are keeping?'

'What is that supposed to mean?'

'I know you have a secret.'

'What?'

'I was told.'

'This is crazy. Who told you?'

'I had a letter.'

Robert sat up. 'Another one? Who from?'

Angela was feeling sicker and sicker. 'The same. Anonymous.'

'Where is this letter?'

'Another one? What do you mean?' Mamie did not understand.

Angela answered Robert. 'In my bedside drawer.'

Robert leapt to his feet and, crossing the room, wrenched the lounge door open. 'I'm going to get it.'

Angela got unsteadily to her feet and said, 'I think I'm

going to be sick. Please don't tell Robert. You know his phobia about people being sick.' She ran to the downstairs loo.

Upstairs in the bedroom, Robert found the letter and read it with growing revulsion. Downstairs, he showed it to Mamie. 'Where is she?' he asked.

'Still in the loo.'

Robert paled. 'I can't deal with sick, you know that.'

'I know. Don't worry. My fault. I mixed one or two extra things into the punch. I forget that she doesn't have the stamina for alcohol the way I do.'

'Who do you think wrote this?'

'How the hell should I know?'

He sat down and said quietly, 'I would never cheat on her. Never. When we first met, I don't know if she ever told you, but I was very insecure. I had no faith in myself. Lack of self-esteem, the doctor called it. I was doing well but felt like an imposter, about to be found out. She was the only person I told and she stood by me. Got me help. She believed in me when I thought I was pointless. I even . . .' He hid his head in his hands. 'One night, I decided that I couldn't go on. I just wanted all my wretchedness to stop so I laid out a line of painkillers and began taking them, one at a time, in between sips of brandy. After about five pills my phone rang. It was her. I told her what I was doing and she made me promise to stop. She was there in minutes. Why would I betray her? I need her probably more than she needs me.'

The door opened and a shaky Angela came back in. Mamie held up the letter.

'We've read it. It's a lie.'

Robert stood up and took Angela into his arms. 'I'm so sorry. I wish you had shown me this as soon as it came.'

Angela was chilled and trembling. 'I thought it was a joke. A bad joke. I thought the "secret" must have been the dress. But that would mean Helen must have sent it. And it would mean that Helen was jealous of me and wanted you.'

She began to sob.

Mamie took control. 'Robert, take her upstairs and wash her face and teeth.'

Robert was reluctant. 'You're not going to be sick again, are you, Ange?'

She shook her head.

Mamie tutted. 'Robert dear, it's time for you to grow a pair. Get her upstairs and I'll bring water.' She looked at her niece's grey face and added, 'And a dry biscuit. This could be a long night.'

26

The warm sunshine of the garden party vanished the following day. A cold easterly pushed heavy cloud across the entire South West and heavy rain was forecast for later in the day.

Mamie, shaken by Angela's outburst the evening before, wrapped up and set off for Queenie's. She needed to get away from the tension at the vicarage.

'Do you want one of me pasties? Fresh from the oven this morning.' Queenie pointed at a tray with a dozen golden pasties on it. Mamie's stomach was not ready for them.

'No, thank you, darling.' Mamie swept her blond hair from her face. 'I barely slept last night. I need coffee.'

Queenie chuckled. 'What a caper that was, yesterday. Any news on Malcolm?'

'Angela is popping over after the service this morning to check on Evelyn. It was all very upsetting. Angela was rather disturbed by it. It's a wonder she's managed to get to church but she'd never let everybody down. She got herself very upset.'

'Well, she would. She's a kind woman.'

'Not just about Evelyn . . .'

'Oh?' Queenie's eyes lit up as she sensed fresh gossip. 'What's rattled her pearls then?'

Mamie bit her lip; she had promised Robert and Angela that she wouldn't discuss Angela's unfounded jealousy, with Queenie or anyone else.

'She, er, had a little too much sun and perhaps I made the punch a bit too . . . punchy.'

Queenie cackled. 'She got pissed, did she? Hungover? Well, we've all done it, ain't we?'

'Yes. She was rather sick and I sat with her until she slept.'

'Poor gel, but it's Evelyn I feel for. We never knew none of that was going on. What's going to happen to the farm? I mean, it's been in Malcolm's family for donkey's years. I suppose those two lummocks of sons will have to pull their fingers out. Evelyn won't be able to manage on her own.'

'She'll need a ton of support. And not just on the farm.'

'She loves them boys. One of 'em's all right. The other's a right little terror. Always was.' Queenie began to get out of her chair, bending from the hips, and groaning in discomfort. 'I'll get the coffee on.'

Mamie had seen this ruse too many times to be sympathetic. 'Just ask me and I'll do it. You don't have to do this old lady act for my benefit, you know.'

Queenie looked sharply at Mamie, then sat down again, cackling. 'It was worth a try.'

Mamie went to the stairs that led up to Queenie's living quarters.

'There's a tin of biscuits by the sink. Bring them down too,' shouted Queenie over her shoulder.

'What did your last servant die of?' Mamie called back before disappearing.

Alone in her shop, Queenie closed her eyes. Mamie would be gone long enough for her to have a little snooze.

The front door of Pendruggan farmhouse, short and wide, was built of oak so ancient that lichen was clinging to its silvered panelling. There remained scars of locks long gone and heavy boot scuffs. Angela lifted the heavy, copper knocker, stained with verdigris.

Angela heard some quiet scuffling as footsteps approached from the other side of the door. Evelyn opened it, just enough for her cautious eyes to glance at Angela and check that no one else was around.

'Hello,' Angela said. 'I've come to see how you are. I thought you might need a friendly ear.'

Evelyn said nothing but the door was widened just enough for Angela to slip through.

She shut the door behind them and walked the long, dark, uneven passage to the kitchen.

'Will you want tea?' she asked.

'Thank you.'

'Find a seat.' Evelyn's voice was flat.

Angela looked around at the kitchen strewn with wellington boots, newspapers, and a dog basket by the old Rayburn. The dog, a collie mix, lifted her head and barked.

'Shut up, Prim,' Evelyn ordered.

Prim gave Angela a warning growl then settled back to her doggy dreams.

Angela pulled the nearest chair out from the cluttered table and disturbed a bony cat sleeping on a thin feather cushion.

'Don't worry about her. Blossom, get off that cushion.' The cat stayed where she was.

'I won't disturb her. I'll sit here instead.' Angela pulled out another chair – this one animal free – and sat down.

Evelyn brought an old brown teapot, covered by a knitted cosy, and two mugs to the table.

'Prim is missing Malcolm. She's normally out all day with him.'

'And how about you?' asked Angela. 'Are you missing him?'

'No.' Evelyn was very firm.

Angela nodded. 'And where are your sons?'

'Tommy's out somewhere. I'm expecting him back soon. He did the milking this morning. He's a good boy. And Jimmy, he's at the police station.'

'Seeing his dad?'

'No. Been arrested. Last night police stopped his car. Drunk driving.'

'Oh, no.'

Evelyn shrugged. 'He's too much like his dad. Always been trouble. But he's old enough now to clear up his own mess.'

'I'm so sorry,' Angela said.

'Oh, don't be. Me and Tom, we'll be all right. He said to me this morning that we're best off without Malcolm. Mum, he said, we can be happy with him gone. Him and Jimmy won't be drinking and gambling away all the farm profits, what there is, anyway. And it's quiet. I feel safer than I have since before I was married.'

'Have the police been in touch?' Angela asked.

Evelyn nodded. 'Yeah, they released Malcolm this morning on condition that he doesn't come within two hundred yards of me or the house.'

'Good.'

They drank their tea, the old kitchen clock ticking in the silence between them.

The first drops of light rain spattered on the windows. Evelyn pushed her foot under Prim's legs and tickled the dog with her socked toes.

'I been unlucky, that's all,' she said.

'How?'

'Marrying that arsehole. Some women seem to marry the right one first go. Look at you and your husband. You can tell he loves you. He'd never run off with a fat, brassy bint, would he?'

Angela felt ashamed, remembering all the accusations she had thrown at Robert last night. Did she honestly believe he would have an affair?

'No.'

A shard of lightning lit the gloomy room as the rain increased.

'Here it comes,' said Evelyn.

A crack of thunder jolted them both.

'I'd better get home.' Angela did up her jacket. 'But, Evelyn, anything you need, please know I am here for you.'

As the old farmhouse door closed behind her Angela looked at the sky. It was darkening. Black rainclouds billowed like bruises. She made a dash for home, desperate suddenly to see Robert and ask for forgiveness. He and Mamie had been right. She had been doing too much. She needed to take things more slowly. Get some perspective. Be a good and proper wife.

In the village shop, Mamie and Queenie were deep in the realms of storytelling.

'But in those days, Marrakesh was wildly romantic. No package tours. No rules. We all did yoga, naked, in the early morning. I can still feel the warmth of the mosaic floor beneath my bottom and hear the fountains splashing in their timeless pools.' Mamie stretched her arms over her head, reliving the moment.

Queenie was gaping. 'But what happened with Warren Beatty?'

'I turned him down, of course,' Mamie said virtuously. 'Sweet, sweet boy that he was. But not my type.'

Outside the rain was beginning to gather pace and weight. The shop grew dimmer. Only the peach light of Queenie's table lamp on the counter offered a glow as Mamie, her mind still in Morocco, continued.

'Did I tell you about my dinner with Churchill? That was in Casablanca. We were both en route to Blighty and found ourselves on the same train to the ship. I have always found talent and intelligence the ultimate aphrodisiacs.'

Queenie's mouth dropped. 'Winston? Winston Churchill?'

'Yes.' Mamie laughed. 'Not the prime minister. His grandson. Winston Junior. So charming and damnably handsome.'

'Did you . . . er . . . you know . . . with him?'

'He was already in love with the woman who became his first wife, but he was an excellent flirter. He gave me a necklace and matching anklet of silver bells. He said he wanted me to wear them always. To remind me of him and the innocent fun we had. Of course, we were both so young. In our twenties.'

'Have you still got his jewellery?'

'Certainly.'

'Can I see them?'

'I shall dig them out for you.'

The rain began to hammer against the shop windows, bouncing off the pavement beyond and battering Queenie's geraniums in their tubs.

The flash of lightning lit the village green, giving it an almost emerald quality.

'But enough of my stories.' Mamie knew when to stop.

'What about you? I hope you had some misspent adventures?'

'Oh, I had my moments when I was courting my hubby.' A roll of thunder bounced around the village.

'That's God telling you off for being a naughty girl,' Mamie laughed.

'I certainly was not as naughty as you!' Queenie told her. 'I was evacuated, you see. Had to leave my mum in the East End and come here, to Cornwall. Bloody long train ride, that was. The last time I saw my mum, she was waving to me from the platform at Paddington. My mum caught a bomb in the Blitz. Nothing much left of the house, but they told me they found her all in one piece under the kitchen table. Sheltering, you see. Bless her. But I wasn't allowed to go to the funeral. Train would be too expensive and I was considered too young to go. That it would upset me too much.' Her fingers found a cotton hanky under her sleeve and she wiped her eyes. 'It still upsets me. I don't even know where her grave is.'

A second lightning bolt lit the heavy sky.

Mamie remained silent, knowing that Queenie would rebuff any hug; she was too proud for that. So instead she asked, 'What about your father?'

Queenie coughed her rattly cough and reached for her tobacco bag. 'His ship was sunk by the *Bismarck*. Killed in action. To be honest I'm glad my mum never knew about it.'

'And no brothers or sisters?'

'I'm the only one left.' Queenie cleared her throat and rolled one of her fags. 'You never said, but did you never marry?'

Mamie laughed her throaty laugh. 'Never. Not for me.'

'Never wanted no children?'

'God, no. My sister did all that for me. Married, had Angela and then when Angela's father died, I stepped up to be Alpha Aunt. That's quite enough for me.'

Outside the black sky continued to let drop its torrential rain. Another clap of thunder rattled the shop's windows. Both women jumped nervously as the shop door blew open, jangling the bell above it.

'Sorry,' said Angela, standing drenched on the threshold. 'The wind took the door from my hand.'

'Well, close it quick. The rain's coming in,' Mamie told her. 'You look half drowned.'

Angela forced the door shut. 'I've come for a good bottle of wine. What have you got?'

Queenie arranged herself a little more comfortably into her chair. 'First of all, what's the news about Evelyn and that brute of a husband?'

'Oh, Queenie, you know how I feel about gossip. I'm sure Evelyn will tell you herself. Now, I'd like a good bottle of red, if you have it?'

Mamie smiled. 'Ah. I get it. You and Robert have made up?'

Queenie was on it like a cat on a catnip mouse. 'Had a falling-out, have you?'

Angela's eyes darted to Mamie, but Mamie shook her head in denial. Angela's eyes narrowed slightly but decided to believe that her aunt had not been indiscreet after all.

'Robert and I have never been better, thank you.'

Queenie rustled up a dusty bottle of Merlot. 'I hope it does you good, duck,' she told Angela as Angela was leaving the shop. 'It'll sort your hangover out a treat.'

Angela threw her aunt an accusatory look.

'I told her nothing.' Mamie held her hands up. 'Honestly.'

27

Angela put away her jealousy and decided to at least try to forget the anonymous letters. Both Robert and Mamie agreed that they must have been written by someone very unhappy but not dangerous.

Angela made even more effort to be the perfect vicar. Helpful and welcoming. Although she still felt slightly threatened by Helen, there was no evidence to suggest that Helen was interested in anyone but Piran.

Mamie told her, 'You are not going to be here for ever. You can afford to trust them. Have them over for dinner. They are good people.'

Angela knew her aunt was right.

Gradually, June gave way to July and thoughts began to turn to the next Pendruggan event: the Big Village Pond Dig.

Mike had worked tirelessly to gather the relevant paperwork and permissions from the council, and digging was confirmed for the first weekend of the summer holidays.

He arrived at the vicarage two days before it was due to begin, pink with excitement.

'I say,' he beamed at Mamie and Robert, 'a crew from Coast Atlantic TV want to do a background piece on the search for the pond.'

Robert was impressed. 'That's excellent. If you'd like me to be around that day, offer some guidance, I'd be glad to. What day are they coming?'

'Friday.'

'Oh damn. I won't be here. I'm over in Lostwithiel reviewing the antique shops and auction rooms. They're having a sale of vintage garden equipment.'

Mamie patted Robert's shoulder. 'I am sure we can do without you. Coffee, Mike?'

'Don't let them make you out to be yokels,' Robert said knowingly. 'Stick to the facts.'

'I'm sure we'll be OK.' Mike accepted Mamie's coffee. 'You look very lovely today, Mamie.'

Mamie was wearing a figure-hugging summer dress exposing just enough cleavage and leg.

'Oh, darling. This old thing? I bought it yonks ago in St Tropez.'

'St Tropez, eh?' Mike settled himself on a kitchen chair. 'I was there in the sixties.'

'Me too! Did you ever see Bardot?'

'Sadly not, but I remember one morning . . .'

Robert excused himself. 'I'd love to stay and chat but I really must get on.'

Closing the door behind him, he bumped into Angela in the hall. 'If I were you I wouldn't go into the kitchen. Mike is busy chatting Mamie up. Or it may be the other way around.'

'Not again. He's been here almost every day this week. I wish he'd just ask her out to dinner or something.'

The kitchen door opened and a giddy Mike and Mamie stepped out. 'Mike is taking me for some lunch.' She turned to him. 'Are you sure I look all right in this old thing?'

'My dear, it is I who should ask if I look smart enough to escort you,' Mike replied.

Robert opened the front door. 'Go on, you two. Shoo and don't come back until teatime. Angie and I have a lot of work to get on with and we could do without any interruptions.'

Mamie handed Mike the keys to the Jensen with a flirty, 'Would you like to drive?'

'I'd be honoured.'

Robert and Angela waved them off and were finally on their own.

'Have you got a copy deadline?' Angela said to Robert as she headed for her office.

'No.' He leant against the doorframe. 'Have you got urgent stuff to see to?'

'No. Not urgent. Why?'

He held his hand out to her. 'Come to bed.'

'It's the middle of the day . . .'

'Which means that somewhere in the world it's midnight and the stars are shining.'

'Oh.'

'So?'

'Well, I do need a lie-down,' she said provocatively, 'and you,' she pinched his tummy, 'could do with the exercise so . . .'

'Race you.'

It was early in the morning before the Big Dig that the local TV crew rolled into the village.

The reporter, a handsome, cocky young man called Brad,

climbed out of the Land Rover Discovery with his cameraman and adjusted his tie.

'You get the gear out, Nige, I'll go and knock up a few locals.'

His first pick was Candle Cottage, home to Polly, the white witch and paramedic.

Polly answered the door in her dressing gown.

'Can I help you?' she yawned.

'Hi, good morning. I'm Brad Taylor of Coast Atlantic TV. I'd like to talk to you about the Big Pond Dig.'

Polly tightened her dressing gown around her and rubbed her eyes. 'What time is it?'

'Just coming up for seven.'

'I haven't had my breakfast yet.'

Brad was not to be put off. He turned on the full beam of his telly persona. 'I've arrived at a bad time. I can see that. I know it's early. Nige, my cameraman, and I haven't had a chance to have breakfast ourselves. But my boss is very keen that I capture the whole story of the Big Pond Dig, right from the start.'

Polly looked over Brad's shoulder to Nige, who gave her a cheery wave. 'I'm making tea if you want some. And I could make some toast?'

Brad put his hand behind his back and gave Nige a thumbs up.

'That's very kind of you. Only, I prefer coffee.'

Over breakfast, Brad drew a lot of information from an unwitting Polly. 'So you work in the NHS but off-duty you are the village witch?'

'Oh, yes. There's always been one here. There's talk that if the pond is there, they'll build a ducking stool and drown me.' Polly smiled at the idea. 'It's a joke, of course.'

'Golly, I hope so. Lovely woman like you.' Brad looked deep into her eyes. 'Suppose Nige and I clear up these breakfast things while you get dressed and you can take us down to the pond site? Give us a little interview?'

'I suppose I could.'

'It'll be so interesting to our viewers and I can tell you'll be a natural on camera.' He started to help her towards the stairs of her tiny cottage. 'Nige and I will get everything shipshape down here.'

'I don't have to put make-up on, do I? 'Cos I don't wear it.'

'A natural beauty, now off you go.'

Half an hour later, standing in the bright morning sun, Polly was put in front of Nige's camera.

'Just look at me,' said Brad. 'Not at the camera. Forget it's there. And if you could try not to squint.'

'But the sun's right in my eyes.'

'All the better to light your radiant beauty. OK, Nige?'

'Rolling.'

Brad began, 'With me now is a woman known as the White Witch of Pendruggan. Polly, you were telling me earlier that many people believe this spot to be haunted.'

'I haven't ever seen anything myself, but I remember my friend's mum telling us when we were little that she had seen the ghost of a woman wearing an old-fashioned dress and a sort of mobcap on her head. She said it was Loony Lydia, a witch what lived here hundreds of years ago. She told us they drowned her. My friend and I used to come down here and scare ourselves half to death. Funny really.'

'I understand that, on certain nights,' Brad continued, 'screams are heard right here in Shellsand Lane? The very place where the lost pond is supposed to be?'

Nige slowly pushed his lens into a big close-up on Polly.

'Yes, I have heard that said. There's always someone who swears they heard something. Especially on Halloween.' Polly laughed. 'But it's probably a gull on his way home.'

'So, Polly, as a white witch, will you be on hand to channel any spirits, good or bad, that may be disturbed by the dig?'

'Erm, I am interested to see if the pond is there and I will certainly cast a protection spell around the volunteer diggers . . .'

'A protection spell!' Brad almost wet himself with excitement. Polly the fruit loop was telly gold.

'Yes. Of course.'

'So you think the disturbance of the land here could awaken some negative energy?' He was almost rubbing his hands with glee. His editor was going to love this.

'It's possible that the earth goddess may be upset.' Polly tried to pick her words carefully. 'Which is why I will keep a vigil, camping out, and keeping an eye on any adverse happenings.'

'What exactly are you worried about?'

'Unexplained accidents, people falling ill or feeling unwell. Just the usual sort of thing when negative forces are released.'

'Or a curse?' He was hitting his stride.

'Yes,' Polly agreed. 'A hundred years ago or so there was talk of a curse. We don't know if this is true or not but there was a story of a farmer losing his entire herd after they had been watered at the pond.'

'So it may be poisoned, even today?'

'I don't know about poisoned but—'

'And who will join you for the vigil? I mean, there can't be many people, who'd want to sit up all night, in the dark, next to a haunted pond.'

'Oh, I won't be on my own. I will have my cat, Myrtle, with me.'

'A familiar? Isn't that the right term for a witch's cat?'

'Yes, but Myrtle is more a moggie.'

'Does she sit on the back of your broomstick?'

'Don't be daft.' Polly laughed nervously.

'Does Myrtle help in your spells?'

'Of course not. No. Nothing like that. She is my friend. She likes to cuddle up to me. She will keep me quite warm in the tent.'

'One last question. Will you be prepared to perform an exorcism if needed?'

'Oh, no. That's more the vicar's line.'

'Thank you, Polly.' Brad turned to the camera. 'Sounds like the vicar is my next port of call on my search for the Lost Pond of Pendruggan.'

He was more than pleased. Dropping his professional smile, he said, 'Cut there, Nige,' before turning to Polly and shaking her hand. 'Thank you for your time and good luck with it all. Rather you than me!'

'Rev Whitehorn?' He smiled as Angela opened the vicarage door.

'Yes?'

'Hello. I'm Brad Taylor from Coast Atlantic TV. I'd love to talk to you about the Big Dig.'

Angela welcomed him. 'Do come in.'

'Actually, I was wondering if I could interview you, on camera, outside your beautiful church. Would you be free in, say, half an hour?'

Angela checked her watch. 'Yes, but I can't give you very long. I have a meeting with the chair of the parish council.

Do you know him? Mike Bates. You might want to interview him too.'

Brad couldn't believe how easily this was all falling into his lap.

'Super. But I'd like you on your own first. My cameraman and I will have a look around the churchyard and find the best spot to use.'

'OK. Give me twenty minutes?'

'Perfect.'

Standing with the church clock tower behind her, in a spot where buttercups mingled with the long grass and forget-me-nots, Angela took a couple of deep breaths to calm her nerves.

'Just look at me, not the camera. Nige, are you rolling?'

'Yep.'

'Angela Whitehorn is the vicar of Pendruggan Church.'

'Hello,' said Angela.

'Where does the church stand on rumours that the pond might be cursed?'

'I am not a believer in curses.' She gave what she hoped was a reassuring smile. 'But I do believe that scary stories can feed the imagination.'

'You mean people can believe that a curse is real?'

'Without any proof whatsoever, yes.'

'I have been talking to Polly, your village witch, and she firmly believes that the pond is haunted by the women who were drowned there as witches.'

'Does she?' Angela frowned.

'Oh, yes. She has told me that she will cast protection spells in case of negative activity from paranormal energies.'

'I don't believe in spells but there are many ancient rites that are used today as a bit of fun.'

'She seemed very serious.' Brad rubbed his chin, hoping to look deeply intelligent. 'She also told us that, if necessary, you would perform a service of exorcism. That doesn't sound like "just a bit of fun" to me.'

'What?' Angela was thrown off-balance. 'There will be no need for any exorcisms. This is nonsense. This is a family fun weekend.' She turned to look straight down the camera lens. 'Come and join us as we dig to discover the mystery of the Pendruggan pond. Thank you.'

She held her hand up to cover the lens. 'Thank you, Mr Taylor. That is quite enough. Now, if you'll excuse me, I have pressing things to do.'

Angela went back home and immediately alerted Mike Bates and anyone else on the Big Dig committee not to speak to Brad Taylor. She watched from her office window as Brad and Nige climbed into their crew car and drove out of the village.

Then she picked up the phone and rang Polly and was relieved to hear exactly what she had said.

At six o'clock that night all Pendruggan inhabitants were in front of their televisions.

Polly invited Tony, who lodged in her old shepherd's hut in the back garden, to watch the report. Tony didn't like what he saw and heard.

'I don't want no ghosts and spooky things coming to find me. I will fight them but I will be scared,' he told her.

Polly opened the box of crystals she kept by her chair and gave him three. 'Put one by the door, one in your pocket, and one under your pillow and you'll be fine. And, just to be sure, I will draw a circle of protection around your hut. You won't see me do it. I'll do it when you're asleep. Nothing will get you or me. I promise.'

Tony felt a bit better. 'OK. And the vicar said she'd make sure I was OK too. Going to say a prayer for me.'

'Double protection,' smiled Polly. 'That's good.'

'Are you sure you will be safe?' he asked again. His deep brown eyes, as trusting as a Labrador puppy's, melted Polly's heart. 'I don't want the spookies getting you.'

'Bless you, Tony. I am strong. The force of good always wins over evil.'

'Like the Doctor in her Tardis?'

'Exactly like the Doctor.'

'That makes me feel a lot better.'

Piran appeared at the vicarage with a couple of very old survey maps and spread them on the kitchen table.

'Who doesn't like an old map?' Robert said as he pored over the sepia markings. 'The vicarage looks a different shape to what it is now. Smaller.'

'Aye,' Piran said. ''Twas added to around 1912 and some of the land sold off to the farm, see.' He pointed a thick-knuckled finger to the east.

'How old is this map?'

'There's a date at the bottom. 1881.'

'Let me see,' said Angela, getting in between the shoulders of the two men. 'Where's the pond supposed to be?'

Piran pointed again. 'There. The lane to Shellsand was only a footpath in those days.'

'And where is the pond source coming from?' Angela asked, peering at the faded lines and shading.

'Probably diverted water from an old mine shaft.'

Angela straightened up. 'What's your theory as to why it's dry now, Piran?

'Mebbe there's a blockage. Mebbe the underground source

found a different path to the sea or mebbe it's still there, just hidden by undergrowth.'

Robert rubbed his chin. 'I thought you and Gasping Bob found signs of marshy ground?'

'Oh, aye, we did. Which is hopeful. But we won't be sure of anything till we dig.'

The doorbell rang.

'That'll be Digger Pete,' said Piran. 'Sure you don't mind him parking on your drive for the night?'

'Not at all,' replied Angela. 'Robert, let him in and I'll find some beers for you all.'

Robert and Piran went out together to admire the old pale blue digger. Pete was only too happy to demonstrate its skills. 'Stand back while I turn 'er on again. Can get a bit smoky.'

He turned the key and a black plume of hot exhaust belched into the warm evening air.

The three men stood rapt as the old digger rattled and chugged, changing its tune each time Pete adjusted the choke or revved the throttle.

'How long have you had her?' Robert shouted over the noise.

'Since 1988. Second-hand. Had her rebuilt and fine-tuned. Lovely bit of kit.' Pete turned the engine off.

'Can anyone drive one of these things?' Robert asked.

'You'm want a go, do you?' said Pete, jumping down from the small cab.

'Course he does,' Piran smiled. 'Don't we all?'

'I'd love to.' Robert stuck his hands in his pockets, feeling fourteen. He was desperately keen to have a go.

'The answer's no,' Pete said in a way that brooked no argument. 'You'm not insured.'

Robert was disappointed. 'Understood, understood.'

Angela appeared at the front door and called them in. 'Beers are in the kitchen.'

While the men had been outside, she had made a pile of cheese and pickle sandwiches, which were now sitting in the middle of the kitchen table.

'Oh, ideal,' said Pete, rubbing his hands hungrily.

'Take a seat, Pete,' Angela offered. 'And if you don't mind, I shall leave you three to it. I'm going to have a bath and an early night.' She gave Piran a pat on the shoulder as she walked past. 'Have a lovely time talking about maps and diggers. By the way, there are three more beers in the fridge.'

'Thank you, maid. See you in the morning,' Piran said, reaching for a sandwich.

Robert smiled lovingly at her. 'You all right, darling?'

'I'm fine.' She kissed his head.

'I won't be late myself.' Robert kissed her hand. 'Love you. And thanks for the beer and sandwiches.'

Robert had been a model husband since the upsetting night of the garden party.

Angela had fought hard to take the fantasy images of him and Helen out of her head, but every now and then a spasm of hateful doubt triggered a tsunami of anxiety through her.

Robert came up to bed just as she was closing her book, ready to sleep.

'Hey,' he said, bending over her and pushing her short curls from her forehead. 'I thought you'd be asleep.'

'Almost.'

He kissed her. 'Give me a minute and I'll join you.'

Once in bed, he curled himself around her. 'Piran's a good bloke, you know.'

'That's why Helen is with him.'

'Yes,' he said smoothly. 'Pete's a good lad too. He's giving his time for free this weekend. Great, isn't it?'

'Very kind.'

'That's life in a village, I suppose. Everyone mucking in to help. By the way, have you got your pond blessing all written?'

'I'd like you to look at it in the morning. It was quite hard. I checked the internet for blessings of water, and although there are a few, nothing seemed quite to fit. I hope I've sort of got a good balance between the religious and the secular. I'm looking forward to the weekend. I wonder what we'll find.'

Robert didn't reply. 'Robert?'

She lifted herself to see his face. His lips were slightly parted, eyes shut. Asleep already.

He looked so handsome, sometimes she couldn't believe he was actually her husband. 'Night night, my love,' she whispered and turned the light out.

28

The sun rose in a crystal-sapphire sky. Not a cloud or a breath of wind would spoil the day's excavations.

Around the village, Pendruggan families were having breakfasts, making packed lunches and rummaging for wellies and sun cream.

They had been asked to be at the site of the pond by nine o'clock, for Angela and Polly to each bless the day's work and workers.

The television piece had attracted many sightseers. Cars and camper vans were arriving packed with fold-up chairs, dogs and excitable children. Soon, the outer edges of the village green were blotted out by a tight line of glinting windscreens and hot metal.

The lane to the pond was clogged with pedestrians and pushchairs, picnic hampers and cool boxes. An ice cream van rumbled behind them, its painted bodywork covered in pictures of 99s, lollies and cold drinks, cranking the children's excitement to beyond any warp factor known to man.

By the pond, Pete was standing next to his digger. Hands

in his overalls. Proud of his role. Next to him, Gasping Bob leant on one of Pete's grave-digging spades, smoking.

Piran had been collared by a group of French holiday-makers who wanted to know about the pond's curse. 'You need to speak to Polly over there,' he grunted. 'She's the one believes in all that crap.'

'*Merci, Monsieur. Merci beaucoup.*' They rushed to Polly, overwhelming her with questions and selfies.

Angela stood quietly by with Mamie and Robert.

'What a great turnout.' Mamie patted Angela's arm. 'Queenie's going to make a bomb on her pasties today.'

'Do I look all right?' asked Angela, fiddling with her dog collar. 'Does this work with my shirt?'

Mamie swept her eyes over Angela's outfit. A short-sleeved checked skirt and denim shorts. 'The picture of a modern vicar, my dear.'

'Thank you.'

Robert was unsure about any of it. 'Do you really need to do this? I mean, Polly will do her earth goddess bit, which is fine, but do you need to bring God into this?' Having read through her short speech of blessing that morning, he had misgivings. 'After that ridiculous report on the local news.'

Irritated and nervous, Angela said, 'It is a blessing. That's all. Very simple. I'm not giving a sermon or conjuring up lucky djinns.'

He reached for the phone in his pocket. 'Text from Faith. She wants me to fix the brakes on her bike.'

'Now?' asked Angela.

'Yeah. She's going on a ride with Ben, apparently.'

'I thought she was coming down here?'

'She will later.' He pecked her cheek. 'I'd better go. Give me a call if you need me. Good luck.'

Angela watched as he walked away. Mamie took her arm. 'Buck up, darling. Men are a shower of utter shites. Don't worry about Robert. I am here for you. Today is very much your day.'

Piran strode to the centre of the surrounding crowd and clapped his hands for attention.

'Can I have a bit of quiet, please? Right.' He turned on the spot, eyeing them up, until the crowd hushed. 'All villages have or had a pond at some point in their history. Back in the day they were a valuable water source for humans and animals. They were also the laundry place, the gossip place and, as I'm sure you will have heard on the telly last night, a place to put the local witches on trial by ducking.'

He turned to find Polly, standing with Simple Tony, and pointed at her. 'Polly there is a true twenty-first-century woman. A paramedic. A good one. Five hundred years ago a woman like her, with medical knowledge, would have been placed on a ducking stool and probably drowned, right here.' He pointed to the ground beneath their feet. The crowd laughed nervously.

Piran continued, 'But Polly, modern woman that she is, has a foot in the history of the sixteenth century. Polly,' he held his arm out to her, 'come and tell us your story.'

Polly stepped forward, receiving a spattering of uncertain applause. She was wearing a loosely floating, long dress; her dark hair, parted in the middle, hung in curly clouds either side of her pale Celtic face.

She was barefoot and holding a branch of what looked like dead leaves woven with twine.

'Hello.' She smiled and lifted her arms, the sleeves of her

dress falling back to her shoulders to reveal strong arms. 'Are there any children here who believe in magic?'

A few children put their hands up. Others crept into their mothers' skirted knees and buried their faces with maybe half an eye uncovered.

'I do,' she continued. 'I do a little bit of good magic to help people now and again because I am a white witch. Have you heard of white witches?'

A couple of families began to look uncomfortable, passing looks to their partners that said, *Let's get the kids away from this mumbo jumbo.*

'Is that your wand?' asked a small boy boldly. A small girl with bunched hair grabbed his hand and shushed him. 'Get off,' he told her. 'You wanted to know.'

'I'm scared,' she whispered loudly.

'There is nothing to be scared of,' Polly said cheerfully. 'This is a sort of wand.' She held it out for all to see. 'It is made from the leaves of sage and myrtle. Very good plants that will protect us and help with psychic awareness. I like myrtle so much, I named my cat after it. You might see her later. A little tabby with green eyes.'

The little girl pulled the corners of her lips down and showed her teeth. 'I'm scared,' she said again.

Polly smiled. 'Don't be sacred of my Myrtle. She likes a tickle round the ears so give her one of those and she'll be your friend.' The little girl managed a tiny smile. Polly went on, 'I am here today to make sure that the spirits guarding this place are happy.'

'What sort of spirits?' asked the boy. 'Are they like fairies? My sister believes in fairies. Don't you?' He looked down at the little girl gripping his arm.

'Yes.'

'Ah well,' Polly said. 'Fairies, elves and all sorts could be here and I don't want them to be upset by the digger so, in case they are listening, I'm going to tell them it will all be all right. Would you all please hold hands to form an unbroken circle.'

She closed her eyes and took a deep breath. Slowly she began to turn on the spot, waving the sage and myrtle branch. 'Mother Goddess, purify this long-lost water and bless this sacred land with your ancient powers and bless all here with your loving light.'

She stopped turning, held the branch high, opened her eyes and smiled. 'Perfect. What marvellous energy you have given me. You may feel a little woozy after that but it will pass quickly. Now, may I ask the vicar of Pendruggan, Angela Whitehorn, to give us her blessing.'

Angela stepped forward and Polly returned to Simple Tony's side. 'Well done,' he whispered.

'Thank you, Polly,' said Angela. She looked over to Mamie for reassurance, who gave her a thumbs up.

Angela took a breath and began, 'Let us pray. Dear Lord, bless the work we do here today. May we find water that is pure and may the workers stay safe. Help us make this a day that will be remembered well. We thank you. Amen.'

Before Angela could open her eyes, she heard the unmistakable tones of Audrey Tipton. 'Mrs Whitehorn! Mrs Whitehorn!'

Angela opened her eyes. Audrey was pushing her way through the throng. 'That ice cream van cannot, cannot, stay where it is. Geoffrey is bringing the off-roader down in a minute. You must tell the driver of the van to move.'

Audrey was a sight. The normal tweeds and brogues had been replaced with ageing tennis shorts, at least three sizes too small, which showed her Queen Anne legs to the worst possible advantage. Her top half was sporting a T-shirt with the message 'Beethoven at Bognor, 1983'.

'Can you not ask the driver, Audrey?' Angela asked, trying not to laugh.

'He will not listen to me.' Audrey was scarlet. 'Is Robert here?'

Angela thought she saw a flush of extra red in Audrey's face. 'He's at home.'

'Well, get him down here,' ordered Audrey.

Angela felt in her pockets and then in her shoulder bag, then in her pockets again. 'Gosh. I must have left my phone at home.'

Mamie, watching, sighed and stepped in. 'Audrey dear. Whatever is the matter? Let me help.' Audrey allowed herself to be swept off.

Mamie glanced over her retreating shoulder and gave Angela a big wink.

Angela blew her a kiss.

Piran took centre stage once more. 'May I have your attention, please? Would you all step back to behind the blue paint-line on the grass?' He pointed to the digger next to him. 'This is a dangerous bit of kit. Kids, listen to me, that big bit on the front,' he pointed to the heavily toothed digger arm. 'That bit there will swing from side to side, digging and emptying whatever is under here. So, keep your parents from being stupid, would you?'

The adults smiled. The children giggled. Piran carried on. 'As long as you keep yourselves and your dogs behind that line, you'll be safe. OK? And to make sure you don't step over the line. Bob there, and Mike Bates, are going to put up a temporary barrier.'

Gasping Bob helpfully indicated the blue line and encouraged people to move out of the way. 'Right back, please. Right back. We'm putting up some poles and orange tape for your safety so step right back please.'

The site was at last made safe and ready. Mike Bates checked that all was secure and, after a final reminder to keep back behind the orange tape and blue line, Digger Pete started up the old machine.

'Ooh,' went the crowd, one or two of the younger children screaming with shock at the sudden noise.

''Tis all right,' shouted Piran. ''Tis a noisy beggar but by lunchtime we could be down to the water level. OK, let's have a countdown. Three. Two. One.'

He lifted his right arm and dropped it, signalling to Pete to roll the digger forward and begin.

The caterpillar tracks moved him to the centre of the irregular circle. The heavy arm dropped towards the deep grass. Pete manoeuvred the stick handles in the cab, and the great metal teeth bit into the vegetation. The Big Dig had begun.

The sun was rising fast in the bright July sky and the crowd was growing by the minute.

After every scoop was dragged out and tipped into the nearby skip, Piran, Bob and Mike Bates went to see what lay beneath. Each time they turned to Pete with thumbs down and Pete would start again.

The morning wore on . . . with nothing to see.

Those who had been there since the beginning began to drift down the lane and onto the beach of Shellsand Bay.

The ice cream van had found a good vantage point at the top of a slight slope, a spot that was shared by a burger van that had turned up out of the blue. Geoffrey arrived in his four-by-four off-roader, parking it sideways across the lane to stop any other hawkers arriving without permission.

Audrey strode to the dig team, her thighs rubbing painfully together. 'Geoffrey has stationed our vehicle up there. Traffic prevention.'

Piran ignored her but Mike, being well-mannered, said, 'Do thank him, Audrey. Very kind.'

'Yes, it is,' she said without humour. 'We have a comprehensive selection of first-aid equipment on board. I don't suppose anyone else has thought of that. So if there are any problems, wasp stings, bites, grazes, I have everything.' She was very pleased with herself.

'That's excellent,' Mike replied. 'Thank you.'

Audrey, catching sight of a dog fouling near the ice cream van, cried, 'Oh, for heaven's sake. Look at that. Some people,' and marched off to have words.

Piran sauntered over to Mike. 'What did Captain Mainwaring want?'

Mike couldn't help but laugh. 'Oh, you are bad, Piran. She's got a heart of gold really. She's brought some first-aid supplies down in case of accident, apparently.'

'I 'ope she hasn't forgotten the sun cream. Her thighs are getting burnt.'

Mike looked at Audrey, who was now berating the elderly dog owners. 'Oh dear me, yes. Those shorts of hers are rather skimpy.'

Piran threw away the last dregs of tea from his mug. 'Never mind her. Right, let's push on. Two hours until lunch break . . .'

By lunchtime, the whole area, roughly forty metres square, had been scraped back to underlying seams of shale and sand. The sand was damp, giving the team a boost.

'Looks like we might find something after all,' Piran told Simple Tony, who had been watching from the slope by the ice cream van. 'I'm going to get some lunch. Want anything?'

Tony shook his head and patted the pocket of his blue overalls. 'Polly did me some Marmite sandwiches.'

'Right you are. I'm going for the burger and chips, with fried onions and a mug of tea.'

Angela returned to the vicarage for lunch and found Robert in the kitchen with Mamie.

'Hello, you.' He kissed her as she came into the kitchen. 'Just making a chicken Caesar. Fancy some?'

'Yes, please.'

'How's it going?'

'OK. Some damp sand that looks promising. It's very hot out there.' She slumped into a chair.

Mamie got a glass from the cupboard and filled it from the cold tap. 'There you are. You'll be dehydrated.'

'Where's Faith?' Angela asked after she'd drunk the glass empty.

'Still out on her bike,' replied Robert, mixing the salad dressing. 'She said she and Ben might come down to the dig to have a look later.'

'Her bike was OK, was it?'

'I pumped up the tyres and greased the chain. Everything else was fine. The brakes will need replacing soon but they will be all right for today.'

Angela remembered something. 'You haven't seen my phone, have you?'

'No,' Robert replied.

'I wonder where it is. I was sure I put it in my pocket earlier. I'll have a look.' She wandered upstairs and checked her bedroom, Faith's bedroom, the bathroom, and the handbag she hadn't bothered to take with her to the dig. Nothing.

As she came back into the kitchen, Mamie looked up. 'Any luck?'

'No.' Angela frowned, thinking.

'Checked all your pockets?'

'Yes. Odd. I was sure I had it with me when I went to the dig.'

Robert finished shaving parmesan on top of the salad and placed the bowl on the table. 'Get that down you before you do anything.' He made Angela and Mamie sit down as he spooned the salad onto their plates. 'Have you checked your office? The sitting room?'

'No.' Angela moved to get up.

'Uh-uh, stay there and eat first. Then you can look. I don't know. You'll lose your head if it wasn't screwed on.'

'It's stress and exhaustion,' said Mamie. 'Your mind is whirring with too many things.'

Robert added, 'Take a hat with you this afternoon. We don't want you getting sunstroke.'

'Sunstroke is not funny.' Mamie broke the end off a baguette and started to butter it. 'I remember skiing in Aspen with Goldie Hawn back in the eighties. It got very hot at the top of the mountain and the sun was scorching. One woman was taken very ill and Goldie and I had to get her down on the ski lift. Horrible. She needed hospital treatment.'

Angela was getting irritated with the assumption that she was unwell and/or forgetful. 'I'm fine. Really. My phone will turn up. It's no drama.'

Piran finished his tea and brushed the burger-bun crumbs from his fisherman's smock. He had spent the lunch hour with Gasping Bob and Digger Pete, sitting in the dunes of Shellsand Bay. The tide was out and the long stretch of wet sand between them and the water's edge had people scattered over it. Some were dragging body boards to the virtually flat sea, others were playing boules or throwing Frisbees.

A sandy tennis ball landed at Piran's feet followed by a wet dog and a small child.

'Watch where you're going,' he said, patting the dog and smiling at the laughing child.

'That's our ball,' the child told him with youthful menace.

''Tis that. Want me to throw it for you?' Before the child could answer, Piran threw the ball high. 'There you go.'

The dog and child left Piran in a shower of sand as they dashed off after it.

He began to pack up his rubbish. 'Right fellas, fit to go again?'

'Aye.' Pete checked the time on his phone. 'Reckon we'm got a few hours left in the day.'

Gasping Bob stubbed out his latest roll-up and burped. 'Do you think we're going to find anything? How much further do you think?'

Piran shook his head. 'Just scratched the surface. I'll bet my dog's life on us finding something this weekend. Why else would there be such an enormous clump of gunnera growing there? They'm only grow that strong where there's water.'

'Maybe it's a stream and not a pond,' Bob said.

Whatever it was, the villagers hadn't had so much fun together in years.

At the vicarage, Angela was wiping the last of the Caesar dressing from her plate with some French bread. 'Delicious, Robert. Thank you.'

'I'll clear this up.' Mamie began to collect their plates. 'You two go and check on the dig.'

Angela sighed. 'I'm beginning to wonder if this is going to turn out to be a wild-goose chase. The boys found some damp sand under the top soil and, if there ever was a pond, it may have disappeared.'

'Hey.' Robert, sitting next to her, nudged her arm with his. 'No negativity. If there is a pond, great. If there isn't, well, it's been a good community project. History. Myth. A day out. What could be better?'

'Yeah, I know all that, but an awful lot of people have given a lot of their time to this. If it all fails I'll be remembered as the newcomer vicar who got carried away . . . If I'm remembered at all.'

'Oh for heaven's sake,' said Mamie. 'Self-pity is not worthy of you. Robert, take her away and have a lovely afternoon in the sun together. You might be surprised yet.'

Robert and Angela arrived at the site in time to see Digger Pete start the first excavation of the afternoon. The crowd had thinned considerably since the morning, most of them heading for the beach where the ice cream van had also relocated. Just about a dozen die-hard gawpers remained.

Angela and Robert made their way to the orange-taped barrier.

'Ah, Mrs Whitehorn. You haven't missed much,' Audrey said. She was very sunburnt now, her legs, out of her unsuitable shorts, like sausages in tight skins. She walked unsteadily towards them. 'Robert, I have been waiting for you.' She smiled at him.

'Hello, Audrey. How is it all going?' Robert could see she wasn't quite herself.

Audrey placed her hand on his shoulder. 'You do look very handsome. So strong.'

Robert raised his concerned eyebrows towards Angela.

'Are you quite well, Audrey?' Angela stepped closer. 'You look a little flushed.'

'Flushed?' Audrey slurred. 'Flushed? Mrs Whitehorn, I have never . . . oh, the ground is being silly . . . I may need to sit down a moment . . . Robert, can you help?'

Robert put an arm out for her to lean on. She looked giddily into his eyes.

'Such a lovely man, you are, and so strong and handsome. Oh dear, I'm . . .' She collapsed against Robert and he tried to catch her but she tumbled to the ground, pulling him with her. He felt his balance going and, whirling his arms helplessly, he fell on top of her. His knees hit hard ground but his face was saved by her bosoms.

'Oh my God!' He could feel whale bone against his nose. 'Angela! Help.'

Angela bent down to lift Robert off her but Audrey had got Robert in a sort of Boston crab.

'Don't touch him,' Audrey growled. 'He's mine.'

'What?' yelped the trapped Robert.

'Audrey,' Angela said gently. 'I think you need to get into the shade and have some water. You are not yourself.'

'Oh, I am.' Audrey began to stroke Robert's hair. 'I have never been more myself. I have tried to fight this but it's just too strong. Robert . . .' She puckered up. 'Robert . . .'

'Angela!' he squealed.

'*AUDREY!*' Geoffrey was thundering towards his wife and Robert. 'Let her go, you utter bastard.' Geoffrey fell to his knees and got hold of his wife's face. 'Audrey, it's me, your Geoff-Geoff.'

'Geoff-Geoff?' Audrey sounded surprised. 'What are you doing here?'

'It's not what it seems,' Robert attempted, unable to breathe inside Audrey's arm clamp.

Geoffrey's fury was unleashed. 'Oh-ho-ho. I know your game, *Mr* Whitehorn. Men like you, they see an attractive woman dressed provocatively and they think she's there for the taking. You are a *sex pest.*'

Angela was open-mouthed. 'Geoffrey, I rather think that Audrey is unwell. Robert was trying to help her.'

'I feel sorry for you, Vicar,' roared Geoffrey. 'You are married to a philanderer!'

Quietly Audrey bleated, 'Geoffy, I think I'm going to be sick.'

'Oh God, please, no. I'm not good with sick,' said Robert.

Angela urged Geoffrey to help Robert off Audrey. 'If she's sick, Robert will be sick. We need to get her in the shade. Get her some water.'

Piran walked over from where he'd been watching from inside the dig circle. 'Geoff, don't just stand there like a bleddy idiot, get your wife out of the sun. Angela, there's water in my truck, bring a bottle. Audrey, listen to me. It's Piran. Geoff and I are going to get you to the shade. Do you understand?'

'I can't stand,' she mumbled.

Piran tried to peel her arms from Robert's back. 'Let go of Robert.'

'I don't want to.'

'He'll come with you if you let him go.' Piran tried to sound patient. 'There's a good girl.'

Geoffrey was furious. 'How dare you infantilise my wife. She is not a *girl*, she's a *woman*!'

Piran had had enough. 'Bore off, you right-on PC knob, your wife needs to get to the shade.'

Audrey finally let Robert loose and was helped to her feet by Piran.

'I don't feel very well, Geoffy.' Her face was grey under the sunburn.

'I think my back's gone,' groaned Robert as he got painfully to his feet, brushing grit and grass from his jeans.

Geoffrey glowered at him. 'If you have hurt one hair on her head—'

But Robert interrupted him. 'Geoffrey. Look out. She's going to be—'

Audrey threw up over Geoffrey's back.

Angela shouted, 'Robert, close your eyes. Don't look.' But it was too late.

29

Mamie, alone in the vicarage, dialled Queenie.

'Darling, it's me. Shut the shop and come over. Use the back door. We have all afternoon without being disturbed.'

Minutes later, there was a quiet knock on the back door. 'Come in, come in.'

Queenie wheezed her way into the kitchen.

'Did anyone see you coming over here?' Mamie asked.

'No. Not a single blighter out there. All on the beach or staring at that bleeding hole in the ground.'

'Good-o. This is going to be such a fun afternoon for us. Look.' On the kitchen table was a tea tray set with two mugs, a teapot, a milk jug and a sugar bowl.

Queenie's face fell. ''Ere, I haven't come for tea. I thought we was going to—'

'Shhh.' Mamie whipped her head round from filling the kettle and frowned at Queenie. 'Afternoon tea is our cover. Look in the sugar bowl.'

Queenie lifted the small lid and smiled. 'That's the stuff, is it?'

'Yep.'

'Where are we going to have it?'

'In the garden. The smell will linger in the house.'

'You've thought of everything, entcha?' Queenie cackled. 'What could be more normal than having a cuppa and a smoke in the garden?'

'Exactly.' Mamie gleefully filled the teapot from the kettle. 'I'll take the tray, you open the door and we'll head to the bench under the tree. I've checked. We can't be seen from the road there.'

'I ain't 'ad this much excitement since I met Alan Titchmarsh. Have I ever told you I met him?'

'Many times. Have you brought the cigarette papers and loose tobacco?'

'What do you take me for?' Queenie sat down on the bench and reached in her bag. ''Ere they are.'

'Good stuff. Your job is to roll the things, while I pour the tea.'

'Right you are.'

Mamie watched intently, admiring Queenie's skill. The ritual of pulling the cigarette paper carefully from its packet, the precise placement of the rolling tobacco within it, and now, 'How much of this marryjuana do we need?'

'Oh. I'm not sure.' Mamie decided to err on the side of caution. 'Not too much to start with. We don't know how strong it is.'

Queenie lifted the lid of the sugar bowl and pinched a few strands of dried cannabis leaves from it. 'This enough?'

'I think so.'

Queenie rolled the bundle expertly and licked the glued strip to seal it down.

'Who goes first?' she asked.

'I'd better try first. It's a long time since I have done this but I will be able to tell if it's too strong for you.'

Queenie passed it to her. 'Don't have too much too quick.'

'I have done this before.'

'You was younger then, gel. It might affect you different at your age.'

Mamie put the drugged cigarette to her lips and struck a match. 'Here goes.'

The paper flared, making the cannabis and tobacco crackle as they caught the flame.

She inhaled.

'Well? What's it like?' Queenie's eyes were bright and eager.

Mamie held the smoke in the bottom of her lungs for a second or two then blew out and coughed. 'Nothing yet.'

'Give it me then.' Queenie, a professional roll-up smoker, took a deep drag, held it, exhaled and waited. 'No. Nothing. What's it supposed to do to us?'

'It should make us feel relaxed and happy.'

'When does it stop my hips hurting?'

'Have some patience.'

They finished the first one with some disappointment, and took a tea break.

'Right, shall we try again?' Queenie took her cigarette papers from her bag and began the process for a second time. 'I'll put a bit more of the stuff in this time. I don't think we had enough for it to work.'

Five minutes later, both women were sitting quietly, looking at the cloudless sky.

'Isn't sky amazing?' breathed Mamie. 'So blue and yet . . . so white. Can you feel the sky, Queenie?'

'Oh, yes. I'm feeling it but not feeling it. I wonder what it would be like to swim in the sky?'

'Oh, it'd be warm. Definitely warm.'

'Don't it smell nice?' Queenie was inhaling deeply. 'Like fresh air and like sky.'

Mamie took a deep sniff and smiled. 'You're so right, Queenie. I love the smell of sky. Pass me another drag.' She held her hand out.

'We've finished that one.'

Mamie's smile dropped. 'Oh. That's sad. So sad. Maybe we got a duff batch. Nothing is happening for me. How about you?'

'Nope. Nothing. Nada. Zilch.'

The two women sat in silence on the bench, enjoying the warmth of the sun and the relaxed state they were in. The drone of bees busy in the borders and the soft breeze caressing their faces was better than any spa.

'Would you like a biscuit?' asked Mamie.

'I would. Tell you what, you get them, I'll roll us another.'

Mamie stood up very slowly and walked carefully towards the house.

Queenie began rolling up again, talking softly, reminding herself how to do it.

'Who are you talking to?' asked Mamie, returning with a packet of Mr Kipling's Viennese whirls, one already in her mouth.

'I'm not talking.'

'Yes you were. I saw your lips moving.'

'Did you?'

'Yes.'

'Oh.'

'Have one of these biscuits.' Mamie put one in front of Queenie. 'I have never tasted anything like them. Try one.'

'Just let me finish this.' Queenie licked down the paper

and handed it to Mamie. 'There you go, girl. I made one each.'

'Did you? You know what you are?'

'Tell me.'

'A bloody wonderful woman.'

'I know.' Queenie reached for a Viennese whirl. 'I sell these in my shop, you know.'

'Do you?' Mamie lit up and inhaled. 'Do you really? I didn't know that.'

Queenie was puffing too. 'Didn't know what?'

'I don't know.' Mamie began to laugh. 'Do you think this is beginning to work?'

'I think I could dance right now. Got any?'

'Got any what?'

'To dance to?'

'Music?'

'Yeah.'

'Can you dance?'

'Course I can flipping dance.'

'I feel a bit light-headed.'

'Me too. Lovely, innit? What's this cigarette called then?'

'A joint.'

'I love a joint of lamb.'

'Pork and apple sauce.'

'Bacon sandwich.'

Mamie stood up a bit too quickly but steadied herself on the arm of the bench. 'We are going to make bacon sandwiches.'

'Are we?'

'Yes. Bacon and tomato and, and . . . what's it called?'

'What?'

'That salad thing, lettuce. What's that called?'

'Lettuce.'

'That's it.'

'I like ketchup.'

'Well, you shall have some. I shall make you the best ketchup bacon sandshoe you have ever eaten. Come with me.'

Faith and Ben cycled into the village, feeling hot and thirsty. Together they had explored the lanes and coves, cooling their feet in rock pools and buying a couple of pasties to eat on the cliff path.

'Race you to the vicarage!' shouted Faith, her tanned legs pedalling faster.

Ben picked up speed and, neck and neck, they turned onto the vicarage drive. Pulling to a halt, they walked the bikes round to the back of the house and leant them against the wall.

'I smell bacon.' Faith sniffed the air. 'Maybe Mum's home. Are you hungry, Ben?'

'I'd like a drink first, please.' Ben put his rucksack down and followed Faith to the open back door.

Faith stood in the doorway and observed the carnage inside. 'Oh my God.'

Ben arrived and looked over Faith's shoulder. 'Oh holy shit.'

A half-empty packet of sliced white bread lay on its side among butter, ketchup, lettuce, and a jar of pickled onions.

Sprawled in two chairs were Mamie and Queenie, warming their feet against the Aga. They seemed to be chatting but without any sense that Faith and Ben could make out.

'Auntie Mamie?' Faith said uncertainly. 'Are you OK?'

Mamie popped a block of Cadbury's Fruit and Nut chocolate

into her mouth. 'I'm fine, thank you. How are you? Have you met my friend?'

'Yes.' Faith was unsure of what was going on. 'I know her. Is that my chocolate you're eating?'

'How would I know?'

'Are you drunk?' asked Ben, making Queenie burst into laughter.

'How dare you, young man?' Mamie managed with some dignity. 'I am not drunk. I am stoned. Quite, quite, different.'

'Stoned.' Faith was worried. 'You've been doing drugs?' She took a deep breath. 'If you have, it's OK. Don't worry. I am not going to be cross. Just tell me what you have taken.'

Queenie and Mamie burst into uncontrollable laughter.

'We just smoked a little cigarette, darling.' Mamie brushed her hands through the air. 'Don't go all po-faced teenager. It's nothing.'

Ben knew exactly what it was. 'They've got the munchies. They've had a spliff.'

'But only a whiff of a spliff.' Mamie grinned stupidly.

'I think this is more than a whiff,' said Ben. 'I think we need to find your mum and dad, Faith.'

Faith wasn't sure. 'They're at the pond dig. Are these two going to be all right on their own? Shouldn't we stay with them?'

'Ring your mum. Tell them to come back.'

Faith dialled her mother's phone. As it connected, a phone began to ring in the kitchen.

Ben began to look around for it. If it was Queenie's or Mamie's it could be anywhere.

After eight rings, Angela's phone went to voicemail, and the phone in the room stopped ringing. Ben bent down to Mr Worthington's basket and found a phone under the old rug.

Angela's.

He picked it up and stood in front of Faith, who was finishing a message to Angela.

'Is this your mum's?' he asked.

'Yeah. Where did you find it?'

'In the dog bed.'

'Oh shit.' Faith shook her head. 'My mum's losing her marbles and my aunt and her mate are doing drugs. What kind of family do I have?'

Ben looked towards the Aga. 'Look at the pair of them. Fast asleep now. So, here's the plan. We tidy up in here. Remove all evidence. And go down to the dig as if nothing happened. OK?'

Faith smiled over at the sleeping Mamie and Queenie. 'Those two are going to owe us big time for this.'

Back at the dig, Polly was using her paramedic skills on Audrey.

Audrey was sleeping in the cool shade of a small tree, on a soft blanket, in the recovery position. Polly had put up a saline drip suspended from a low branch, loosened Audrey's clothing and was now checking her pulse.

'What the hell were you thinking?' she scolded Geoffrey. 'No hat. No sun cream. No water. Sunstroke can be very serious.'

'She insisted on the shorts. She knows how damn good she looks in them.' He was holding Audrey's left hand and stroking it. 'I can't believe I allowed it. My precious Audy.' He choked back imminent tears. 'I shall never let anything like this happen again.'

'Right,' said Polly. 'You sit with her and make sure the drip stays upright.' Geoffrey obeyed meekly. 'I'll be back to check on her.' She stood up and wiped her sweating forehead.

'Thank goodness you were here, Polly,' said Angela.

'It's my job. How's Robert?' She looked over to where Robert was propped against a car in the shade.

'He's OK. His knees are bruised.'

'Has he had some water?'

'Yes.'

'Make sure he has plenty.' Polly looked over to the dig circle, about fifty yards away. 'Have they found anything yet?'

'I'm not sure. While Robert was being sick, Piran was called away to look at something. I don't know what.'

Just then, Faith and Ben rattled down the lane, brakes squeaking in the kicked-up dust. Faith dinged her bell. 'Mum. You OK? What's happened?'

'We are all fine, darling. Poor Audrey got sunstroke and tumbled into Dad and then she was sick so . . .'

'Oh God. Dad was sick too. Euugh.'

'Well, yes, but he's OK now. He's in the shade of that car over there. Anyway, how are you two? Had a good day?'

Ben and Faith looked at each other slyly and giggled.

'What's the joke?' Angela was curious.

'Nothing,' Faith said innocently. 'We've just had a really funny afternoon.'

Angela's attention was suddenly taken by a huge and triumphant roar, coming from the dig site.

'The pond? Have they found it?' She began running towards the noise.

'Come on!' Faith urged Ben, taking his hand and scrambling off after her.

In the middle of the cleared site, where they must have dug down almost two metres, a shallow pool of clear water was bubbling up through the shale and sand.

Pete was lifting away another mechanical scoop of spoil

and, as he did so, Mike Bates came along his blindside. Wreathed in smiles, laughing with excitement, his hands on his hips.

Pete lifted the digger bucket and turned its long arm with jerky swiftness. The movement was so quick and the bucket so heavy, poor Mike didn't have a chance of escaping it. It knocked him off his feet and dumped the wet spoil on top of him, before he had a chance to scream.

30

Polly, mistress of the calm emergency, sprinted into action once again. She shouted, 'Piran, Bob, dig him out, with your hands,' while simultaneously dialling 999.

She ran for her kit bag and prepared herself to start CPR.

'We've got him,' Piran panted as she arrived. 'He's got a bad gash on his head and it looks like he may have broken a leg. It's at a very nasty angle.'

Polly looked down at Mike. He had a large swelling on his left temple and blood was seeping from his left ear. His skin was grey.

'Is he breathing?' She took out a pack of sterile medical gloves.

Piran put his ear to Mike's nose. 'I'm not sure.'

'Move over.' Polly checked Mike's nose and mouth for obstructions, felt for a pulse and then, seeing the deterioration in his colour, began chest compressions.

In the distance she could hear the wail of sirens.

'What have we got, Polly?' Derek, an ambulance colleague, jumped out of the emergency vehicle and ran to her. The female driver, Janet, ran to the back of the ambulance to bring out the wheeled stretcher.

'No heartbeat. Not breathing. CPR for the last seven minutes. May have fractures,' Polly told Derek.

Digger Pete, shocked and distressed, stood over Mike. 'I didn't see him. I just didn't see him.'

Derek, ignoring him, called out to Janet, 'Bring the defib.'

He knelt next to Polly. 'What's his name?'

'Mike,' Polly said without pausing in her chest compressions.

'OK.' Derek took one of Mike's hands and began talking to him. 'Mike, my name is Derek. I'm part of the emergency medical team. You've had an accident but we are helping you.'

Janet arrived and handed over the defibrillator case. 'Trolley ready when you are.'

Before Derek could open the defibrillator case, Mike suddenly coughed and took a deep breath.

'That's it, Mike. Well done,' Polly told him calmly. 'We're going to get some oxygen in you and get you to hospital.'

As Mike was driven away, Polly looked at an ashen Digger Pete, and put her arm around his shoulder for support. 'Sit down, Pete.'

'No. I need to follow Mike to hospital.'

'Not right now. Sit down. You're in shock. I'll take you to see Mike once I've checked you over.'

The village may have thought her an oddball, but she had saved Mike and now she ushered Digger Pete into the back of the ambulance with such care and patience that everyone looked at her in a new light.

Angela and Piran had stood back while Mike was being treated, knowing they would be more hindrance than help. Angela had sent Faith and Ben back home.

'Tell Mamie what's happened,' she had instructed them. 'She's very fond of Mike. I will bring Dad back as soon as he's feeling better.'

At the vicarage, Mamie had woken up with a dull head.

Queenie was snoring.

The memory of their lurid afternoon came back to her in tiny pictures. Making tea. Smoking. Laughing. Bacon sandwiches. Chocolate.

Faith and Ben.

Oh God.

Faith and Ben.

She looked around the kitchen. Spotless. No evidence of bad behaviour. Had it happened? Was she hallucinating?

The back door opened and Faith came in with Ben behind her.

Mamie stood up, hanging onto the Aga rail to stop the room from tilting.

'Hello,' she said. 'Queenie and I have been having a little nap.'

'Hmm,' said Faith. 'And a lot of weed.'

'Not a lot of weed.'

'We haven't time to talk about it now.' Faith had to act fast. 'Mum and Dad will be here any minute. Mike was knocked over and buried by the digger. You need to tidy yourself up.'

Mamie sat down heavily. 'Mike? Is he OK?'

Faith's eyes were darting around the kitchen, checking she and Ben hadn't left any evidence of Mamie and Queenie's druggy afternoon.

'Well, Polly was pumping his chest so I'm guessing he's not.'

'Oh my God.' Mamie was stricken.

'Yeah. And you two were getting stoned,' Ben said wryly. 'In the vicarage.'

'We did it in the garden, actually,' Mamie whimpered with some dignity.

'What the hell were you thinking?' demanded Faith.

'It was to help Queenie's arthritis.'

'The garden!' Ben ran to the back door. 'Faith, we didn't check the garden.'

'Hellooo.' Angela called out as she came through the vicarage front door holding Robert's arm. 'We are hoo-oome.'

Faith sauntered from the kitchen into the hall. 'Oh, hi. How are you feeling, Dad?'

'I have had better days.'

'Ben's just putting the kettle on for you,' smiled Faith, replacing her mother's helping arm for her own.

'Bless him,' said Robert.

Angela was dumping her bag on the stairs. 'I'm thinking of making us a bacon sandwich. What with all the hoo-ha this afternoon we forgot to have lunch. Would you and Ben like one?'

'Never say no to a bacon sandwich,' said Faith, 'By the way, I found your phone in Mr W's bed. I've told him he has to break his online shopping addiction.'

'You found it! Oh, thank goodness. He must have taken it out of my bag.'

'Maybe.' Faith shrugged and escorted her father into the kitchen.

Ben was standing by the kettle, hands in pockets and whistling innocently.

'Where's Mamie?' Robert asked, heading for a chair.

'Just taking Queenie home,' Faith said, smiling. 'Are you comfy there, Dad? Another cushion?'

Robert stared hard with narrowed eyes at both his daughter and Ben. 'What's going on?'

Faith laughed, brightly. 'What do you mean? Ben and I have been out all day on our bikes. Haven't we, Ben?'

'Yes.' Ben smiled. 'Great fun.' The kettle boiled behind him and he quickly turned to the mug cupboard, hiding his face from Robert.

'And Mamie?' Robert queried, looking at Faith. 'What has she been up to today?'

Ben and Faith exchanged grinning glances. 'Having fun with Queenie, I think.' Faith's voice broke on a giggle.

Robert's antenna was up. 'Something is going on here.'

Angela came into the kitchen. 'What a day.' She went to the fridge.

Robert continued to pin his gaze on his daughter, who refused to catch his eye.

Faith said brightly, 'Is there anything I can help you with, Mum? You must be in shock after what happened to Mike Bates.'

Robert became more suspicious.

Angela had her head in the fridge. 'I can't find the bacon. It must be in here. I bought some really good streaky rashers from the butcher up in St Columb. He hand-sliced them for me.'

Robert rolled his eyes. 'Keys, phones, iPads and now bacon! Let me have a look.'

'Stay where you are, I don't need you to find a pack of bacon for me.'

Mamie arrived at the back door, the sun behind her, her tall shadow falling over the room. 'Bacon? I had a little with Queenie earlier.'

Angela turned from the fridge and smiled at her aunt, feeling a slight moment of relief it wasn't something else she'd mislaid. 'Well, a couple of rashers won't have made much of a dent in the amount I bought. Where did you put the rest?'

Mamie flicked a pleading look towards Ben and Faith. 'I, er, put it back where I found it.' She made her way to the nearest chair and sat down slowly. 'We were . . . hungry.'

Angela was now opening the bread bin. 'I bought a tiger loaf too. Where's that gone?'

Ben stepped in, 'I'm sorry, Angela. I asked Faith to bring the bacon and the bread. For crab-fishing. I didn't realise. I shall replace it.'

Angela looked at him, annoyed. 'Well, I hope they liked it because it was some of the best you could buy.'

'I am really sorry,' said Ben.

Faith dropped her folded arms and gave her aunt Mamie a stern look. 'I think you ought to tell them what really happened.'

'Tell us what?' Angela rubbed her forehead with her fingertips; a dull headache was making itself known. 'What's been going on?'

Mamie hung her head. 'It was me. I cooked all the bacon and used all the bread. And you'll find the lettuce and tomatoes have gone too. And the Hellmann's. I am so sorry.'

'I don't understand,' Angela said. 'Did you have friends over?'

'No. It was just Queenie and me. I was trying to help her arthritis.'

Angela was flummoxed. 'Bacon helps arthritis?'

Mamie took a deep breath. 'No, but cannabis does, I think.'

Faith sighed. 'Mum, Auntie Mamie and Queenie got stoned on weed and then got the munchies.'

'WHAT!' Angela's eyes were wide in fury. Mamie had never seen her like this.

'Darling.' Mamie stood up and managed to totter towards her niece while hanging onto bits of furniture.

'Don't you "darling" me. Look at you. You can hardly walk!' Angela was truly angry. 'For God's sake, could this day get any worse? The godawful Audrey has heatstroke and was sick all over *him*!' She pointed wildly at Robert.

'Not my fault. You know how I feel about other people's vomit.'

'Oh, shut up,' Angela told him. 'I've had enough of it. I am more concerned about poor Mike.'

'Oh, goodness, yes.' Mamie buckled onto a hard kitchen chair. 'I must go to see him.'

'Not in that bloody state you won't,' snapped Angela, picking up her keys.

'Shall I come with you?' asked Robert, trying to get back in favour.

'No, you damn well can't. Fat lot of good you'd be in a hospital, full of *sick* people.'

31

Angela slammed her car door shut and sat shaking with anger. How the hell was she going to handle this shit-storm? She leant her head on the steering wheel, the backs of her eyes prickling with tears of frustration. She sat up straight again and took three slow deep breaths. How could Mamie and Queenie have been so very stupid? She'd have to clear that mess up later but, for now, top of the priority list was Mike. The poor man could have died. He could still. Oh God, she hoped he had covered the event sufficiently with insurance. The health and safety lobby would be all over this. Why had she ever thought that digging out a stupid pond was a good idea? She'd just been trying so hard to bring the village together and it had nearly killed poor Mike. With another deep sigh, she put the key into the ignition, slammed into first gear and set off for the hospital.

Angela's mood didn't improve when she entered the hospital car park and found it full. She cruised around for twenty minutes, praying to Saint Philomena (who had never let her down for a parking space before), until finally, she saw the blessed white reversing lights of a small red car come twinkling about ten spaces from her. She pulled over, indicating her intention, and waited and waited.

A young man in an Audi stopped close behind her and beeped his horn.

She opened her window and waved him past, which he did while tapping his temple as if she were a moron.

Swallowing a searing spear of anger, she ignored him, focusing on the space she wanted. She could see that the driver was an elderly man in a trilby hat, and she moved her car a little closer so that he could see her. He spotted her and waved affably.

Her grin, she hoped, suggested that she was in a bit of a hurry, and she added a thumbs up to encourage him to get a move on.

Returning her thumbs up, he very slowly got himself settled.

He readjusted his rear-view mirror, found his spectacle case, took out his glasses, polished them and then placed them on his face.

'Come on you, stupid man,' Angela muttered with a clenched jaw.

He was pulling on a pair of driving gloves now.

Angela drummed at the steering wheel, mumbling under her breath, 'Comeoncomeoncomeon.'

He began to pull out, then move forward six inches, then pull out again, and move forward a few more inches.

'Oh Jesus Christ,' she shouted. 'Please please please get this man OUT OF THAT SPACE.'

Finally, he slid out and drove away, touching the brim of his hat in gratitude.

She swung into the space and drove straight into a concrete

bollard. The noise brought a young couple and an older man over to gloat at her misfortune.

'You've hit the bollard,' said the older man.

She unwound the window and said through gritted teeth, 'Yes, thank you.'

The young woman threw her pennyworth in too. 'My mum done that as well. My dad was really, really cross with her.'

The young man got onto his haunches and looked at the damage. 'That's gonna cost you.'

'Right,' Angela said tensely.

'Do you want me to call anybody?' he asked.

'No, thank you.'

'Your hubby's going to go mad,' the young woman said.

'Very probably.'

Finally, after they'd squeezed as much pleasure from her misfortune as possible, she was left on her own and gave herself permission to cry a little.

She opened the glove box for the travel tissues she always kept there. But the box was empty, bringing fresh tears of anger and frustration. She wiped her eyes on her sleeve instead and, taking a few more deep breaths, got out of the car and headed for A&E.

She finally found Mike in a curtained bay with a drip attached to his arm and very sleepy. But, thankfully, very much alive.

'Hi, Mike. It's Angela. I am so sorry that this has happened. How are you feeling?'

With some effort he opened his eyes. 'A bit better. My leg is bad.'

'Have they X-rayed you?'

'Yes. Just waiting to hear what the damage is.' He closed his eyes again. 'I'm so sorry, I'm very sleepy.'

'You sleep and I will stay with you.'

'Thank you, my dear.'

The hospital staff were overloaded with casualties but Mike's injuries bumped him up the list pretty quickly. The X-ray revealed that there were three breaks and that they would need surgery to pin them that evening. The force of the digger had also cracked two ribs and given Mike some internal bruising.

'You are a lucky man, Mr Bates,' said the orthopaedic surgeon who looked about fourteen. 'Things could have been a lot worse.'

As Mike was wheeled down to theatre, Angela reassured him that she would be there when he woke up. 'I want to make sure you are OK, and anyway, they don't need me at home tonight. They have enough to keep them busy.'

While she waited for his return, she texted Robert.

Mike in theatre pinning broken leg. Two ribs broken and internal bruising but comfortable on painkillers. I shall wait here until I know he's settled. Tell Mamie I will talk to her tomorrow.

She pressed send, then turned her phone off. Her stupid, irresponsible, and selfish family could fend for themselves for once.

Mike came up from theatre very late but the surgeon was pleased with the results.

'The op has gone well and the fractures should heal in six to eight weeks. He was lucky that the breaks were clean. When the swelling goes down over the next few days, we'll plaster the leg and get him home. He will be on crutches and we'll schedule some physiotherapy appointments. He won't be driving until the plaster is off. Has he got anyone at home to look after him?'

Angela rubbed her scalp, feeling exhausted. 'He lives alone but I'm sure I can sort something out.'

Saying goodbye to Mike and promising to look after his dogs and to bring Mamie with her the next day, she headed home, leaving a chunk of bumper on the tarmac.

Angela got home to a dark house. Letting herself in, she walked through the dark hall to the kitchen where the glow of a soft table lamp led her.

Robert was sitting up. 'Hi,' he said. 'How is he?'

Angela dropped her bag and went to the fridge. 'He's OK. He'll be home in a couple of days but will need help at home. I've said we can have his dogs too; at least Mr Worthington likes them. It feels like the least I could do.' She took out a bottle of rosé and poured a glass.

'You must be exhausted,' Robert said quietly.

'Yep.'

'I have spoken to Mamie and Faith,' he said.

'I'm too tired to hear it.'

'They promise it will never happen again and that nobody will find out.'

'How can they be sure?'

'No witnesses.'

'Well, that's something, I suppose.'

'Ben has promised not to say anything either. He's a good lad.'

'Yes.' She took a deep draught of the chilled wine. 'What a terrible day.'

Robert got up and went to rub the back of Angela's neck. She tipped her head back. 'That's good.'

He moved his hands across her shoulders, kneading her muscles gently. 'Do you want to hear the good news?'

'Is there any?' she groaned.

'The water level at the pond site is rising. It looks like we have a village pond, after all.'

The next morning, after walking Mike's spaniels, Danvers and Davey, a weary Angela got ready for church.

What would her parishioners be thinking of her after yesterday's débâcle? She had messed up very badly. She wouldn't blame them if they had lost their confidence in her entirely.

She journeyed across the churchyard, which was pricked with cornflowers and buttercups, dew glistening from them like diamonds, but saw nothing other than her shadow in its long robe wavering towards the vestry door.

Processing down the aisle to the first hymn, she saw from the corner of her eye people watching her. One or two touched her arm gently as she passed. She heard, 'You OK, Vicar?' from one of the Bible group mums. The hymn came to an end and, as the last organ notes died, Angela faced her congregation.

'Good morning, everybody. As you will have heard, Mike Bates had a serious accident at the pond dig, and was taken to hospital with suspected fractures. The good news is that his broken leg was operated on last night and he could be out of hospital in a few days. He also has a couple of broken ribs but the doctor has reassured me that his lungs have not been pierced. He does have some internal bruising but the superficial bleeding has stopped. And the main thing is he's stable and will just need time to get back on his feet.

'This is the real time that us – the parish of Pendruggan – can pull together. I set out to do the Pond Dig because I wanted to pull the parish together, but it's the people that make the parish, and each and every one of us can make a difference to Mike to speed his recovery.'

Her voice wobbling, she paused and searched the upturned faces for Polly.

'May I thank Polly for her swift action and CPR, which, to my mind, saved his life.' Polly was embarrassed as a murmur of thanks swept the nave. 'She also helped Audrey Tipton, who suffered from heatstroke and was very unwell. How is she this morning, Polly?'

Polly stood up. 'Feeling a lot better. Geoffrey wanted to apologise for them not being here today. But I told him to keep her cool, hydrated and rested for another twenty-four hours.'

'Thank you, Polly.'

Polly remained standing. 'And how is your husband? He didn't seem too well after Audrey's vomiting spell? I see he and your aunt aren't here this morning.'

Angela's pale face flushed. 'He's a lot better, thank you, Polly. Mamie is keeping an eye on him.' Moving on, she continued, 'I haven't been down to the pond site this morning, but I have heard that we seem to have found a water source and that the pond is beginning to fill.'

Digger Pete, who she hadn't noticed earlier, stood up. 'I don't care about the bleddy pond. I didn't sleep last night, worried about Mr Bates. I can't believe what happened. I keep thinking about suddenly seeing him fall. It was my fault. I will never forgive myself.'

'It was an accident,' said Angela. 'No blame is attached to you and nor should it be. Piran Ambrose is shutting the dig site down until the council health and safety team have inspected the site. However, Piran will be spending today with a couple of his archaeological team to see what is coming to the surface, if anybody wants to take a look. As long as you keep outside the orange tape you will remain safe.'

She stopped for a moment and after a deep breath said, 'On a personal note, I want to apologise for pushing the whole idea forward. I thought it would be fun. I take full responsibility for it.'

'It was my fault,' Simple Tony piped up from Polly's side. 'I wanted to do it. It was me who let the curse escape.'

Polly took his hand and shushed him. 'Be quiet. I told you it's not your fault.'

Angela held her hands up. 'Tony, let me make this clear. There is no curse and nothing is your fault. You may come and see me later and I will reassure you. OK?'

Polly put a gentle arm around his shoulders and hugged him. 'There. I told you.'

Angela took a deep breath. 'Right, please stand for our second hymn, "Lord of all hopefulness".'

When she returned from church, she found Mamie in the kitchen attempting to cook a Sunday roast.

'Hello, darling.' Mamie was on a charm offensive. 'How was church? I've made some fresh coffee for you, and Robert nipped up to Tesco for some croissants.' She produced a pretty plate with two warm and flaky croissant arranged carefully with a knob of butter and a small pot of raspberry jam. 'Sit down and relax. *The Archers* omnibus has just started. I know how much you love it. Shall I pop the radio on for you?'

Angela sat down at the kitchen table and crossed her arms. 'What the hell were you thinking?'

'I'm thinking of you, darling. You work so hard I wanted to show my appreciation.'

'No. What were you thinking when you decided to bring

drugs into this house? Into a vicarage. And how did you get hold of them?' A sudden terrible thought crossed her mind. 'Oh, no. You didn't get them from Ben, did you? Or Faith?'

'No, darling. They are a couple of dear little prudes. I got them from a man who happens to be a doctor.'

'Not from Trevay Health Centre? Not Dr Adam?'

'Of course not. Just a nice man who lives on the moor and sells a little bit of medicinal cannabis.'

Angela was shocked. 'He could have been selling anything. I read all the time about drugs that are contaminated with brick dust or ant powder. It could have killed you and Queenie.'

Mamie tutted and pushed a blond lock of hair out of her eyes. 'I know good dope when I see it. I was young once, you know. In India I remember, Jack Nicholson and I, we . . .'

Angela stood up fast, knocking her chair backwards where it crashed to the floor, making Mamie jump. Angela unleashed her fury.

'Shut up! Shut up! I can't bear to hear another of your stories. THIS IS SERIOUS! I can see you now, sometime soon when you'll be telling your cronies all about the time you brought drugs into your niece's vicarage and ate all the bacon and got a telling-off because your niece, me,' she jabbed herself in the chest with a shaking hand, 'is such a square head that I didn't see the joke. And no, I do not see the damn joke.'

Mamie said quietly, 'The phrase is square, not square head.'

Angela burst into tears. 'I don't care what it is. I am trying to be a good vicar. I want to do so well here that I'll be offered a parish of my own where I can live out my days and be a real part of the community, not just another newcomer, blown in on the breeze and out again. The one remembered for digging a stupid pond, nearly killing the chairman of the parish council, having a drugged-up aunt and, and . . .' she was sobbing now and losing her strength '. . . the one they hated so much that she deserved two poison-pen letters.'

Angela crumpled and Mamie flew to her side.

'Darling, darling,' she said, cradling Angela in her arms. 'You are the best person I know. I am a feeble stupid old woman but you are strong and thoughtful and caring. I am so, so sorry.'

'So you should be,' Angela sobbed.

'I am, truly.'

Someone knocked at the front door, as often happens at the wrong moment.

'I'll get rid of them,' said Mamie as she left the room.

Angela got some kitchen towel, blew her nose and sat down. She hoped that whoever it was at the door would go away quickly. She listened for Mamie's voice.

'Polly,' Mamie said overloudly, so that Angela would hear, 'I'm so sorry, if you've come to see Angela, but she's having a rest. It's been a difficult time for her.'

Polly was sounding upset. Angela pricked her ears up. 'I wouldn't trouble her but I don't know who else to talk to.'

'Can you tell me?'

Angela heard Polly sniff and blow her nose, then her voice, full of emotion. 'It's the curse.'

'What curse, dear?'

'The pond. We should never have touched it. I feel so bad. I've unleashed the spirits.'

Angela wearily rubbed her eyes, got out of her chair and went to meet Polly.

'Come on, Polly,' she said, taking the distraught woman's hand. 'Come into my study. Mamie, would you bring two cups of your coffee, please?'

Angela offered a chair to Polly and then a box of tissues. Polly accepted both.

'I heard you telling Mamie about the curse. I told Tony, all of you, in church, that there is no curse,' Angela said.

Polly wiped her nose and eyes. 'But supposing there is?'

'There really isn't. Mike had an accident, that's all. Nothing else is going to happen.'

'It has already.' Polly's eyes were full of anxiety. 'I got a horrible letter last night when I got home. I only popped in to get the cat and a Thermos, then I was going to spend the night down at the pond like I said. But when I opened the door the postman had been and there was a few letters, rubbish mostly, but there was one I didn't recognise. Marked "Personal".'

Angela felt a chill in her chest. 'May I see it?'

Polly pulled a crumpled envelope from the pocket of her cardigan. 'Here.'

As with Angela's letters, there were no distinguishing marks. White envelope. White address label stuck to it. White sheet of paper inside. The words were all in black type:

WITCHES LIKE YOU NEED DROWNING.

Angela examined it carefully then folded it and put it back in its envelope.

'We must call the police.'

'No, no,' said Polly. 'I don't want more trouble.'

'Whoever has written this needs help and needs to be stopped.'

Polly chewed her lip in anxiety. 'What have I done to upset the spirits?'

'You have done nothing. There are no spirits to upset.' Angela was fed up with hearing about 'the spirits'. She opened the top drawer of her desk, and took out two envelopes addressed to her. One blue. One white. 'Long before the pond was dug,' she said, handing Polly the letters to read, 'I received these.'

'What?'

'Read them.'

Polly opened the letters and read the malicious words. 'Oh, no,' she said. 'These are horrible.'

'Indeed. So, you see, we have to call the police.'

'Yes, I do see.'

'Do you mind if I show your letter to Robert?'

'No.'

Angela stood up and opened the door onto the hall outside her study. 'Robert?' she called. 'Can you come here for a moment, please?'

Mamie appeared from the kitchen end of the hall with two coffee cups. 'He's just getting something from the car. Here's your coffee.' As she handed over the two drinks, she saw the two letters on the desk and looked at Angela questioningly.

'I'm afraid Polly has received one too,' Angela said.

The women looked at each other in shock.

'My God,' Mamie whispered. 'Who the hell is doing this?'

Robert came into the house via the back door and shouted Angela's name. 'Where are you?'

'In the study,' she called back.

As he came into the room, she could see he was angry. 'When were you going to tell me about crashing the damn car?'

'I'm so sorry. I had forgotten all about that. You see—'

'Forgotten? How can you forget writing the bloody front of the car off?'

In answer, Angela calmly held up Polly's letter. 'There's been another one.'

32

'What?' Robert said. 'Show it to me.' He read the five words. 'Oh, Polly, I am so sorry. This is horrible.'

Mamie was peeved. 'You should apologise to Angela while you're at it. Coming in here accusing her of crashing the car.'

'Mamie, I did damage the car,' said Angela.

'I'm sure you haven't done any lasting damage.' Mamie was in full-on defensive mode. 'What men think of as a write-off is just a little scuff on a wheel arch, or a small little bump.'

Angela stopped her. 'It is more than a bump. It was when I went to see Mike in hospital yesterday. As I was parking I drove straight into a concrete post. I wasn't concentrating. I was worried about Mike.'

'But why didn't you tell me?' Robert asked.

'What with everything else, it skipped my mind, and I didn't want to bring another problem into the house.'

'There,' said Mamie indignantly. 'Happy now, Robert? If she's pranged the silly car, it is because of all the extra pressure we put on her.' She took Angela's hand and glared at Robert.

He ran his hand through his hair, calming himself. 'Yes.

You are right. I suppose it's only a new bumper and radiator grille. Possibly a new radiator too, but—'

'Oh, do shut up,' Mamie snapped. 'What are we going to do about Polly's letter?'

'Well,' he looked at the three expectant faces, 'we should call the police.'

'You should have done that weeks ago, when the second letter came to Angela,' Mamie said sniffily.

Polly made the decision for them. 'Let's talk about this in a day or two. The main thing is to see how Mike is and get him back home.'

'Are you sure?' asked Angela.

'Quite sure. I feel better knowing it's not just aimed at me and that it's nothing to do with the curse.'

'There is no curse,' sighed Angela.

'I know that, but I might just go down the pond tonight and cleanse its aura.'

'If it makes you feel better.' Angela put the three letters into her desk and picked up her bag. 'Robert, would you take over the Sunday roast that Mamie has started? I am taking her to see Mike.'

'Sure. When will you be back?'

Mamie swept past Robert. 'She'll be back when she's back. And I am driving her so you don't have to worry about her driving into any more bollards. Come along, Angela.'

Mike was looking a lot better when they entered his ward and, when he saw Mamie, his face lit up.

'How lovely of you to come,' he smiled.

Mamie bent and kissed his forehead. 'Darling, the whole village sends love to you.' She pulled the one available chair up to his bedside and sat down. 'How are you feeling?'

'Oh, you know. Not too bad. Surgeon is an awfully decent chap. Done a good job. I could be home in a couple of days.'

'That's excellent,' smiled Angela, standing at the foot of the bed. 'The dogs are fine. I took them on the beach this morning with Mr W. Faith and Ben are taking them out later.'

'Very kind. Is there enough dog food?'

Mamie took his hand. 'Now don't go worrying about dog food. We'll sort all that out. I am more concerned about how you'll manage when you get home.'

'That reminds me.' Angela looked towards the nurses' station. 'I need to talk to someone about what happens when you are discharged. I won't be long.'

When she'd gone, Mamie looked around at the occupants in the five other beds in the ward. 'Not exactly a lively bunch, are they?'

'That man in the corner,' whispered Mike, 'I think he has a wife *and* a mistress.'

'Really?'

'This morning I heard the nurse saying that Bridget had called and was coming in to see him at teatime with the children, and half an hour later a rather attractive woman, whom he called Georgie, rolled up wearing a skirt so tight I could see the tops of her stockings.'

'You know you shouldn't have been looking,' Mamie said primly. 'Although I have never got on with tights myself.'

Mike swallowed too quickly and began a coughing fit.

'Oh, darling, here, let me get you a glass of water.' She poured some water into a white plastic cup and offered it to him. 'Better now?'

'Fine.' He coughed a little more, then settled back. 'Mamie, you are a joy in a dull world.'

'That's the nicest thing anyone has said to me all week.'

She smiled at him. 'So, now, what are we going to do with you once you're home?'

'I'll be fine.'

Mamie rolled her eyes. 'Oh, really? You won't be able to use your bedroom because the stairs will be too much. You can't drive. You can't let the dogs out. But you'll be fine?'

Mike set his shoulders. 'I will employ someone to help. An agency nurse.'

'That'll cost you an arm and a leg. And one of your legs is already duff.'

Mike couldn't help but laugh. 'You are a tonic.'

Angela returned. 'The doctor says if we can move your bed downstairs and make sure we have a rota of friends coming in to bring food and walk the dogs, they will arrange for a carer to come twice a day to help you wash and dress in the morning and then get you ready for bed at night. You could be home in a couple of days.'

Mike shook his head. 'That's very kind of you, but I really don't think I want to trouble people in that way.'

Angela put her hands on her hips. 'Do you want to come home or don't you?'

'Well, of course I want to come home. Can't block a jolly good bed like this when other people deserve it more than me. But really, I—'

'Mike.' Mamie winked at him. 'Let my niece do her job. This is what vicars do.' She smiled at Angela. 'And it'll look excellent on her CV.'

Motoring home in the old Jensen, Angela sat quietly.

'What's going on in your head, young lady?' Mamie asked.

'Nothing much.'

'Oh, come, come. I've told you before, you can't kid a kidder.'

Angela looked at her hands in her lap. 'The last few days have been awful. All I was trying to do was bring the village closer together, to make a difference to the community, and I ended up nearly killing one of them!'

'I know it's been awful, love, but nothing is your fault. Accidents happen.'

'Poor Mike. I'll see if one or two of the Pals can pop in to help him. Robbie might help, and do you think Evelyn would mind?'

'I think they'd be only too happy to help, but I have an even better idea.'

'Oh?'

'Me. I shall be his carer. I shall move into the house tomorrow, give it a spring clean, you and Robert can move the bed downstairs, and I shall look after him.'

'No, no, it'll be too much for you.' Angela was dismissive.

'Why?' Mamie pursed her lips.

'Well, it will be so tiring and, no offence, but you are not getting any younger.'

Mamie was very offended. 'Thank you for nothing.'

'You know what I mean.'

'No, I do not know what you mean. I am strong and fit, and besides all that, I want to help. I like Mike and—'

Angela snorted. 'He likes you!'

'Is that so strange? Why wouldn't he like me? I am an attractive woman and I know how to cheer him up.'

'Oh, for goodness' sake, spare me the details.' Angela couldn't hide her amusement.

Mamie gave her niece a sidelong glance before turning left into the lane to Pendruggan. 'Don't worry. There will be no hanky-panky.'

*

Over a supper of the delayed roast chicken lunch, Mamie outlined her plan.

Robert was very supportive. 'It's a great idea. You'll perk the poor man up no end. Just don't send his blood pressure rising too much.'

Mamie tutted. 'For heaven's sake, you and your wife have sex on the brain.'

Faith put her knife and fork down with a clatter. 'Oh, pleeeease. I do not want to hear this.'

'Sex is not just for the young, young lady,' Mamie told her.

'Eugggh. Stop it. Can I have my pudding upstairs?'

Angela shot Mamie a warning glance and received a 'what have I said?' look in return.

Robert stood up and began clearing the empty plates. 'Pudding is ice cream and strawberries and, yes, Faith, you can take it to your room.'

When Faith had left and the others were sharing out the strawberries, Robert set out a workable plan.

'Right you two, tomorrow morning, I'll get Gasping Bob to come and help me move Mike's bed. Angela, you get the dogs walked and fed. Mamie, you get the house ready for Mike's return, and any shopping that needs doing I'll pick it up on my way back from the police station.'

'You're going to tell them about the letters?' asked Angela.

'Definitely. We need to find this person,' asserted Robert. 'I phoned the police station earlier and made an appointment for two o'clock tomorrow afternoon.'

The next day, bright and early, the troops arrived at Mike's house.

'How did he get this bed up here in the first place?' panted

Robert. Mike's bed had a heavy wooden frame, which was currently stuck on the turn of the cottage stairs.

''Tis lovely bit of carpentry, though,' Bob said.

'Try turning it a little more on its end so that we can somehow slide it on the banisters.' Robert was holding the full weight of the bed in his arms.

'Righto.' Bob gave it a push and a shove.

'Ow. Not that fast.' Robert's head was now squashed between the bed and the wall.

'Anything I can do, boys?' Mamie appeared at the bottom of the stairs. 'I could get under it and take the weight on my back?'

'We are fine, thank you,' Robert said through clenched lips.

'Maybe if you went back upstairs and turned it onto the other end?' she proffered.

Robert's head was beginning to throb with the squashing. 'We are totally fine.'

'As you please.' Mamie left them to it.

Mike's handsome drawing room had already had its sofa moved to the chilly, unused dining room. Mamie had vacuumed the rolling dust balls that had accumulated beneath it and was now pushing his favourite armchair in a position near the window, close to his bookshelf and in front of the television.

She stood up and inspected the space left for the bed.

'Plenty of room,' she said to herself, then spotted his small desk. 'I wonder if that would sit nicely in the opposite corner?'

His desk was a well-organised bureau, with four drawers and several cubby compartments. She noticed that one held his cheque book, one some writing paper with matching envelopes and another a bulldog clip gripping a bunch of receipts. On the flat writing area was his laptop, hardwired to a small printer on the floor beneath.

'Now then,' she said to the desk. 'If I can just manage to push you to the other corner, without having to unplug things, we'll be laughing. It's not far.'

She began to pull. The chubby legs, resistant at first, gradually gave way and shifted along six inches of carpet.

'Good.' She straightened herself up. 'Now, if I can give you a shove from the other side . . .' She stepped into the space she'd revealed. 'OK. Come on, boy. You can do it.' As she applied her strength the desk moved a few more inches and then would move no more. 'What's the matter with you?' By her feet she could see the power cable to the printer was stretched taut. 'Sod it,' she said. 'Right, let's unplug you and see if there is another socket where I want you to be.'

On her hands and knees, and at an awkward angle, she reached round to unplug the machine. As she did so she spotted a small sheaf of three envelopes that had somehow fallen behind the desk. Brushing away a couple of strings of dust-laden cobwebs, she reached for the envelopes, intending to put them back on the desk. Then she saw the address labels on the front of each one.

'Oh, no,' she said softly. 'Please no.'

She wriggled out of the tight space and sat on her heels reading each address.

She felt sick.

Neat black type.

White notepaper and envelope.

One to Robbie, one to Piran and one to Mamie herself.

A wave of sickness lapped in her stomach.

Not being able to face the one addressed to herself, she opened the one to Robbie first.

332

CANCER? YOU ARE A LIAR

Mamie gasped in horror. This couldn't be Mike's work.

With trembling fingers she opened the one labelled with her name.

DRUGGIE HIPPYCRIT

She closed her eyes, feeling the room spin around her. How had Mike found out?

She felt her skin flush and cold perspiration spring onto her top lip. How could Mike do this?

Finally, she opened the envelope for Piran.

A photograph fluttered out. An image of Robert and Helen; unmistakably kissing. On the back, a printed label spelling out the words:

POOR PIRAN. YOUR TART AND THE VICAR'S HUSBAND. NICE.

'Oh my God, my God.' Mamie was struggling to think.

'Mamie?' Robert called from the hall. 'We've got the bed downstairs. Are you ready for it to come in?'

33

Stuffing the letters into the pocket of her jeans, Mamie took hold of her emotions and replied, 'Yes, all ready. Just replugging the printer.'

Robert stuck his head around the door. 'Any chance of a cuppa before we move the bed in here?'

Mamie wanted to smack the smug smile from his face. How could he cheat on poor Angela – this would shatter her, tear apart the family. Oh God. She bit down on her lip; it would be wiser to keep her powder dry until she figured out what on earth was going on. On her hands and knees she hid her expression from him as she found a socket and pushed the printer plug into place.

'There,' she said, standing up and brushing the dust from her knees. 'I think the bed will fit well here.' She indicated the space in the middle of the room. 'A good view through the window to the front garden and TV and books all reachable.'

'Jolly good job you've done too,' Robert beamed.

Mamie looked straight into his lying eyes. 'For a woman?'

'Ha-ha.' He laughed uneasily. She could see that he couldn't judge whether she was joking or not.

She smiled sweetly. 'I'll get the kettle on.'

She walked past him and out into the hall where Gasping Bob was opening the front door to have a quiet smoke. Mike's upturned bed was blocking the way to the kitchen.

The thought of Mike and his nasty letters filled her with a fresh fury. Bob copped it.

'If you want a bloody tea break, you'd better move this bloody bed so that I can get to the bloody kettle.'

'Sorry, missus,' said Bob. 'I was told it would be OK there.'

Robert, who had heard all this, appeared from the drawing room, smiling apologetically. 'So sorry. Stupid of me.'

'Yes. Very. Move it.'

Waiting for the kettle to boil, Mamie stood at the sink staring out into the back garden. How could she have been so wrong? Mike the poison-pen-letter writer? Robert an adulterer? Helen a scheming bitch? How was she going to tell Angela? After all the things Mamie had said to her about how Robert adored her; what a good friend Helen was.

Mamie had always prided herself on her ability to read people's characters. Now she felt stupid.

Stupid, silly and old.

She looked down at her hands. They were cold and white as they clenched the rim of the china sink. Only yesterday she had imagined those hands caring for Mike. Plumping his pillows. Fetching his glasses. Stroking his face. The hands of a lover.

Now she saw them as they were. Liver-spotted and arthritic. The hands of a fool.

She needed to think. Allow this shock and revulsion to pass, and to plan her course of action.

She made the tea and took it into the men, where the bed was now set up and in place.

Robert held the door open for Mamie and the tray. 'Lovely.' He rubbed his hands together, overemphasising his gratitude. 'Thanks, Mamie.'

She said nothing as she handed over his mug. She knew she had put him on edge and was delighting in his confusion. The bastard.

'Here you are, Bob,' she said warmly. 'Thank you so much for all your help. Robert would have been quite useless without you.'

Always a man of few words, Bob said, 'Ta.'

The three of them stood in the sunlit room and sipped their hot tea silently.

Gasping Bob appeared to have an asbestos tongue and finished his first. Putting it on the tray he took his leave. 'Got a shed to put up this afternoon.'

Robert pulled out his wallet and handed over a twenty-pound note. 'Thanks for your help, mate.'

Bob accepted it. 'Very kind.' Taking a well-thumbed red notebook out of the top pocket of his overalls, he folded the money carefully and put it under the rubber band that kept the book from falling apart. 'Thanks for the tea.'

He set off, whistling as he went down the path.

'Well,' said Robert, checking his watch, 'I'd better get going myself. The police are expecting me at two o'clock.'

'Ah, yes,' said Mamie. 'I forgot to tell you. They called earlier and cancelled. Some sort of panic on and they can't see you today. They said they'd ring you when things calmed down. In a few days.'

Robert was puzzled. 'Really? They rang here?'

'No, no,' Mamie said easily. 'While you were upstairs sorting the bed out, I had to nip home to get my rubber gloves. Good job, too. Angela was out with the dogs. Faith was in her room. The phone was ringing and I took the message.'

'Oh. I see.' He rubbed the back of his neck. 'In that case, I'll go and do the shopping for Mike's homecoming. Do you have a list?'

'Yes.' Mamie went back to the kitchen and retrieved the list she had been adding to all morning. 'Here you are.'

He looked at it. 'There's quite a lot here.'

'Yes,' she said pleasantly.

'I think I'll go and have some lunch at home before I go. Angela should be back by now.'

'I'll be over in a while. I just need to finish off a few bits,' she said. 'Ask Angela to hang onto Danvers and Davey until I have fully spring-cleaned their part of the kitchen.'

'OK,' he said nervously. 'Erm, has anything happened?'

'Happened?'

'You seem a bit . . . upset?' he tried.

'What makes you think that?'

Her smile, he noticed, did not reach her eyes. He tried again. 'I wondered if, well, if I had done something to upset you?'

'Have you?' she parried.

'I hope not.'

'So do I.'

She watched until he had shut the gate and was heading towards the vicarage, then she picked up the phone and dialled.

'Hello,' she said as it was answered, 'I would like to cancel an appointment made for two o'clock this afternoon by Mr Robert Whitehorn, to meet with one of your officers. He does apologise but he has been delayed by circumstances beyond his control.'

For the next hour, as she polished and vacuumed, she was thinking. She had to stop Robert from going to the police or else Mike would be arrested. She wanted to talk to Mike first. So many questions; all of them starting with, *why?*

Then she had to tackle Robert and Helen's affair situation. Should she have it out with them face to face? Or, if she told Piran, he could drop the bombshell perhaps? That way she could keep out of it. No, that was not her style. Protect the innocent. Expose the guilty. That was her strategy. But then why did she want to protect Mike? And how was Angela going to cope?

She pulled off her rubber gloves and looked around at the now sparkling cottage. She knew what she had to do.

She pulled her mobile from her handbag and rang Angela.

'Hi, darling.'

'I was just about to ring you,' Angela said. 'You missed lunch. Robert has just got back with all the shopping. I could bring it over now with the dogs?'

'That would be helpful. Would you mind putting everything in the fridge and larder over here while I nip home and get cleaned up? I want to go and visit Mike.'

Mamie had never been afraid of confrontation. It was one of the reasons she had never married. She adored the company of men and was always pleased, if surprised, that she could attract them so easily. But she had learnt as a young woman that men were, very definitely, the weaker sex. They needed to be coaxed and praised, adored and unchallenged, which eventually made them less attractive to her.

When it was over, it was over, and she was always the first to leave.

With Mike, she had almost believed differently. A man confident in his single life. Charming, polite, unpushy, intelligent. Someone who had lived a life of danger and deprivation in the army, yet had quietly accepted the failure of his marriage as his own without sinking into self-pity.

If you had asked her yesterday if maybe he was 'The One', she might have answered, 'Possibly.'

But twenty-four hours is a long time in the spirit level of love.

She was nervous as she drove to the hospital.

He was sitting in a wheelchair in the day room, playing bridge with three other male patients, all exhibiting a variety of broken limbs.

He saw her immediately. 'Ah! What a wonderful surprise!' he said delightedly. He introduced her to his card-playing chums, then excused himself to them by saying, 'Do you mind if we take a break in the game, chaps? I'd like to take my friend for a cup of afternoon tea.'

They all approved.

'Of course, old man.'

'Understood, dear boy.'

'I need to stretch my legs anyway.'

Mike reversed his chair with dexterity and pointed it in the direction of the lift.

'There's a decent little restaurant on the ground floor, I'm told,' he said. 'Rather good lemon drizzle.'

Mamie followed, her knees weak with subdued rage.

In the lift he babbled away cheerfully, showing her his new plaster cast and demonstrating his wheelchair skills.

'Spins on a sixpence,' he laughed, turning a three-hundred-and-sixty-degree circle. 'Marvellous, eh?'

In the restaurant he wheeled himself to the counter where two helpful volunteers were waiting in their RVS uniforms.

'Hello, Mr Bates,' the older woman said. 'How are you doing?'

'Better than yesterday,' he grinned.

'You look it!'

He turned to Mamie. 'Mrs Johnson and her colleague here came with a trolley to the ward. Very good tea and sandwiches. They told me they do a cream tea so I thought, when you come to visit, I shall treat you. And here we are.'

'How very nice,' Mamie managed.

'We'll bring it over to your table,' said Mrs Johnson. 'There's a good one over by the window. Lovely breeze coming in and you can smell the roses.'

'Shall I be mother?' Mike smiled, as the teapot arrived.

'Thank you.' Mamie pushed her cup and saucer towards him.

Tea poured, he lifted his cup. 'To you, my dear.'

She looked at him carefully, searching in hope for a sign that would tell her he was innocent.

'To you,' she said.

'So,' he sipped his tea. 'What news from the Rialto?'

'I remember asking Queenie that,' she answered with a faint smile. She wished so much she could turn the clock back. Never bought the blasted cannabis. Never tempted dear, innocent Queenie into this scandal. 'She thought I meant the cinema in Plymouth.'

'Marvellous woman, Queenie.'

'Yes.'

The younger of the RVS women arrived with a brimming

cake stand of cucumber finger sandwiches, Genoa slices, and scones with little dishes filled with clotted cream and jam.

'Here you are, Mr Bates.'

'You spoil me. Thank you.'

'My pleasure. I like to spoil the patients. Good food, good health, is what my husband always says.'

'He's a lucky man,' grinned Mike.

Mamie watched the woman go.

'Have a sandwich?' Mike asked.

'Thank you.'

'How are the dogs?'

'They are fine. Angela has been looking after them. Mr Worthington has enjoyed having his friends to play with.'

'I miss them,' he said, biting into a sandwich. 'Oh, these are very good.'

'Yes,' she began, 'after seeing you yesterday, I decided that I would move into your cottage,' he looked up in happy surprise as she went on, 'to look after you.'

'But I said I would get in an agency person—'

'Yes. I think that would be better. You need someone living in. To take the dogs out. Take care of you. So we – that is, Robert and Bob – took the liberty of bringing your bed down into the drawing room. The downstairs cloakroom will double as your bathroom. I have made up the bed in your guest room for . . . for the agency nurse, and Angela and I have stocked the fridge and the larder with basic provisions.'

He reached a hand out to hers. 'That is so kind.'

She moved her hand back to her half-eaten sandwich sitting on her plate. 'I hope you don't mind?'

'Not at all.' He was looking at her with utter tenderness. 'My dear, no one, since my wife left me, has meant as much to me as you have.'

She pushed the remains of her sandwich around her plate and looked out at the garden rather than him.

He was worried. 'May I ask why you changed your mind? Is it because of me? Would it have been too, I don't know what the word is, too personal, perhaps? To be under the same roof?'

Mamie took a deep breath and said, 'No. Nothing like that.'

Confused, he asked, 'Then why?'

'Mike, when I was moving your desk to make room for your bed, I came across something.'

'Oh, yes? Dead spider? Mouse? Wouldn't surprise me.'

'No.' She felt for her bag and pulled out the three envelopes. 'I found these.'

His warm and kindly smile died on his lips and his skin became almost grey. 'I . . . oh, my dear.'

Mamie sat still and waited for his shock to pass.

Eventually he lifted his head and wiped his eyes with a handkerchief from his pocket. 'You've read them?'

'Yes.'

'What must you be thinking?'

'What made you do it?'

He was finding it hard to speak. 'You think it was me?'

'Why else were they hidden in your house?'

He looked around the café. 'Can we find somewhere quieter to talk?'

The hovering RVS women were very understanding.

'Oh dear,' bustled in Mrs Johnson. 'Appetite is the last thing to come back after trauma. Never mind. He'll feel better tomorrow. Done too much today, I expect. We see it all the time, don't we, Louise? Especially with the men patients. Bye, Mr Bates. Take care of yourself and have a lie-down.'

Mamie pushed Mike out onto a small patch of grass outside

the hospital entrance, overlooking the ambulance bay. Under a spreading tree there was a single bench, thankfully unoccupied. She parked Mike to one side of the bench and sat next to him.

'OK, I'm all ears.' She folded her hands in her lap. 'Talk.'

'I was hoping that none of this would get out.'

'I'm sure you were.'

'It's going to hurt Angela and Robert so very much.'

34

'How was Mike?' asked Angela when Mamie got back to the vicarage. 'Is he coming home tomorrow?'

Mamie went to the fridge. 'Yes. After lunch. I shall get him.'

'I bet he was happy to hear that you are going to look after him.'

Mamie ignored her. 'Any wine in here?'

Angela laughed. 'There's some in the door. Bad day? It's not six o'clock yet.'

'It is somewhere in the world.' Mamie found a half-open bottle of Chablis and poured two large glasses. 'Robert in?'

'Yes. In his study. Why?'

'Just thought he might like a drink too.'

Robert looked up from his laptop as she came in. 'Hi, Mamie. Is one of those for me?' he asked, spying the wine glasses.

'Yes. You're going to need it.'

He looked baffled. 'Oh dear. What can be this bad that it requires wine before dinner?'

Mamie flopped into the nearest armchair and took a slug of wine. 'Worse.' Robert saw the glint of tears in her eyes.

'What? What is it? You're worrying me.'

She pulled the three envelopes from her bag. 'Read these.'

He opened each of them, reading them carefully. When he got to the letter addressed to Piran, and the photo of Robert and Helen kissing fell on his lap, Mamie could see his bewilderment.

'Who took this picture? Who wrote these?'

'Oh God, Robert.' Mamie leant forward, her elbows on her knees, cradling her wine glass. 'This is so awful. I don't know how to tell you.'

Robert's blood ran cold. 'Tell me.'

'It's Faith.' Mamie's voice cracked as tears began to fall.

He jumped up and went to her, crouching in front of her, looking into her eyes to see if this was a joke. 'Faith?'

Mamie took two or three rapid breaths, calming herself. 'She is the person sending the poison-pen letters, and that photo.'

Robert shook his head and said calmly, 'No. Not Faith. Who told you that?'

'Mike.'

'How the hell does he know?'

'Apparently, he saw Faith and Ben standing at the bus stop, waiting for the Trevay bus, and he offered them a lift.'

'And?'

'She must have been going in to post the letters, because after he'd dropped them off he found them in the footwell of the back seat, where she'd been sitting. They must have fallen out of that stupid floppy bag she has.'

'And he read them? What kind of creep does that?'

'He said he had a feeling something was wrong. Why would

Faith be posting letters addressed to Piran, me and Robbie? You had already told him about the first letter, to Angela, and he put two and two together.'

Robert shifted in his chair. 'He should have brought them straight here. To me. It can't be her, it must be that awful boyfriend of hers—'

'No, Robert, it's her. Mike talked to Faith. She was mortified and admitted it all. She promised never ever to do it again if he promised not to tell anyone.'

Robert stood up and reached for the wine glass sitting on his desk. He took a large swig and wiped his mouth. 'The only way to get to the truth of this is to confront her. Where is she?'

'Maybe in her room?'

'Right.' He stalked out of the study and Mamie heard him calling Faith from the bottom of the stairs.

'Faith?'

Her voice came back muffled through her bedroom door. 'What?'

'Come down to my study now, please.'

'Hang on. I'm just talking to a friend—'

'*Come down this minute,*' he roared.

Angela came out of the kitchen. 'What's going on?'

Faith slunk down the stairs in loose jogging bottoms, her hair wrapped up in a towel and a green face-pack on. 'What?'

'In my study,' growled Robert.

Angela followed them and sat near to an obviously upset Mamie. 'What's going on?' she asked.

Faith was beginning to look nervous. 'What's happened?'

Robert picked up the three envelopes. Faith's eyes widened. Her cheeks began to burn.

'Recognise these?' Robert asked.

'No.' Her eyes slid to the floor.

Sighing, Robert asked again. 'One more go. Do you recognise these?'

Faith began picking at her nail polish. 'I don't know.'

'What are they?' Angela asked.

'Tell your mother what these are, please.' Robert's voice was dangerously calm.

Faith burst into tears. 'I'm sorry. I'm so sorry. He said he wouldn't tell anyone. I promised not to do it again.' She grew more hysterical with every word. Angela jumped up and held her.

'It's OK, darling. It's OK.' She looked at Robert, confusion and worry furrowing her brow.

'No, Angela,' Mamie said. 'It's not OK. Read them.'

Angela took the envelopes and read each letter silently. When she saw the incriminating photograph she raised her head to Robert. 'What is this?'

Robert exhaled deeply. 'I know what it looks like.' He turned to Faith. 'Did you take this?'

Faith's expression was one of pure anger. 'Mum was scared you were having an affair with Helen,' she spat. 'Spending so much time with her at her *cosy* little cottage. I heard Mum talking about it. How much you were hurting her.'

Angela gasped. 'When did you hear me saying that?'

'I can hear everything you and Mamie talk about in the garden from my bedroom window. I wanted to find out if it was true so I followed him,' she indicated Robert, 'and her. On my bike. They went and had lunch at a swanky restaurant. Afterwards they kissed each other. And there's the proof.'

Angela was stunned. 'It was you? You wrote those letters?'

'Yes.' Faith's jaw jutted out defiantly. 'And I would do it again if it was to protect you.'

Angela was thinking. 'But the first letter was to me. Telling me to leave the village. That I wasn't wanted here. You wrote that?'

'Yeah.'

Angela felt sick, shock rippling through her. 'Why? It doesn't make sense.'

Faith's jutted lip began to tremble, 'Because I didn't like it here. I missed my friends and stupid Helen wouldn't leave Dad alone. I was scared that you and Dad would get divorced or something. I just wanted everything to be all right, to go back to normal. I thought if you got a letter telling you you weren't wanted here, we could leave and get back home again.'

'So that's why you sent me the one about Dad having a secret?'

'Yeah.' Faith wiped strings of snot from her nose onto her sleeve. 'Yeah. But it just got you more upset, so then I thought you'd know it was me so I had to write to other people as well.'

'To put them off the scent?' Mamie raised an eyebrow. 'Too many letters coming just to us otherwise?'

'Yeah.' Faith shifted the weight from one hip to another, looking at floor, not able to look her mother, father or Mamie in the eye.

'Oh, Faith, what have you done? And how on earth did you find out about Robbie's cancer scare?'

'Your stupid weekly Pals meetings.' Faith's voice was defiant. 'I listen in. Upstairs. When we first moved here, little Jenna showed me a secret hiding space under the floorboards in her room. She kept her sweets and little things there. So, I did the same thing. But when I lifted the board up one night, to show Ben, we could hear you all talking.'

Robert ran his hand over his face. 'This just gets worse.'

Angela was horrified. 'That's a breach of confidentiality! I encouraged the girls to share things in safety here. Things they did not want to share with anyone else.' She dropped her head in her hands. 'Dear God.'

Mamie broke the ensuing silence. 'Since we seem to be playing the truth game, Robert, for the record, are you having or have you had an affair with Helen?'

'Jesus Christ, what do you think?' he exploded.

'A simple yes or no will do,' Mamie said.

'*NO!*' he roared, making the three women jump. 'Angela, look at me.' He was desperate. '*Look at me.* How could I ever be unfaithful to you? You and Faith are everything to me. I could never, would never do that to you.'

Angela tried to swallow an uncomfortable lump in her throat. 'Truly?'

'Yes.' He went to her and knelt at her feet. He held her hands tenderly. 'It's always been you. You didn't really think, did you . . . that I could . . .'

'I was jealous,' Angela said simply. 'My sin was to be jealous and untrusting. Helen is everything I'm not. Can you forgive me?'

Robert held her to him. 'It's me who should say sorry. I shouldn't have given you cause for worry.'

Mamie snorted, 'I told you he was not having a fling with her.' Conveniently ignoring the fact that up until a few minutes ago she'd fallen for the lie hook, line and sinker!

'Then why are they kissing in that picture?' Angela asked quietly.

'I'll tell you,' Robert said. 'I kissed her to thank her for being my plus one for the restaurant review I was going to write. As I bent to get her cheek, she moved her head and I accidentally caught her lips. I apologised, she laughed. End of.'

'Is that what you saw, Faith?' Mamie asked.

'Well, yeah,' Faith said miserably. 'And I have stopped. I promised Mike . . .'

Mamie gave her a cool look. 'But you did do it again, didn't you?'

'No. I swear.' Faith was panicking.

'Yes, you did,' Mamie told her. 'After Mike's accident at the Pond Dig, you sent one to Polly. Telling her that witches like her should be drowned.'

'No, I never.'

Robert looked at her. 'You're lying.'

Faith collapsed into Angela's arms, smearing wet green face-pack onto her mother's T-shirt.

'It was you, wasn't it?' asked Angela gently.

'Yee . . . ss,' Faith sobbed.

A thought suddenly occurred to Mamie. 'If you wrote the letters Mike found, weeks ago, how did you know about my cannabis? That was before you caught me in the act.'

Faith stopped crying. 'I . . .'

'You went into my room and went through my things.' Mamie knew instinctively that this was the truth. 'Well, well. A snoop, a nasty letter-writer and a liar.'

Faith's sobbing grew louder.

'I am disappointed to my core, Faith,' Mamie said with contempt. 'To. My. Core.'

Faith disentangled herself from her mother and ran upstairs.

'I'll go,' said Angela.

'I'm coming with you.' Robert followed her.

They found Faith curled on the bed, her back to her parents, eyes closed and miserable.

Swallowing her anger, Angela sat on the edge of the mattress and stroked Faith's hair. 'Have you been unhappy ever since we got here?'

'I was,' mumbled Faith. 'Things got better when I met Ben, but when I thought Dad was having an affair things got worse again.'

'I see. And what about now we have found out the truth and you know that Dad and I are OK?'

Faith rolled over, her tear-streaked face and puffy eyes telling Angela with more than words how sorry she was.

'I'm embarrassed,' Faith said. 'I want to go back home because everyone will know what I did and they'll hate me and people at school will hear and I'll get left out again as the new girl with the funny "up country" posh accent.'

'No, they won't.' Angela tried to soothe her.

'But that's what they do.'

'You were bullied?'

'Of course.'

'What? Why didn't you tell us?'

'Would have made things worse. Then one day, when the girls were picking on me at break, Ben sort of rescued me. He was being bullied too. He was called all sorts of names for being gay.'

Robert, who had been pacing the room as he listened, stopped. 'I'm going to have words with that bloody head-teacher. How can she not see that bullying is going on in her school?'

'She does, Dad. But not everyone reports it because bad things happen to sneaks. Ben handles it. He's been great. He's respected loads. Even the bullies respect him.'

'Well, that's as may be, but the school needs to know.' Robert was insistent. 'I will not have my child bullied.'

'Darling.' Angela reached up to him. 'One thing at a time.'

She turned back to Faith. 'As it happens, we may be leaving here a bit earlier than we thought. I've been put forward for a job in Oxfordshire. A village called Wallingford. My own church. I have been putting off telling you because I was sure you were happy here. I didn't want to drag you off to another school so soon.'

'You've not mentioned anything to me,' said Robert. 'When would they want you?'

'Soon. Before Christmas. It's on the London train line if you want to commute.'

'London?' Faith's eyes were round with hope.

Robert brightened up. 'Interesting. So, do you have to have an interview?'

'I had one,' Angela admitted. 'Over the phone. Last week.'

'And?' asked Faith.

'Well, they have actually offered me the job but I wanted to talk it through with you both . . . when the time was right.'

Faith sat up and swung her arms around her mother's neck. 'The time is right now! Please, please can we go?'

Angela smiled. 'There's a lot to think about.'

'Hold on,' said Robert. 'I am not going to allow Faith's recent, appalling misdemeanours to be forgotten this quickly.' He frowned down at her. 'You and I, young lady, will be having a very serious talk tomorrow morning. We are all too tired and emotions are heightened this evening. But tomorrow, this family is going to do some serious talking before we even consider moving away. Understood?'

'Yes, Dad.'

'Good. Ah, and one other thing I need to know. Where is the loose floorboard?'

Faith got off her bed and went to the corner of her room beneath the big window. She lifted the carpet edge to reveal an old, oak plank. Pressing the far left corner, Robert saw that the bottom edge lifted enough to put a small finger under it and pull.

'There,' said Faith.

Robert put his hand inside, right up to his elbow, and felt about. 'Aha.' He pulled out Mr Worthington's whistle.

He went in again. This time he retrieved the parish cheque book.

Then the keys to the garage, and finally a small box of blue Basildon Bond stationery.

'I presume this is the paper you used for the first letter telling Mum she wasn't wanted here?' he said to Faith.

Faith said in a quiet voice, 'Yes.'

'And Mr Worthington's whistle is the one I have accused Mum of losing?'

'Yes,' she said in a tiny voice.

'And shall I presume that this is where you hid Mum's iPad? Her phone? Her keys? So that I would think she was losing her memory?'

Faith nodded, ashamed.

Robert and Angela stared at each other in shock. It was as if they didn't know the daughter that stood in front of them, suddenly looking so young in her PJs, the face-mask now all rubbed off with the tears that had run down her face.

'All this because you were so unhappy and wanted to go back towards London?' asked Angela.

'Yes.'

'Well then,' said Robert, replacing the floorboard and flopping the carpet back into place. 'I think the sooner we leave here the better.'

35

'My word!' Mike used his new crutches to push the drawing room door open and gazed in wonder at his perfectly organised temporary bedroom. 'That must have taken some doing to get the bed down here. Heavy piece of kit.'

Mamie kicked the front door shut behind her and dropped his bags on the stairs.

'Cup of tea?' she asked.

'What time is it?'

She pushed up her sleeve and checked her small wristwatch. 'Coming up to four o'clock.'

Mike swung himself and his crutches towards his armchair. 'In that case, we are just in time for *Tipping Point* and a glass of Scotch.'

Mamie shook her head. 'Uh-uh. No alcohol with the pain-killers. I promised your doctor.'

'Oh, for goodness' sake.' He lowered himself into the chair. 'A small one won't do any harm. Have one with me.'

'You are a bad influence,' she laughed. 'Just the one then. Here, let me pass you the telly clicker.'

As she poured two generous glasses of Scotch with a drop of soda, he turned the television on to *Tipping Point* and she handed him his glass.

'Cheers.'

'*Salut*,' he returned.

As they sat together, Mamie felt the stresses of the last forty-eight hours slip away. She was giving Angela, Robert and Faith some space and found refuge by Mike's side. She surprised herself with quite how much she enjoyed shouting out the answers to the quiz questions, both of them happily pouring scorn on any wrong answers supplied by the contestants.

'He's a bloody fool,' Mike said of a hapless young man who didn't know the first names of Morecambe and Wise. 'Eric and Ernie, you numbskull,' he shouted at the screen.

Mamie patted his arm. 'The poor boy's not even twenty. How is he supposed to know?'

'General knowledge, my dear. I wasn't alive when Churchill made his great speeches but I sure as hell know what he said.'

'That's because everyone does.'

'Not that idiot. I bet he doesn't even know who the Prime Minister is.'

'Shh. I can't hear the question.'

Quiz host Ben Shephard was speaking. 'Who won the 2017 Nobel Prize for Literature?'

'Ha, he'll never know this,' scoffed Mike.

'Do you know it?' asked Mamie.

'Of course I don't. Who would!'

The young contestant was looking anxious.

'Come on, Toby. You need this to stay in the game,' Ben urged.

'Is it,' Toby hesitated, 'is it Kazuo Ishiguro?'

Ben's grin lit up the screen. 'That is correct! How did you know that?'

'*The Remains of the Day* is one of my favourite books,' Toby said without showing off.

'A-ha!' crowed Mamie. 'Never assume anyone knows less than you, Michael Bates.'

'Fair play to him,' Mike allowed. He tipped the last of his whisky into his mouth. 'Any chance of another one?'

'None.' Mamie stood up. 'I'll get you your supper. Pork pie and salad OK?'

The carer to get Mike ready for bed arrived just after eight, by which point Mike was tired and happy to get an early night.

'It's been a very exciting day,' he yawned. 'So happy to be at home and so thankful for your company.'

Mamie placed a glass of water on the table by his bed and a little metal bell next to it. 'If you need me, just ring. I'm only at the top of the stairs.'

He took her hand and said sincerely, 'Thank you, my dear. For all you have done. Means a great deal to me.'

'It's my pleasure.' She kissed his brow. 'Sleep tight.' And for the first time in her considerably adventurous life, Mamie could see that a simple life could indeed be an adventure she was ready for.

As the week went on, Mike got stronger and more mobile, while Mamie, although tired, enjoyed their daily routine of doing the crossword, listening to music or simply snoozing together on separate armchairs after lunch.

On Thursday Mamie decided that lunch would be one of Queenie's pasties.

'I haven't seen her for days,' she told Mike. 'I miss her.'

'And her gossip?' he suggested.

'Well, maybe a little. Would you like to come? I can get the wheelchair out of the car?'

It was now August and the village children were enjoying the summer holiday by playing rounders on the green.

Mamie and Mike stopped for a few minutes to watch. 'I suppose before too long Faith will getting herself ready for school.' Mike smiled. 'I remember the fun of getting smart new pencils and rulers for the start of term.'

'Me too.' Mamie thought back. 'My poor mother would take my sister and me to buy new shoes because our feet would have grown so much since the beginning of the summer. There would be terrible rows over what styles we wanted and what styles our mother said we had to have. All of us would leave the shop in tears, every time. Those poor shop assistants. They must have dreaded us coming in.'

A light breeze blew up and Mamie noticed Mike had goosebumps on his unplastered leg. He could only wear shorts for the time being.

'I told you I should have brought a rug for your knees.'

'Don't fuss, darling. I'm fine.'

She turned his chair towards the village shop. 'It'll be warmer in Queenie's.'

Queenie was delighted to see them and busily set about making tea and selecting two of her best pasties.

'Fresh this morning,' she told them, licking her fingers to open a paper bag and popping the two pasties inside. 'There you go, my ducks. On the house.'

'Thank you. They smell very good,' Mike said. 'Have you got the latest *Country Life?*'

Queenie bustled to her magazine shelf. 'Here we are. I'll

bring the little heater closer for you and you can have a read while I catch up with Mamie.'

'You go ahead,' said Mike, finding his reading glasses and putting them on. 'I'm happy here.'

Queenie nudged Mamie while Mike was engrossed. 'Here.' She winked and pointed to the back of the shop. 'Come round the back for a quiet chat. Is it true your Angela is moving back to London?'

Meanwhile at the vicarage, the night Faith's sins were revealed became a moment that, when they looked back at the thread of time, had a red flag planted upon it.

As happens in families, all three of them had not noticed that the bonds that kept them close had loosened. Each of them, without recognising it, had drifted on the current of their own wants and needs. Angela focused on the parish and her future. Robert looked for things to occupy his mind while not admitting to himself that he couldn't wait to get back to London and the dog-eat-dog world of political journalism. And in between the two of them a fifteen-year-old girl dispossessed of her friendship group, afraid to tell her parents she was being bullied at school, and investing all her anxieties in working on a plan to get her family back to the home she knew.

Angela could understand why Faith had done the terrible things she had done but Robert found it harder.

'It's as if I don't know you any more,' he told her. 'I don't know what to think or what to say to you.'

Faith was exhausted by her tears and her father's reaction. 'I've said I'm sorry and I truly am.'

Angela, sitting between them on Faith's bed, appealed to Robert. 'We can learn from this. I'm grateful that we know the truth. Faith needs us to listen and hear what she's saying. We can be angry or we can rebuild ourselves and face the future. Together.'

Faith began to smile.

Robert glared at her. 'I'm glad you think is funny.'

'No, Dad, I don't, but Mum sounded just like a TED Talk then.' She started to giggle.

Angela's lips twitched. 'Oh golly, I did, didn't I!'

'I'm sorry, am I missing something?' Robert was still angry. 'What is a TED Talk?'

The girls began laughing helplessly. 'It's like a podcast, Dad. Inspirational motivational . . .' Faith couldn't finish the sentence and rolled on to her back shrieking with laughter.

Angela tried to explain, 'It's all very modern and trendy and . . .'

Robert interrupted, 'Bloody claptrap is what it sounds like.' Which set mum and daughter off again.

'Oh, Dad, I do love you.' Faith reached over to him and hugged him.

'Yeah, well, I love you too.' He kissed the top of her head. The smell of her overwhelmed him as it had since the day she was born. 'It's going to take me time to forgive you for doing that to your mum, young lady. But I do love you, nothing will ever change that. So what happens now?' He asked.

'We go back home,' said Angela. 'As a family.'

As anyone knows, news spreads fast in a small community but in Pendruggan it spread infinitely faster than in most.

Within forty-eight hours, Angela's front door had seen more visitors than it had in the previous six months.

Her larder was filling with welcome gifts of homemade

marmalade, local honey, artisan gin and Sea Salt Scented St Eval candles, and each day several invitations to lunch or tea would arrive.

She couldn't possibly accept every one of them, because her date to leave the village and take up her new job had been confirmed. It was in three weeks.

It was with mixed feelings that she announced her plans at church the next Sunday.

'Good morning, everybody.'

'Mornin', Vicar,' replied Tony from his pew, his glossy sleek hair slicked down for the occasion.

'I believe you have all heard that it won't be long before I have to leave you, earlier than I intended, but as it turns out, not earlier than God intended. I have been called to another parish, one that will be my own. My first true parish.

'I am due to start in just a few weeks, but you won't be left in the lurch. Rev Rowena, of St Peter's in Trevay, is going to share you with her parish until Simon gets back in the New Year. But I want you all to know how much you and this church, in Pendruggan, will forever be in my heart as the place where my life as a vicar began. Each and every one of you have given me courage, friendship and memories that can never be erased.

'Yesterday I received an email from Simon in Brazil, wishing me well and asking me to leave notes on how to run the animal blessing service. He seems determined to make that an annual event.' A ripple of amusement ran round the church and Tony clapped.

'The running club is doing very well. OK, there may be only five of us who run regularly,' she paused for more laughter, 'but we five are up to ten miles non-stop now, which I count as a huge success.' She looked around the faces gazing up at her. 'Where are my runners? Stand up, would you, and take a bow.'

Dorrie, Ella, Ben's mum Sarah and Helen stood to a polite round of applause.

Angela went on, 'One of my least successful events was the digging of the old pond. It led to Mike Bates having his leg and several ribs broken. If it hadn't been for Polly's quick medical attention, he might not have been here today.' Her voice faltered as she felt her guilt and stupidity. She searched for Polly. 'Polly, stand up and take a well-deserved round of applause.'

'Oh, 'tis nothing.' Polly smiled, flapping her hand to make the noise stop, before sitting down.

Simple Tony put his hand up. 'It was my idea, miss. To dig the pond.'

Angela smiled at his anxious, innocent face. 'But I made it happen. It was my responsibility,' she reminded him.

Digger Pete stood up at the back of the church. 'It was mine, really. 'Twas me who swung the bloody digger arm at Mr Bates and bloody buried him.'

'No, no,' said Angela. 'It was not your fault.'

Mike, balancing on his crutches, got to his feet. 'I can't have this. The fault was all mine. I was too damn nosy and put myself in the firing line.'

Piran stood up. His height and bearing, and the general respect in which he was held, stopped the chatter instantly.

He walked to the front of the church.

''Twas nobody's fault. Accidents happen and that's that.' He turned to Angela. 'We did find a little water on the weekend of the dig – not enough to write home about but it was there and it was clean. Since then we have kept the site fenced off. But me, being an inquisitive sort of bugger – beg pardon, Vicar

– have been going down there most nights, doing a bit of my own digging. There was plenty of rubbish down there, but not the modern stuff. Looks like it had been used as the village tip and that's what clogged it up. Hobnail boots, pottery, glass bottles, clay pipes, you know the sort of thing. Anyway, I've been slowly clearing all that and a few nights ago I got a helluva surprise when I pulled out a great clump of clay and silt and the bleddy spring only started running like a tap.'

He looked at Angela and grinned. 'Pendruggan has got a bleddy pond and it's beautiful!'

Angela gasped. She closed her eyes, put her hands together and sent a silent, personal prayer of thanks.

'Can we go and see it?' asked Tony, his sleek otter head bobbing with excitement.

Again Piran looked to Angela. 'What do you say?'

'Well, what can I say but, yes!'

Mike, sitting next to Mamie, whispered to her, 'I don't think I can go that far on my crutches.'

She frowned. 'Bring back the bad memory, you mean?'

'Good God no, woman. I want to go. Just haven't got the legs to do it.'

'Oh, that's easily sorted.'

She beckoned Piran and Don over. 'Boys, can you two give this old soldier a shoulder to lean on?'

Outside, the sun was low and warm. A slight breeze ran off the beach and up the lane towards them, rustling the long grass of the verges and pulling at the first autumnal leaves on the trees. It seemed the perfect place for Angela to leave this community that taken her to their hearts.

'There,' said Piran, stopping the crowd a few yards from the pond. 'Can you hear it?'

Everybody stopped and listened. They could hear the gentle waves lapping onto the beach and the chuckle of a seagull skittering on the wind above them, but nothing else.

But then, as ears old and young filtered out the waves and the gull, they heard the faintest trickle.

Like a tiny garden water feature.

'I can hear it,' said Tony, so excited he was almost skipping.

'I can't hear a bloody thing over your racket,' Queenie scolded.

'Sorry.'

As quiet fell again and every ear strained, they all began to hear the same thing. A faint but definite sound of bubbling water.

'You all hear that?' asked Piran.

Everyone nodded.

'Then come and see it.'

Just a few steps on and there it was. Not yet a boating pond but a small clear pool of water about six metres in circumference.

'It's beautiful,' said Polly with reverence. 'The earth goddess is pleased.'

Faith wriggled out of her Doc Martens. 'Can I paddle in it?'

'I wouldn't recommend it,' warned Piran. 'There's glass and all sorts still in there.'

'Oh. Well, can I just dip my toes?' she asked, looking at her mother.

'Be careful!' said Angela.

Polly delved inside her large bag and pulled out a small, clean, empty jam pot, the type served with cream teas. 'I'm going to fill this with the water and bless it. Powerful stuff, this is.'

Angela hid a smile. 'You bless the water, I'll bless this place.'

She held her face to the sun and put her hands together.

'Dear Lord, we thank you for this beautiful pond and the joy it will bring to our village. Bless this ancient spot and keep all who visit here safe. We don't want any more accidents.'

A wave of laughter swept the group.

She went on, 'May Mike continue his recovery. Thank you too for bringing me to this place and teaching me so much about life, love, friends and family. I shall miss everyone and will return as often as possible. Amen.'

'Amen.'

36

'You know what?' Angela announced one morning at breakfast.

Robert lowered his newspaper and peered at her. 'I'm not sure I'm going to like this.'

'I am going to host a dinner party for the key people of Pendruggan. To thank them and to say goodbye properly.'

Robert groaned and lifted his paper again. 'Yep, I knew I wouldn't like it.'

'Don't be so mean. I'm thinking of maybe Thursday night.'

Robert gave up reading and folded his paper. 'That's three days away.'

'Plenty of time then,' she grinned. 'Mamie will help me.'

Robert stood up and made for the hall. 'Don't let her cook. Please.'

'Where are you going?'

'To sit in my study and read my paper.'

'OK. Coffee at eleven?' she asked.

'You spoil me,' he said before closing his study door.

Angela watched him go then found the kitchen notepad and began scribbling down a guest list.

Mamie found her sitting there ten minutes later.

'Good morning, darling,' she chirped. 'Thought I should check in to see how everything is going without me here.' She put the kettle on and helped herself to the biscuit tin. 'Oh, good. Chocolate Hobnobs. Mike is a bit of a puritan where biscuits are concerned. His favourites are Rich Tea. I mean, they are no good at all. Very dull. The sort of thing a vicar might have for the nuns.'

Angela gave her a withering look. 'Thank you for that.'

Mamie made her tea and brought a handful of Hobnobs with her. 'You are a much more exciting vicar, darling . . . although there was that Christmas when you only had those ghastly pink wafers in the house.' She shuddered. 'I can't bear to think about them.' She dunked her biscuit and took a mouthful. 'Bliss. What are you up to?'

'We are giving a dinner party on Thursday.'

Mamie raised her eyebrow. 'Oh, are we?'

'You will help me, won't you?'

'Tell me who is coming and I shall decide.'

'Well, you and Mike of course.'

'Of course.'

'Helen and Piran. Ben and Faith. Robbie and Gasping Bob. Don and Dorrie from the pub. Ben's mum, Sarah. Queenie. Evelyn and . . .'

Mamie waited for Angela to reveal the next name and then realisation dawned. 'Oh, no. I will not sit at a dinner table with that ghastly woman and her cringing husband.'

'They have to come.' Angela was firm. 'Audrey and Geoffrey would be very hurt to be excluded and for all her—'

'Rudeness.'

'Little foibles, she does have a good heart.'

'Good heart my arse.' Mamie dunked another Hobnob. 'And Geoffrey is King Bore of Bore Land.'

'He thinks you are gorgeous.'

'Well, he would! Having to wake up next to that gargoyle every morning. If they share a bed. I bet she has the bed and makes him sleep on the floor next to her, like one of her bloody dogs.'

'Mamie! That's a terrible thing to say. I don't like it when you are so nasty.'

'You still need my help, though, don't you?'

'I can do it on my own,' Angela sniffed. 'But yes, I would like your help as long as you keep your horrible thoughts to yourself.'

'I shall be the model hostess.'

'Good. I'm working on the menu.'

'Ah now, I'm good at that. I am cordon bleu trained, after all.'

'No, you're not.'

'Well, I attended a one-hour cookery demonstration when I was a student at the Lucie Clayton Charm School.' Mamie stretched her slender legs out under the kitchen table, her mind going back to the sixties. 'The chef was an absolute dish. I can't remember what he was making but I can see his eyes now. Like amber pools in his tanned face. Of course his French accent was le icing on le cake. But it wasn't to be. He went off with bloody Lumley. Took her out for dinner and expected more. Typical French. She told us the next day that she had to smack him. Only made him more keen, of course. We had to hide her under our coats and smuggle her into the school every day. Such fun. Such a great girl.'

'The last time you told me that story, the chef was Italian,' Angela said.

'Maybe he was.' Mamie ran her hands through her hair. 'Who cares? Why spoil a good story for a bit of truth?'

'Can we get back to our dinner menu?'

'Of course, darling. You have my full attention.'

'I was thinking of a small salad to start with. Pear, stilton, walnuts and spinach with a sweet French dressing and some walnut bread?'

Mamie narrowed her eyes suspiciously. 'Oh, yeah?'

'Followed by garlic roast leg of lamb with buttered mashed potato, sautéed leeks and roast cauliflower.'

'Yeess,' said Mamie.

'And for pudding, vanilla ice cream with sherry poured over the top.'

Mamie leant her elbows on the table and began giggling. 'And where, my fair niece, did you come up with all that?'

Angela lifted her bum and pulled out a copy of a cookery magazine that she'd been sitting on. 'Page 102 to 106.'

Mike was thrilled with the invitation. 'How jolly kind of Angela and Robert. Do I need to get my dinner jacket dry cleaned? It's a long time since I've been out in such exalted company.'

'Dinner jacket!' Mamie was thrilled. 'Oh, yes. I love a man in black tie. I shall wear my silk kaftan.' She came back to her senses. 'But how are you going to wear a dinner suit with that plaster on your leg?'

'I have black shorts.'

Thursday arrived and Mamie and Angela started early. Robert had been made to pack up his study the day before, so that they could reclaim the old vicarage dining room.

Faith polished the table with lavender-scented wax and dusted and vacuumed every crevice.

Ben turned out to be very good at choosing interesting foliage from the garden, which he wound around three silver candlesticks.

Angela popped in to see how he was getting on and was very impressed. 'Ben, that's fabulous. Have you done that before?'

'No I haven't, but I'm quite pleased with it.'

'Well,' Angela replied, 'you are very artistic.'

Faith stepped in. 'Don't you dare say it's because he's gay, Mum.'

Angela, who had been thinking something along those lines, quickly defended herself. 'Of course I wasn't thinking that, I was just saying Ben has an artistic talent . . .'

Ben burst into laughter. 'It's all right. Really. Faith is pulling your leg.'

'Oh well, in that case . . . um . . . would you write out some place name cards for who sits where?'

'He's on it, Mum,' Faith laughed, and chucked her duster at Ben, who began to wrestle with her. Angela left them to it.

In the kitchen, Mamie was pricking the lamb with garlic. 'The recipe says to cook it in the top Aga oven for around twenty minutes then leave it for a couple of hours in the bottom oven. Does that sound right?'

'Yep. I think so. Let's do the back timing. If guests are due at seven for seven thirty, and the lamb will need thirty minutes to rest, we'd better get it started at about five?'

'Good. Plenty of time.' Mamie checked her watch. 'I'll get the veg prepped and then I'll go back to Mike's to get us both ready. What are you wearing?'

'I thought the green dress that Robert bought me for my birthday. The one I didn't wear.'

Mamie gave Angela a slow smile then hugged her. 'Perfect.'

At six forty-five, Mamie returned in a mist of Shalimar, her jewelled black kaftan glittering in the late evening sun.

Mike had now graduated to a simple polished wood walking stick and was very dapper from the waist up in a white shirt, black bow tie and well-cut dinner jacket. However, below the waist he was wearing a pair of black chino shorts with black socks and white trainers.

'It's all the rage, you know!' he laughed. 'Robert, you should try it!'

'Let me get you a drink first,' Robert smiled. 'Come into the sitting room.'

Mamie pulled Angela to one side. 'You look gorgeous, darling, and the house looks so pretty. Love the candle arrangement on the hall table.'

'Ben,' Angela smiled.

'That boy will go far,' winked Mamie. 'Right. What can I do?'

'Sit down and have Robert pour you a drink.'

'I can do that.' Mamie kissed her niece and swept off to join the men.

On the dot of seven Audrey and Geoffrey arrived. Audrey had had her hair permed very tightly and was wearing a most unsuitable low-backed, strappy evening dress, two sizes too small. Geoffrey was in tweed.

Audrey looked Angela up and down. 'I thought you might have dressed up for tonight, Angela.'

'I, oh—' said Angela.

Geoffrey interrupted. 'Dearest, not every woman can carry off formal evening wear in the same way as you do.'

Angela bit her lip to stop her laughter escaping. 'Quite so, Geoffrey. Audrey, you look wonderful. Give me your coats and then do go into the sitting room. Robert's pouring the drinks.'

In quick succession everyone else arrived. Sarah, Queenie, Don and Dorrie, Helen and Piran, Robbie and Bob and finally Evelyn, and she was not on her own. A tall, slender, gentle-looking man in jeans and a patterned shirt was standing next to her.

'Vicar, I hope you don't mind but I have brought a friend with me. This is Graham.'

Angela shook his hand. 'Good evening, Graham.'

'Hello. I hope you don't mind me just showing up, only Evelyn was sure you wouldn't mind.'

'I don't mind a bit. Come on in and join the others.'

Angela took them to the sitting room and introduced Graham. He and Piran knew each other and were soon absorbed in a male group that included Don and Mike.

'So how did you meet him?' Queenie went in for the kill.

'You dark horse,' Mamie teased Evelyn.

'Don't laugh nor nothing, but we met at the cattle auction up Launceston.'

'So he's a farmer.' Mamie approved.

'Yeah. Bigger farm than ours, though. He does dairy and arable, and dabbles in old-breed pigs.'

Queenie couldn't help herself. 'Married? Children?'

Evelyn shook her head. 'No. Nothing. He looked after his parents until they died and the farm's his own now.'

'Well, good on you,' smiled Angela. She chinked her wine glass against Evelyn's gin and tonic. 'To happiness.'

'To happiness.'

*

At the agreed signal from Angela, Robert ushered everyone into the dining room. The sight of it, bathed in candlelight and smelling of the white phlox that Ben had gathered from the garden and studded with spires of blue salvia, was stunning.

Audrey sniffed in disdain. 'Smells like a tart's boudoir,' she muttered to Geoffrey.

'Geoffrey,' Mamie called from the other side of the long table. 'You are sitting next to me, and Mike . . .'

'Yes, my dear?'

'You are sitting on my other side.'

Geoffrey fairly sprinted around to his seat while Audrey quietly fumed.

Robert was placing Dorrie in the seat to his left and then called to Audrey.

'Audrey, would you care to be seated next to me?'

For a large woman, Audrey could move like a whippet.

The first course went down well and the consumption of wine helped the conversation to run smoothly. The lamb was perfect. Succulent, slightly pink and tender. The look of it rather reminded Robert of Audrey on the day of the Pond Dig when she had heatstroke, but he didn't mention it.

The entire table was now relaxed and merry. After pudding they returned to the sitting room and Faith and Ben were dispatched to make the coffee.

Geoffrey made sure he was on a seat next to Mamie. 'My dear, what scent are you wearing?'

'Oh. Do you like it?' she asked flirtatiously.

If he'd had a moustache he would have stroked it. 'I certainly do.'

'It's very old-fashioned. One of Guerlain's classic fragrances.

I have just had a spritz. I keep it in the downstairs cloakroom for when I need a lift.'

'It's absolutely delightful.'

'What does Audrey wear?' Mamie asked, all innocence.

Audrey, who had been watching from the other side of the room, approached. 'What are you two getting so cosy about?'

Geoffrey blanched. 'Ah, my dear. We are talking fragrances. Mamie would like to know what you wear.'

Audrey at once became superior. 'I like the classics, of course. Freesia is my go-to signature scent.'

'Oh, yes?' asked Mamie. 'By which of the perfume houses?'

'Woods of Windsor,' preened Audrey. 'One of the Queen's favourites.'

'Fascinating,' Mamie smiled. 'Now if you'll excuse me I shall chase up some brandy to go with our coffee.'

'Ladies and gentlemen.' Piran was standing by the fireplace with a second large brandy in his hand. 'I'd like to propose a toast to our vicar. When Simon and Penny left for Brazil, we had no idea how a new vicar, and a woman at that, would fill the gap left. I have known Simon all my life and, although I don't believe in all the church stuff, I do know that Simon brings a sense of belonging to our village. When folks are having a tough time, church-goers or not, he helps them, and that is what you have done too, Angela. We'm gonna miss you.' He raised his glass. 'To Angela.'

'Thank you,' Angela said through tears. 'Thank you so much.'

'Right, everybody.' Mamie got to her feet. 'I have some news of my own. I haven't even told Angela, or you, Queenie!'

'Oh my good Gawd. You tell me everything,' Queenie said crossly.

'Well, I'm telling you now.' Mamie held them in suspense for a moment. 'Angela, Robert and Faith may be leaving Pendruggan, but I am not.'

'What?' gasped Angela.

'Mike has asked me to stay and live with him. In sin!'

'Woo hoo!' shouted Faith. 'Good on you.'

From his armchair Mike raised his glass. 'I'd like to propose another toast. To darling Mamie. Thank you for agreeing to stay with me for as long as that may be. I love you.'

After all the excitement, and too much booze, the party began to thin out. Mike was tired and Piran walked him home, with Mamie promising she would be back in the morning, but tonight she'd help clear up and stay at the vicarage.

The last to go were the Tiptons, Geoffrey hanging on to get a last glimpse of Mamie, who was already in the kitchen washing up. Angela was encouraging him out of the door.

'They don't make women like her any more,' he told Angela.

'They certainly don't.' Angela smiled. 'Now look, Audrey is waiting for you.'

'*GEOFFREY!*'

'Yes, my love.'

'*COME,*' Audrey commanded.

Finally Angela waved off the tiddly Geoffrey and shut the door. Mamie insisted that she and Robert were to go to bed.

'You have to get up in the morning,' she told them. 'I can have a lie-in. I've got all the time in the world now, haven't I? I'm not going anywhere.'

37

Mamie turned off the lights and climbed the stairs. The sound of gentle snoring was coming from Angela and Robert's room – she presumed it was Robert – and all was quiet behind the closed door of Faith's room.

In her own room, Mamie cleansed her face, and got into her pyjamas.

She unrolled her yoga mat and sat cross-legged in front of her long mirror.

How extraordinary life was, she said to herself. Here she was, in her seventies, embarking on her first journey into true love.

For all her talk about her great and exciting life, which by and large was true, she had never fallen in love with anyone.

And suddenly, here was Mike. A good and certain man. Not a braggart or a womaniser. No notches on his bed post. The night he told her he loved her had been an ordinary one. They had played Scrabble and talked. Had a cup of tea before bed. Laughed at how their joints ached and how their sight and hearing were going, and quietly he had taken her hand and told her, 'I love you.'

'Why?' she had asked.

'Because I couldn't imagine our lives without each other. Do you understand?'

She took his hand. 'I do.'

'I'll marry you if you like, but honestly, what's the point? I'd rather both of us were together because we wanted to be together, not because we had to.'

'That would suit me very well.'

'Is that a yes?'

'Yes.'

She smiled at her reflection. *You're OK*, she told herself. *You are happy.*

She began doing her nightly stretches and then settled into her meditation routine. She hadn't done it since she'd been at Mike's and tonight she was ready for one.

She closed her eyes and began the slow breathing. She stilled her thoughts and concentrated on the sounds around her. Someone snoring. The dishwasher quietly churning. The wind beyond her open window.

Her breathing slowed and she focused her mind on her body. The feel of the mat beneath her. The cool breeze coming from the window. Her hands loosely resting on her knees.

Peace was coming to her. Mind and body were stilled. She breathed slower and deeper and then . . . What was that?

A noise in the hall?

Had she not shut Mr Worthington into the kitchen? Had he nosed his way out?

She didn't move, her brain listening again for a noise but otherwise undisturbed.

Footsteps.

Definitely footsteps.

Walking from the front door and down the hall. Stopping halfway.

Mamie opened her eyes.

She would have to go and check.

Rousing herself, she stood and went to her bedroom door. She opened it quietly and shut it behind her, not wanting the light to alert any intruder.

She stood at the top of the stairs, in the dark, and listened.

She heard breathing and it wasn't hers.

She began to inch her way down, tread by tread.

Staring into the darkness of the hall, she was sure she saw a dark shape in the shadows.

'I can see you,' she whispered. 'I know who you are.'

The shadow moved quickly up the hall towards the front door. Mamie took the last few stairs as quickly as she could but the intruder got to the front door ahead of her.

Mamie misjudged the last three steps and floundered, her feet desperate to touch solid ground.

The front door opened. The shadow looked around at Mamie and saw her fall. Head first. Her skull hitting the solid oak wainscoting.

With a tiny strangled cry the shadow ran through the open door and closed it as quietly as possible before disappearing into the night.

Mamie, dazed, sat up and tried to stand, but the pain in her head made her weak. She felt blood running down her face and knew that poor Angela would be the one who had to clean it up. Oh dear. What a bother that was going to be.

Without asking, her body fell back to the floor. She knew it was the end.

'I'm sorry, Mike,' she said. 'This was not how it was supposed to be. I'm so sorry.'

The coroner's office had been very helpful and released Mamie's body for burial before the inquest. The coroner had been satisfied with the reports from the doctor and police who had attended the scene, and had accepted their opinion that no foul play had been involved.

Mamie's wishes were to be buried in a wicker coffin woven with ivy and lilies.

Angela, Mike and Faith had gone to the florist together to describe exactly what Mamie would have wanted.

'Can we have fairy lights too?' asked Faith. 'Mamie loved fairy lights. Little ones that twinkle? They'll make it look so pretty.'

Mike put his arm in Faith's. 'I think that's a marvellous idea.'

'No problem,' said the florist. 'As long as the vicar officiating thinks it's OK. Some of these vicars are very traditional.'

'I'm sure the vicar won't mind,' said Angela.

Mike took them out for tea after that. 'We need teacakes and crumpets,' he told them.

Sitting in the cosy teashop garden, Mike settled himself with his walking stick at a sturdy cast-iron table and ordered for the three of them.

'Thank you,' said Angela. 'I can't seem to be able to make decisions about anything at the moment.'

'Understandable, my dear. I rather feel the same,' he said.

'I can't believe she's not here.' Faith began to cry. 'I miss her.'

'We all do,' said Mike. 'We all do.'

*

The church was full. Mamie was carried in on the shoulders of Robert, Piran, Don, Bob, Digger Pete and Faith, who insisted on it.

Mamie's coffin sat in front of the altar, its fairy lights twinkling magically in the winding whips of ivy and the stems of the lilies.

'She looks beautiful,' said Queenie, taking Faith's hand as she returned to the pew.

'She does,' nodded Faith, wiping her eyes.

Angela had assisted at many funerals but never conducted one on her own and she was determined to do it the way she hoped Mamie would have wanted it.

'Good afternoon, everybody. We are here to celebrate my Aunt Mamie's life. She was an incredible woman. Courageous. Loving. Fun. She lived life to the full wherever she was. Many of you have told me what light she brought into the village and how fond you had grown of her in the short time she was here. She's been in my life all of my life and today I am bereft. I feel orphaned. My father died when I was young. My mother, Mamie's sister, just a few years ago. But I always had Mamie. My mad and eccentric and wonderful Mamie. And now she's gone.'

Angela swallowed hard. Tears threatened her ability to carry on. 'I make no apologies for my tears,' she managed. 'I am with you all, my friends, and . . .' she coughed, 'and I am so grateful to you all.' She dug into the pocket of her cassock and pulled out a tissue. 'Excuse me.' She wiped her eyes and blew her nose. 'Shall we stand for our first hymn. "Lord of the Dance".'

As the hymn finished, Mike limped to the altar and stood next to Mamie's casket.

'This woman, lying here, in sweetest lilies, gave me more

in the few months I knew her than any other person I have ever known. I have been an old bachelor for many, many years. After the breakdown of my marriage I accepted that I would never find anyone who I would want to share my life with, or indeed vice versa. But Mamie has a way of getting under your skin. Her silly jokes and rackety stories. Her blithe dismissal of the ordinary. I thank God that I did break my leg. If I hadn't she might never have come to look after me and I might never have had so much laughter. God, how we laughed. She did have some faults, though. She was a dreadful cook.' He laughed as the congregation laughed. 'But she could pour a damn fine whisky and soda. We may have lost her but I know not one of us will ever forget her.' He bent and kissed her coffin. 'God bless you, my love. Until we meet again.'

Mike walked back to his seat, his heart breaking, while all around him people wept.

Simple Tony stood up and walked to the altar. Nervously, he smoothed his hair down and looked at Angela, who gave him a tearful nod of approval.

He began.

'Missus had a lovely car. A Jensen Interceptor sports car. 1976. Seven-point-two litre. She let me clean it. Once, she let me sit in it while she turned the engine on. We didn't drive anywhere because I told her I didn't like driving in cars, so she put the radio on and this song came on. She said it was her favourite and I would like to sing it for you today. It's called "Unforgettable" because she was.'

He cleared his throat and then began. His beautiful clear singing of the great love song swept along the aisles and swooped up into the vaulted roof and gradually people joined in, as best they could through their tears.

Angela's final words before they headed out to the churchyard for Mamie's burial were heartfelt.

'This is my last service here. How well I remember sitting in this empty church with Mamie just before I started. She told me that all parishes, small cosy ones like Pendruggan or large inner-city ones with knife crime, racial tension and poverty, were the same under the skin. She told me that humans couldn't help but make a mess of their lives and will keep on doing so. That is the challenge of being human and being alive. It's a challenge that my family have faced and that your families have faced. I came here a newcomer, but I leave as your friend.'

Mamie's grave was in a pretty corner of the churchyard. A cherry blossom tree stood at one end and the other was open to the sunny skies.

As the service drew to a close and Angela committed Mamie to her final resting place, Audrey, who had been unusually quiet, suddenly fled, a concerned Geoff calling after her.

Queenie watched her go with her shrewd eyes. She spoke under her breath as though Mamie were standing next to her. 'Now where the 'ell does she think she's going? Summink's not right there, I'm telling you. And by the way, Simple Tony done you proud, didn't he?'

The wake was in the village hall. It could have been at the vicarage but Angela felt that only the most macabre of guests would enjoy stepping on the exact spot where Mamie had died.

The trestle tables were covered in cakes and sandwiches, and tea flowed constantly, oiling the conversations and the anecdotes about Mamie.

Angela found Queenie sitting in a corner chatting to Mike. 'May I interrupt?' she asked.

'You go ahead, me duck. Mike and I were just saying how well you did today.'

'That's kind of you. Actually, Queenie, Mamie wanted me to give you something of hers. She thought you might like it.'

'Ooo-er!' said Queenie, thrilled. 'Whatever has she left me?'

'You know her fur coat?'

Queenie began to cry. 'Yes?'

'It's yours.'

'Rita Hayworth's coat?'

'The very one.'

Queenie patted her heart with shock. 'Oh my good Gawd. Oh, me heart. That lovely coat? Mine? Has anyone got a drop of brandy? My heart's going ten to the dozen. Can I come and get it now?'

'I'll bring it over to you tomorrow. How about that?'

'Oh, yes. That would be lovely. Oh, I don't know how I'll sleep tonight, I really don't.'

'I'll get Robert to walk you home now. I think we are all tired.'

No one wanted any supper that night. Angela had asked Mike if he would like to stay with them for a bit, but he made his excuses and went back to his cottage. Angela could see the pain of his grief and promised herself that she would always stay in touch. As Mamie would have wanted.

Angela decided on a hot bath and an early night and was on her way upstairs, thinking always of Mamie, when there was a knock at the door.

Robert appeared from the sitting room. 'Who the hell is that? Bit late, isn't it?'

He went to the door and opened it. Outside were two police officers with Audrey and Geoffrey.

'Mr Whitehorn?' asked one of the officers. 'May we come in?'

'Er, yes. Of course. Can I offer you some tea? Coffee?'

'That's kind, but no thank you.'

Robert stepped aside, allowing the visitors to come in. He had no idea why they were here. Angela came back down to join him.

In the sitting room, Audrey and Geoffrey were sitting mute and small on the sofa.

'Do you know these two?' asked one of the officers.

'Yes. Mr and Mrs Tipton,' said Robert. 'Why? Are they in trouble of some kind?'

'Possibly. You see, Mrs Tipton handed herself into the station this afternoon claiming she murdered a woman in this house.'

Angela felt her knees shake and she sat down quickly. 'What?'

'I believe your aunt is recently deceased?'

'Yes.' Robert went to Angela and put his hand on her shoulder. 'My wife's aunt. We buried her today.'

'Well, that concurs with the story Mrs Tipton told us earlier. She feels she was responsible for her death.'

'In what way?' asked Angela.

Audrey spoke. 'It was me. You see, the night of the dinner party, Geoffrey was talking to Mamie about her perfume and when we got back home he wouldn't stop telling me how much he liked it and that I should get some. I was so, so . . . jealous that, once Geoff was asleep, I came over here and let myself in with the key Simon gave me as guardian for when he was away. Geoff had told me that Mamie had told him

385

she kept a bottle of perfume in the downstairs cloakroom so I thought, if I crept in and made a note of the name of it, I could creep out again and no one would be any the wiser. But . . .' Her face fell and she began to cry. 'But Mamie heard me and she came out onto the landing and she said, "I can see you. I know who you are," and I got scared and bolted for the door. I got it open and she was coming down the stairs and as I was about to run off, she fell and banged her head and . . . and . . . God forgive me, I ran away.'

'Did you touch her? Push her?' Angela asked angrily.

'No, no, I promise. But if it hadn't been for me she wouldn't have fallen on the stairs.'

Robert addressed the police officers. 'Is there a case to be answered here?'

'We can definitely investigate it now we have this witness statement from Mrs Tipton.'

'Good,' said Robert loudly. 'Mrs Tipton is a busybody.'

Audrey squawked in horror. 'Please don't let me go to jail.'

'I doubt you'll get a prison term,' said Robert, opening the sitting room door. 'But perhaps some community service would do you good. Now if you don't mind, my wife and I have had a very difficult day and we are tired. Goodnight.'

38

'Serves her right. Nosy cow.' Queenie was in full flow. 'How could she just run away when Mamie had hurt herself? I know what I'd do to her. I'd throw the bloody book at her.'

Angela rubbed her tired head. 'Mamie would have forgiven her.'

'Forgiveness, my arse. I've lost me best friend. Mike's lost the love of his life and you've lost your aunt.'

'I know that, Queenie, but it was an accident.'

'Humph.' Queenie folded her arms across her bosoms. 'You're too nice.'

Angela passed Queenie the large bag she was carrying. 'This is for you.'

'The fur coat?'

'Yes.'

Angela watched as Queenie pulled out the fur coat and held it to her face. 'I can smell her perfume.'

'Shalimar,' said Angela. 'Here, let me help you on with it.'

Queenie slipped her arms through the satin-lined sleeves and wrapped the coat around her.

'Oh,' she breathed, 'I feel like the bloody Queen herself.'

'It suits you.'

'Does it? I can't thank you enough.'

'It's yours.'

'By the way,' said Queenie, 'I wonder if you found the silver bell anklet what Winston Churchill junior gave her in Marrakesh so that he could always hear her coming? I think she said there was a necklace that went with it.'

'No, I haven't seen that. I don't think I even know the story behind it.'

'Well, if you find them, be sure to keep 'em safe.'

'I will.'

Queenie took Angela's hands. 'You will be sad. And there's no shame in being sad and missing her. But one day you'll think of her without getting all upset and you'll remember funny things you'll have forgotten at the moment. But she loved you. With all her heart. You were the daughter she didn't have. She talked about you all the time.'

'Did she?'

'Oh, yeah. How clever you are. What a good mum. How Robert loves the bones of you. You see, you have what Mamie dreamt of. She told me that once. She admired all the work you put into juggling your life. She could never have done that. Not until she met Mike. And even then, I'm not sure she would have been able to stay put. But don't tell Mike that.'

Angela reached for Queenie and hugged her tight. 'Thank you. Thank you for telling me that. It makes me feel a bit better.'

'And so it should.'

Angela left the shop and found herself heading for the church. Mamie's grave was filled in, the earth heaped up in a mound on top of her. The temporary wooden cross gave her name and dates.

Angela sat down next to it.

'Darling, I hate to leave you here but I know that your spirit will be on every breeze and in every gin and tonic and smile and thought I have. Thank you for getting me this far. I couldn't have done any of this without your confidence in my ambition. I am going to miss you for ever but we will come down to visit very often. Robert's even talking about us buying a little cottage down here. Something for our retirement. Queenie and Mike will take care of you. Mike's got a planting plan lined up so that you will always be surrounded by flowers, the sun and the soft rain. I'll be back soon. Send my love to Mum and all my love to you. I'm off to be a newcomer in another parish now, but you have shown me I have nothing to be scared of. Where there is love there will always be open arms to welcome me.'

ACKNOWLEDGEMENTS

Dear all,

How happy I am to be back with you. The last year has been rather wonderful and very difficult. *The Newcomer* was written in many places. It began at home and then, after my amazing mother died, on a mad whim and need for solace, I wrote a huge chunk on the QM2 Atlantic crossing. I hope you can hear the waves!

One morning I got ready for the Captain's Cocktail Party but instead that night I found myself in the middle of the ship's choir. They were singing songs from *Les Mis*. After a couple of bars, my tears started flowing and I hastened to my cabin, embarrassed. I'd rather have had a cocktail!

The second part of the book has been written in hotel rooms around the country as I tour with *Calendar Girls The Musical*. How easy I thought that would be! Theatre at night and writing during the day. What could possibly go wrong?

Turns out that grief and a big schedule, whilst being a salvation, was also rather exhausting. I missed several deadlines. My many big thank-yous go to:

My cycling girls who are the greatest support and succour.

The crew of the QM2 who befriended this lost soul. Thank you for the curry night.

My wonderful editor Kim Young who held her nerve and supported me through deadline after deadline. There would be no book without you.

My literary agent Luigi Bonomi who carried me with support and kindness.

My friend and agent John Rush. The Best.

Elizabeth Dawson, publicist and soul sister.

And, last but not least, Lucy, Toby, Damian, Pauline and all my *Calendar Girls* colleagues who have put up with me these last nine months.

I really do love you all.

Fern xx

There are lots of ways to keep up with

Fern

Sign up to her newsletter
www.fern-britton.com

/officialfernbritton
@Fern_Britton

Discover more fantastic reads from

Fern

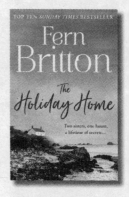

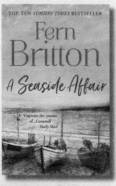

Cornwall is only a page away...